DR. INTERN

LEXIE WOODS

To those of you who prefer dreamy over steamy.
I couldn't leave out the steam.
So you get both.

CHAPTER 1

BEAU

"**B**uffington, get your meaty paws off of the patient," my attending yells from across the operating table. "When I tell you to do something, you do it, son. Do you understand me?"

"Yes, sir."

"Get out of my goddamn sight before I tell everyone just how incompetent you are."

The scrub tech gives me a sympathetic glance as I nod, slowly stepping away from the surgical field.

Just another day in paradise.

I'm three months into my orthopedic surgical residency, and at this point, I'm wondering how I'm going to make it through the next three months, let alone five years. Almost every day has been filled with self-doubt and a constant anxiety that I'm doing something wrong. Everyone says the intern year is the hardest, and to take it day by day, but that's a little challenging when you have a seventy-year-old drill sergeant screaming in your ear for hours on end.

I've been trying to remind myself that this is my dream—the thing I've worked harder for than anything in my life. That everything I sacrificed will be worth it when I make it through to the other side. But, words of affirmation can only get you so far when your eyeballs feel like sandpaper from lack of sleep.

Fortunately, this was my last case of the day, and we're about to give our evening sign-off to the resident on-call tonight. While I would love to swing by the bar afterward with the rest of my coworkers, I have a date with my surgical textbook and YouTube. We have several big cases tomorrow, and I'd love to get in on the hip replacement with Dr. Michaels, which means I need to forgo any fun and keep my head in the game.

The more you get a surgeon to trust you, the more leeway they give you during a case. And the only way to get them to trust you is to appear competent. Not that I am in any way competent, but like I said, the keyword is to *appear* competent.

On my way out of the hospital, I finally check my phone after hours of focus. Six of the unread texts are from my mom, checking in on me because I've let her messages go a week without response. She isn't what I would call a helicopter parent, but because I'm the younger of her two kids, she worries about me more. It also doesn't help that she's an endocrinologist, and I happen to be blessed with type 1 diabetes. If my A1C is even one point higher, she somehow knows and bullies me into compliance. I still don't understand how she gets the information, though, because HIPAA is something she should be compliant with . . .

I shoot her back a thumbs-up emoji to let her know that I'm alive, even though I think I'm closer to a zombie than a human at this point.

The next text is from Parker, my best friend and an attending surgeon at my hospital. He wants to know if I'm still down to play golf this weekend.

Parker doesn't have a lot of people that he's close to. I can count on one hand the number of friends he talks about when we're together. Part of that is his unwavering dedication to his career, but the other part is his personality. He may act cocky and confident at the hospital, but he's actually really reserved and introspective. For some reason, we hit it off when I was shadowing him during med school, and getting to know him on a personal level became like a fun challenge.

Now, though, I can't imagine my life without him in it. I can't explain our friendship—we're opposites in so many ways, but it just works. I've got plenty of friends from various stages of my life, but over time Parker has become like a brother to me. He's taken me under his wing and believed in me, going out of his way to provide positive feedback in a field that doesn't give very much of that.

So even though I'm more exhausted than I've ever been in my life, I'm going to golf with him. It just so happens that neither one of us is on-call, and I know he's desperate to get out of the house while his fiancée, Cassidy, is wedding planning.

The final text on my phone is from a dating app, letting me know that I have a new match. Truth be told, I don't use the app to date. I use it to meet women who are down for a good time without any strings attached. Sometimes they see it that way, and other times they want more from me, which is when I swiftly exit the scene.

It's not that I'm opposed to having a girlfriend, but I've never really felt the urge to choose a specific woman. Plus, working a hundred hours a week doesn't exactly make me prime boyfriend material.

As I hop in my truck, I catch a glimpse of myself in the side mirror. I look like complete dog shit. My light brown hair is disheveled and in desperate need of a good cut. The shadows under my eyes look like they were carved by mountains of coal and I'm pretty sure I smell like moldy cheese.

Being a surgeon is definitely not as glamorous as it looks on television.

I run my fingers through my itchy facial hair. Prickly stubble covers my jaw and upper lip like a rough carpet. Fortunately, none of the red is visible at this time of day. My facial hair tends to lean ginger in the sunlight, much to my friends' amusement. The number of times I was teased for being a daywalker in college because of my stubble was enough to always try to keep it shaved. Though, at this point, I don't have enough time to eat a real meal, let alone shave my face, so it's going to have to stay.

Starting the engine, I open up the dating app and click on the profile: Brunette, twenty-six, new to Atlanta, likes country music. Normally, I would snooze on a plain Jane like that. I have a predilection towards busty blondes with daddy issues, not a woman who wants a love like Johnny and June.

But as I skim past her details to her photos, something makes me pause.

In the first image, she's at a gala, draped in a gown that looks like it was made from the thinnest material imaginable, yet she radiates elegance and sophistication, like she belongs in that environment. Icy blue eyes, unlike any color I've seen before, shine against her pale features. There's a cold, almost detached quality in her gaze, as if she's become indifferent to the world.

However, the second photo tells a different story. Her eyes appear almost wolf-like, playful, and full of life as she's standing on top of a mountain. She seems to be howling with the wind while she laughs, wild and carefree.

It's confusing to me, like the life she's living and the life she wants to live are at odds with each other.

I'm usually good at reading people, it's one of the reasons I thought I'd make a good physician, but the two people I see on this profile are different, and it has me wondering which one I'll meet. Kind of like when you open a mystery airhead flavor—you don't know what you'll get until you taste it.

Which is exactly why, despite my reservations, I find myself typing out a response to her.

Unpopular opinion: Ring of Fire isn't Johnny Cash's best song.

Just as I pull into the driveway of my parent's place, my phone vibrates with a notification. Ever since my residency began this summer, I've been house-sitting for them as they galavant through Europe. While I'd prefer to have an apartment of my own, turning down free housing would be stupid, especially when I make less than minimum wage on a per-hour basis.

Once I put my truck in park, I read her message.

What makes you think I'm interested in your opinion?

Ouch—cold heart to match her cold eyes. Guess she really is the icy, elegant girl from the first photo. I bet she loves missionary and never sucks cock.

Just as I'm about to close the app and forget her, I get a second message.

;)

Interesting way to flirt, but I'll bite. I type out a response, doubling down on her comment.

> I think you're interested in a lot more than just my opinion, pretty girl.

Three dots appear, to indicate that she's typing back.

I can't bring myself to get out of the car, like I'm glued to my phone and need to know what she'll say next.

> Maybe I am… Maybe I'm not. Guess you'll never know.

Like hell, I won't. All of my plans to focus just went out the window.

> Meet me at GJ's in an hour.

After a much-needed shower to wash my stench away, I change into jeans and a button-down before heading out. By the time I get to the pub, I still don't have a response from her. But I'm not the type to send desperate, repeated texts. If she shows up, that's great. If not, I've got my laptop with me. I can grab a booth, order a bite, and dive into work.

Settling into a secluded table, I pull out my computer to begin prepping for the case tomorrow. The chatter of the pub surrounds me as I immerse myself in my work. Every now and then, I glance at the entrance, trying to ignore the slight twinge of disappointment when I don't see anyone—it's not like I'm invested or anything, I tell myself.

Normally women don't make me chase them—they're eager, willing, and desperate for my attention. But there's something different about her, something that tells me she isn't going to beg, that she might be the one who makes me beg.

As I'm focusing on a case video, a flicker of movement catches my eye causing my stomach to tighten with uncertainty. If I were a big drinker, this is when I would down a shot of whiskey to steel my unexpected nerves. It's odd, really, since I'm not typically rattled like this.

I look up, my gaze landing on the most beautiful woman I've ever seen.

Piercing blue eyes, somehow more striking than the photos, meet mine as she skips in my direction.

She legitimately skips.

What grown woman skips?

She has workout clothes on—black leggings and a cropped gray pullover covering a body that looks nearly perfect at first glance. Her hair is pulled back, attempting to tame the wild dark curls that threaten to escape a clip. She looks like she put absolutely no effort into coming to see me, and for some reason, that turns me on.

"Hey there," she greets me, her voice a soft melody that lingers in the air.

I close my laptop, offering her a smile. "Hey. I was starting to think you might bail."

Her laugh, easy and genuine, fills the air as she slides into the booth across from me. "I like to keep people guessing."

"Speaking of guessing, care to tell me your name?" I ask.

The app that we use doesn't include first names, which I prefer because it keeps me from judging too much at the beginning.

Her genuine smile reveals a set of perfectly white, straight teeth. Teeth that, for some reason, I want to run my tongue over.

"What do you think it is?" she asks, batting her naturally full eyelashes at me. "Do I look more like a Jackie, or a Marilyn?"

She's fun. Damn.

I take a sip of my water, considering the question. "Both—let's call you Jacquelyn."

Her eyes dance with amusement as she chuckles. "I don't hate that actually," she says, reaching across the table for my water.

My eyes drop to her chest, the metal zipper on her sweatshirt clanking against the wood as she takes a long sip from my glass. At first glance, it doesn't look like she has a bra on, but then I see a peep of black lace, and all of the blood in my head rushes to my cock.

Not what I was expecting.

"Claire," she introduces herself confidently, returning her body to the seat across from me. "And you are?"

"Thirsty," I grumble, narrowing my eyes on her.

Her naturally pale cheeks flush as she realizes her faux pas. "Well, Thirsty, it's great to meet you. I have to say, that's such an unusual name. Do you have a sibling named Hungry?"

I chuckle at her playful response, relaxing in the booth and crossing my arms. "No, but I do have a cousin somewhere in Georgia named Ravenous."

Speaking of ravenous, I'm starting to feel that way for her.

Claire grins, her expression brightening as she tucks a stray curl behind her ear. "I'd say you got the better end of that deal."

As the waitress comes to get our order, I can't take my eyes off her lips. They're rosy and soft, without even trying to be. No lipstick. No chapstick even. Just bare lips that are clouding every thought in my head.

"You're distracted," she states, snapping me back to reality. Her eyes are glued to me, watching me with a curious expression.

Get your head in the game, man, you're practically drooling over her.

"Sorry," I reply, offering her a small smile. "Just had a long day, and I wasn't planning on doing anything tonight."

"Oh? What changed your mind?"

"That's one secret I'll never tell." I wink at her, and her eyes light up with delight.

"Oh my god, Gossip Girl?" she squeals, clapping her hands together. "I feel like I was just transported back to high school. That was, like, my favorite show."

I chuckle, completely drawn in by her bounding enthusiasm and the unexpected ease of our conversation. It feels like I've known her for my whole life.

"Yeah, my mom was a huge fan," I admit. "She worked a lot, so watching her trash TV was our way to bond."

"Ugh, that's sweet. My brother won't even let me change the channel when he's in the room."

"Well if your taste in television is anything like Gossip Girl, I'm not sure I can blame him."

"Hey!" she protests, dramatically thumping her fist on the table. "I'll have you know that the Real Housewives of New York just had a reboot and the ratings are insane."

I roll my eyes. "I'm sure they are."

We continue bantering back and forth, the conversation flowing effortlessly between us as we eat. The only thing she doesn't ask about is work, which I appreciate because it's genuinely the last thing I want to discuss. I can tell family is the same way for her, because when I broach it, she skillfully redirects us into a light-hearted debate about what truly constitutes a sandwich.

Not sure how she did it, but I'm completely captivated and find myself hanging on every word that comes from those sweet lips. Obviously, I want to fuck her silly, but it feels like something more is sparking between us—like somehow, her enthusiasm has brought me back to life after months of lying in a grave of exhaustion.

When the waitress brings the bill, I toss some cash down and suggest that we head out together. A bit presumptuous, but hey, you gotta shoot your shot sometimes.

By the time we get through the door of my parent's house, I'm about ready to bust out of my pants. My cock is aching from having to control itself for the past few hours, and while I want nothing more than to pin her against the wall and taste every inch of her soft skin, something is holding me back.

She's so unlike any woman I've taken home before—naturally sexy and confident in a way that unnerves me. But she also seems so innocent too, like she hasn't been properly touched by a man.

I join Claire further inside, watching her run her bony fingers over the bookshelves that line the entryway.

"These are your books?" she asks as I walk up behind her. She's tall for a woman, probably only half a foot shorter than my six-foot-four frame.

Wrapping my arms around her waist, I lightly press my body against hers and inhale. She smells fruity and warm, like oranges and vanilla combined. It's the kind of scent that matches her personality perfectly—cozy, yet full of zest.

Claire leans into my arms, pressing her plump ass against my erection. Her breath catches slightly as she no doubt feels my arousal, but she continues staring at the bookshelf.

"The books are my parents," I finally reply, drawing my gaze to the crowded shelf. "I'm house-sitting to save some money."

I notice her quick glance around, likely wondering if anyone else is in the house. "Don't worry," I assure her with a chuckle, "they're in Europe, or something. Honestly, I have no idea what country they're actually in at the moment."

She visibly relaxes, and I briefly consider peppering her neck with kisses, desperately wanting to taste her, but decide instead to hold back for a little longer.

"I've looked through some of these," she comments, skimming fingers over the spine of a radiology book. Given that my mother was an endocrinologist, and my father a surgeon specializing in interventional radiology, our house is practically a library of medical literature.

Raising an eyebrow, I look down at her curiously. "You've read medical textbooks?"

She doesn't turn her head, but I can sense her eyes rolling playfully. "Yes, despite my taste in television, I do enjoy reading."

I chuckle into her wild hair. "Funny, I took you as more of a romance girl."

Claire shrugs, a hint of sadness briefly crossing her face. "Gotta try to fit into my family somehow."

Swiftly shifting the mood, she turns within my embrace, looping her arms around my neck with an easy familiarity.

"Though, these days I do enjoy my dirty books too," she says, her eyes sparkling with mischief, like she's daring me to press her for details.

My hands fall to her waist, pulling her closer so that our bodies are flush.

"Is that so?" I muse, letting my fingers fall on her juicy ass. "Let me guess. Vampire romance? Pretty sure Twilight was in our era, right?"

She shakes her head, tilting her hips into mine slightly. "Guess again."

My dick twitches at the increased pressure and I venture another guess. "Fairies and shit? I can totally see you liking those bat boys, or whatever they call them."

She throws her head back in a burst of genuine, unrestrained laughter, her wild hair cascading free from its clip and framing her face. All I can think about is how I want to wrap those curls around my hand as her lips wrap around my cock.

"It's like you don't know what I like at all," she chides playfully, rubbing her finger across my neck in a way that feels far too natural for someone I just met.

I lean down, our faces inches apart, my lips dangerously close to hers. The air between us changes, now charged with the tension that's been brewing between us all night, and I know without a doubt that I'm less than thirty seconds from a point of no return.

"Tell me then," I say, my voice lowering. "What *exactly* do you like?"

I want her to tell me. I want to know so that I can give it to her.

A quiet gasp escapes her pillowy lips, but no words come out. It's as if she's embarrassed by what she's thinking, which I don't understand because she had no problem verbalizing anything before.

"Use your words, Claire," I breathe, stroking my thumb over her cheekbone. Her eyes flutter closed at my touch, her pulse is pounding so fast I can practically hear it through her skin. "Tell me what types of things you like to read in those *dirty* books of yours."

She breathes in deeply, slowly opening her eyes to meet mine. "You won't judge me?"

I run my thumb from her jaw to her collarbone as I consider the question.

How can she think I would judge her for something like that? It's hot as fuck. All women should read books that enlighten them about sexuality. Hell, if I had time, I would read them too.

"Absolutely not," I reply, noticing tiny goosebumps form on her neck beneath my touch. "Please tell me, pretty girl. I'm hard as fuck just thinking about it."

The corner of her lips twitches up as she looks down at the massive erection pressing against her belly.

"Fine," she concedes, her cheeks flushing bright red as she pauses.

I move my fingers to her chin, tilting her head so that she's forced to look at me.

With a sigh of resignation, she meets my gaze. Her pupils are so dilated that her eyes have lost almost all of their color. "I like a filthy-talking, dominant man who overuses the phrase 'good girl.'"

Fuck—she's going to ruin all women for me.

"Well then," I say smugly, unable to stop the ridiculous grin forming on my lips. "You've come to the right guy."

I crash my lips against hers, stealing her breath as I kiss her like she's the last person I'll ever kiss in my life. Her lips feel soft and warm as they adjust to my insatiable pace, letting me lead just the way she wants—the way she needs.

I sweep my tongue across her lower lip, forcing her mouth open so I can taste all of her. She moans into my throat, the sound ricocheting through my body and landing on my weeping cock.

Her fingers sweep through my hair, finding purchase and tugging slightly. The sensation makes my cock jump in my pants, and I force us to walk backward towards the bookshelf, trying to regain control of myself.

If I don't slow my ass down, I'm going to fuck her against the wall until I bruise her hips and take what I need. And if there's one thing I know without a doubt, it's that Claire is not that type of woman. She's the kind of woman that you spend hours worshiping, deliberately learning how each nerve reacts to your touch, and studying how she comes apart for you. She's the kind of woman that even a lifetime of intimacy wouldn't satiate your hunger for her.

"You're insanely beautiful," I murmur in her ear as I push her against the shelves and peel her jacket over her head. I know it's not what she wants to hear, but it's what I need to say before I add, "Now take my dick in your hands like the good girl that I know you are. I want you to know what you're getting into."

Her cheeks flush crimson with my words as one of her hands traces its way down my chest, the other remaining firmly planted in my overgrown hair. Her touch sears into my body with each inch that her fingers sink lower, and I feel like I'm going to come in my pants like a fucking teenager before she even touches my cock.

Distracting myself, I bend down and kiss along her neck as my hands cup her perky tits. I was right about the bra—it's made of delicate black lace that leaves very little to the imagination.

Not what I was expecting from a woman who could barely tell me what she liked to read in a sexy book. But damn, if that doesn't make me want to explore her even more.

Her hand finally reaches my cock, first rubbing her palm over the entire length before firmly gripping the outline. I push my hips into her hand and she lets out a gasp, either from the surprise of my size or from the way I just pinched her swollen nipples through the lace of her bra.

"Fuck yeah," I growl as she begins rubbing her hand down the length of my hard cock. "You like the feeling of my cock in your hand? It's big, isn't it? But you can take it."

Her eyes go wide as I flex my dick in her hand, making sure she feels all of me because I'm pretty sure I've never been this turned on in my life. My balls tighten at her surprisingly confident touch, and I reach down, cupping her ass cheeks as I lift her into my arms.

There's no way in hell I'm coming from an over-the-pants hand job.

My mouth finds hers again as I walk us toward the back of the house. Her shaking fingers work to unbutton my shirt as I pull back to suck on her neck in a frenzied haze of desperation.

"More," she whispers, as we enter the guest room that I've been using as my bedroom. "I need more."

I couldn't agree more and I nip at her flushed skin, feeling my phone vibrate in my pocket and ignoring it. Whatever it is can wait.

"How much more?" I ask, reaching the foot of my bed and tossing her down.

I need to know how far I can go. How far I can push her. Because if it were up to me, we wouldn't stop. If I showed up to work tomorrow exhausted because I was playing with her body all night, it would have been worth every consequence.

Reaching down to unbutton the bottom of my shirt, I pull it from my pants and toss it on the floor as I wait for her response.

"All of it," she replies, watching me with hooded eyes. "Give me everything you've got, big boy."

My cock nearly leaps out of my pants as she runs her tongue over her bottom lip, her gaze slowly traveling across my bare chest. Leaping forward, I drag her to the edge of the bed, suddenly overcome with the need to know if her panties match her bra.

She giggles, arching her back as my fingers dig into the waistband of her skintight leggings. As I'm about to inch them down, my phone's insistent ringing interrupts the moment. It's set to ring louder when I receive repeated calls in a short span, signaling urgency.

Pausing my movements, I close my eyes and take a deep breath to calm myself down before verbally berating the person on the other side of my phone. Shooting Claire an apologetic glance, I stand and pull my phone from my pocket, glancing down at the number before answering. Of course—it's the hospital calling to tell me to get my ass over there for some emergency.

Fuck my fucking life.

Surgical residency is the biggest cockblock known to man.

CHAPTER 2

CLAIRE

I have no idea how my brother Parker and his fiancée Cassidy work at this hospital every day—it's loud, busy, and so boring. And please don't get me started on the cafeteria. I heard someone refer to it as the worst food in the state of Georgia, and I definitely agree.

Did I want a half-baked pizza slice for dinner tonight? Nope.

Did I want to drink full-calorie soda? Double nope.

Fortunately, Mom and I liven up the place with our fun every week. The nurses all love us because we bring them our home-made oatmeal raisin cookies. Baking them has become a hobby of ours to pass the time—well, a hobby of mine. Mom's a little too weak to spend hours standing in the kitchen, so she watches and directs from the couch, which is a good thing because I barely know how to use an oven.

Since my brother Parker is a physician, he pulled some strings to get Mom into the top cancer doctor at Midtown Memorial. Mom's treatment has been palliative, which means it's focused on prolonging her life rather than curing her cancer. While she could have just continued her chemo in Virginia, Mom wanted to be closer to my siblings, especially now that my sister Caroline is in Atlanta for medical school.

I quit my advertising job to care for her once Parker started his full-time doctor job this summer, and Caroline started classes. Truthfully, I hated advertising anyway, so this move has been a great thing for both of us. We get to spend uninterrupted time together, which basically consists of two things—doctor's appointments and reality TV.

And I wouldn't have it any other way.

"Hey Cass!" I call out, jumping up from my seat beside Mom's infusion bed.

Cassidy looks completely worn out, probably coming straight from a grueling twelve-hour shift in the ER. Her blonde hair is frazzled, piled on top of her head, and there's a dark stain of some sort on her chest, like she was dragged through the mud or something.

Now that I'm in a new city, Cass has taken over the role of my best friend, which is a good thing because she's also my brother's fiancée. They met in the hospital last year since she's an emergency room nurse and he's a cranky surgeon.

"How's it going?" Cassidy greets me, pulling me into a hug while peering over at my mom.

I won't lie, Mom isn't doing great. I've been doing everything in my power to ignore the inevitable, but it's getting harder each day. Her breathing has worsened lately, and now she's reliant on oxygen while she sleeps. She says she's fine, always masking her emotions with a practiced smile, but I know better.

"Oh you know, dear, same old same old," my mom responds softly.

As Cass pulls away from our hug, her eyes catch mine and I can sense the worry in them.

"Though you know," she adds with a sly smile, "Claire went out with some boy last night and didn't come home until the early hours of the morning."

Cassidy's hazel eyes widen, a mix of shock and playful irritation radiating in them. "Claire! Don't say I never tell you anything when you're also holding out on me."

I sigh, glaring at my mother who's watching us with amusement. "You won't tell me who your maid of honor is going to be!"

"That's because I haven't chosen yet. Now spill."

"Nope," I say, gesturing with my hand as if I'm locking my lips shut. "My lips are sealed. You don't share your sexual escapades with me, so I will not be sharing mine with you."

"I'm happy to share . . . you just probably don't want to know," she retorts, a sinister grin forming on her lips.

I bend over, forcing my finger halfway down my throat in a mock gag. "Excuse me while I vomit."

When I look up, the two of them have their eyes glued on me, their expressions identical, like they're not going to let this go until I give up some information.

I roll my eyes, plopping back in my chair as Cassidy situates herself at the end of the infusion bed.

"First of all," I begin with a long sigh, "I only went because Mom forced me."

"Oh hush," Mom chides lightly.

"It's true! You said it wasn't nice to talk to guys on there if I didn't intend on meeting them in person. Though if you ask me, meeting internet strangers in person seems like a great way to get kidnapped. But what do I know?"

"And?" Cass interjects, fluttering her eyelashes at me in an overly dramatic manner.

"I didn't get kidnapped if that's what you're wondering."

Neither of them cracks a smile. They just sit there, slowly blinking as they keep their gaze trained on me, evidently waiting for the rest of the story.

Ugh—they're lucky I love them.

"And nothing," I snap, feeling my cheeks redden. "He was hot. We had fun. He took me home. End of story."

Truthfully, he was the most gorgeous man I've seen in my life, and that's just with his clothes on. Once our night progressed to his house, I found that he was practically a chiseled statue of human perfection.

But, he's some sort of doctor, and everything that I know about doctors tells me to run far, far away from them. They're serious. And boring. And have no fun.

Though to be fair to him, last night was the most fun I've had with a guy in a long time . . . maybe even ever.

"Young lady, I hope you're being careful," Mom cautions, adjusting herself in bed. "I'm too young to become a grandmother."

"Ugh mom, gross," I snap, feeling a little flustered. "First of all, I've been on birth control since I was sixteen so that isn't even a concern. Second of all, we didn't do *that*."

But god, do I wish we did.

From the little time that we had together, I could tell that he knew his way around a female body. Unfortunately, we didn't even get past second base, because he was urgently called into the hospital. He apologized profusely with that southern drawl of his, and dropped me at home, leaving me dripping for more . . . literally.

Cass eyes me with suspicion. "Are you going to see him again?"

"Maybe I will. Maybe I won't," I reply nonchalantly, fiddling with a hangnail as I try to act casual.

He asked for my number when we pulled up to the condo, and it really seemed like he was going to call, but it's been almost a full day without any word whatsoever. So I've decided that I hate him, and will not think of his gorgeous stubbled jawline ever again. Or the stupidly sexy light brown waves covering the top of his stupidly smart head.

"Must you make everything so difficult?" my mother teases, a grin lighting up her face. Her eyes shine bright with affection, and I try to try to etch that image in my mind, knowing these moments are precious and finite.

Standing up, I move to lie next to her, cuddling into her warmth while Cassidy carefully adjusts the chemotherapy lines to accommodate me.

"Yes, and that's why you love me."

"Yes, my dear, but I love you for many other reasons too," she replies, planting a kiss on my forehead. I cling to her, breathing in deeply, committing her scent to memory. "Let's do something fun tomorrow. The three of us."

Mom turns toward Cassidy, extending her hand to clasp hers. "You're not working tomorrow, are you darling?"

"No ma'am, and I think Parker is going golfing with his buddy."

"God, I'm surprised he even has friends. He's so serious all the time, I doubt he's any fun to be around," I add, half-joking, half-serious.

Cassidy laughs, squeezing my leg playfully. "That's why he needs us in his life."

Isn't that the truth.

My older, yet absolutely not wiser, brother has become a completely different person since meeting Cassidy. He's grown more patient, more kind, and more affectionate. He's even started responding to our family group texts, something he used to dodge, claiming he was "too busy."

"Claire Elizabeth," Mom begins in her firm parental tone. "Please promise me to be nice to your brother when I'm no longer here to mediate."

"But . . ."

"No buts, young lady, or I will haunt you from the grave," she teases.

My heart sinks and I feel a prickle of discomfort form in my throat. Like I want to argue, but I also want to sob at the same time. The reality of her words, playful as they may be, brings a poignant reminder of the inevitable.

Cassidy seems to sense my internal battle because she quickly changes the subject. "So what's the plan? We can rewatch *Vanderpump Rules* starting at season one."

The lump in my throat dissipates, replaced by a surge of excitement. "Ooooh yes, and then we can go shopping . . . but only use Parker's credit card."

Mom playfully swats me on the back of my head. "If we're using anyone's credit card, it's mine," she says, pulling my wild hair from my face. "But actually, I was thinking we'd go wedding dress shopping for you, my dear. I'd love to buy your dress."

I spring upright, almost pulling my mom's chemotherapy infusion out in the process. "Yes, Cass, oh my god! Please, please, please say yes."

Cassidy's face, usually pale, is flushed with surprise. "That's way too generous, Mrs. Winters," she protests, shaking her head. "I couldn't possibly accept that."

"Nonsense," Mom insists. "I already spoke with your mother. She's working, but she trusts our judgment completely."

"Are you sure you can handle the outing?" Cass asks quietly, her eyes filled with worry.

Mom flicks her free hand dismissively. "Of course I can. And afterward, we can return to the condo to watch Real Housewives, just like old times."

I give Cassidy a knowing wink, recalling our first meeting. Parker brought her to the lake house for a romantic getaway, not knowing Mom and I had plans to watch reality shows and drink wine up there the same weekend. I almost fell on the floor from shock when my brother came down the stairs shirtless, making some sexually deviant comment about my perfect future sister-in-law.

But seriously, she is perfect.

Cass is gorgeous, smart, funny, and kind—I couldn't ask for a better sister. Not that my actual sister, Caroline, lacks those qualities, but Caroline is much more like Parker. The two of them gang up on me and suck the fun out of most of the things we do, so Cass brings the perfect balance.

"Caroline's going to be so jealous," I squeal, delighting in the fact that I get to experience this with the two of them. "I'm totally scoring major points for maid of honor."

Cassidy rolls her hazel eyes. "We'll just have to video call her then. Everyone gets a say in the dress choice, it's only fair."

"But my opinion is the most important, right?" I tease, playfully batting my lashes at her.

"Ahem," Mom clears her throat, drawing our attention to her. "I believe the person footing the bill has the most important opinion."

Leaning in closer to Cassidy, I whisper, "Yes, followed by your favorite sister."

Her reddened cheeks transform into a crimson color, like she's trying hard to remain diplomatic. "You've got to stop saying that, Claire. I love both you and Caroline equally."

"Don't worry," I reply, ignoring her comment since I know the truth. "I promise not to make you try anything too outrageous. Just feathers, and sequins, and all the tulle in the world."

"Be careful," she warns, her gaze narrowing on mine. "Remember, I'm in charge of what you wear as part of the bridal party."

"You wouldn't."

Cassidy raises an eyebrow, in a playful challenge. "Try me."

Mom chuckles at our banter. "I think I'm going to need to sleep for days after this."

CHAPTER 3

CLAIRE

The wedding dress shop is nestled on a quiet street in Buckhead, the bougiest part of Atlanta. Because of the intimate nature of the store, we're the only people with an appointment this morning. I think Mom must have pulled a few strings to get us in on such short notice because this seems like the kind of place where everyone would want to go dress shopping.

Hundreds of dresses line the walls, including some from the most famous designers in the industry. I immediately notice one of my favorite dresses from an Australian designer in the window, and it takes every ounce of self-restraint that I have to not sprint over and run the delicate fabric through my fingers. I've always been into shopping and fashion, so this place is like paradise for me.

I'm glad that Mom gave me a heads-up on the vibe of the store because I would've felt very out of place in my everyday athleisure. While I love nice things, there's not really a reason to get dressed up when we're only leaving the condo to go to the hospital. Most of my regular clothes are back in Virginia, but I somehow managed to pull together leather leggings, an oversized toffee-colored sweater, and black booties. While it's not my best 'fit, at least I don't stand out like a sore thumb.

As we enter the boutique, an elegant woman welcomes us with glasses of champagne. She's dressed in an all-white pantsuit and appears only slightly older than my mother. "Hello, ladies. Who is the lucky bride-to-be?"

Mom is quick to respond, her head leaning affectionately on Cassidy's shoulder. "This one right here."

"Perfect, I'm Helen," the woman introduces herself. "Let's take a seat, and I'll walk you through our unique process. Dress shopping can be quite the adventure, and we like to make it as seamless as possible here." She gestures to the white leather chairs in front of us, and we follow.

Cass and I help Mom sit down between us, holding her arms tight to make sure she doesn't fall. The chemotherapy from yesterday seems to have taken its toll, leaving her noticeably weaker, and it's hard not to worry. Last night, after we returned home, I was on the verge of calling Cassidy, overwhelmed with the need to talk to someone who could understand.

This morning, we both tried to convince her to postpone the appointment, but Mom refused, adamant that she was just tired from the night before. Though, now that I think about it, that makes no sense because we went to bed around nine last night.

Helen takes a moment to explain that she's going to ask us a few questions before going to pull a few dresses that she feels would be the best fit.

"Now, Cassidy, what style bodice are you looking for?"

Before she can answer, I pipe up. "Definitely something to show off her curves. She has the hottest bod."

Mom squeezes my hand, probably trying to get me to reign in my excitement.

"I was thinking of an A-line dress. Is that what you call it?" Cass asks, her face flushing slightly.

Helen smiles warmly, pulling up an iPad with examples of dress shapes on it. She points to the A-line style. "This is an A-line gown. It has a fitted bodice, but flares out slightly." Her eyes narrow as she fixes her gaze on Cassidy, assessing her for a moment. "I think your sister is right, though. A mermaid silhouette might be a better option for you."

I dramatically turn my head to Cass and stick out my tongue.

Told her so.

"But will I be able to walk?" she asks, letting out a nervous chuckle. "I'm imagining an Aquamarine kind of situation, where I'm bound to the bathtub all night."

Helen laughs, her perfectly bleached teeth showing. "No, honey. There's lots of variations on the dress." She pulls up another picture on the tablet. "See how the tightness stops after her hips? You can boogie all night long."

I cringe—this lady is probably old enough to have danced in the '70s, but I have to admit, she knows what she's talking about.

"Now, what about fabrics?" Helen asks, her attention shifting back to Cassidy.

Cass hesitates before answering. I know she's out of her element and if it were up to her, she'd probably just order something online and call it a day. But over time, I've nudged her out of her comfort zone and convinced her to embrace her style more.

And you know what?

She looks absolutely amazing when she does.

Today she's rocking light-wash jeans, a fitted white bodysuit, and sneakers. I like to leave things better than I found them, which in Cassidy's case wasn't hard considering her wardrobe when we met included stuff she'd had since high school. Not that there's a problem with that, but nobody looks good in low-rise jeans. Nobody.

"I think we should pull multiple options," I suggest, taking charge. "But definitely one that's sparkly, one that has feathers, and one that's got both."

My mom chimes in, her voice soft. "An all-lace dress, and a satin option too, please."

Helen nods, jotting notes down on her tablet. "That sounds like a great starting point ladies. Feel free to browse the store while I pull some dresses. Cassidy, could you please come with me?"

Cass shoots us both a hesitant small smile as she follows the sales associate to the dressing room.

As they disappear, I can feel my mom's eyes on me. Turning my head dramatically, I offer, "Someone had to take charge!"

She sips her champagne, a bemused expression on her face. "I didn't say a word, dear."

"You didn't have to, Mother."

Mom sighs, reaching out to intertwine her cold fingers in mine. "You know that I love everything about you. You march to the beat of your own drum, and have always been the liveliest of my children."

The champagne must have loosened my tongue because I ask, "You don't ever wish I was more like Parker or Caroline?"

She scoffs, closing her eyes for a moment before responding. "I hope you don't really think that, Claire."

I just shrug in response. There's no point in pretending with her—she's always been able to see right through me.

I've always felt like the odd one out in my family—the black sheep. Parker and Caroline are reserved, controlled, and impenetrable, while I'm spontaneous, filterless, and sensitive. I've tried my hardest to appear like them on the outside, only allowing my true personality free in private. But it's exhausting always trying to be who you think other people want you to be.

Mom squeezes my hand, her eyes searching mine. "Want to hear a secret?"

For some reason, the pesky ball in my throat has returned, and all I can do is nod.

"When I was pregnant with you, I prayed that you would be just who you are. Someone outgoing. Someone who takes risks. Someone who carries a childlike enthusiasm for life."

"But why?" I croak, desperately attempting to hold off my tears. Our family never talks about emotions, so this conversation is completely unexpected and slightly uncomfortable. "Parker and Caroline are perfect. They fit the mold of who you wanted us to be so much better than me."

She gently kisses my hand, her touch filled with regret. "Claire, you are perfect in your own way, and I regret not making that clear to you." There's a wistful tone in her voice as she continues. "I've recently realized how much you change yourself in public compared to when you're with us. That was never my intention, and I'm sorry if I ever made you feel like you had to dim your light."

"Well, you never outright said it . . ." I whisper, almost to myself.

But it's true—there was always this unspoken expectation to conform. At school and in public, I was often reprimanded for being too loud or too expressive. Home was the only place where I felt free to be myself.

Mom sighs, pain evident on her face. "If I could redo anything, it would be to let you know, every day, just how proud I am of you."

"But, I'm not a doctor," I murmur, looking down at my hands.

Despite my interest in medicine, I chose a different path, eager to shape my own identity. It was the only thing I felt like I could control at the time, and I guess I thought that working in health-care meant pretending to be someone I wasn't for the rest of my life.

"And thank god for that!" Mom replies with a warm chuckle. "Because your talents would be wasted."

Her words coax a small laugh from me, though I still can't bring myself to look at her.

"You breathe life into our family, my darling. Without you, our memories together would be far more dull. Your siblings appreciate your unique impact too, trust me."

I huff skeptically. "Yeah, well they sure don't let me know that."

"One day they will," she assures me. "Promise me something, Claire?"

I finally meet her eyes. "Anything, Mom."

"Don't try to be like them. Embrace who you are and always remember that I love this version of you. You are my greatest blessing."

A single tear falls down my face. Her words mean more to me than I can even explain, and I'll hold them in my heart forever. "I promise."

"Good, and one final thing before we turn into blubbering messes."

"Yes?" I ask, wiping away the salty water from my cheek.

"Any man worth being with will love you just the way you are. That ex-boyfriend of yours was all wrong for you."

I sigh dramatically. "Just because he asked me to move to New York with him? I honestly should have done it. It's such a great city."

"No, Claire," she shakes her head exasperated. "It's because he gave you an ultimatum to either move with him or break up completely. That's not how love works."

She's right on this one, of course, but I was trying to inject a little levity into the conversation.

My ex-boyfriend, Thomas, was perfect on paper; a southern gentleman who came from a similar upbringing as me. We dated through college, and I genuinely thought he would be the person I married. I pictured a future with him that was just like the one I always imagined as a girl—comfortable and filled with anything I could ever want or need . . . except a voice.

And the funny thing is, it's not even his fault for being surprised when one day I finally found mine.

In hindsight, it was a relationship defined more by expectations and limitations than by genuine love and acceptance. I always wore a practiced mask with him. The same one I was so comfortable wearing from years of being told that's who I needed to be.

I played the role of the perfect woman and called it love. In truth, I don't know what it was . . . but it wasn't real love.

Love shouldn't require you to diminish yourself with the hope that you'll be tolerated.

"Yeah that was pretty fucked up, wasn't it," I offer, finally able to smile about it after a year. "Though I can be a little much."

"When the right man comes along, he won't see it that way, my dear," she reassures me. "He'll embrace all that you are and make your light shine even brighter than it already does. He won't see you as a burden, he'll see you as a gift."

I dramatically slide down the couch, falling in a heap on the fur rug. "Am I the prettiest gift you've ever seen?" I joke, contorting my face into the silliest expression I can muster.

I've had enough sentimental conversations for a lifetime. This is the most heartfelt discussion my mom and I have ever had, and while I value it deeply, I'm emotionally drained.

Mom laughs, pure joy radiating from her face as Helen comes out from around the corner. "Alright ladies, are you ready to see our beautiful bride?"

I sit up and crawl over to my mom's chair, settling at her feet as we wait for Cassidy to come out.

A few moments later she emerges from behind the curtain, and my breath catches in my throat—she looks absolutely stunning. The dress Cass is wearing has long sleeves and a fitted bodice that hugs her curves in all the right places. The fabric at her hips flares out gently, creating an elegant and timeless look.

I can't help the words that come out of my mouth. "Shut up, that dress was made for you."

Cassidy blushes, clearly feeling a little self-conscious under our gaze. "You really think so?"

My mom beams at her. "Absolutely, my dear. Why don't you give us a little twirl?"

Cass spins, her long blonde hair falling over her shoulders as Helen adjusts the long train behind her. While the front of the gown is modest and classic, the back is sexy and provocative. The fabric completely exposes her spine, draping so low that it lands barely above the top of her ass.

Helen steps back, her eyes sparkling with excitement. "What do you think? How do you feel in the dress?"

She looks between me and my mom, glowing with a radiance I've never seen before. "I feel like a bride."

"Well duh, Cass. But do you like it?" I tease, standing to get a closer look.

She nods subtly, seemingly in awe of how perfect the dress feels for her.

I run my fingers over the train's material. It's a thick satin fabric that only shines once you get close enough to touch it—kind of like her in a way, I think. From a distance, she's this intimidating badass nurse, but once you get to know her, she's witty, and fun, and vibrant.

"It's perfect," I whisper, peering up at her. "Though I would have preferred more glitter." I shoot her a wink as I pull her into a hug. "What do you think Mom?"

"I think my son is a very lucky man," she responds, her eyes shining with pride.

CHAPTER 4

BEAU

"**F**ore!" I yell, watching the ball I hit land near the group in front of us.

Golf has never been my best sport, though I can't say it's my worst either considering I just about drowned during diving class in high school. Why they made us go off the twenty-meter board as a graduation requirement is beyond me. Whoever made that rule clearly never did a trauma rotation in med school . . .

Parker chuckles as he cleans his driver off with a towel. "You've got to take lessons man. You're embarrassing me at my club."

"Yeah, because I have so much time at the moment," I reply sarcastically as I toss my driver at him. "You're lucky I'm even here today."

"It'll get better after this year, I promise." He puts my club away before taking a few practice swings of his own.

"Will it though? The second years look pretty damn miserable too," I say, grabbing a beer from the cooler on the cart.

I'm pretty sure I saw one of them leave an OR in tears earlier this week. I may be exhausted, but at least I haven't cried yet.

Parker looks over at me, an amused expression on his face. "Honestly, it was all just a blur of surgery and sex."

Ever since completing his residency, Parker has turned into a wildly more relaxed version of himself. He's become someone who golfs for fun and makes crude jokes—it's like our roles have completely reversed.

"Oh, it feels like I'm getting fucked every day. Just not in a good way." I take a sip from my cold Budweiser as Parker swings, dropping the ball straight into the fairway ahead.

Lucky bastard.

"Well, maybe you need to change it up," he offers, putting his club away before hopping in the driver's seat of the golf cart. "Start giving rather than receiving."

A massive smirk forms on his face at the innuendo as he presses the gas pedal to take us to the next hole.

New and improved Parker is irritating.

While I would have loved to have spent the night *"giving"* to the brunette bombshell with eyes like arctic ice, I got called into the hospital for an emergency just as we were getting to the good stuff. All I could think about as I scrubbed for the case was how I wanted to sink my teeth into her smooth skin and mark it as my own. I felt feral for her, like I've never felt before in my life.

I've been at the hospital for the past forty-eight hours straight, and have barely had a chance to eat, sleep, and piss, let alone think of a witty text to send Claire as an apology for cutting our first date short. But once this game wraps up, I'm planning on heading home and doing some serious groveling.

"Look alive Buffington," Parker shouts, jolting the cart to a stop near his ball. "We've got six holes to go, and you look like shit."

I shake off my exhaustion and glare at him. For someone who used to constantly have a scowl on his face, he's certainly enjoying my downfall.

Fucking sadist.

"Go hit your damn ball," I snap, finishing my beer with a quick swig.

Parker hops out of the cart with a shit-eating grin on his face, grabbing his five-iron. I follow him, hoping that getting on my feet will wake my body up enough to finish this round.

"So, how's the new house?" I ask, watching him line up for his shot.

"Good, man," he replies, taking a few practice swings. "Though Cass has been giving my credit card a workout recently."

I laugh, imagining the conversations they've gotten into. The two of them are perfect together, and I love watching Cassidy push Parker's buttons any chance she can get. I've spent a lot of time with them in the past year, and she's welcomed me with open arms, probably because she knows she needs someone in her corner to handle his grumpy ass.

"Women tend to do that don't they," I comment, leaning on my club.

He takes a perfect swing, driving the ball only feet from the hole. "They sure do."

"What about the condo? Planning to sell it?"

He shakes his head. "Nah, my mom and sister are living there for now while she gets chemo." A flicker of emotion clouds his blue eyes for a moment before he shrugs it off and looks away.

"How's she doing?" I ask as we walk over to my ball in the woods, the fresh pine needles crunching beneath our golf shoes.

He keeps his eyes ahead, not meeting my gaze. "She's fine."

I don't press the subject, knowing he'll tell me if he wants to. "Cass is actually with them right now, wedding dress shopping," he adds after a moment.

I nudge his arm playfully and his cheeks redden—he knows he bagged a dime piece, for sure. "Hell yeah. When's the wedding again?"

He shrugs. "All I know is that it'll be in June. For everything else, ask my fiancée."

I pat him on the back with a smirk. "Well, my friend, it looks like you're well on your way to domestic bliss."

He manages a laugh, but his smile fades as he stares into the distance. "It would be nice if that bliss could hurry up . . . it's been a tough few months. I'll be happy once we come out the other side."

I can't even imagine, but I'm really glad he's opening up like this.

"I'm sorry, man," I say, clapping my hand on his back. "But remember, you've got Cass. Lean on her, and I promise you'll get through it."

Parker nods, his freshly shaven jaw tight.

"Plus, I'm always here to kick your ass at golf whenever you need it," I add, trying to lighten the mood before shimmying my hips between two skinny pines to reach my ball.

This is without a doubt going to be a terrible shot. It's a good thing we're not playing for money because the chance that I make it between the two trees is minimal.

"If this is your version of ass-kicking, I'm not sure I want to see you when your game is off," he chides, watching with amusement from the rough. "Don't shank it."

I shift my focus to the ball as I channel my inner Rory McElroy. To my surprise, it lands only a few feet from Parker's—close enough to still make Par.

I raise my hands in the air, my club still in my hands. "That's fucking right," I yell, narrowing my eyes at him with pride.

Serves him right for talking shit.

"Lucky shot," he grumbles.

As he starts walking toward our balls his phone rings, and he waves his hand at me to suggest it'll be a minute before he can play again.

I nod, returning to the cart to grab my putter and check my phone. Fortunately, nothing from the hospital has come through. Not that they would even have a right to call me in at this point. I'm drastically over my hours for the week already.

As I skim through all of my unanswered messages from the past few days, I glance over to Parker, wondering if I should open another beer while I wait. He's been helping with the residency program a bit, so if he's on the phone with one of them, this could take a minute.

When he turns to face me, his face is ashen and stunned, completely unlike any expression I've seen on him before. Normally Parker is the poster child for remaining cool under pressure. He could accidentally cut a patient's radial artery, and he wouldn't flinch under the stress. Robotic isn't exactly the right word to describe him, but it's damn near close.

Hanging up the phone, he jogs over to me with panic in his eyes. "We've got to go."

CHAPTER 5

CLAIRE

"**D**o you want to do that?"

I blink, trying to focus on my brother's words. On any word other than the one flashing through my brain like an LED billboard.

The only thing going through my head for the past several days has been a string of letters. Six letters to be exact. Letters that when merged together change the course of your life.

Orphan.

I was young when my dad died, so I never really considered that there would be a time in my life when that word would describe me. But it does now. And it will for the rest of my life.

Isn't it weird how the more you say something in your head, the more it doesn't sound real? As if it's completely made up and means nothing. Maybe that's why I keep repeating this particular word. Because if I don't give it meaning, it can't define me.

My beautiful, perfect mom went to heaven exactly one week ago. We were walking out of the bridal shop, having just finished purchasing Cassidy's dress, when she collapsed to the ground. By the time we got her to the car, she could barely breathe and almost seemed like she was a fish out of water, desperate to be thrown back to sea.

Cassidy rushed us to the hospital, practically running every red light in the city to get us there in less than ten minutes. She was the epitome of a calm, collected nurse in a crisis situation, directing our actions with poise as she slammed on the gas. I would have thought everything would be fine based on her confident response, but her eyes were a giveaway to the severity of the situation—filled with terror, as if she knew what was about to come.

By the time we made it to the hospital, they were ready for us and met Mom with a wheelchair and oxygen. I guess Cass called my siblings at some point, but truthfully, the whole situation was a blur, and all I could focus on was holding my mom's hand. Feeling her cool skin in mine. Reassuring her that everything was going to be okay.

Caroline met us at the door, having come straight from Decatur where she's in medical school. While she couldn't do anything directly, it was nice having her there as we waited for my brother. When we got inside, the staff managed to stabilize Mom and get her oxygen saturation up, allowing us a moment of peace. But then, over the next hour, it started going down again.

When Parker showed up in his golf clothes I remember thinking that we were going to be okay because my brother was there. Mom was going to be okay because he was going to start yelling at everyone. He was going to fix this.

But he didn't.

Parker just sat next to us and held her hand, resignation written all over his face.

I screamed at him, trying to get him to do something, to say something. To use his stupid doctor voice and start doing his job.

When he ignored my pleas, I turned to Cassidy, collapsing into her arms as I begged for her to help. For her to make this better.

But she didn't.

She couldn't.

All she could do was hold me tight while I sobbed on her shoulder.

Apparently, Mom had made her wishes known; she was DNR status, meaning they couldn't legally do anything more than give her oxygen and medication for comfort. We just had to watch her die. To sit by her side, holding her hand as she got worse and worse, until she eventually took her last breath.

"Claire," Parker says, his tone curt as he draws me out of my head.

"What?"

His sapphire eyes soften as they meet mine. "Do you want to speak?"

My brother and sister are looking at me expectantly. "Um, sure P, whatever you want."

A man who looks like he's my non-existent parents' age comes to greet us at the front of the church. His hands are tucked into his tailored gray suit, despair written on his face.

"Kids, I'm sorry that we have to meet like this," he says, glancing between us without really meeting our eyes. "I'm Mike Dickerson, the attorney who was appointed to execute the will."

I scoff, unable to hide my irritation. He had to choose now to talk with us? Could he not wait until after she was in the ground?

"I'll let you guys handle this," I say, attempting to make a run for the bathroom. Maybe I can hide there until the service, so I don't have to talk to anyone. Nothing they say is going to make this better, and quite frankly, I don't want it to.

Before I can get far, Parker grabs my arm. He doesn't even look at me as he pulls me back into the discussion.

I glance at Cass, hoping she'll have my side in this, but she keeps her eyes lowered to the ground.

Coward.

"I promise that I won't bother you with the details today," he says sympathetically as his gaze lands on mine. "I just wanted to introduce myself, and let you know that in the next several weeks I will be reaching out with more information regarding assets."

He shifts his feet nervously as I glare at him, trying to convey my distaste for his interruption. "Your mother and I knew each other growing up. She was one of my best friends and helped me through some of the roughest times in my life. I can't tell you how sorry I am for your loss. She was the definition of a servant leader in the community, and I hope you guys can meet all of the people she helped."

I can already feel tears threatening to spill, despite my hope that I'd be able to keep them at bay until after the service. "Is that all you need Mr. Dickerson?"

Parker and Caroline shoot daggered glares in my direction, their identical blue eyes silently chastising me like always.

"Excuse my sister, she's taking this hard," Parker says, as if I'm not here.

My siblings continue to make insignificant small talk with the man as I shift my eyes anywhere but this conversation.

The lobby of the church is massive, with high ceilings covered in intricate white molding that has to be hundreds of years old. Stained glass windows cover the walls, depicting various religious events from thousands of years ago. Not that I really know much about them. Most of the time I spent here growing up was filled with socialization and being told to shush when I was being too loud.

We grew up coming to this church and most of my memories here are happy—Christmas, Easter, that type of thing. Occasions to see and be seen, because this is where all of the hoity-toity people in the suburbs of D.C. go. My parents were both active in the community, and while I know they did a lot of great things like that lawyer guy said, I never really paid attention.

But now I wish I had.

As people adorned in black begin to enter the lobby, the man tells us goodbye and Parker's grip on my arm loosens.

To my surprise, he doesn't say anything. Instead, my sister Caroline turns her head to me, her eyes glowering at me. "Would it kill you to be polite?"

"I'm sorry that we were having an important discussion and he interrupted," I snap. "He's an adult, shouldn't he also have manners?"

Parker sighs, the circles under his eyes appearing to darken with his exhale. "You're an adult too, Claire."

Good—two against one, just like always. Why couldn't my parents have four kids? At least things would be even.

"Cass, will you come to the bathroom with me?" I ask, shooting her a hopeful look.

My one ally.

Her face falls, glancing between my brother and me hesitantly. He nods almost imperceptibly, as if he's her goddamn keeper.

"Sure, let's go."

As we enter the bathroom the tension between us is palpable. I can tell she's torn between supporting me or supporting my brother. Why does she have to even choose? Why can't we be on the same side and just support each other?

I lean against the counter, letting out a frustrated sigh. "I can't believe Caroline. Why is she always taking Parker's side?" The tears that threatened earlier have given way to rage—an easier emotion for me to process.

Cassidy stands in front of me, her expression tender yet filled with something else I can't place. She looks perfect, dressed in a velvet black long-sleeve dress that hangs from her body. Her blonde hair is curled loosely, falling casually over her shoulders. Despite the situation, her presence is warm and comfortable, like an old friend that I've known my whole life.

She reaches out, plucking a piece of lint from my black Dior cap-sleeved dress.

I've always hated black—it's so somber. If I had it my way, I would have worn something from Mom's colorful closet in homage to her. But Dr. Jerkoff told me that it would be distracting and that we needed to put on a united front. Though I'm not sure how united we look after the argument we just had . . .

"They love you," Cass says softly. "You know that right?"

"Yeah, so everyone says." I scoff, tilting my head back to look at the ceiling as the lump starts to form in my throat again. "It doesn't ever feel like it."

"Claire, I think everyone's just on edge with everything that's happened," she sighs as she smooths out her dress. "It'll get better once we make it through today."

I can feel her hazel eyes on me, but I refuse to meet her gaze. "I thought you of all people would defend me."

She lets out an exasperated laugh. "You know you're one of my best friends, right? I value our relationship more than anything."

I nod, peering down at the too-tall strappy heels that are cutting into my ankles. These are definitely not standing heels. I need to remember to only wear them on occasions where I'll be sitting only, because even the walk from the car was painful.

"But you know that your brother is my fiancé?" she asks, and I know it's a question that doesn't need an answer, so I keep my mouth shut. "It's not fair to ask me to choose between the two of you every time you go at it."

I let out a small huff because while I know she's right, it doesn't make me feel any better. "That's fine, you can just tell me in private each time that I'm right. He won't know any better."

Cassidy smiles, her laugh easing the tension between us as she gently pushes a stray curl behind my ear. For some reason, the simple touch, both caring and gentle, makes the ball in my throat bigger, and I can feel the tears in my eyes threatening to fall.

I tried hard to tame my hair today, pinning it behind my head in an intricate updo. It took hours, but it also allowed me to sit and process my feelings by myself. I really thought I had gotten over the hump of despair and could hold it together for a few hours. Apparently, I was wrong.

Finally meeting Cassidy's eyes, I wait for her to say something as the silence between us simmers. Her eyes shine with sympathy, and I know if I speak, I'm going to cry.

"Do you know what you're going to say?" she asks gently, assessing my expression. "You don't have to speak if you don't want to. I didn't speak at Carter's funeral."

Her brother died last year before she met my brother. I think he was in a bad car accident because she still refuses to drive anywhere. Normally, I would ask for every explicit detail, but something about the situation has held even my untamed tongue. She'll tell me when she's ready.

"I want to," I admit. "But no, I don't know what I'm going to say. I figure it'll just come to me up there."

She grins at me, pulling me into her arms. "You're the bravest person I know, babe."

I let out a small laugh, attempting to lighten the mood. "Or the most unhinged. Jury's still out on that one."

"You ready to go back out there?"

I run my fingers over my face, thankful that I wore absolutely no makeup today. "If we must."

Chapter 6

Beau

The great thing about my friendship with Parker is that he can control my schedule if he wants to, though this wasn't a particularly great use of that power, considering I used it to fly to Virginia this morning for his mother's funeral. He was able to get me a day off, but tomorrow night I have to head straight from the airport to the hospital. It's going to be a shitty twenty-four hours, but I'm just glad I can be there for him.

After Parker got the call on the golf course, he didn't say much on the drive to the hospital, though his body language implied there was a serious emergency. When we pulled into the entrance, he tossed me the keys and asked me to drop his car at his condo for him. I assumed that it was something serious with a patient, but Cassidy reached out a few hours later to give me the heads-up about his mom.

When the taxi drops me at the front entrance of the massive church, part of me questions if I'm in the right place. A sea of people crowds on the front lawn, chatting and conversing happily. If they weren't all in black, I would seriously question if this was a funeral because there's a shit ton of people here.

I haven't wanted to bother Parker with anything since I'm sure he's got a lot on his plate, so I've been going back and forth with Cassidy about logistics. She told me that they had several seats reserved at the front of the sanctuary, and as I step inside, I feel thankful. Every pew in the cavernous room is full, except for a few seats that have coats marking the place for someone.

I hesitate as I walk through the crowd of unfamiliar faces, feeling incredibly low-class compared to the people surrounding me. My suit is a hand-me-down from my older brother, and I don't think it cost more than a hundred dollars at the time. Some of these people look like they're dripping in wealth, and I swear to God I even recognize the Secretary of State on the end of a pew in the back.

Spotting Parker, and a woman who looks to be related to him, standing in the front corner of the room, I snake through the crowd to join them.

"Damn—this is really something," I say, pulling Parker into a hug as I draw my eyes over the room.

A small smile forms on his lips. "Thanks for being here."

"Anything for you," I say before turning to the brunette woman. "I don't think we've met. I'm Beau."

She looks like a miniature version of Parker, her face trained into the same cool and composed expression that he wears daily. "Nice to meet you. I'm Caroline."

I shake her hand with a friendly smile. "Are you the pain in the ass sister, or the angel sister?"

Her cheeks flush like she's surprised by the direct nature of my question. "I'll let you guess."

I stroke my chin, trying my best to add a bit of levity to a somber situation. "Well, considering his jaw isn't clenched right now, I would go with the second choice."

Caroline's lips twitch, almost in a smile. "You're very intuitive."

"That's what they teach us in doctor school," I say, shooting her a wink.

Parker rolls his eyes as he runs his fingers through his slicked-back dark hair. "If you could stop flirting with my sister for a moment, I think we need to get seated."

"Where's Cass?" I ask, scanning the room for his better half.

He shakes his head. "God knows—I think she went somewhere with Claire."

Caroline leans into me as she whispers, "The pain in his ass."

"Noted," I chuckle. "Where do y'all want me? Looks like the front is for family only."

"Nah man, you're sitting with us. I made sure there was room."

As the three of us take our seats in the pew, we leave room for the stragglers at the end. The room settles as the pastor begins to shuffle papers at the front of the congregation. Parker and his sister fall into hushed conversation, so I take a minute to look at the booklet.

Grace Woodward Winters
August 21, 1955 - October 7, 2023
Devoted wife. Loving mother.

His mother was beautiful, the kind of beauty that transcends age. She shared a lot of features with her children—dark hair, a thin nose, and full lips. Compared to Parker and Caroline, though, her eyes were bright and icy blue, compared to their darker hue. They almost remind me of that lagoon in Iceland that everyone visits after college.

Out of the corner of my eye, I notice Cassidy's blonde hair pushing past people to get to the front of the sanctuary. Turning my head to meet her gaze, I grin as she huffs dramatically, falling heavily into the seat next to me.

"Glad to see you made it in time," I joke, wrapping my arm around her and pulling her close.

"Thanks for coming," she says, leaning into my embrace. "You know he appreciates it."

Parker leans over, eyes narrowed on his fiancée. "Where's Claire?" he whispers as the music from the string quartet begins to play.

Hearing that name for a second time triggers a memory, reminding me to reach out to the girl from the bar again. I haven't been able to get her out of my head and need to figure out a way to see her again.

Cass reaches over me, patting his leg to try to calm him down. "She's coming. She was right behind me, I promise."

Parker's sharp inhale gives away his feelings, but he holds his tongue, apparently thinking better of whatever he was going to say.

"Do you want me to switch places with you?" I whisper to Cass.

She nods briefly, releasing her comforting grip on Parker's leg as we stand and swap spots.

A few moments later, as the musicians are finishing their prelude, Parker's missing sister slides into the open seat next to me.

The first thing that I notice before I turn my head is her scent—it's familiar, like bourbon and oranges combined. I let my gaze travel up her long legs as she reaches to adjust her high heels, lingering a second too long on the hem of the dress, which stops halfway up her thigh.

My stomach drops when my mind finally connects the dots—the unique eyes, the perfect legs, the familiar scent—she's not the pain in the ass sibling of my best friend, she's the girl from the bar that I haven't been able to stop thinking about. The one that turned my world upside down and made me feel alive again.

Fuck me—she was Parker's sister?

I ended up reaching out to her that night after golf with some flirty text about how I had numerous ways to make things up to her that didn't involve clothes.

But now it makes sense why she didn't reply—her mom had just died and I was the douche who was trying to get in her pants. If I were her, I'd hate me.

As Claire sits up from adjusting her shoe, I lean over and whisper in her ear as if we're old acquaintances, "Nice to see you again."

Her spine visibly stiffens, like she recognizes my voice immediately. Those lagoon blue eyes stare straight ahead as her lips part, like she's considering whether to acknowledge our previous history or pretend it never happened.

"Beau isn't it?" she replies sweetly. "What the *fuck* are you doing here?"

Yep, she hates me.

"Your brother asked me to come," I answer casually, forcing myself to keep my eyes trained ahead. "Though trust me, I had no idea you were his sister until now."

Her breath catches as Cass leans forward and whispers, "Claire—this is Beau, Parker's buddy from work."

I give her my best All-American grin as I turn and hold out my hand. "Nice to meet you, Claire. I'm sure we'll chat more later."

She narrows her eyes on mine as she places her palm in mine, her grip surprisingly firm. "Nice to meet you," she replies, the words sounding forced.

It seems we've both decided to keep that night a secret for now, and I'm more than okay with that. Parker doesn't need to know that I've been obsessed with his sister since the moment I met her. And he definitely doesn't need to know that seeing her today is the highlight of my entire month.

Before Claire and I can continue our game of who cares less, the elderly pastor stands to begin the service, a hush falling over the crowd.

"We are gathered here today to celebrate the life of Grace Winters," he begins, eyes surveying the congregation. "As many of you know, she was well-loved in the community for her generosity and her vibrant personality."

As the pastor goes on discussing the accolades of their mother, I can't stop my eyes from drifting to Claire's tense body beside me. Her hands are clenched in her lap, knuckles practically white from gripping each other. She seems much more frail than the last time I saw her.

Everything inside me wants to reach out and ease her pain, to let her know that I'm here for her, even though she doesn't want me. But I can't do that without drawing suspicion from her family, so I sit still and brood over how much of a jerk I am.

We stand to sing a hymn, and I notice her body tense further as a single tear runs down her face. On instinct, I pull a handkerchief out of my suit pocket and hand it to her.

Surprisingly she takes it with a faint nod of appreciation, using the fabric to dab away the lone tear that escaped her control. For a brief moment, our eyes meet, and I see a mixture of gratitude and vulnerability in her gaze. It's a stark contrast to the confident and fiery woman I encountered at the bar and my heart aches for her.

God, I just want to hold her in my arms and never let go.

Once we sit, I'm surprised when the pastor calls her up to speak. Not that I don't think she can handle the situation, but shouldn't Parker be the one doing that kind of thing? He's much more refined and controlled than his sister, and I doubt speaking in front of an audience like this would phase him.

I glance at Cass, who shoots me a look that says she'll explain later as I redirect my attention to Claire.

She stands gracefully, her posture exuding confidence despite the clear pain she's masking. I watch her as she moves toward the front of the church, her eyes scanning the room briefly before she takes a deep breath to begin.

"Do any of you know the name of the OG of the OC?" she asks, peering into the crowd.

Hushed murmurs surround us, and I can sense Parker stiffening to the left of me, probably wondering what the hell is going to come out of her mouth next.

If Claire notices the crowd's response, she doesn't let it affect her. She just softly smiles before continuing. "What about the name of Dorinda's estate?"

She pauses again, allowing her tired eyes to shift across the sea of people.

"Do you remember where you were when Theresa flipped the table?" Her throat bobs with a forced swallow, as if she's trying to push down the emotion threatening to break free from her control. "Because I do. I was with my mom."

Claire's hand drifts up to her head, nervously pushing a stray curl behind her ear. "It's funny, because I don't think she even liked reality television," she admits to herself, her lips parting to let a small chuckle escape. "I think she found the fights exhausting and petty. But she loved me. And she showed her love in ways that I didn't even realize until this very moment."

Claire peers down at the ivory pulpit, her chest heaving like she's holding back a wave of emotion that's threatening to break at any moment.

"She also loved all of you in this room. You want to know how I know?" she asks, shifting her gaze to the back of the congregation. "Because when she wasn't listening to me ramble about my life, she was updating me on yours. She knew that Mrs. Kay just finished a baby quilt for her third grandchild."

Her eyes scan the room, landing on someone in the far right. "She knew that Mr. Richardson just had a triple bypass surgery, and we spent hours choosing the perfect flowers for his recovery."

As if realizing her mistake, her porcelain skin flushes bright red. "Oops! Sorry! Forget I said that." Everyone in the room chuckles, unfazed by her divulgence of private health information.

"What I'm trying to say is that she was actively involved in all of her friends' lives. She cared deeply about what was important to each and every one of you . . . probably more than she cared about the things that were important to herself."

She swallows and closes her eyes for a moment.

"I think we can all learn a lot from my mom," she says, voice trembling slightly. "So I ask that when you leave here today, you take a piece of her with you in your heart. Live like her. Live as if you're interested in the lives of those around you because you might just gain a perspective that you never knew you needed."

Claire's eyes glass over, the flood of tears that she's held back now taking over. From the side of the pulpit, I can see her hand unclench slightly, revealing the white handkerchief that I gave her.

"Thank you all for coming today to celebrate our mom," she chokes out, barely holding it together. "Parker, Caroline, and I will be holding a reception at our family home after the service. Everyone is welcome."

The heartfelt eulogy ends with a round of applause from the congregation, and Claire steps down from the pulpit with the weight of the moment clearly etched on her face. She returns to her seat next to me, and I can feel the tension in her body slowly easing with each tear that she finally allows to stream down her cheeks.

Leaning in, I whisper, "You did a great job."

I know she probably doesn't care what I think, but something tells me that despite her irritation with me, she needs a friend right now.

Her glistening eyes flick to mine as she nods, silently handing me back the crumpled handkerchief. I take it, my fingers lingering on hers a second too long before I pull them away.

As the crowd begins to disperse following the final hymn, Parker and his siblings stand at the front of the church, receiving encouragement and embraces from friends and family. I watch from a distance with Cassidy, still unsure of my role at this moment. This would be a hell of a lot easier if someone ordered me to get food or clean the house before guests arrive.

"How's everyone doing?" I ask Cass, eyes drifting to Claire standing beside her siblings. Claire's gaze is distant, almost glassy as people pass by to give their condolences.

Cassidy sighs, her concerned eyes following mine, though they land on her fiancé instead of Claire. "You know Parker. He's ordering everyone around and hasn't rested at all. Honestly, if I didn't know his mother had just died, I would just think he was just stressed at work."

"Sounds about right."

"Caroline is the same," she adds, shifting her focus to Parker's youngest sister. "Though she would never order people around. She's much more reserved. I'm sure she's hurting, but she seems to be channeling her emotions into studying for her med school exams."

"And the other sister?" I ask, trying to sound casual despite the emotion hammering through my chest when I look at Claire.

She was so poignant during her eulogy, so emotionally aware in a way that her brother isn't. It struck me as interesting that two completely opposite people could come from the same family.

"Claire wears her heart on her sleeve in everything that she does," Cassidy explains as her eyes fall on her future sister. "She's having a tough time, which only makes her brother more frustrated with her. It's been hard, feeling like I'm caught between them. They won't stop going at it."

I can't explain it, but I feel my pulse quicken at the thought of Parker's frustration with his sister. Like I need to protect her. To tell her it's going to be okay—that she can feel how she needs to feel.

"We all grieve differently, Cass. He should lay off," I comment, grinding my teeth to control my building rage.

She sighs, her weary eyes finding mine. "Trust me, I've told him that. Every day."

"Her speech was really good," I offer, drawing my eyes to Claire again. She's looking at an elderly funeralgoer's phone and beaming as she zooms in on a photo.

Fuck what Parker thinks, she's more together than I could ever expect to be at this point.

"She's so much like her mom," Cassidy points out, watching her with the pride of an older sister. "She's intuitive, empathetic, and extraordinarily friendly to everyone she meets."

I nod, because I remember exactly how she bounded up to me that night, completely unafraid of a stranger who had messaged her just hours before. It was like meeting me was a challenge to her, and she wanted to unpack every piece of me in that finite encounter. Surprisingly, the only thing she didn't ask about was my job, as if who I am as a person had nothing to do with what I did for work. And as someone who only works, talking about anything else for a few hours was like a beacon of light.

She was my beacon of light.

"I just worry about her," Cass adds quietly. "Claire put her life on hold to move to Atlanta and help her mom. I'm not sure what she'll do now that she's gone."

"I'm sure she'll figure it out," I assure her, watching the final few people trickle out of the church. "Fortunately, that's a problem for another day. For now, let's go back to the house, entertain these people for a few more hours, and then drink ourselves silly."

Cassidy's spirits seem to lift at my suggestion. "Rematch in beer pong tonight?"

I grin, glad to see that her mood is improving. "You're on Callaway."

CHAPTER 7

CLAIRE

After the funeral, we hosted hundreds of family friends at our childhood home. I felt like a volleyball constantly being passed between people that were clamoring for my attention. Fortunately, by the time the reception was over, it was late enough that I could credibly claim exhaustion and go to bed.

I would have truthfully enjoyed spending the evening with my siblings and Cassidy, but having Beau around threw a massive wrench in my already horrible day. When I'm around Parker and Caroline I already feel like the odd one out, no matter how much I try to fit in. I didn't need to make my feelings of inadequacy worse by spending hours with a hookup who never texted me.

For some reason Beau's presence didn't send me further into my rage spiral like I anticipated. He was tender and overly kind to me, which, while comforting, also left me wondering if it stemmed from pity—the rejected girl now facing a family tragedy. Fortunately, by the time I went downstairs the next morning, Beau had vanished, and no one seemed aware of our prior connection.

The days after the service were spent going through the house and spending time together as siblings. We reminisced on our favorite memories, took evening swims by the pool, and made cocktails by the fire. We laughed. We cried. We allowed ourselves to feel. And for the first time in a long time, the three of us felt like a single unit, banded together through tragedy.

By the end of the week, my sister had to go back to Atlanta for school, and I decided to go with her. The life I had in Virginia just doesn't exist anymore, and no single twenty-six-year-old girl should live alone in a ten thousand-square-foot house. I'm sure Mom made plans for what she wanted to do with it, but I've been letting Parker deal with that stuff. If I had to guess, it'll probably be sold and the money funneled into the trusts set up for us since childhood. The only thing I was adamant that we keep was the lake house, which my siblings didn't fight me on—it's their favorite place in the world, too.

Back at the condo, the quietness has been stifling, especially when the highlight reel of memories I made with my mom plays through my head every moment that I'm alone. The funny thing about grief is that if you have people to share it with, you almost forget you're in pain. But when you're on your own, the silence forces you to experience emotions that you've been pushing away. And it sucks.

When Parker moved out of the condo, he left practically all of his furniture because Cass made him buy new stuff. Fortunately for me, he forgot about his stash of wine in the upper cupboards of the kitchen and I won't lie, it's been the only thing to quiet my mind at night. I've been slowly working through his collection, limiting myself to only one glass a night to help me sleep.

Tonight, I'm lying in my bedroom staring at the ceiling as I work on a bottle of merlot from France. The spinning fan is making the glow of the city appear like scattered disco lights on my walls, and I wonder briefly what it would look like in a painting. I would call it mirrorball, or something like that because the dots are shimmering like a thousand pieces of sadness.

It's ironic that in a city of lights, surrounded by millions of people, I've never felt more alone.

Just as I'm about to toss on an episode of *The Bachelor* and let the buzz from my wine whisk me into a dream, my phone rings. Rolling onto my stomach to check who's calling, I see the picture of Cass from Christmas last year light up my screen, and I immediately swipe to answer the phone.

"Want to come help me finish this wine?" I ask, looking over at the half-full bottle on my nightstand.

"Claire," a deep, controlled voice says.

Ugh—I should have known.

Choosing violence, I reply, "Who are you, and why do you have my sister-in-law's phone? I'll call the police."

I've been dodging Parker's calls since I got back to Atlanta because he's been nagging me to get a job. While I recognize that it's just his way of ensuring I get out of the house, and work is the only thing he knows, it doesn't mean I'm ready for life to go back to normal. Because if it goes back to normal, that means that my mom is really gone.

And I'm not ready to admit that.

I'm not ready to forget her.

Also to be fair, it's not just him that I'm ignoring—it's everyone. Currently, my phone has three hundred and eighty-seven unread messages, because I haven't looked at them since the day we went wedding dress shopping. I just can't bring myself to read the pitying messages from people—I have enough pity for myself.

Parker audibly exhales into the phone. "Can you act like an adult for once in your life?"

I roll my eyes, a reflexive response even though he can't see it. "I know you are but what am I?"

"Claire, I swear to God," he growls, his patience wearing thin. "Sometimes I want to strangle you."

"The feeling is mutual, big brother."

In the background, I can hear Cassidy's soothing voice, trying to temper Parker's frustration. It's almost comical how she manages his moods, and I let out a little giggle.

He takes another deep breath before asking, "Can we please just have a normal conversation for a moment?"

I echo his sigh, putting the phone on speaker as I get up to walk to the bathroom. "If we must."

"What have you been up to this week?"

I place the phone on the counter, pulling my wild hair into a bun on top of my head. "Oh you know, this and that."

"Care to explain to me how you maxed out your credit card?"

Oooof.

I forgot that my card was still linked with Mom's. He must have access to all of the accounts now.

My eyes sweep over the piles of brand-new beauty products on the counter.

"If you'd like, I sure can," I say, smirking at my new purchases. "The Dyson Air Wrap is supposed to be the best product on the market for hair like mine. And the sales associate at Sephora said I needed a special shampoo and conditioner for it, so I got that. When I was leaving the store, the new MAC line caught my eye, so I decided to replace my—"

He cuts me off, his voice heavy with exasperation. "Please stop."

I lean closer to the mirror, admiring the smoothness of my face thanks to the Botox I got earlier in the week. "But I was just getting to the good part."

Parker's tone turns serious. "I know Mom was fine paying for your lifestyle, but you can't do that anymore. Please tell me you understand that spending fifteen thousand dollars in a week is not sustainable."

Truthfully, I never really considered money when I was spending it in the past. And yes, I recognize that is a super annoying thing to say. But I've always had whatever I wanted or needed.

Sure—Mom might have funded my shopping habit, considering my salary at my old advertising firm was pennies on the dollar, but I've never gone anywhere near as overboard as I have this week. I just don't want to be alone, and if I'm spending money, people are talking to me and distracting me for a few hours.

It feels nice.

"Yes, idiot, I understand that," I reply, spinning to admire my new silky pajama set.

Money can't buy happiness, but it can buy a hell of a lot of lingerie.

"Good," he says, his tone finally more controlled. "Listen, I know you're struggling. And I'm sorry that I haven't been around this week. But please promise me that you'll stop spending money like it grows on goddamn trees."

I'm barely listening when I turn off the bathroom light. "Got it. Goodnight, P."

He sighs. "Goodnight. I love you, you know?"

Maybe he tells himself that.

"I know."

CHAPTER 8

BEAU

If you've ever wondered what it's like to get constantly railed before the sun rises, I would recommend becoming an intern in an orthopedic surgery residency. I've been up all night, taking pages and scrubbing in on surgeries. Now, I have to do it all over again while somehow remaining competent enough to not completely fuck up or kill someone.

They call morning meetings with our chief resident pimping, but really they're just putting a name to blatant verbal abuse.

Each day we run through the case list—the patients who came in overnight, the patients who are scheduled for the day, and the follow-ups who are still hospitalized. The chief resident asks you question after question, hoping to trip you up or find a gap in your knowledge. Eventually, they succeed, resulting in a loud torrent of slurs and degradations.

And listen, I get it—they're teaching us the same way they were taught. But if you're purposely asking me a question that I don't know the answer to, just to prove that you're smarter than me . . . well, congratulations. You're four years ahead of me in your training, so I'd fucking hope you're smarter than me.

"Buffington," my chief resident, Walker Chastain, yells from across the room. His dark eyes flicker with irritation, like he knows I was about to fall asleep in my chair. "Care to explain to me why you ordered twenty-four hours of azithromycin for Mr. Peterson?"

God, this sucks.

"Uh," I grunt, looking down at my notes as I try to remember who the hell that patient is. "To prevent infection."

The three other interns in my class chuckle, though I know it's not critical. It's because they're just as delirious as me.

Walker runs his fingers through his jet-black hair, the expression on his face fluttering somewhere between annoyance and disappointment. "Tell me about that case."

I pause, hoping the answer will magically come to me. On any given day we have over sixty cases under our care, so patient names aren't always top of mind. It's much easier to think of them by specific case descriptions. If he had said the seventy-year-old male, two days post-op from a hip replacement, that might have jogged my memory.

"When you played rugby in college, did it completely obliterate all of your brain cells?" he asks, narrowing his gaze on me.

I know this is rhetorical, but I can't resist a smart-ass response.

"Some of them, probably," I admit, a cheeky grin forming on my lips. "But mostly just my self-confidence, since I have this crooked ass nose ruining my pretty face."

He rolls his eyes at me as my coworkers stifle their laughter.

"If you don't get your shit together, I swear to God—"

He doesn't continue his threat, because I know he's just trying to be an asshole, he doesn't actually mean anything by it. Walker would be a hell of a lot more terrifying if I didn't know he had a soft spot for me. Most people see him and are instantly intimidated because of his full sleeve of tattoos and tall stature, but I just see a big ol' teddy bear.

Walker whips his head toward the other interns. "Y'all need to know your patients backward and forwards. If I ask you a question, I expect you to know the details of the case without looking it up. We go over this every day."

He pauses, as if expecting us to echo his criticism. "Can anyone else tell me why ordering twenty-four hours of azithromycin is problematic?"

The only girl in our small intern group, Sam, answers. "Azithro is only effective if it's given for forty-eight hours or longer."

I shoot her a glare, but she just shrugs. It's not her fault I'm a dumbass who can't remember basic pharmacologic principles.

"Bingo," Walker replies. "Buffington has essentially ordered a cocktail that's not going to even get our patient tipsy."

"What's the fun in that?" my friend Matt jokes, hoping to lighten the mood.

Unfazed by our antics, Walker clenches his jaw. "Higgins, you're with Dr. Hunter today in the clinic."

I fist bump Matt discreetly under the table because the clinic is the most chill assignment for us, and while I love operating, sometimes we need a break.

He's a lucky bastard.

Matt gives me a ridiculous grin while Walker doles out the other assignments. God help me if I'm on trauma today I'm going to lose my mind. It's the busiest service, and I already had a shitty night.

"Buffington—you've been requested by Dr. Winters in general today. Get your ass out of here."

Walker's expression is blank, but he's definitely unamused by the choice for my cases today. He probably thinks that because Parker and I are close, I'm getting special treatment. If Walker had his way, I would be on the shittiest service as punishment for my tomfoolery this morning.

I hop up, working hard to stifle my grin. It's been about a month since I've seen Parker, and our only communication has been shit-talking each other in the app where we play chess, so I've been wondering how everything's been going since the funeral.

As we funnel out of the tiny on-call room, Matt elbows me in the ribs. He's a lot smaller than me, both in stature and build, but he's hilarious and always keeps the mood light on days when we're running on empty.

"I think you're Walker's favorite, man," he jokes, a massive grin forming on his sly face.

"Well, he certainly can't pick on you every day. It would be too easy, little guy."

Matt rolls his eyes, following me down the hallway past a group of pre-op nurses who are chatting as they wait for their patients to trickle in. One of them, a short blonde with her hair in a braid, jumps up when she sees us coming and walks in stride next to me.

"How are things going this morning guys?" she asks, batting her eyelashes and ignoring Matt completely.

I glance down at her. I'm pretty sure I've hooked up with her before, but I'm so fucking tired I can't think straight.

"Better now that I saw you," I reply, enjoying the way her cheeks redden with my words.

Sometimes I can't help myself. Flirty banter just flows out of my mouth.

Sue me.

"So listen," she starts, practically jogging to keep up with our pace down the hallway. "I was thinking we could continue what we started in the call room at my place this weekend."

Ah, so we did hookup. Makes sense considering she's my type to a tee.

Well, she was my type, until I met my best friend's sister.

I can hear Matt's chuckle next to me and I discreetly pinch his arm. "I'm on call most of the weekend," I admit, not wanting to make promises. "But shoot me a page with your info, and I'll figure something out."

Her face lights up with excitement as she nods and turns back to her friends.

It's about damn time I hop back on the horse. I haven't gone this long busting a nut since I was a teenager, and sex is the only thing in my life that I don't completely suck at.

Matt chuckles, breaking the silence as we reach the elevator. "It's gotta be tough being you."

"It is when you have to remember all of their names."

***

Before I meet Parker for his surgery marathon, I make a quick stop at the cafeteria. His caseload has been heavy since he returned from his time off, and I don't anticipate a break at all today. While he may be a robot who can power through without basic needs like food, I'm at the mercy of my blood sugar and have to make sure I plan accordingly.

Deciding on a breakfast biscuit and a handful of snacks for between cases, I swipe my card and plop down in a quiet corner of the cafeteria for a moment of peace before the insane day. The plush booth squeaks as I slide in, and despite the sterile appearance, it's incredibly comfortable.

If I could just close my eyes . . .

As I'm about to nod off, my phone rings, Luke Bryan blasting from the pocket of my scrub pants.

"Hang on a sec, Mom," I say into the phone as I place it on the table and put in my headphones. "You still there?"

"Can you hear me?"

"Yep, I've got you. Sorry, I had to put in headphones since I'm in the cafeteria," I explain, pulling out my biscuit and taking a huge bite.

I hear tapping on her end, and then a brief pause. "Sorry, was just texting with the realtor," she says, sounding distracted.

I'm too tired to delve into her comment, so I just grunt in response, focusing on my food.

"Beauregard, I can hear you chewing through the phone. Can this not wait a moment? I swear, it's like I completely dropped the ball on teaching you manners."

I swallow my bite quickly to reply, slightly annoyed. "You're the one who's always on me about my A1C. I feel like you should be glad that I'm nourishing my body."

She huffs into the phone. "I would be if you weren't putting complete crap into it. I swear your numbers are worse than an eighty-year-old man."

She's wrong—nobody that's eighty years old has type one diabetes because insulin has only been around commercially for fifty years. They would likely have died long before they made it to their forties.

For some reason, my mom has been on my ass about my A1C since I started residency. It's like she's channeling all of her energy into me now that she's retired. Honestly, considering she isn't pulling thirty hours straight without sleep every couple of days, I don't think she can judge what I put into my body.

I'm just doing my best to make sure I don't pass out, regardless of the nutritional value of the food. Plus, they're already working on an artificial pancreas, so in five years I won't have to manage any of this shit on my own.

"Did you call just to lecture me?" I ask, half-joking and half-serious. "Because while this has been a pleasure, I've got a case soon."

"Oh, of course, I live to point out your flaws," she retorts sarcastically.

I smirk. She said it, not me.

"Glad you finally admit it."

"You exhaust me," she sighs, clearly tired of our conversation, which is a good thing because I need to get my ass to the OR. "The reason I'm calling is because your father and I are coming home early."

I take a sip of my lukewarm coffee. "Remind me where y'all even are?"

It's been months since they've been home, and it's not like keeping up with them on my mother's blog has been at the top of my priority list.

"London," she replies swiftly. "We booked a flight home tomorrow because we're meeting with our realtor this weekend. Someone made an offer on the house that we just can't refuse, and we need to be out by the end of the month."

I nearly spit out my coffee as I look down at my watch. It's already the 20th.

"It's not what we intended, of course. We wanted to keep the house for you to live in while you were in residency, but our realtor said we would be incredibly foolish if we didn't take the deal. You know how the housing market is right now."

Yep—the housing market in Atlanta is at the top of my mind at all times.

My mind races as I work through what this means for me. As if I didn't have enough on my plate already, now I need to find somewhere to live at the last minute.

Fan-fucking-tastic.

"And where will you two stay?" I ask, hoping they have something else lined up already. My mom is a planner so I can't imagine she would accept without a plan B.

"Bradley has a whole guest house in Houston. With the three kiddos, he suggested that we stay with them until we decided on where to officially retire."

Of course he did. Brad has been, and always will be, the golden child.

"That sounds like a great way to spend your retirement—taking care of his little demons for free," I snort, rubbing my eyes to try to wake myself from this nightmare. "Don't worry about me though."

"Young man," she warns, her tone sharpening. "You knew this arrangement wasn't forever. I'm sorry about the timing, but we'll help you find a solution."

I brush off her offer. "It's fine. I'll figure something out."

"Are you sure? We have thousands of hotel points that you're welcome to."

"Don't sweat it. I'll see you tomorrow."

CHAPTER 9

BEAU

S tanding at the scrub sink, I feel like I'm in a complete daze. Not only am I physically and mentally exhausted, but now I have something on my plate that needs to be dealt with immediately, and no fucking time to do it.

I don't blame my parents for taking the offer on their house, nor do I blame them for moving halfway across the country to live with my brother and his family. It's just hard to be excited for them when I feel like my life is spiraling.

Walking backward into the OR, I glance up to see Parker already deep in conversation with his scrub nurse. Despite arriving a solid fifteen minutes early, he's there ahead of me, meticulously checking every detail. The man takes the term control freak to a whole new level.

"Pretty sure the intern is supposed to be here before the attending," he comments with a soft chuckle.

I hang my head and sigh as I step next to the sterile field. "If I hear one more thing today about how incompetent I am, I might just fake an injury to get a break from this hell hole."

Parker steps forward, his body positioned across from me as he eyes me with concern. "You know they're just busting your balls right? It happens to all of the interns, though I hear it's worse in ortho than general surgery."

I nod, taking a moment to compose myself. This self-pity bull-shit I have going on in my head isn't going to help anything. "So they say."

"Trust me, my first year was horrible. It gets better."

He proceeds with the first incision. The surgery isn't particu-larly long or complex—a few hours at most—and doesn't demand much from me besides basic assistance. But fatigue is a constant battle, and I struggle to stay alert.

Some residents physically harm themselves to stay awake, pinching their skin or kicking the base of the operating table. Oth-ers resort to drugs—uppers, downers, and beta blockers to keep them regulated. My method is simpler—I chew gum. It keeps me moving and somewhat helps stabilize my blood sugar by keeping me from going low.

As the surgery progresses I assist Parker where I can, even though this procedure isn't directly relevant to my specialty. There's always something to learn, regardless of the case, so I do my best to focus on his explanations despite my mind trying to parse through all of the things I need to get done this week.

"Buffington," I hear out of the corner of my mind as I debate where to move within the city.

I know Parker loved living in Midtown, and it definitely would be nice to roll out of bed and get to work in a few minutes. Buckhead could be cool, but it's expensive as hell, and I doubt I could afford a place on my intern salary.

"Buffington," Parker yells again, snapping me out of my daze.

"Sorry," I respond sheepishly.

"Is my surgery boring you?" he drawls, his tone clipped.

I can see how people at the hospital steer clear of him when he's like this. Hell if I didn't know the other side of him, I'd join them and run in the opposite direction.

"No, sorry," I apologize as I shift my feet slightly. "Just got a lot on my mind, that's all."

"Your charm is only going to get you so far. People love you and you're smart as hell, but you've got to focus. If it were any other surgeon in here with you, you'd be out and your chief would get a report. So I suggest you get your shit together."

I nod as Parker shifts his gaze back to his work. He's almost done with the case and just has to close the abdomen once the sutures are tied on the bowel.

"So what's going on? I've never seen you like this," he asks as his hands work in precise movements to tie tiny knots inside the patient.

"Just family stuff," I answer, cutting his stitches off. "My parents abruptly sold their house, and I've got to be out in the next week."

Parker pauses his work momentarily, looking at me thoughtfully. "That sucks man, I'm sorry."

I shrug it off. "It is what it is."

"You know where you want to move?" he asks as his scrub nurse pulls his headlamp off his face.

"No clue. Feels like I already live at the hospital anyway, so it's not like it fucking matters."

His midnight blue eyes narrow as if a thought has come to him, but he's not sure he should voice it. "You know . . ."

I grab a fresh suture set and prepare to close. "Yes?"

"My condo has two extra bedrooms and all of my old furniture is still there. You could stay there for a while."

I laugh at his suggestion. "Dude, I bet your mortgage is insane. I can't afford that."

The man used to live in the penthouse of one of the nicest condos in Midtown. I've got a decent amount in my savings but not nearly enough to pay his bills. Probably not even enough to cover one month's payment.

"The condo's paid off." Parker tilts his head, indicating that I should start working. "You'd be doing me a favor, actually."

"How do you figure?"

Parker's gaze lingers on me, not scrutinizing my surgical technique, but gauging my reaction to his next words.

"I've been worried about Claire since the funeral," he begins. I can sense his hesitation and doubt he wants to talk about this at all, let alone in such a public setting. "I think she's struggling and I need someone to keep an eye on her."

My pulse quickens at his mention of Claire and I have to force myself to focus on my hands so I don't look up at him. "You want me to spy on your sister?"

He corrects me quickly. "Not spy. Just look after her. I don't have time for her right now."

"And you think I do?" I ask skeptically.

We just talked about how I spend all of my time at the hospital. He can't think I have the capacity for this, can he?

"No, but at least you'll be around more than me. It's a win-win. You need a place to stay, and I need someone to check in on her."

I'm doing my best here to find a reason to refuse.

"Why not have Caroline move in?" I suggest, looking for alternatives to his offer. "It's not like University Hospital is that far away."

"She's locked into a lease for the next year. Plus, I'm pretty sure they would kill each other," he responds with a slight chuckle.

I glance at Parker, noting the genuine concern on his face. "And you think we won't?"

"I think you're the most patient guy I know. If anyone can handle Claire, it's you."

I want to do a lot more than handle her . . . but I'm pretty sure she wants nothing to do with me, and I highly doubt this will go as smoothly as he thinks. The first thing that comes to mind is yelling—lots of yelling.

"Let me think about it," I reply cautiously. "Have you even talked to her about this?"

"I'll handle it."

CHAPTER 10

CLAIRE

It's been a month since Mom left us, and I wish I could say that the hurt in my heart has gotten any less prominent. But the truth is, the hole in my chest isn't healing at the rate I thought it would. I still feel a gaping emptiness inside.

In Virginia, I was constantly surrounded by friends and on the go. I hated being alone and would spend practically every day with someone important to me. Lots of them have called me asking when I'm coming home and offering their support. And I just tell them—soon. I'll be home soon.

But that's a lie; I don't have a home anymore.

Because home isn't a place. It's not a city or a house or a set of walls. It's a person. And for me, home was anywhere that my mom was.

Home was my childhood house, surrounded by lush evergreen trees and laughter as we rolled down the grass surrounding the driveway. Home was the boat rides we took around the lake during endless summers and the fire pits on the dock. Home was the hand I held as I went through heartache last year.

And now, home is a memory.

For the first time in my life, I don't want to be surrounded by people. I want quiet. I want silence. I want to hold onto this feeling deep inside because at least if I am still grieving, I'm keeping her memory alive.

"You need help carrying anything inside, young lady? This is quite the shopping haul you have here."

I smile at my condo's doorman as I pull my keys out of my black Longchamp purse. "No, sir. Thank you so much for the banana bread. I survive mostly on Lunchables and takeout, so this will get some fruit into my diet."

His large belly shakes as he chuckles. "Don't tell me that, now. I'll start worrying about you."

"Get in line," I reply, waving at him as he turns to the elevator.

The doorman, Mr. Bill, and I have become best friends. He's old enough to have retired twenty years ago, but it genuinely seems like he works because he loves his job rather than a need for money. Whenever I walk through the double doors from the parking garage, he greets me and offers to carry my bags even if I don't need help.

I don't mind though, because somehow his presence is comforting. It's like he's an old friend who won't judge me or pity me like everyone else.

Opening the lock to the condo, I gather my shopping bags in both hands, determined to make it through the doors in one trip. While I originally intended to go to the store for a pickup order from weeks ago, there was an insane sale at Dilards that was calling out to me. And who am I to deny the shopping Gods?

Kicking the door closed with my foot, I balance the shoe box full of brand-new fall boots under my chin as I walk into the chilly condo.

"You've got to be fucking kidding me," Parker's grating voice mutters from the living room. "Shopping again?"

The normal instinct for anyone caught doing something they promised they wouldn't do, is to apologize and feel guilty. But my brother clearly came here to fight, so why not give him what he wants?

I drop the bags on the kitchen counter, bracing myself for the verbal battle about to ensue. "Do you have a problem, dear brother? Or have you decided to stop by out of the kindness of your heart?"

His precious surgeon hands clench and unclench, as if he's trying to stop himself from reacting. "The kindness of my heart? Do you really want to go there?"

I shrug my shoulders in indifference, patiently waiting for him to erupt.

"You're living in my condo for free, Claire," he states, weariness evident on his face, as if he doesn't want to fight with me. Parker's dark brown hair, the same shade as mine, is disheveled like he came here straight from the hospital. And while most people would take pity on him and retreat, I just can't.

I love poking him where it hurts.

"Oh wow, P. The condo that you bought in cash with your trust and didn't have to work for?" I say, narrowing my eyes at him. "You're such a philanthropist."

Our late father's invention revolutionized surgical procedures, setting our family up financially for life. It grates on me when Parker acts like he's self-made. Yeah, he's successful in his career, but he wouldn't have nearly the same lifestyle on a surgeon's salary.

His jaw clenches and the thick vein in his forehead throbs with his rapidly escalating pulse. "This isn't about me, Claire. This is about responsibility and accountability." He looks over at the shopping bags on the chair. "Qualities that seem to elude you."

"Did you have nothing better to do than ambush me with your criticism?" I ask, walking into the kitchen to get a Diet Coke out of the fridge. "Because I would rather not listen to your constant disapproval of me. I get enough of it from my own head."

Parker runs his fingers through his hair. "No," he says, his expression softening. "I'm sorry. I know this past month has been hard on you."

I crack the can open, watching him quietly.

He looks so much like our dad with his angular face and prominent jaw. I barely knew my father—he died when I was five but my mom always made a strong effort to keep him alive through stories and photos. Sometimes I wonder how much Parker remembers. Have his memories of Dad faded like the ones of my mom already are?

"I wish I could be here more for you," he confesses.

"It's fine," I croak, feeling my chin start to quiver.

"No it's not," he insists, rising from the couch to take me into his arms.

I let him, leaning into his embrace as his chin rests on the top of my head. He may piss me off and try to control me, but he will always be my older brother. My protector. My idol.

Just don't tell him that.

"Cass keeps reminding me that we all handle grief differently," he says, rubbing his hands across my back. "And I know I've been taking it out on you instead of confronting it myself. That's not okay and I'm going to do better."

I manage a small smile as I step back.

"Thank God for her," I joke. "And just so you know, I haven't made any job decisions yet. I promise I'll let you know when I'm ready. But, I really have been better about shopping, I swear."

I've been mostly spending my days reading and taking walks through Piedmont Park. It's more than I was doing a week ago, and even though it might feel like a baby step to him, it was a huge hurdle to even get out of bed at first, so I'm proud of myself.

That's not to say every day is easy, but they're at least getting easier.

Parker nods, acknowledging my efforts. "I know. I'm still getting bank notifications every time you spend money. We need to get that sorted out."

I bat my eyelashes at him. "Relinquishing control? Look at you making progress. Though if you're looking for something to control, I think the thermostat is broken."

His expression shifts, hesitating before he speaks. "That's actually why I came over to see you."

I pull from his embrace and slide onto a barstool. "Oh thank god it wasn't actually because you followed me around shopping today. I was debating calling your boss to tell him that you seriously needed to sort out your priorities."

"Right." He scrubs his hand over his face, completely ignoring my joke. "I wanted to chat about the spare bedroom. Do you ever use it?"

I furrow my brow, taking another sip of my soda. "Your old room? Ew gross, absolutely not. Mom and I stayed together in the guest room and I honestly don't think I've even opened the door."

"Why did you say ew?" he asks, amusement in his voice.

"Are you kidding? I don't know what kind of weird shit you did in there. It probably needs to be sterilized."

"You're ridiculous." Parker shakes his head. "Glad to see a bit of your old self shining through."

I grin, happy to see that part of me too. "Why do you ask?"

"Beau needs a place to stay for a few months, and I offered him my room."

"What?" I sputter, nearly choking on my drink.

Parker looks confused by my reaction. "Beau's going to stay here for a while."

"I heard you the first time," I stammer, trying to control the torrent of emotions flowing through me. "But don't you think you should've checked with me first?"

"We're discussing it now, are we not?" he responds defensively.

"A question and an order are two different things, Parker," I shoot back, feeling cornered.

My brother can be the most dense person sometimes, good lord.

"He's barely around anyway," he explains, ignoring my comment. "The guy works over a hundred hours a week."

I don't know why he thought this would go smoothly. Even if you ignore the fact that Beau has seen me half-naked, I don't want someone living with me. Being alone is the only thing I have right now. It's helping me heal.

"I'm assuming my opinion on this doesn't matter."

"Of course it matters," he says, though his tone suggests he's already made up his mind. "But I don't see why it's such a big deal."

I take a deep breath, working to calm my racing heart. "What if I said I don't want him here? What then, Parker?"

He shrugs dismissively. "I mean, it is kind of my condo."

And there it is—the same old overbearing big brother. Just when I thought he had gained a few points of emotional intelligence, he goes and does something like this. It always seems like one step forward and two steps back with him.

"So, what, you'd rather I move out so that your buddy can move in?" I demand, crossing my arms against my chest.

Honestly, I totally would move out. But I have nowhere to go and this condo is the last thing I have that ties me to my mom. I still feel her all around me, and I'm not ready to let go of that.

"No, Claire, that's not what I'm saying at all," he tries to clarify.

"It kind of seems like that's what you're saying," I fire back, working hard to keep my voice steady.

"Do you have a problem with him? You seemed fine at the memorial."

I groan, feeling like I'm talking to a brick wall. "He's fine."

Parker smiles, taking those words as my submission to his grand plan. "Good, because he's bringing his stuff over tonight."

CHAPTER 11

CLAIRE

There is genuinely nothing better than Southern Charm on Bravo. Not only is the show an incredibly accurate representation of Peter Pan Syndrome, where the men in the South simply refuse to grow up, but it also has the best drama and makes me feel like my own life is a little less chaotic.

I mean, at least I'm not hooking up with my best friend's ex-boyfriend and lying to their face about it. I just have my brother's best friend, who saw my tits and then ghosted me, moving into my home without my consent.

Life's all about perspective.

Just as the drama on the screen starts heating up, several loud bangs come from the area outside my room.

I guess my new roommate is here.

Sighing, I press the volume button on the remote, desperate to drown out the noise and keep as far away from him as possible. I thought about leaving for the night but quickly realized that the only place I had to go was Parker and Cassidy's house, and I couldn't hang with Cass without the threat of Parker lurking. And he's on my shit list right now so his stupid face is the last thing I want to see.

Unfortunately, that left me with only one option—locking myself in my room and avoiding Beau Buffington at all costs.

When I've settled into the show and almost forgotten about my unwanted houseguest, a loud knock echoes through my bedroom door, shooting my pulse through the roof. My eyes fly to the door and I can see the shadows of his feet darkening the bottom of the frame.

Maybe if I pretend I'm asleep he'll go away.

The thumping continues followed by a deep southern voice murmuring my name as if it's the most beautiful word in the English language. I'd almost forgotten how sensual he sounds, and I instantly sit up and hold my breath, hoping he can't detect the rapid beating of my heart through the door.

"Claire," he repeats himself, my name sounding like honey on his tongue, as if he's purposely drawing out syllables that aren't normally there. "I know you're in there."

He knocks on the door a third time and my trance quickly shifts into irritation. Who the hell does he think he is banging on my door at midnight? Some of us require sleep. Not that I'll be getting any with this brute living in my condo, but that's beside the point.

"I'm sleeping," I yell, hoping it'll shut him up and make him go away. I turn off the TV and burrow under my covers to emphasize my point.

"And I'm Beau," he replies, his chuckle echoing through the door. "Just wanted to say hi to my new roommate."

"Hi," I reply, my voice normal now that I don't have to yell over the TV. "It's midnight. Can this wait until tomorrow?"

"I was wondering if it was okay if I cleaned up a bit? There's dishes in the sink you know."

Oh god, is he some sort of clean freak? The kind of guy who makes you put your dishes in the dishwasher facing a specific direction? If that's the case, he's going to hate living with me . .

"Sure, do whatever you want. Just let me sleep," I concede.

"Whatever I want?" he drawls, inexplicably sending a flush of warmth to my cheeks.

"Within reason. Goodnight, Beau."

The next morning, bright light pours through my floor-to-ceiling windows, reminding me of my mom. Any time the rays stream through, I picture her and her vibrancy for life. Sometimes, they shine directly onto my face, warming me in the crisp fall air. Other times they glimmer beside me, like a tangible presence of her, silently encouraging me from wherever she is now.

At first, I thought I was crazy for feeling like she was there with me, but one night over a glass of wine Cass said she experienced a similar thing when her brother died, only with a cardinal. It's common, she said, especially in hospitals—loved ones witnessing some physical symbol representing the departed's soul. I'm not entirely sure about that. To me, it feels more like we're all just trying to keep the memories of those we've lost alive in any way we can. Either way, we do what we need in order to move forward with some semblance of peace after grief.

I stretch my arms above my head, groaning dramatically as I check social media, ignoring the ever-growing number on my green messages app. After aimlessly scrolling for a bit, I roll out of bed and pad across the warm carpet of my bedroom to the door. Turning the handle, I trudge across the living room and into the modern kitchen to make myself a cup of coffee.

But then I pause, confusion setting in as the smell of warm vanilla and hazelnut washes over me. Blinking the sleep from my eyes, I glance around the kitchen, my gaze landing on a folded piece of paper next to a half-filled coffee pot.

Claire-
Went to the gym. Hope you like coffee.
Beau
P.S. I ordered groceries. If I'm not back by 10 am, can you bring them inside?

Absorbing the words, I can't help but notice Beau's scrawled, almost illegible handwriting, typical of a doctor. I read it multiple times before crumpling it up and tossing it in the trash. Why would he bother leaving me a note? That seems like something someone courteous would do . . . and he certainly wasn't courteous when he took me home and never tried to reach out to me again.

Memories of that night come flooding back to me and it feels like a lifetime ago, though it's only been a little more than a month. Beau made me feel like for the first time, I was enough. The true version of myself was enough. Like I could let him see all of me and wouldn't be asked to tone it down. So I guess it's not a surprise that I never heard from him after that. Nobody wants a woman with no filter.

Part of me wonders if he's going to bring it up, or if we're just going to dance around the topic until the day he moves out. For a moment at the memorial service, I thought he was going to say something, but he never did. I'm no stranger to confrontation, but I also refuse to be the one to break first in this game of nonchalance that we're playing.

My mom used to say that I was the most stubborn person she knew, which is funny because her son is just as bad. Growing up was a battle of wills between me and my brother, the two of us always going at it while my sister watched from the sidelines. One time, when Parker was an intern, he told me that I couldn't get into medical school if I tried.

So what did I do?

I spent my last semester of undergrad buried in books to prove him wrong. Sure, I missed out on a few fun nights with my friends, but the satisfaction of scoring higher than him on the MCAT still brings a smile to my face, so I'd say it was worth it.

Stepping onto the balcony, I'm hit by a surprisingly brisk October chill. The contrast between yesterday's sundress weather and today's cooler air against my silk pajamas is stark. I could go in for a robe, but the cold is oddly refreshing, a reminder that I'm very much alive, not just going through the motions.

As one of the only penthouses in the building, the condo has plenty of outdoor space. The modern finishes of the interior continue to the patio with exposed concrete ceilings and sleek all-weather furniture. I have to admit, when Parker furnished this place, he did a great job. It would honestly be the perfect spot for a party, with plenty of room for people to stand and views of the city that are to die for. The entirety of the exterior space has to be over a thousand square feet.

Though it's not the tallest building on the block, our condo has unobstructed views of downtown facing one direction. The other is caged in by another massive condominium, which I've come to appreciate because it gives me the option to be alone or people-watch from the couch. This morning, I opt for the latter, a bit of entertainment to go with my morning coffee, as I settle into the sectional.

There's a couple who live across the street that look to be around my age, and I've come to find them fascinating. I've watched them dance around the living room and chase each other through their apartment with wide grins on their faces, like they can't get enough of each other. This morning, they're eating breakfast at the counter together, nuzzled close as they share a bowl of some sort of food. They just look so happy, and it makes my heart soar knowing that a love like that is possible.

"I didn't take you for someone who liked to watch." Beau's voice booms from behind me, making me jump with surprise.

I turn to face my new roommate, who's leaning casually on a concrete pillar a few feet away. His shirtless body, covered only in gray joggers and tennis shoes, glistens with the remnants of his workout, highlighting the contours of his well-defined chest.

Why does he have to be so hot?

It's distracting and unfair.

Forcing my eyes to meet his, I muster the best glower I can. "And I didn't take you for someone who bangs on their roommate's door in the middle of the night."

His lips twitch into a smirk as he takes a leisurely sip from his water bottle. "How else was I supposed to get your attention?"

"Maybe something with a little less brute force," I suggest, struggling to keep my eyes away from the way his throat moves as he swallows. It's absurd how sexy a well-defined Adam's apple is, something I've never really considered until I noticed it on him.

Beau's tongue clicks with amusement as his eyes lock with mine. "I don't know if you know this, Claire," he says, drawing out my name in a way that makes my blood stir. "But I'm the kind of guy who thrives on brute force."

Oh, I know that all too well.

The way Beau took me into his arms and threw me onto the bed the night after our date gave that away—not that I'm complaining, because it was hot as hell. He acted like I weighed nothing at all and I remember wondering what else he could do with that strength.

My eyes inadvertently drop to his thighs—thick and muscular, the size of tree trunks. They look like they could squat two of me without issue, something I imagine he just did at the gym based on how sweaty his body is. I try my hardest to avoid looking at his dick, but it's just sitting there, outlined in the tight-fitting joggers like a completely separate and large appendage.

He's probably a shower, not a grower—at least that's what I'm going to tell myself.

"How distinguished," I mutter, darting my eyes back to his face. "I didn't know they let heathens become doctors."

He laughs, a rich, joyful sound that echoes through the crisp air. "They do in orthopedic surgery. We're just heathens with hammers, baby."

I roll my lips under my teeth to hide my smirk. It's hard to not like the guy, especially with his thick accent. Everything he says just rolls off his tongue like smooth wine.

Beau's chocolate eyes narrow, scanning over me as they drop to my chest with absolutely zero discretion whatsoever. For some reason I feel my nipples harden under his gaze, my body responding to him despite my mind's intentions.

A bra would have probably been a good idea now that I have a roommate. But then again, why should I adjust my habits for his comfort? He's the one intruding in my home, not the other way around.

"Aren't you cold?" he asks, forcing his gaze from my chest to my eyes once more. Despite the stubble, I notice a slight flush on his cheeks which surprises me, because it's definitely not from the chilly morning.

"Nope," I reply, slightly amused by his reaction. He doesn't seem like the kind of guy to get flustered easily. "Are you?"

He lets out a visible breath, the cold air accentuating it. "Not in the slightest. Besides, I know a few ways to stay warm in this weather."

"Judging by your attire, I highly doubt that."

He smirks mischievously, a devilish twinkle in his eyes. "Clothes aren't necessary when you've got someone else's body heat."

My cheeks flush at the image of exactly how he could do that. How his thick arms could reach out and wrap around me, pulling me into his sweaty wall of muscle without a word of complaint from me. How his large hands could trace down my spine as I pressed against his hard body, breathing in his purely masculine scent. It's hard not to get lost in the fantasy, but I shake the thoughts away, reminding myself of our past.

Rising from the couch in a rush, I gather things without looking up.

"Well, I'm not sure where you're going to find another body," I stammer, clearing my throat as I practically sprint towards the condo, "but it certainly won't be mine."

And as I'm halfway through the sliding door to the condo, I swear I hear him say, "We'll see about that."

Chapter 12

Sometimes I'll stare at an object in a trance as I wonder about its history. Who invented it? What led them to the idea? How long has it existed?

Right now, I'm sitting in my truck staring at the love of my life, beef jerky, as I consider those very questions. It's practical, portable, and fucking delicious. Not to mention the fact that it's got minimal carbs, something that's constantly on my mind given the diabetes that has plagued my body since age ten.

Up until this week, the circle of people who knew about my diagnosis was pretty small—just my folks, my brother, and a few old roommates from college. It's not that I'm secretive about my illness, it's just that I don't see it as a big deal, so I don't feel the urge to bring it up. But now that I have a new roommate, I figured I should give Claire a heads up, just in case she has to shove sugar down my throat, or something.

Truthfully, the only way that you would know something was wrong with me was if you saw the quarter-sized monitor on the back of my upper arm. It's so inconspicuous that I don't think Claire even noticed until I pointed it out to her. The device continually checks my blood sugar and sends notifications to my phone when my glucose goes out of range. Not that this has been particularly helpful in surgeries that have me tied up for hours at a time, but at least it allows me to completely forego finger sticks. I'm no pussy, but pricking yourself multiple times a day fucking sucks.

All I can say is thank god for modern medicine. Now all I have to do is give myself a long-acting insulin shot to keep my blood sugar regulated through the day. If I decide to eat whatever I want and completely disregard carb counting, I also have quick-acting insulin to bring the numbers down. If I go too low, I keep Skittles on me at all times to pump my numbers back up. It's a constant game of regulation, and while it sounds exhausting, I try to look on the bright side—I'm alive.

As the street light turns green and I pull out of the hospital, Parker's name pops up on the console as an incoming call.

Pressing the answer button on the wheel of my F-150 I say, "Please say you don't need me to come back. I'm finally leaving."

I was just at the hospital for the past twenty-four hours, and though there's a team of general surgery residents that Parker could call if there was an issue, I did have a few consults today that I passed to his team. In theory, I could have missed something that was orthopedic-related and be completely fucked.

"Dude chill, I've been in the clinic all week," he laughs into the speaker.

Fucker.

"Must be nice," I grumble as I turn onto Peachtree Street, grateful that Parker's condo is only a five-minute drive from the hospital. If it was any further, I might pass out from exhaustion.

"Sure is, big guy," he replies, clearly amusing himself. In the background, I hear clattering and a muffled curse.

"Everything okay?"

Parker chuckles into the phone. "Yeah, my fiancée is just a clutz and ran into the coffee table."

Faintly I can hear Cassidy reply to him, though I can't hear exactly what she says.

It must have been good though, because Parker's voice is muffled, as if he's covering the phone, when he says, "Say that again, sweetheart, and you'll be over my knee in ten seconds."

I look out the window trying to distract myself from their banter. This isn't the first time I've been caught in the crossfires of their uncontrolled lust for each other, and I'm honestly just glad they finally stopped arguing and gave in to it. When I was Parker's med student, he once used me as a buffer during a fight, and the tension between them was something I'll never forget. Fortunately, they took things outside and worked them out like adults—by hooking up in the supply closet.

"Sorry," Parker says into the phone after a moment, his breathing slightly labored. "Had to handle something."

A giggle erupts in the background, and I hear the rustling of what sounds like a zipper.

"No worries."

"I just wanted to check in to see how the move went."

I pull up to a light a few blocks from the condo and drum my fingers on the wheel, anxious all of a sudden. I haven't been around for more than a few hours in the days since I moved my shit into the spare bedroom. Not because I haven't wanted to, but because my time isn't my own. Though, for some reason the thought of going back there now, at a time when Claire might be up, makes my heart race.

"Not bad," I answer, trying to sound casual. "I took the loft in case y'all want to ever stay in the city."

Well, that and because I didn't trust myself sleeping across the hall from his little sister. At least this way I have to walk down a full set of stairs to get to her.

"Well, thanks, man. I know I didn't say this before, but you're welcome to stay all residency if you want. It's paid off, so you can just handle the utilities."

"That's too much," I admit, slightly stunned by his generosity. "But I may take you up on it for intern year."

I was only intending to stay a few months while I got my shit together, but the commute has already been a godsend. And for a surgical intern who is starved for sleep, the few extra minutes in bed are precious. So precious, in fact, that I'm seriously considering sticking it out in a condo with a woman who hates my guts.

"Whatever you want," he responds, his tone more rushed. "I've, uh, got something I need to—" His voice trails off and then the line goes dead.

I roll my eyes and try not to think about what they're doing as I pull up to the valet for my new home.

It feels weird living in luxury like this given the way I grew up. Back in South Georgia, where I spent the majority of my childhood, life was simpler and more grounded. Our family wasn't poor by any means, especially with both my parents being local physicians, but our circumstances were a far cry from the opulence I'm surrounded by now. My days were filled with mudding, fishing, and a freedom that only a small town can offer. Our town, with its lack of high-rise buildings and close-knit community, was a paradise for my brother and me.

The shift to city life hit me like a freight train when my parents took jobs in Atlanta during my freshman year of high school. The move was enough of a culture shock as it was, but then they put me in private school which made me truly feel like a fish out of water. Initially, my thick southern drawl made me the target of bullying, but I quickly learned that it's easy to charm the pants off your peers when you're outgoing, friendly, and play sports.

While private school is easy to judge for someone with my upbringing, it taught me how to talk to pretty much anyone. Now I can find some sort of commonality with each person I meet, regardless of their background.

I wouldn't be surprised if that skill was the only reason I got into the orthopedic surgery residency, because I had to network my ass off in addition to leaning on Parker's recommendations. Though now that the exhaustion of my day has finally settled in, and I have several hours of studying left before bed, I'm kicking myself for not choosing a specialty with a better lifestyle.

As I pass through the front door of the condo, I'm half-expecting some kind of standoff with Claire, but the place is quiet, almost too quiet. Part of me wishes we could just address whatever tension there is head-on, but I haven't yet figured out how to explain to her that I'm not an asshole who flirted with her the same day her mom died.

I'm just a busy asshole who has incredibly poor timing.

Dropping my keys on the stainless steel countertop, I head to the fridge to grab something for dinner. My life these days is all about efficiency, including my meals. The stuffed peppers from Costco are a lifesaver—healthy enough and easy to prepare. Cooking used to be a passion of mine during med school, but now it's just another chore squeezed into a packed schedule.

Surprisingly, the only stuff in the refrigerator belongs to me. I didn't question it at first, assuming Claire just needed to go grocery shopping, but it's been a week and there's still nothing but my food.

I rub my face as I place my dinner in the microwave, telling myself that her nutrition is a problem for another day. Right now I just need to shove something in my mouth, take a shower, and watch case videos until I pass out. I've got to be back at the hospital in less than eight hours for rounds, so time is not on my side.

Thank god, though, that tomorrow is Friday and I have Saturday off. I may still be spending the day thinking about surgery, but at least I'll be doing it from the couch with a cold beer in my hand.

Once my meal is warmed up, I slouch on the black metal barstool at the counter. I barely pause for breaths as I inhale the combination of peppers, meat, and cheese, while simultaneously watching a YouTube video on a potential surgical case for tomorrow. The case itself is simple, but I prefer to know exactly what to expect before I encounter something in the OR for the first time. My old rugby coach used to say, "Perfect preparation prevents piss poor performance," and I guess that mantra always stuck with me.

"Well, well, well, I was beginning to think my new roommate had already moved out," Claire's lively voice appears beside me. I haven't heard a peep from the condo, and considering the late hour, I assumed she was asleep.

I'm glad she's not.

"You haven't scared me off just yet," I answer, swallowing the last bite of my dinner as I look in her direction. "Did I wake you?"

Her dark hair is piled on top of her head in a messy bun, a few untamed wisps of hair falling around her delicate features. She's wearing a thin, black silk robe, loosely tied, revealing more than it conceals. It would be almost too easy to reach out and tug on the loose tie holding it together. Too easy to determine if she's completely naked beneath the haphazardly tied fabric.

There are four total barstools in the kitchen, but for some reason Claire chooses to perch on the one directly next to me, spinning to face me. My blood stirs as my eyes drop to her bare legs, noticing the way her robe stops halfway up her thigh, exposing more of her toned legs than I've ever seen before. They seem to go on for days, and I have to bite the inside of my cheek to get a grip on myself.

Fuck—I'm going to need to go jerk off after this. It's been too damn long since I got laid.

I force myself to look away, focusing on her words as she responds, "No, you didn't wake me. I'm a bit of a night owl these days." Claire lets out a soft moan that makes my cock jump as she looks down at my plate. "Plus, whatever you made smelled so good."

"I'm sure anything would smell good when you don't keep any food in the house."

She rolls those perfect eyes of hers with practiced precision, as if she's done it every day since the moment she was born. "I finished my last Lunchable and can of Diet Coke today, I'll have you know. Normally I at least have those in the fridge."

"The epitome of a balanced diet," I say, shaking my head in mock dismay. "Aspartame and preservatives. Are you sure you come from a family of doctors and nurses?"

"We all have our vices."

Yeah, we do. And unfortunately, I'm realizing that she's mine.

"Well, go on," I offer, gesturing my chin to the fridge. "There's plenty of food for the both of us."

Her face lights up with delight as she hops off the stool like a kid who's just been picked first for a game during recess. Fuck, I'd pick her first any day. Every day.

I try to avert my eyes, attempting to glue them to the YouTube video on my phone, but something about her is like a fucking siren that I can't look away from.

She's beautiful, magnetic, and fearless—exactly like I remembered her. I don't know why Parker is so worried. She seems to be doing just fine.

After Claire removes the warmed-up food from the microwave, she returns to her original perch, facing me as she shovels a bite of pepper and meat through her lips. "Mmmmm," she hums, chewing slowly as she studies me. "I think you're officially my favorite roommate."

"I'm your only roommate," I remind her, returning my focus to the screen.

Claire finishes her meal, making a satiated sound that goes directly to my crotch as she pushes the plate across the counter. I expect her to get up and head back to her room, but instead, she moves closer to me, her leg now resting against mine as her gaze lands on my phone screen.

"Whatcha watching?"

"Oh, uh," I fumble my words, not expecting her question. "It's a shoulder arthroplasty where they substitute the—"

"Woah," she gushes, interrupting my train of thought as she leans in, her chin resting on her hands. Her blue eyes widen with fascination as they focus on the video playing on my phone. "That's so freaking cool. Except the camera angle kind of sucks, so I don't know how you can tell what the heck is happening."

"You get used to it," I reply, trying to focus as I explain to her exactly what's happening in the video, despite this being the first time I'm also seeing it.

Claire's eating it up and asking me questions as I walk her through the procedural steps. For someone who didn't pursue a medical career like the rest of her family, she sure seems drawn to it.

"Interesting," she whispers in awe as reaches for the screen to get a closer look, our fingers briefly touching in the process. "It's like you're piecing together a puzzle."

I nod, my passion quickly reignited by her genuine interest. It can sometimes be hard to remember that while I'm going through hell, my job is actually exciting, and can even be fun sometimes.

"Honestly, that's a pretty good way of describing it," I admit. "Each patient's body is different, and you never know what you're going to see until you open someone up and take a deeper look inside."

Just like the woman next to me. On the night we met, I braced myself for someone aloof and uninteresting, but she turned out to be the complete opposite.

"So," she says, her voice softer now. "Do you ever get nervous before surgeries?"

"Only when your brother is my attending," I joke, unable to help my smile when she giggles at my remark.

It's not true—Parker doesn't scare me in the slightest. But I'm desperately trying to remind my logical brain that she's my best friend's little sister, and therefore she is completely off-limits. That night was a one-time thing, and it can't ever happen again.

"He's not that scary," she assures me, pausing the video. "Especially not when you've seen pictures of him playing dress up as a kid."

I chuckle. "I would pay a lot of money for those."

"Hmmm." She hums thoughtfully, sliding the phone back to me. "Maybe if you're good."

I run my fingers over my stubble, trying to work out why she's talking to me like this, as if I'm a friend and someone she genuinely wants to get to know, not a complete douche. I don't deserve it, but I'm sure as fuck not going to complain.

So while I'm not proud of what's about to come out of my mouth, I can't stop it.

"And what if I'm bad?" I ask, my voice dropping to a level that I didn't know existed.

"If you're bad," she considers, her voice surprisingly steady given the flush creeping down her neck, "I might have a few *other* photos in my stash that you might like."

Fuck me sideways.

Now all I can think about are the pictures of her naked body just sitting on her phone completely unappreciated. At least I hope nobody has had a chance to appreciate them . . .

"Oh, Claire," I say, trying to maintain some semblance of self-control. "You don't want to know just how bad I can be."

For a moment, neither of us says anything. The room seems to have shrunk, and I can practically hear the rapid beating of her heart. My pulse pounds to match hers, desperately trying to figure out what the fuck is happening here.

I should get up and walk away—should take an ice-cold shower and get in bed. But I can't bring myself to move, let alone breathe.

Deciding for us, she pushes the stool back and stands up, leaving me aching with a mix of desire and frustration. I need more, but I'm not going to push her. Even this tension is better than nothing.

"Goodnight, Beau," she says, her voice a little breathy as if she's trying hard to maintain her composure. "Or should I call you, bad boy Beau?"

Her small smirk sends me over the edge, and I reach out to grab her arm, wanting to keep her a moment longer. "Call me whatever you want, pretty girl. Just make sure it's my name on your lips."

She inhales sharply, a visible reaction to my touch, before gently pulling away. Crossing the living room, she heads towards her bedroom, casting a playful challenge over her shoulder. "Try to behave yourself."

I swallow, watching her disappear into her bedroom. Behaving myself around her is going to be damn near impossible.

CLAIRE

Every morning for the past week, I've woken up to the scent of vanilla hazelnut and a fresh pot of my favorite coffee. And every morning, despite my best intentions, I smile because there's a cheeky note in Beau's chicken scratch sitting next to one of my mugs. At first, I tossed them, but now, they've started to fill the drawer under the coffee machine. He might not realize it, but the small gesture is one of the first things in a while to bring me happiness. And after Mom died, I'm trying to hold onto any little bit of happiness that I can.

Parker took most of his kitchen stuff to his new house, so the only mugs in the condo are from my personal collection. Over the years I've collected a slew of reality TV-themed ceramic coffee mugs that range from quotes of my favorite stars to photos of iconic scenes. They're not the most sightly things, but they remind me not to take life too seriously—Sonja Morgan certainly doesn't.

The mug that Beau left out on the counter this morning has cursive pink letters with the words, "A new bombshell has entered the villa." It's a reference to the show Love Island UK, and while there's now a spin-off in the US, I will forever read the phrase with a British accent.

The note read:

I felt like this was fitting given we're now roomies.
(I'm the bombshell, in case you were confused)

I couldn't help the laugh that came out of me as I tossed the note in the drawer and grabbed my coffee. Something about Beau is just so endearing, like he's a big softie stuck in this massively intimidating body. I can see why my brother is friends with him and can practically picture Beau immediately melting Parker's ice-cold shell.

Speaking of things that are melting—my heart is at the top of the list. Beau opened up about his diabetes last night, a topic he evidently doesn't share widely. I expected a brief explanation, but when I bombarded him with questions, he didn't shut me down or show annoyance. Instead, he just smiled that warm, engaging smile and patiently indulged my curiosity. Which, it turns out, was short-lived, because after a few moments of intense eye contact with my strikingly handsome roommate, my stomach started doing backflips, and I fled to my room.

He's just really hard not to like . . . that's the problem.

But at the same time, Beau is also a bundle of contradictions. He blatantly flirts with me, yet made zero effort to contact me after our date. No calls, no messages, only deafening silence—as if the night we shared simply vanished into thin air.

I feel like any normal guy would act awkward around a girl that they ghosted. But not Beau. He's in his own world, breezing through life as if we can casually switch from a fling to friends without missing a beat.

The problem is—I've never once felt like an adult in my life.

And, a massive part of me is dying to make things as awkward as possible between us. But because I'm stubborn as hell, I'm not going to let him know how he affects me. I'll flirt back, and make him see everything he missed out on until he's kicking himself for not calling me. After all, he's just a man. And anything men can do, women can do better.

Following my coffee and morning walk through the park, I decided to curl up on the balcony with my Kindle. While my most recent read is a slow-burn rom-com, I can't bring myself to open it. I'm a mood reader and switch between books at a wildly unhinged rate. Maybe it's my ADHD, but I have a hard time focusing on one thing for too long. And right now, I need a good old smutty story to take my mind off my brother's best friend.

As I'm settling into a hockey romance that's already making me laugh out loud, my phone rings.

"Cass!" I exclaim into the phone. "You're going to die. This goalie just put his main character on the Zamboni and, well, you know."

Cassidy is the one who introduced me to spicy books this year. At first, I was hesitant because none of my other friends read smut. Or if they do, they definitely don't talk about it. But once I started reading, I couldn't stop. It's a completely different world than the one I'm used to, where books like this are seen as taboo and uncouth.

While I have zero filter around my family, growing up like I did made me super aware of how everyone sees me. It was like I was always two different people. One version of me at home and another out in public and at school.

I never wanted to be an embarrassment to my family, especially considering the circles my parents moved in, so I did everything I could to portray on the outside that I fit in.

Which is why I'm always assessing how much of my true self I can let free. How wild I can be. It's also why at twenty-six years old, I'm still discovering so much about myself.

"What?" Cass pauses before replying to my greeting because I'm pretty sure that's the last thing she expected me to say at noon on a weekday. "Oh, nice. Send me the name of the book."

She sounds distracted and I can barely hear her, which makes me worried given everything that's happened the past month. Sometimes it feels like once you experience a tragedy, you're just waiting for the next one to strike.

"Is everything okay?" I ask, closing my Kindle and setting it on the cushion beside me. In the background, there's a muffled commotion, then silence.

"Cass? I can't hear you." I put the phone to my ear, trying to catch her distant words.

She comes back clearer. "Sorry about that. Can you hear me now? There was a wild patient in the hallway, and I had to slip into the supply room."

Relief washes over me as I take a deep breath, trying to calm my racing heart.

"Yep, I gotcha sister."

She chuckles. "I'm not your sister yet."

"You might as well be," I reply honestly. "Like it or not, you're stuck with me, even if my idiot brother fucks things up again."

Cass and Parker had lots of ups and downs in their relationship before they got to where they are now. I like to think that I'm the reason they're happy and together because I brought her to our house on Christmas last year to reconnect. He was being a mopey asshole and wouldn't swallow his pride to call her. I forced her to get on a plane and surprise him. After an hour, they made up and the rest is history.

"He won't," Cassidy says, "because I honestly think he's more scared of you than he is of me."

I take a sip of the Diet Coke sitting on the table in front of me. "As he should be. I'm a very formidable force."

"Speaking of formidable forces, I have a bone to pick with you."

"Uh oh," I tease playfully. "What did I do now? Did Parker see my credit card bill again? Because I've been good, I swear. Whatever he says is a filthy lie."

Something rustles in the background as she replies. "I texted you last week about getting my stethoscope from the condo and you never responded. I wanted to give you space, but now I'm kind of desperate. We ran out of the cheap ones at work which is why I'm currently on my hands and knees in the supply closet searching for a spare."

My brain must still be in the book I was reading because I say, "Don't tell Parker that."

And then I remember that he's my brother, and I almost vomit. Sometimes I have a hard time separating the fact that Cassidy is my best friend, but also the person marrying my brother. It's like I want to know everything, but at the same time, I don't want to know anything at all.

"He's in surgery all day, don't worry," she responds with a light chuckle. "So the stethoscope?"

"Ah yeah, about that," I say sheepishly. "I deleted all of my texts on Monday, so I didn't see it."

"Why on earth would you do that?"

"Well, when you have hundreds of unread messages it can get a little overwhelming," I admit, smiling as I pull up the nice clean message box. "It felt nice to start fresh."

I haven't looked at my texts once since that day in the hospital. Messages just started pouring in once news got out about my mom and I couldn't bring myself to read them. My phone's been on do not disturb for texts ever since.

"I'm glad," Cassidy replies, and I know she genuinely means it.

"Do you think you could bring the stethoscope to me? I'm almost positive that it's inside the nightstand in Parker's old room. Sorry to rush you. I really want to chat, but I'm desperate and we're short-staffed."

"I'll be there in fifteen minutes," I promise as I walk into the condo. "Do you want me to just pull up to the emergency room entrance and honk my horn?"

"No, no," she says quickly. "Just call me when you're here and I'll run out."

By the time I'm able to find the stethoscope, which was not anywhere near the nightstand like she said, and drive to the hospital, over thirty minutes have passed. A pang of guilt hits me for taking so long, given how hectic her day is. I'm just hoping she can spare a second to meet me outside. If not, I'll just dash in and leave it at the front desk.

On the way over, I was clutching the steering wheel as tight as I possibly could, anticipating the range of emotions that would come with returning to the last place I saw my mom alive. But surprisingly when I put the car in park and turn my flashers on, a sense of calm washes over me. I don't picture my mom at all, because where she died isn't where she lived. Instead of imagining her gasping for breath, I see my brother and sister-in-law, and the incredible work they do each day. I see the lives they save and the people that they help.

I know I like to give them shit, but it's really remarkable that they have a calling. A passion.

After trying to reach Cass three times without any luck, I decide to park in the garage and head inside the hospital, not wanting to obstruct the entrance.

On my way in, I find myself trailing behind a young boy on crutches. He looks like he can't be much older than eight and is clad in a green baseball uniform, smeared with red clay as if he's been sliding through the dirt. I slow my pace, noticing how he's struggling with each step, like he's never been on crutches before.

Glancing around for any sign of his parents, I find no one. The thought of him falling and worsening whatever injury he's got going on urges me to help him.

Quickening my pace, I pause in front of the boy. "Hang on bud," I tell him, taking in the black streaks of eye paint smeared down his cheeks. "Let me grab you a wheelchair."

The young boy nods, his dark eyes wide and grateful. "Okay, thanks," he manages to sniffle, wiping his muddy arm across his face.

I rush inside, quickly spotting an unattended wheelchair in the breezeway. Grabbing it, I return to the boy and position the chair to his right, making sure to lock it in place so it won't go anywhere. I used wheelchairs occasionally with Mom when she was too weak from chemo, so I've learned the importance of putting the brake on before someone sits down.

There will be no falls on my watch.

"Alright, pass me the crutches first and then reach down to the chair so you don't tumble over," I instruct, holding out my right hand as I toss Cassidy's stethoscope around my neck because the dang leggings I'm wearing don't have any pockets. I may hate cargo pants from a fashion perspective, but I'm now understanding why scrubs are designed the way they are—with lots of room to hold things.

The kid follows my lead, hobbling over and wincing as he settles into the chair.

"Thanks," he mumbles, placing his hands on the wheels to move forward. He doesn't know the brakes are engaged, so he grunts as he tries with all his strength to push himself forward.

I stifle a grin, admiring his independence.

"Just a sec," I say, bending down to release the brakes. "We're heading the same way. Mind if I give you a push?"

He nods and I hand him the crutches, too big for his small frame.

"So what happened?" I ask as we start moving toward the entrance. "Hurt your ankle sliding home?"

He shakes his head. "Into first."

"I thought you weren't supposed to slide into first?" I don't know much about baseball, but in the games I've been to you never see the pros do that.

Apparently for good reason . . .

"It's way more fun to slide," he explains as we cross the threshold to the hospital. "Plus, I was safe and it helped us win."

"Totally worth it then," I joke as we stop in front of the triage desk. An elderly woman is checking in with the nurse so I crouch down to the little dude's eye level while we wait.

"You should tell my mom that," he says, flashing me a semi-toothless grin. I'm not sure when kids start losing their teeth, but it's super cute. "She's upset that I got hurt and was crying in the car."

"She's probably just worried about you. Speaking of that, where is she? Do you need me to wait with you?"

"She went to park the car and said she should be back in a sec—Mom!" His face lights up as his mom comes running through the automatic doors to the emergency room. They share strikingly similar features; dark hair and dark eyes, though hers are slightly reddened like the kid said.

"I'm sorry it took so long," she apologizes, bending down to squeeze her son. "Parking here is a nightmare. Are you okay?"

"I'm fine," he reassures her, his small hand patting her back as he watches me. "This lady got me a wheelchair and helped me. Plus, she thinks sliding into first base was smart, not silly like you said."

My eyes widen with alarm. I don't know these people and definitely don't want to get yelled at for saying, or doing, the wrong thing. "I did not!"

"Did too," he replies, sticking his tongue out at me.

I mirror his gesture and he giggles. His mom, slightly exasperated but grateful, thanks me for assisting him.

"No problem at all," I reply with a smile. "I'm just here to drop something off for my sister-in-law, so I've got plenty of time."

The woman in front of us moves aside, and I gesture for the woman and her son to go ahead of me so they can check-in. I don't have anything going on for the rest of the day, so I'm fine waiting. Plus, it's kind of interesting to people watch.

The massive room is packed to the brim, with every single chair full, and multiple people standing. It's actually kind of beautiful when I think about it. People of all shapes, sizes, and backgrounds all gathered in one place. How their stories all probably differ so much, but here they are in one place with the same goal—to heal.

"Are you Claire?" a petite brunette in light blue scrubs squeals, appearing out of nowhere. Her short ponytail is coming undone and she looks slightly disheveled, like she just ran miles through the hospital to meet me.

"Uh, yeah," I answer, caught off guard. "Sorry, do I know you?"

Her green eyes light up as she leans in and pulls me into a hug, tiny arms somehow circling my whole frame as her head crashes into my chest. I can't help but let out a laugh, because this is exactly how I would act all the time if it wasn't ingrained in me to hold back in public. It's endearing and I can instantly sense a potential friendship despite never having met her before.

"Oops! Sorry." She quickly steps back, a sheepish grin on her face. "I have zero self-control, and my friends say I struggle with boundaries. I'm Morgan and I work with Cass, though I'm sure you gathered that by the scrubs and chaos."

I can't help but smile. "People say that about me too."

"I know." She takes my hand, pulling me through the crowds of people. "Cass has told me everything about you."

"Hopefully only good things."

"Are you kidding me?" Morgan giggles, her eyes giddy with amusement. "Anyone who puts Dr. Winters in his place as often as you do is automatically my hero. I still crack up at the thought of the St. Patrick's Day prank you pulled on him this year."

She's talking about the family vacation we took to Savannah where Parker claimed that he could outdrink me. Little did he know that I switched to non-alcoholic beer halfway through the day and was practically sober by the end of the night. He was so confused and wouldn't stop grumbling about how he only lost because he hardly ever drinks. To this day I'm not sure if he knows the truth about what I did.

I roll my eyes at the memory. "He's such an idiot."

"Can't argue with you on that," Morgan agrees, pausing in a more secluded section of the hallway. "Grady is on diversion, so it's a bit of a shit show today. I've been at the triage desk, so Cass told me to look out for you."

Looking back down the corridor, I see the overflowing patient area. "Is it always this crazy around here?"

"Depends on the day, but that's part of the fun," she answers, swinging her arm out like she's showing off something she's proud of. "You never know what you're gonna get."

I can tell working in the ER is something she truly enjoys by the light that shines in her eyes as she describes everything she's seen come through the door today. Shockingly, I find myself hanging on her words and asking a million questions.

I've never really asked Cass what her days were like, because I just assumed it was the same as my brothers. He always made medicine sound so regimented and boring, kind of like how he lives his life. But Morgan's perspective portrays it more like a game with multiple ways to win, and it sounds almost fun.

"Sorry, I don't want to eat up your day, I know you're busy," I offer once she finishes her explanation on the differences between sedatives. Apparently, some new resident only ordered a small dose of Ativan for her patient and she was pissed. I have no idea what it means, but I nod along like I do.

"You're totally fine," she assures me. "I have our charge nurse covering for me, and honestly am in no rush to go back. Triage is the most boring assignment ever."

I smile, appreciating her candor. "Well, tell Cass I said hi and that I miss her."

I haven't seen my future sister-in-law very much recently. She's been giving me space to work through everything, and I know she's been busy with wedding planning plus the move, so I haven't wanted to bother her either.

"For sure," Morgan replies as we start to walk back toward the entrance of the hospital. "And hey, we're grabbing dinner and drinks on Friday if you want to come along. I literally just convinced Cass to ditch your brother for margaritas. She's a hard sell now that she's practically wifed up."

"Tequila is definitely the trick with her. But, count me in. Just have Cass send me the details, and I'll be there."

CHAPTER 14

BEAU

"**G**et your ass in here, Buffington," Walker calls from the operating room as I finish scrubbing my hands with antiseptic soap. "This guy doesn't have all day."

I was only just paged to OR3 and had to scrub properly before entering the room, but I don't say that. He's just trying to be a dick.

"What do we have?" I ask, entering the room and turning to allow the nurse to put my gown on.

Normally there's a little bit of time to prep before a case and I don't have to walk in completely blind. As someone who's used to planning out everything I do, it makes me uncomfortable feeling unprepared, but sometimes that's the nature of the job.

"Thirty-year-old male," the scrub nurse reads from a clipboard with a practiced calm. "Paraplegic for five years. Cut his right foot on a rock at the lake this weekend, and presented to the ED with a t-max of 104 this morning. Bacterial swab positive for necrotizing fasciitis."

"Hell yeah," I mutter as I position myself across the table from my chief resident.

Necrotizing fasciitis, also known as flesh-eating bacteria, is incredibly rare to see, especially in a city hospital. If it's not detected and treated quickly, it can have significantly high mortality rates in patients.

Looking down at the limb, I note how swelling and redness have taken over the whole foot. The chance that he keeps anything below the knee is probably pretty slim, but we won't know until we get in there how extensive the damage is. Sometimes we have to take more than necessary to ensure the infection is gone and we don't have to do a repeat surgery.

"What's the plan, Dr. Chastain?" I ask, feeling my heart start to race with excitement. I likely won't see this again in my surgical career, and I feel grateful that he brought me in on this case rather than another intern.

"I was going to ask you that," Walker asks, watching me carefully.

Okay, remain calm. You know this shit.

I take a deep breath and spout out my plan.

"It's systemic at this point, so we can't just debride the wound. We need to remove the limb above the ankle and then assess the area of involvement once it's open to determine if we got enough. Post-op we'll consult infectious disease to manage antibiotic therapy."

"Bingo." Walker nods with approval. "Let's get it done, Buffington. You're running the show today."

Though the mask hides it, my grin is huge as the scrub tech hands me the blade to make the first incision.

Other specialties always rag on orthopedic surgeons for being idiots with power tools and I totally get it—it's easy to make fun of something from the outside without knowing what it takes to do our jobs. From their perspective, they see a male-dominated field filled with bros who like to listen to heavy metal while sawing off necrotic toes.

And yeah, orthopedic surgery can be all of those things. There are days when it's fun as hell, and we pound our hammers into hips until the sun goes down, but it's also incredibly complex and challenging.

Orthopedics requires you to think mechanically about each patient's life outside of the hospital. I have to consider how they go about their days, what's important to them, and how I can minimize the impact of their injury. If I compromise even a few degrees of motion to someone's shoulder, they might not ever be able to comfortably dress themselves again.

Our patients put a lot of trust in us. And sometimes it's scary as hell, because I still feel like a kid most of the time, and one minor mistake has bigger implications than just a bad grade in med school.

But it's also exhilarating.

There's no other high like it.

By the time the case finishes and we speak to the family, it's well into the afternoon. I was going to scrub in on a septic joint washout with Dr. Franklin, but Walker suggested I catch up on charting before heading out. I've got ten open notes that need to be completed from follow-up visits and procedures today. It might not sound like a lot of work, but when your chief resident starts breathing down your neck about the formatting of a current medication list, it's better to do things right the first time.

As I walk into the empty ortho lounge, I pull out my phone to check my blood sugar, feeling thankful that my numbers have recovered. That case was longer than I anticipated and towards the end, I started feeling a little shaky and lightheaded. Fortunately, I tossed back a few handfuls of Skittles after we closed up and immediately started feeling better. I can handle the shakes as long as I don't pass out on the operating table.

Sinking into the uncomfortable desk chair, I pop in my headphones and give in to the tedious task ahead of me. Truthfully, charting has got to be the worst part of a physician's job—it's repetitive and mind-numbing. I understand why we have to do it, but squinting at a computer screen for hours on end was never high up on the list of reasons I wanted to become a doctor. Nor was the daily dose of getting chewed out, but that's beside the point. At least the berating will taper off after five years. These notes, however, will haunt me for my entire career.

The door opens just as I'm finishing up, the raspy voice of Hinder's "Lips of an Angel" echoing through the cramped room.

I know—I'm a walking, talking stereotype.

"Hey," Walker greets me as he falls on top of the bed in the corner of the room.

Massive feet hang off the edge of the frame, and he makes no effort to move them as he drapes his tattoo-covered arm over his eyes. The man has a couple of inches on me and a much leaner build, almost like a swimmer. Honestly, at one point I think he told me he did swim in college, but everything in the past few months has been a blur that it's hard to keep non-medical details straight.

I pause the song. "How's it going?"

He grunts, not opening his eyes. "Horrible."

Walker is the most literal person I've ever met. He's not one to beat around the bush or make a play on words. He says what he means and he means what he says. And I love him for that.

"Yeah, you kind of look like dog shit," I joke, trying to lighten his mood as I kick back in my chair. "I didn't want to say anything, but you smell like it too."

Walker scrubs his hands over his face, not taking my bait. "It's the fucking beard. How much longer do we have?"

Our department started doing a "No Shave November" challenge, and if you don't make it to December, you have to pick up one additional call day. While this might sound easy to the general population, most ortho guys hate having facial hair because it gets sweaty and hot beneath the surgical masks, though it personally doesn't bother me.

"Three weeks dude," I remind him. "Come on, it's not that bad."

He runs his fingers through his jet-black hair and lets out a dramatic exhale. "It's itchy as fuck, and as you so kindly stated, I look like dog shit."

"I think I said you smell like dog shit too," I add, unable to help myself as I grin over at him.

His eyes slowly open with the singular intent of glaring at me. "I can't wait until you become chief resident one day. It sucks every little bit of life from your body."

"I don't have any life in my body now, dude," I reply as I log off the computer. "Plus, it'll be one of the other interns. I'm too good-looking to be chief. Wouldn't be fair."

Silence settles between us as I pack up my things. I glance at my reflection in the locker mirror, taking in a week's worth of stubble and tired eyes. Yep, I'm definitely starting to resemble a mad scientist more than a heartthrob.

"You did good work today, Buffington," Walker says, finally sitting up from the bed. "Don't diminish your skills."

Walker isn't one to hand out compliments quickly, so I can't help but feel surprised by his praise. In fact, I'm pretty sure this is the first nice thing I've heard him say to an intern.

Something about grumpy chief residents . . . they just love me I guess.

"Thanks," I reply, shooting him a wide grin. "Probably not something we'll see again for a while."

He lets loose a chuckle as he stands. "We might if people keep dumping toxic shit into the Chattahoochee River. Let's get the fuck out of here. I slept like shit on call last night and need some good rest."

I shake my head as I sling my bag over my shoulder. "You try getting good rest when you live with Parker's little sister. All she wants to do when I get back from the hospital is talk."

It comes out sounding like a complaint, but really, I'd give up every additional minute of sleep to talk to her. She reminds me what it feels like to be excited to be alive. Somehow, even though I come home feeling like I'm running on empty, the second I see her I'm instantly recharged.

Whether she talks to me because she's lonely or because she's beginning to forgive me, I don't care. Coming home to Claire has become the highlight of my day, and I hang on every word that comes out of her sweet lips.

"Parker Winters?" Walker asks, raising an eyebrow at me as he gathers his things.

"The one and only," I confirm.

"What's that like?" He smirks, clearly amused by my revelation. "If she's anything like Parker I can only imagine . . ."

For some reason, my pulse quickens with the urge to defend her. I respect Parker, he's like a brother, but comparing him to Claire feels off, especially given his reputation around here. They couldn't be more opposite if they tried. She's vibrant, intriguing, and lively as hell—a stark contrast to Parker's more reserved nature.

She's . . . perfect and all I fucking think about.

But I can't say that, nor should I even be admitting it to myself, so I keep my response simple.

"She's nothing like Parker."

CHAPTER 15

CLAIRE

Are men supposed to be so clean? It's been a while since I lived with one, though when my brother lived with us he was more of a man-child than a man, so I doubt he even qualifies. If Parker doesn't count, then I've officially never lived with a man until now.

In D.C., all of my friends from college would complain about how gross their boyfriends were, leaving the toilet seat up and hair in the sink while they remained oblivious to their mess. Their stories of testosterone-fueled Sundays and beer boxes crowding out the wine in the fridge made me appreciate my living situation with my girlfriends. Honestly, it also made me a little relieved that my boyfriend never suggested we move in together.

So, when Beau forced his way into the nonexistent roommate position, and immediately offered to clean the apartment, it threw me for a loop. It didn't seem on brand for the male population, given everything I'd heard from my friends. Then when he started writing me stupidly cute notes and making my morning coffee, I started to question if I was in an alternate universe.

Because in what world does your brother's best friend, and previous one-night stand, move in with you?

A reality world.

In what world is he also the perfect roommate and insanely thoughtful?

A dream world.

I keep waiting for some reason to hate this arrangement, but I don't. The condo has never looked better, not even during my brother's reign as king of the penthouse. I'd be lying if I said I was the tidiest person, usually content with leaving coats strewn over chairs and dishes in the sink. But now I wake up in the morning and everything is where it should be, like a magical fairy came through overnight and righted my chaos.

Beau even had a grocery order of Lunchables and Diet Coke delivered for me this morning with a note that said:

> **One day we'll talk about what a nutritious meal includes. Thanks for letting me crash here.**

I want to tell him that I'm perfectly capable of buying my food and to save his money for the other women in his life, but I can't. Despite my best efforts to harbor an inkling of irritation for him, I just don't have it in me. He's so stupidly likable.

Which is why I'm currently heading up the set of iron stairs to his loft to make my mother proud and thank him for his generosity. If I had his phone number, I would have just sent him a casual thank you text, but I don't, and I'm certainly not going to be the one to ask for it.

I haven't been up to the loft since he moved in, trying my hardest to refrain from snooping despite the excess of time I have on my hands. Have I wanted to search for skeletons in his closet to give me a reason to dislike him?

Absolutely.

But even I have boundaries.

The impeccable state of Beau's loft catches me off guard, though it really shouldn't, given the way he treats the rest of our living space. The bed, with its black metal canopy, is neatly made, pillows fluffed perfectly as if awaiting a professional photoshoot. Two dark wood nightstands outline the bed, with nothing left out on them except two matching modern lamps. His desk is covered in a pile of neatly stacked books that look like they've been organized by alphabetical order, and his shoes sit lined up along the wall like stinky soldiers preparing for battle. The organization is impressive and so very on-brand for him.

Glancing around, I don't see Beau anywhere, which is strange because I swear I heard him come back from the hospital. He's been gone all day, and while I won't admit that I miss him, it is admittedly nice to have another person around.

After Mom's death, I relished in the solitude of living alone. The silence and space were healing, and the thought of having Beau ruin my peace was irritating. But now, as I'm starting to feel more and more like myself, it's like my viewpoint has turned upside down. Rather than retreating into the quiet like I once loved, I find myself waiting up for him to return from the hospital, desperate for his company.

I try to reassure myself that it's just because he's accessible. My desire to spend time with him has nothing to do with the fact that he's friendly, super hot, or interesting. It would be this way with any roommate. And that's all he is—my roommate.

Just as I'm about to turn around, I notice a stream of fluorescent light coming out of the slightly cracked bathroom door.

A normal person would leave their roommate to their shower and speak with them when they were finished. I was taught to have boundaries for personal space, especially when it comes to privacy, which is why I have no logical explanation for the reason my feet start moving toward the occupied bathroom instead of down the stairs.

The bathroom attached to the loft is the smallest in the condo, with barely enough space to house a stand-up shower, toilet, and sink. Warm steam trickles out of the cracked door and hits me in the face as I push it slightly further open to peer inside.

As my eyes adjust to the haze, I spot Beau's back facing the glass door, droplets of water from the rain shower head cascading down his broad shoulders. One of his arms is pressed against the gray tiled wall in front of him, almost like it's holding him upright while he washes himself clean.

Or at least that's what I assume he's doing.

A white, finger-sized device sits on the back of his bulging tricep muscle, something I never noticed before. It must be the monitor he was explaining to me, though in real life it looks more like a tracking device than an instrument to check blood glucose. I make a mental note to ask him more about it when he's not butt-ass naked in the shower.

Speaking of butts . . . his looks like it belongs in a museum. It's sculpted and firm with two dimples that sit at the base of his hips. The image of digging my heels into them as he thrusts into me makes my blood stir in a way that I wish it didn't.

I should look away, but I can't—especially not when I notice him clench his knuckles against the wall, almost like he's in pain.

Only the sound that escapes his mouth doesn't sound like he's in pain . . .

My eyes widen and I have to slap my hand over my mouth to stop myself from gasping when the realization of what he's doing hits me.

I've never watched porn, but the image of Dr. Beau Buffington getting himself off is surely something that women would pay for. His completely naked body is drool-worthy alone, but when you add in the sounds coming out of his mouth, anyone would have a lady boner.

"Fuck yeah," he groans, his tricep flexing as he slowly pumps himself. "That's it, pretty girl. Take it for me."

His voice is low and gravelly, like he's barely able to form words but needs to let them loose. He used that tone with me that night, and my core clenches at the memory. So damn panty melting.

My mind drifts to who he's picturing as he strokes himself. Probably some perfect blonde with a big chest and fat ass. He has that All-American look about him—the guy who was captain of the football team and ends up with the head cheerleader.

Which is why it makes sense that he didn't want me.

I should turn around.

I should walk out of this door and forget how much better he looks naked than with clothes on.

But the sound of an even louder grunt makes me freeze in place.

My brain is no longer controlling my body or I would stop watching. I would stop imagining myself on the other side of him receiving his praise.

"That's my girl," he breathes again. "You're gonna take it all."

Holy dirty-talking heaven.

All of my brain cells are gone and I don't even care that he doesn't want me. All I care about is staying for the show.

I shift slightly in the door frame, crossing my feet to alleviate the surprisingly strong ache that has grown between my legs.

As his grunts start coming at a quicker rate, I feel my breathing quicken, knowing that he's close to coming apart and wanting more than anything to watch him as he does.

Something tells me that he's not even remotely quiet.

That he doesn't hold back.

That his control evaporates.

Beau's body clenches and he tosses his head back beneath the streaming water, a wild sound escaping his lips, like he's been restraining this sexual tension for his whole life and is finally allowing it to release.

And despite my best intentions, I wish I was the one making him come undone. That he would use me for his pleasure and wouldn't have to resort to his hand.

Would he be rough and bad like he promised?

Or would he be the tender Beau that leaves handwritten notes for me on the counter?

Stuck in my thoughts, I hardly notice when Beau quickly turns off the shower and opens the glass door. His dazed eyes meet mine, momentarily wide at the sight of me standing there like a peeping Tom.

I should move.

Run.

Something.

But I can't.

My body is in shock—insanely aroused shock.

All I can do is stand with my bare feet planted in the door frame as my eyes inexplicably drop from Beau's now amused expression to the monster cock hanging between his legs.

When I gripped it that night, I could tell he was big . . . but nothing like this. Never in my wildest dreams did I think that his dick needed its own zip code.

Feeling my cheeks heat with embarrassment, I mutter an apology as I uncross my legs and force myself to move, unable to meet his gaze.

Beau snickers, his tone low and gravelly as I practically trip on the door frame. "Knew you liked to watch."

Chapter 16

Beau

Claire Winters watching me jerk off in the shower was not on my bingo card for the year.

While it momentarily surprised me, the memory is now ingrained in my mind forever. There's no way I'll ever be able to get in that tiny shower again without picturing her standing in the doorway, her cheeks cherry red with the realization that she had been caught.

What I don't understand, though, is why Claire shies away from me at the first flicker of conflict or discomfort. Whenever we flirt, she dishes it back to me without even a second thought. Then, it's like once the words leave her lips, she realizes her faux pas and retreats completely. Almost like she's embarrassed of her sexuality because she thinks that it's something to be ashamed of. It's fucking not—and god, do I want to teach her that.

Last night I didn't hear a peep from her after she practically fell down the stairs to get away from me. I gave her space, but if I were a betting man, I'd put all my money on the fact that she won't come out of her room today. That even if I were to knock on her door, she would pretend she was out for the day and ignore me completely, just to avoid her perceived awkwardness between us.

But from my perspective, there's nothing awkward about what happened. It was hot as fuck finding her watching me, and if I had known she was standing there, I would have made sure she heard her name on my lips when I came.

Before I left for the gym this morning, my plan to get Claire out of her bedroom included Krispy Kreme donuts and promises to watch her stupid reality shows with her. But then I realized that spending time with me is probably the last thing she wants to do if she's set on avoiding me, so I had to scrap that idea and come up with something else.

Fortunately, and unfortunately, while I was cooling down on the treadmill after my morning workout, my phone went off with an email from the humane society. Apparently, they're renovating their main building and desperate for volunteers to temporarily take in the animals.

Ding, ding, ding—what woman can resist a tiny, helpless creature?

My family has always adopted dogs from them before, so I wasn't sure how that would work with living in a high rise. Instead, I decided to play it safe and went with an orange kitten, figuring he could be a peace offering to Claire and hopefully mend the bridge of awkwardness between us.

In hindsight, I probably should have checked with Parker, since it is his condo . . . but that's a problem for a different day. Plus, this is a completely temporary arrangement. The shelter just needs us to give him a home for a week and then he's off to find his forever family.

Although, at this point, I'm starting to think even a week together is going to be too long because the little rascal hustled me. His originally calm demeanor has now turned feral, and he's throwing himself around the carrier in desperate attempts to break free. Thank god there's nobody in this lobby because I'm pretty sure they would call animal control for a baby mountain lion on the loose.

By the time we make it up the elevator and to the door of the condo, I think I've gone deaf in one ear from his shrill meows. I like to think I'm a pretty patient guy, but this hellion is making me question everything I know about myself.

"One week," I mutter as I push open the door to the condo with my elbow. "You've got one week with us little man, and then back to the shelter you go."

I set the carrier down in the kitchen and take a moment to assess the situation. Frosty is still going strong with his vocal performance, and I'm half-convinced that he's about to break some sound barrier I wasn't aware existed. If he keeps this up, I'm going to have to order earplugs as a legitimate survival strategy to make it through the next few nights.

Rummaging through the box the shelter gave me, I pull out the necessities—a small litter box, food, and a bowl. I plop them on the floor, surveying the living room for a good spot to put the litter box. This is when I realize that, aside from the videos of cute cats that my sister-in-law sends to our family group chat, I know absolutely nothing about cat care.

I scratch my head, contemplating the placement of the kitty commode. Do cats prefer privacy like humans do? Or should I put it out in the open where it's easy to find?

Eventually, I opt for a corner in the living room, hoping for the best.

The kitten screams again, reminding me that he's still trapped in the carrier.

As soon as I lean down and release him, all hell breaks loose. The furry torpedo launches itself at me, charging forward with supernatural speed.

Caught off guard, I stumble backward as I try to escape his fury, but end up tumbling over the back of the sectional and crashing head-first onto the cushions.

A string of curse words flow from my mouth, followed by a sigh of relief when I realize that I'm not injured.

Just as I'm trying to regain some semblance of dignity and determine how I'm ever going to escape this couch, I hear the creak of Claire's bedroom door.

Immediately, I pop my head up from the cushion to warn her. "Watch out! He's probably coming your way!"

Her thin brows furrow with confusion as she emerges from her room, glancing briefly at me and then down at the lion in our living room.

Only she doesn't squeal from terror—she bursts into laughter. I'm talking doubled over on the floor, can't breathe type of laughter. And it's beautiful, because I was seriously questioning if I'd ever hear that sound again.

"You've got to be kidding me," she manages to gasp out as she clutches her stomach. It's mid-afternoon at this point and it looks like she hasn't gotten out of bed all day, those sexy pink satin pajamas swaying against her skin as she rolls back and forth on the floor in a fit of laughter.

Frosted Orange, Frosty for short, prowls over to her and rubs his body against her bare legs, purring so loud that I can hear it from across the room.

Little shit.

"It's not that funny," I snap, standing up from the couch as she rolls to face me.

Claire wipes a tear from the corner of her eye, still laughing. "It absolutely is."

"He was coming for me!"

Picking up the kitten and returning to her back, Claire places him on her chest. "Good boy," she says, running her thumb over his disproportionately sized head.

I cross my arms. "Frosty is a *menace*, not a good boy."

"Well, he seems to like me," she coos, scratching his oversized ears. "Maybe you're the problem. Cats can sense when people don't like them, you know?"

I shake my head, pretending to be irritated, but I'm thankful that the awkwardness has evaporated between us. "I'm the one who got him from the shelter! How could I not like him?"

Claire ignores my comment and chuckles to herself. "I can't wait to tell Cassidy about this. Baby boy Beau, put in his place by a three-pound ball of fluff."

"Don't you dare," I snap, trying to sound serious despite the smirk I'm desperately trying to hold back.

"Or what?" she taunts, bright blue eyes shimmering with amusement.

Happy that our normal banter is returning, I finally let my lips twitch up. "Or I'll have him unleash his terror on you while you sleep. We'll see how much you laugh when he's screaming at two in the morning."

She lets out a mock gasp. "Are you threatening me, Beau Buffington?"

"Consider it a warning," I reply with a wink.

Claire rolls her eyes as she sits up, dark hair falling loosely across her chest. "Well, I'm not scared. This little guy and I are partners in crime now. Isn't that right, Frosty?"

Claire scoops up the kitten into her arms and cradles him like a baby. "Plus, I'm pretty sure he's only interested in terrorizing you."

The kitten seems to purr even louder in response, and she shoots me a triumphant look.

"Worst decision ever," I lie.

It's hard to tell at this point if she came out of her room to witness my takedown or save me from torment. Either way, I'm not going to complain, because my impulsive plan seems to have worked.

"Can we keep him?" she asks, batting her full lashes at me.

I prod my cheek with my tongue as I consider, knowing full well that there's no way I can say no to her. I'd give her anything she wanted if it meant seeing her like this—with pure joy radiating from her face.

Claire pops her lower lip out to make a pout. "Please? I need an ally to help put you in your place."

I chuckle. "You have no problem putting me in my place, Claire."

"True," she admits. "But it would be so much more fun with an accomplice."

"Fine, but the moment he turns on you, don't come running upstairs to me."

She runs her tongue over her bottom lip as her cheeks flush bright red. "I wouldn't dare. We both know how that turned out last time."

CHAPTER 17

CLAIRE

I think Parker is paying Beau to be nice to me.

Why else would he go out of his way to do all of this? The man is already so busy with work, it makes no sense why he would use his precious free time doing things that make me feel comfortable. Whatever his reason, it's working—I feel more at home with him than I could have imagined, especially given our history.

Any time he's around I feel my defenses crumbling. I don't want to like him. I want to push him away and run in the opposite direction. But there's just something about him that just makes me feel like I'm safe to be myself, like he's accepted who I am and supports that version of me wholeheartedly.

That's also why I spent the whole day in my room avoiding him. I was terrified that I had ruined everything last night and embarrassed that I ran away, unable to confront the aftermath like an adult.

I've never been a stranger to conflict with my family, probably because they're sort of stuck with me regardless of what I say or do. Even if I take things too far, I know they'll always be there because that's what they signed up for the day I was born.

But Beau is different—I can't gauge our boundaries. He's been clear that he doesn't want me romantically, yet his flirtatious banter sends mixed signals, and I can't help but send them right back. Every interaction between us feels natural, effortless, until the words slip out, and I'm left wondering if I've pushed too far, if I'm too much for him, like I fear I am for everyone else.

The thought of conflict with him makes my stomach churn. I'm terrified of destroying this friendship between us, or whatever it is. I truthfully don't know what you'd call it, but I do know that I've already lost so much this year, the thought of losing him too seems unbearable.

Fortunately, he seems to know just how to pull me out of my spiraling thoughts. We spent the afternoon figuring out how to care for Frosty, and the awkward tension of last night didn't once resurface. Falling back into our easy, playful exchange felt natural, as if my fears of the previous night were just a fleeting thought.

Beau's lack of experience with cats doesn't stop him from acting like an authority on the matter, typical of his doctor's confidence. He's been dispensing cat care advice all day, citing articles from veterinary journals and adding his interpretations. Mostly, I've tuned him out, amusing myself by watching Frosty dart enthusiastically around the living room as he chases a laser pointer.

Having grown up in a family of medical professionals, I'm used to dealing with oversized egos. Strip away the white coats and the godlike complex, and you're left with someone who was once the underdog on the playground, now overcompensating for their past. It's a perspective I enjoy reminding them of, and my new sidekick seems to be on the same page.

Beau kept trying to establish himself as the alpha male in the house, only to be hilariously outmaneuvered by a tiny, mischievous kitten. The more Beau raised his voice, the more Frosty seemed to rebel, even going so far as to ruin one of Beau's sneakers.

Did the angel baby touch any of my things? No.

He only felt the need to assert his dominance over Beau, and I don't think I've ever been more proud.

I've already made up my mind to adopt Frosty, though I still need to figure out how to break the news to Parker. I know that Beau works a ton and did this for me as a temporary peace offering, but after a few hours together I think I've found my spirit animal. And there's no way I'm giving him up.

We've decided to keep the kitten a secret for now, given Parker's obsession with keeping his condo flawless. If I'm being honest, I love that we have this between us. While he may not be interested in dating, his actions show a level of care and concern for me that's comforting. And right now, that's enough.

As I'm getting ready for the night out with Cassidy and Morgan, my new shadow lays on his back next to the floor-to-ceiling window. His little paws are in the air, bent at the wrist as he sleeps from his eventful afternoon and I already can't wait to come home to snuggle his tiny face tonight.

I'm supposed to be at the Mexican restaurant in five minutes and am still standing in my bra and panties. To be fair, it's across the street from the condo so I've got an extra ten minutes that would normally be spent driving.

Girl math.

Picking up my phone, I dial Cass's number and she answers immediately.

"Sorry! We're running a little late," she huffs like she's out of breath. "Are you already at the restaurant?"

Cassidy is perpetually late, just like me. It drives my brother crazy, but because we grew up together, he's at least used to it.

"Nope," I respond, walking through the heaps of clothes on the floor and into my closet. "What is the vibe for tonight?"

"Hang on." She puts me on a video call and pans the camera over to Morgan. Her ass is out and she's not even making an effort to cover herself up as she crawls into the back seat of their Uber.

"You're insane—it's got to be forty degrees outside and you're in mini skirts!"

"Morg is," she says, turning the camera back to her face. "I'm wearing a bodysuit and pants from Abercrombie."

I sigh, looking at my matching dirty pair crumpled on the floor. "I love their jeans. They've made such a comeback."

Cassidy smiles, wobbling the phone as the car door closes behind her. "Yes, I have you to thank for my newfound sense of fashion."

"She looks hot!" Morgan calls from the other seat.

"Perfect," I reply, scanning my closet for a clean pair of jeans. "I'll just go with something similar."

The phone shakes again, going momentarily black before Morgan's emerald eyes overtake the screen. "Absolutely not. Wear your sluttiest outfit."

I can't help but grin. I like her so much.

"I don't think I have anything that you would consider slutty."

I've always been into fashion, but most of the clothes I own lean more conservative compared to what people my age usually wear. But because that's how I've always grown up dressing, it's how I'm most comfortable, at least in public.

Truthfully, despite the attention I've received from men, I've never felt entirely confident in my skin. Most of that probably comes from constantly playing roles and fitting expectations rather than my distaste for my looks, but either way, I've just never felt like the most beautiful woman in the room. My body isn't curvy, leaning more towards a rectangle shape than anything else. My hips aren't wide, nor do I have big breasts, so sexy is never a word that I would use to describe myself.

My saving grace, though, is my extensive collection of lingerie. I've probably spent more on delicate, lacy undergarments than some people do on their first car, but to me, it's worth every penny. I figure there are worse things to spend my money on. They give me a boost of confidence and a hidden layer of allure that makes me feel beautiful and empowered.

"Not true," Cass chimes, leaning in so both her and Morgan's faces are in the frame. "You bought that mini skirt for the Eras Tour and looked *hot*."

"That was a wear and tear," I say, recalling my outfit from that night.

We had the time of our lives and each dressed as our favorite Taylor Swift album. I chose Red and wore a red leather mini skirt that couldn't have cost more than twenty dollars on the internet. It was intended for one-time wear—hence the name.

"It's perfect! Put on a bodysuit and black thigh-high boots and get your ass over to the restaurant," Cass demands as I crouch down in my closet, looking for the skirt. She's just as stubborn as me, so I know that she's not going to let this idea go until I concede.

"Look at you," I say, spotting the red faux leather in the corner of the closet. "A true fashionista."

"I learned from the best."

My sister-in-law is buttering me up and it's working.

I huff a dramatic exhale. "Fine, I'll see you guys soon."

By the time I get dressed and leave my room, I'm already ten minutes late.

Beau is lounging on the couch with his charmingly crooked nose in some textbook as he sips a Budweiser. His black workout shorts are bunched around his thighs, practically clinging to the bulging muscle and offering a slight peek at his dark briefs beneath. A heather gray t-shirt clings to his torso, somehow accentuating the definition in his arms despite his relaxed position.

It took me an hour to straighten my hair and put on my makeup to the point that I was relatively happy with it, and he looks like *that* without even trying? Being a woman is so unfair.

I cough to get his attention as I pause in the kitchen. "Hey, so I can leave Frosty in my room, and close the door if you want. Don't want you getting eaten while I'm gone."

Beau glances up from his book, his caramel eyes meeting mine momentarily before slowly drifting over my body.

I shift my feet, feeling somewhat uncomfortable under his gaze despite the warm tingle that I get from his attention. I'm wearing the exact outfit that Cassidy suggested, and while I suspected he would be affected by it because of how different it is from my usual outfits, I didn't expect this reaction.

Instead of flirting like normal, he looks pissed.

"No," he snaps, narrowing his gaze on me.

"No, you don't want me to leave him in my room?" I frown, trying to figure out what he means. "Or no, you don't want him around you?"

A muscle in his jaw ripples as his eyes drop to my legs. "No, you're not going out wearing that."

His response catches me off guard and I let out a hesitant giggle. "You can't be serious," I reply, studying his face.

His molten gaze sharpens as it lands on mine once more. He looks pissed. "Dead serious. It's not appropriate."

I cross my arms, more amused than annoyed. "Appropriate for what? I'm just grabbing dinner with friends."

"What friends?"

"Wouldn't you like to know," I tease, knowing I'm baiting him. "Though I still don't know what you mean. I think I look good."

I do a twirl, purposely shimmying my ass as I spin around.

There's a challenge in his tone, and I can't help but grin. "You know *exactly* what I mean, Claire."

Is it wrong to admit that he's hot when he's mad? He's such a carefree guy but the way his arms are crossed right now makes a sharp pang of lust hit my core. The fact that he's so worked up over an outfit makes me wonder if he's having regrets over not taking things further with us.

Good.

He should have regrets.

I raise an eyebrow, feigning innocence. "I'm just wearing what Cass suggested. It's not a big deal."

He sets his beer down. "It doesn't matter who suggested the outfit. You're not going out in that. Period. "

"Oh god," I sigh as I grab my keys from the counter. "Did you learn this alpha-hole stuff from my brother? Because he's really not the person you want to be emulating."

"Your brother would freak if he saw you in that," he counters, his voice raising slightly. "There's barely any fabric."

I roll my eyes. "Parker's never given a shit about what I wear—trust me it's fine. And, how is this any different than what

I wear around here? I'm more covered up now than I usually am, and you've never once complained about *those* outfits."

I practically live in my sexy pajamas and robes when I'm at the condo and I'd be lying if I said I don't enjoy the way his eyes roam over my body when I do.

"The difference is," he starts, pausing for a moment to gather his thoughts. There's almost a pained expression on his face as he continues. "The difference is that other people shouldn't see you like that."

"But you should?" I taunt, knowing I've got him in a vice.

Beau runs his fingers over his face. "Whatever. Leave the cat out, it's fine."

"Yay!" I squeal, practically tripping over the bar stool to run to my room and open the door. "You guys are going to be besties by the time I get back."

"I doubt it," he grumbles.

On the way out of the condo, I purposely sway my hips again, feeling his eyes watching me like a hawk. I smile to myself—let him see what he missed out on.

With my hand on the doorknob, I look back at him and decide to see how far I can push him. "I'll be gone for several hours . . . if you want to have some girl over or something."

I've not seen him with anyone since he moved in and not that it matters, but I'm curious if he's dating. I mean, I know that he hardly has any time, but I'm not naive to the fact that there's stuff that goes down in the hospitals—that's how my brother and Cassidy met.

Do I want him to say that he doesn't want anyone but me?

Obviously.

But I know that's not realistic.

Beau raises a bushy eyebrow at me, clearly not expecting my comment. "Uh, okay thanks."

Ugh.

Me and my stupid mouth need a muzzle. I shouldn't have said anything at all. I should have left the condo and our conversation without another word. But of course, I took things too far.

Once again.

God, now I need a drink.

CHAPTER 18

CLAIRE

Señor Cuervo's is already packed with people on the patio enjoying the happy hour, two-for-one drink specials. I've never been a fan of beer, but something about a frozen margarita with sugar on the rim gets me every time. And yes, I recognize that adding extra sugar to an already sugary drink is ridiculous. But if I'm anything, I'm on brand.

Spotting Cassidy and Morgan in a booth at the back of the restaurant, I weave through the crowd to join them, holding my skirt down with one hand. When I wore this for the concert, I paired it with a floor-length cardigan so I didn't have to worry about flashing anyone. I may have pretended like I was comfortable in this outfit to mess with Beau, but truthfully I'm terrified that someone's going to see my no-no square with every step I take.

"Oh my god," Morgan exclaims as I carefully shimmy into the booth across from them, her eyes wide with excitement. "You look hot."

I feel myself blush at the compliment. I've never been one for words of affirmation or praise. My family signs our cards with our names, and our names alone. No sap. No frivolous sentences about why we love each other. So any time I get a compliment, I don't know how to act or what to say.

So I say nothing, choosing to pick up the menu and avoid the heat of their gaze.

"Doesn't she look hot, Cass?" Morgan whisper-yells, clearly not letting me off easy.

I draw my eyes up over the appetizer list, silently begging her to change the subject. Cassidy smirks and agrees with Morgan. "Super hot. The hottest little sister ever."

She just loves pushing my buttons.

Darting my eyes around the room, I whisper, "Are you guys done?"

"Nope," Morgan says, a wicked grin on her face. "Not until you admit it."

"Stop it," I seethe, trying to signal our waiter so I can order a drink. I'm going to need it tonight with these two.

The waiter appears, and I hastily order a frozen margarita, hoping the icy concoction will cool the heat rising in my cheeks. As he walks away, Morgan leans in, her green eyes sparkling with pride.

"Seriously, Claire, you need to give yourself credit. You have the hottest bod," she insists.

Cassidy nods in agreement, her smirk widening. "She's right. You should embrace it. If I had legs like that I would walk around naked all day."

I sigh, realizing there's no escaping this conversation. "Thank you for the compliments. Can we *please* move on now?"

Morgan raises an eyebrow. "Not until you admit that you look banging."

I roll my eyes, but there's a small smile tugging at the corner of my lips. "Fine, I look good," I concede. "You should have seen

Beau's face when I walked out of the apartment. I thought he was going to have a heart attack."

Cassidy laughs, taking a sip of her margarita before replying, "He's a good ol' southern boy. What do you expect?"

"Yeah," Morgan agrees as she plunges a chip into the salsa at the center of the table. "He's the kind of guy that would totally tip his hat at you in a bar."

I accept my drink from the waiter as I try to think of anything other than Beau and his charm.

"Hola, ladies. My name is Miguel and I'll be taking care of you," the waiter says, as he leans against our table. He looks to be about my age, with thick dark hair and a freshly shaven face that shows off his round jaw. His brown eyes sparkle as he stares directly at me and asks, "What can I do for *you* this evening?"

I drop my eyes to my drink and take a massive sip, suddenly feeling like a bug under a microscope.

Fortunately, Morgan steps in and says, "Keep the drinks coming, Miguel. Also, bring us a queso and guac, por favor."

"No problem, señorita," he replies, winking at her playfully. "I'll be back shortly."

Once the waiter is gone, Morgan starts giggling as she sucks up the rest of her first drink. "He is *totally* into you."

"Is not."

Cass chimes in, "For sure he is. And can you blame him? Look at you!"

Oh lord—we're back to this again.

"He winked at Morgan too you idiot," I counter, deciding to suck down the rest of my drink.

"Everyone winks at me," Morgan states matter-of-factly, flicking her dark hair over her shoulder. "And can you blame them? I'm a hot piece of ass."

Cassidy snorts, shaking her head. "You're a piece of something. That's for sure."

"Jealousy doesn't look good on you, Cass."

"Oh yes, Morg. I'm so jealous of you going out every night and ending up in different men's beds," Cassidy says, sarcasm dripping off her tongue.

"It sounds kinda fun," I admit.

I've never really explored the sexual side of myself, but what better time than now? How will I ever know what I like and don't like without dating?

Cass sneers as she looks directly at Morgan. "It sounds like a way to get gonorrhea."

We all burst out laughing as our waiter returns with a tray of appetizers and fresh drinks. As he passes them out across the table, another man who looks to be in his mid-thirties with a full beard comes up behind him with a tray of five shot glasses.

"Shots on the house for the most beautiful ladies in the restaurant," the bearded man says with a charming smile as he nudges his friend. Our waiter offers an apologetic shrug and starts passing out the glasses as Morgan and Cassidy exchange excited glances.

"What should we toast to?" Morgan asks, licking the back of her hand and pouring salt on it. She's definitely in her element here and passes me the salt shaker, indicating that I should mimic her action.

"To tequila," our waiter says, lifting his glass to the middle of the table.

"To tequila," we echo, clinking our glasses together.

The burning liquid slides down my throat. It's harsh but surprisingly not as awful as I expected. A delicious warmth washes through me, and for a moment, I forget about Beau and the fact that I wish he were here to experience the fun.

As our waiter collects the empty shot glasses, he unexpectedly holds onto my hand, lifting it slowly toward his lips as if he's going to kiss my knuckles. I chuckle uncomfortably, thankful for the alcohol flowing through my veins, easing this somewhat awkward moment. Instead of kissing my hand, he takes my two middle fingers into his mouth and sucks on them, his ink-colored eyes glimmering with mischief as they hold mine.

I nervously giggle as Morgan cries, "Hell yes, you're getting one hell of a tip tonight, Miguel."

The rest of the evening flows in a blur with several more rounds of shots and margaritas. I'm pretty sure that I agreed to go on a date with one of Morgan's friends from college who she had to video call during our meal, because apparently we would, "look so good together."

After Mom died, I deleted my dating apps and have found myself in a serious dry spell. While I doubt Morgan has the best taste in men, I have to admit, the guy is super attractive and could be the perfect thing to scratch that itch. Plus, at least I know he's not a serial killer.

Actually, scratch that . . . Morgan is one hundred percent the girl that would befriend a serial killer.

By the time we pay and make it out of the restaurant, it's close to midnight and I can barely feel my face. I haven't had this much alcohol since college and definitely am beginning to feel a little queasy. I just need to make it across the street and into the warm bed that's calling my name.

My stomach does a backflip.

On second thought, a trip to the bathroom might be necessary before I climb into bed.

"So are you going to call him?" Morg slurs as we wait on the corner for their Uber. She's referring to the waiter who left his number on the receipt and handed it directly to me.

"Noooooo, he's too pretty."

She runs her fingers through my hair, standing on her tiptoes to reach my head. "You're pretty."

I giggle. "No, you're pretty."

"You're both pretty," Cass says deadpan as she takes Morgan's hand and pulls her to the car waiting down the street. She's the responsible one, and only had one margarita the whole night. Apparently, she and Parker are going to look at more furniture in the morning, and she doesn't want to be hungover.

Boring.

Unfortunately, it seems like my brother has rubbed off on her.

"I love you, Cass!" I yell as I watch her shove Morgan in the car. "Have fun at the hardware shop tomorrow."

She shakes her head. "It's Restoration Hardware."

"Right," I nod my head very seriously. "The carpenter shop."

"Please get home safely," she says, bringing me in for a hug. "I'll see you on Thursday for Thanksgiving. Are you sure you don't need a ride home?"

I shake my head. "I'm a strong, independent woman who can cross the street on her own thank you very much."

"That you are," she says, winking as she runs to meet Morgan in the Uber.

Damn right, I am.

CHAPTER 19

BEAU

Waiting up for Claire wasn't part of my plan for the evening, but here I am, unable to allow myself to head to bed until I know she's back safely. Thoughts of her ending up in bed with someone flooded my mind, and it became impossible to focus on studying for the rest of the evening.

By the time Claire comes crashing through the door it's well past my bedtime, especially considering I have to be at the hospital by six tomorrow morning. Her cheeks are flushed a bright red, like the wind whipped them on her way up, and her hair is completely frazzled.

"You're up late," she sings, skipping into the kitchen like an amused child. She nearly loses her balance when her heel catches on the corner of the island and she has to bend to steady herself, inadvertently gifting me with a glimpse of her long legs. As she begins to unzip her shoe, my cock twitches with the fantasy of seeing her completely naked and wearing nothing but those boots.

"Been busy reading about my cases tomorrow," I reply casually as I watch her.

In truth, all I've been able to do is sip my beer and stare aimlessly at the TV, but I'm not going to tell her that.

She giggles, though nothing I said was funny. "Always so serious, Dr. Buffington."

Why the fuck is it so hot when she says my name like that?

"You need some help over there?" I ask, growing slightly concerned as she wobbles with the effort of removing her boot. The last thing I need is to have to explain to her brother why we ended up in the ER tonight.

Claire exhales dramatically, peering up at me through the dark locks that have fallen in front of her eyes. "I'm an independent woman. I don't need a man to help me do anything."

I stifle a grin as I get up from the couch to help her. "I didn't say you did. But an independent woman also knows when she needs someone."

"Fine." She straightens and perches herself on the bar stool, kicking out her leg for me. "I need someone."

"See?" I ask, taking her leg in my hand as my other reaches for the zipper of the boot. "Doesn't it feel good to admit that you're wrong?"

"I'm never wrong," she declares with a theatrical sigh as she throws her head back.

Fuck—I've got to look away or I'm going to lose all control here. All I can think about is running my tongue along her neck and feeling her pulse escalate with my touch. I refocus on the task at hand, gently removing the first boot from her foot.

"You Winters kids are just so stubborn," I chuckle as I place the boot on the ground and tap her leg, indicating that she should switch feet.

Claire's head snaps up and she smirks, kicking her other leg into my hands. "But I'm the most stubborn."

I roll my eyes. "You're right. I should have added competitive to that. Stubborn and competitive."

"Speaking of competition," she muses, watching me pull the second boot from her leg. "Does Frosty still love me more, or did you pull out your stupid southern charm to win him over?"

Somehow the little kitten knew to leave me alone to brood tonight. He lay in the swivel armchair across from the sectional, content to roll around and play with the mouse toy that the shelter gave us. While it pains me to admit it, it was truthfully kind of nice to have a companion. I'm still not a cat guy, but we definitely made progress tonight.

"What charm?" I drawl, keeping my eyes glued to hers as I hold her leg. I'm afraid if I look any lower I'll *accidentally* see the color of her panties.

Claire laughs as she points her toes in my hand. "Don't act like you don't know."

"I'm not sure what you're talking about," I tease, rubbing my thumb along the instep of her foot.

She closes her eyes and groans, the sweet sound sending all of my blood to my crotch.

"Sure you don't," she sighs, tugging her foot from my grasp before stumbling off the stool.

I quickly reach out to steady her, my hands gripping her hips a bit more firmly than I intended. "Easy there," I say softly. "Let's get you to your bed."

The scent of alcohol on her breath is strong as I guide her through the kitchen. After only a few steps, she pulls away from my grip, lunging towards the guest bathroom halfway between the kitchen and her bedroom.

Claire barely makes it in time, her body heaving over the sink as the night's indulgences come back up. I hesitate at the doorway, torn between the urge to help and wanting to respect her privacy.

After a moment, she steadies herself, rinsing her mouth and avoiding my gaze in the mirror. "Sorry," she mumbles. "Not my finest moment."

I step closer, prepared to hold her hair back in case she gets sick again. "Hey, it happens to the best of us. You okay?"

Claire nods, splashing water on her face before meeting my eyes in the mirror with a sheepish smile. "Yeah, you know what they say . . . give me five margaritas . . ."

My brow furrows in confusion. I have no idea what she's talking about. "Think you can make it to bed? Or do we need to sleep on the couch tonight?"

She turns, leaning heavily against the countertop, her eyes reflecting a mix of gratitude and something else I can't quite decipher. "I'm fine on my own. You don't have to stay with me."

"It would make me feel better," I admit, putting my arm around her waist. "Plus, your brother would kill me if you died in your sleep because of my negligence."

By the time we reach her bedroom, Claire stumbles, a hand flying to her mouth. I can tell she's going to be sick again and instinctively, I guide her towards her ensuite bathroom.

"I've got you," I soothe as we make it to the toilet just in time for her to throw up.

"I've got you," I repeat as she leans forward. I gently pull her hair back, holding it away from her face as she continues to wretch.

"Sorry," she whispers between breaths, clearly embarrassed.

"Don't be," I reply softly, rubbing my free hand along her back. "It's okay. I'm here."

Once she steadies herself, I wet a washcloth with cool water and crouch down to her level, gently rubbing her forehead.

"You don't have to do that," she says, sitting back on her heels as she flushes the toilet.

"I know. But I want to."

Claire takes the washcloth from my hands and starts wiping the makeup off her face as she watches me. I know she's drunk and probably won't remember any of this in the morning, but for some reason, it feels like she's staring into my soul. Like she knows that I'm trying my hardest not to cross a line right now, but yet she's daring me to cross it anyway.

"I could have gone home with a guy tonight you know," she admits after a moment.

"I'm glad you didn't." I offer a tight smile, trying to control the thoughts that come to my mind when I consider what would have happened if she had. They wouldn't have taken care of her—they would have taken advantage of her.

"Our waiter gave me his number and wanted me to come over once he was done with his shift." Her blue eyes narrow, watching for my reaction.

I shake my head, getting up to grab her a glass of water. "I don't think that's the kind of guy you want, Claire."

"Oh, isn't it?" she says, taking the full glass from me and sipping. "And how would you know?"

Before I can respond, she laughs into the water and says to herself, "Duh, he's a doctor. He knows everything."

I can't help but chuckle at that comment. We grew up in similar backgrounds, with families who are all medical professionals. You have to fight tooth and nail to get your way, because usually the answer to an argument is, "I know more than you."

"I just want someone to want me," she says quietly, looking down at the floor.

I can tell this side of her, vulnerable and raw, is something she doesn't let people see very often. She's normally so confident and witty, always ready with a comeback. I'd do anything to get that version of her back. To get her to understand just how wanted she is.

"Surely you have higher standards than a one-night stand with a waiter who allowed you to get this drunk," I reply, a bit more sharply than intended.

They should have stopped her several drinks ago, and I need to remember to text Cass in the morning and thank her for making sure Claire got home safely. Cassidy gave me a heads up that they were out together and that Claire was on her way home around midnight, though if I had known she was in this bad of shape, I would have walked over to get her myself.

"Not anymore," Claire huffs, blowing a stray piece of hair out of her face.

"What's that supposed to mean?" I ask, crouching down again to tuck the hair behind her ear.

Claire sighs dramatically and closes her eyes. "The last guy I wanted didn't want me. So now I've gotta take what I can get."

Her words spark a fierce protectiveness in me. The idea of someone rejecting her, and making her feel unworthy, is infuriating. Claire is every man's ideal woman, and some douche who fails to see that isn't worthy of her. Whenever I find out who it was, I'll kick their ass.

"Well he was a damn fool to not want you," I offer, trying to boost her confidence.

"At least you finally admit it," she says with a small laugh as her eyes meet mine. There's a vulnerability in her gaze, a shimmer of unshed tears that makes my heart break.

"What?" I ask, confused by her comment.

She lets out an exasperated exhale as her pretty eyes roll to the back of her head. "For someone so smart, you really are very stupid."

I narrow my eyes on her, trying to understand what she's talking about. When I don't say anything, she quietly adds, "I'm talking about you, idiot. You never called me."

Shit—I've gotta kick my own ass.

Does she really think I never called her? That I didn't want her?

I've spent the past two months thinking about nothing but her.

I deleted the apps.

I ignored the texts, the pages from women.

I shut myself out of sex and dating completely—all because I couldn't get her out of my head.

"I texted you," I explain, needing her to understand. "But I was stuck in the hospital for two days straight after our date and didn't have a chance to send it until I had finally slept."

Her face brightens. "You did? I never saw it. I deleted all of my messages after Mom . . ."

"I did," I confirm. "I thought you hated me because when I finally sent it, your mom was in the hospital. I was convinced you wanted nothing to do with me because my dumb ass sent you a dirty text on the worst day of your life."

She bites her bottom lip, considering my words. "How dirty are we talking?"

"You don't want to know," I smile, glad to see her perking up.

"I don't hate you," she admits quietly as she draws her knees up to her chest. "At first, I tried to be mad at the fact that you were moving in. Tried to find something wrong with you because it was easier that way—to think that you were some horrible guy, and I was better off without you. But I couldn't."

She sighs, closing her eyes as a single tear falls from her eyes. "You're too damn perfect and it's infuriating. Because of course, you wouldn't want someone like me."

I shake my head, surprised by her admission. Surely she can't think that about herself. Unable to help myself, I reach out and wipe the tear from her still-flushed cheek. "Is that what you think?"

She leans into my touch, keeping her eyes closed and letting silence settle between us. Her chin quivers and I can tell additional tears are threatening to fall.

"Is that what you think, Claire?" I repeat, brushing the back of my hand over her cheek.

Her reddened eyes open. "Look at me," she sniffs, gesturing to her body. "I'm a mess. It makes complete sense why you wouldn't want me."

"You're not a mess," I insist, hoping she believes me. "You're a force of nature, pretty girl. A goddamn category four hurricane. And you know what? I'm a storm chaser."

The corner of her lip tilts upwards. "You are?"

"Absolutely," I nod. "Best one there ever was, of course. Belong on *The Weather Channel.*"

"Why am I not surprised?" She giggles and I feel thankful to hear that sound again.

"Not everyone can be good at everything. But that's just a burden I have to bear."

She looks away and sucks in a deep breath, as if she's wrestling with her thoughts. Wanting to encourage her to open up, I gently prompt, "Hey, what's on your mind? Other than the fact that we're both up way past our bedtimes."

She swallows, her eyes distant as they study the tiled floor. "You don't think I'm too much?"

"Why would you think that?"

Her chin quivers as if she's remembering something deeply seeded within her soul. "I've just—"

"Look at me," I say, reaching out to her again. My hands hold her bent knees, rubbing the skin as I wait for her to listen. She needs to fucking hear this.

After a beat of silence, her gaze finds mine.

"Anyone who tells you that you're too much needs to go find less. You are *everything* I've ever wanted in a woman."

She blinks warily at me a few times, as if she can't believe what I just said. "I am?"

"Fuck yeah, you are," I respond without any hesitation. "You have no idea how much I want you, Claire, and living with you has only made that even more painfully evident."

"Really?"

"One hundred and ten percent," I answer honestly.

She rolls her eyes. "That's not a possible score, idiot."

I smirk. "It is when you get extra credit."

"I want you too."

Her words hang in the air and for the first time in my life, I'm stunned into silence. What do you say when the only thing you've been wanting for months finally comes true? I feel like a giddy teenager with his first crush, not a grown-ass doctor who saves lives.

There's a small part of me that wonders if she would have admitted this when she was sober. But truthfully, it doesn't fucking matter, because drunk words are sober thoughts. And I'm just thankful to know the truth.

"Obviously you want me," I tease, the smirk on my face growing into a full-blown smile.

She frowns and kicks her foot out, attempting to hit me on the shin.

Grabbing her leg in the air before it hits me, I warn, "Don't make me put you in time out."

She responds with a huff, her feisty spirit shining through once more. "I'd like to see you try."

As much as I'd love to show her my version of timeout, I restrain myself.

"Let's get you in bed," I say, releasing her leg and offering her my hand. "I'm going to leave a trash can next to you just in case."

She takes it and allows me to pull her up. "Always a gentleman."

I chuckle. "You love it."

While I get her a fresh glass of water, Claire changes out of her clothes and into a set of pajamas. On the way back from the kitchen, I grab a few extra pillows, positioning them beside her so she doesn't roll onto her back and choke in the middle of the night. The rounds of vomiting probably helped a ton, and though she seems much better, you can never be too sure.

Once she's settled beneath her massive white comforter, I toss a pillow and blanket from the living room down on the floor.

"What are you doing?" she asks, peering over at me with wide eyes as I turn off the room light and close the door.

"Going to sleep," I state, dropping to the ground. Fortunately, her bedroom is carpeted, so this won't be the worst sleep of my life. "What does it look like I'm doing?"

"Why are you doing that?"

"Playing twenty questions tonight, are we?" I joke, fluffing the couch pillow as best as I can before lowering my head.

She sighs dramatically, loud enough for me to hear. "Is it fun for you to make everything so difficult?"

I grin at the ceiling. "Seems like you've finally met your match."

Claire doesn't respond for a while and for a second I think she's fallen asleep, which is good because I've only got about four hours until I need to get my ass up.

"You know you can sleep in the bed with me right?" Her voice cuts through the darkness like a warm caress, tempting me with everything I've ever wanted.

"Not yet I can't."

"Why?" she probes, drawing out the simple question on her lips.

"Because I don't trust myself in the same bed as you."

"You can sleep on the other side of the bed," she suggests. "I'll create a pillow barrier between us. We won't even have to touch."

I shake my head, admiring her effort. It would be so easy to give in . . . to slip beneath the covers and tempt myself with her proximity. But I can't. I know myself better than that.

"While I love that you think I have that much control when it comes to you, pretty girl, I promise you that I don't. And I'm not going to touch you until I talk to Parker."

"Why?"

It's not that I feel like I need Parker's permission to date Claire. This isn't the 1800s, and from what I know about their relationship, I doubt his opinion would really matter to her. But, I also respect Parker enough to give him a heads-up about us. So as much as it pains me to draw a line in the sand . . . I have to.

"Because I'm not one to keep secrets from the people I care about," I answer truthfully. "He might be your brother, but he's also one of my best friends."

Claire sighs again, disappointment clear in her tone. "Ugh, he really does ruin everything."

I chuckle, turning to my side so I can face her. Her room doesn't have curtains so the faint glow of city light illuminates her face just enough for me to catch her curious expression.

"Final question, I promise," she says softly.

"Shoot."

"When are you going to talk to him?"

I didn't anticipate this happening between us, so I have to pause for a moment before I reply.

"We've got this intern retreat right after Thanksgiving and Parker drew the short stick as the youngest attending so he's leading it. I'll talk to him then."

Her voice carries a mix of hope and uncertainty, "And once you do?"

"I'll make up for all of the days that you spent thinking I didn't want you. You won't ever question my intentions again, because your entire body will feel me every time you walk. Every move you make will reinforce that you are, unequivocally, the *only* thing that I want."

CHAPTER 20

BEAU

On my way out of the condo this morning, I made Claire a fresh pot of coffee with a bottle of Ibuprofen and a note. Don't ask me why I started writing the notes, because I genuinely don't know. At first, I guess I thought she hated me, so I wanted to do it as a nice gesture. But then, I noticed that she kept them in a drawer underneath the coffee pot, so I figured if she wasn't balling them up and lighting them on fire, she must not entirely loathe me.

Call it a gesture of peace. Call it a manifestation of my obsession with her. Whatever you call it, I haven't been able to stop since the day I moved in.

When I was growing up, my dad used to leave my mom similar notes on days that he had long surgeries. Mom is a physician too, but she was only ever in the clinic all day, which meant she had a much more predictable schedule. I have no idea what the notes said, but I guess the concept always stuck with me.

To be fair, that was also before the days of cell phones and texts, so they were limited in their communication methods, but the smile on her face when she read them in the morning was something that I've always remembered. There's something incredibly intimate about the gesture. Anyone can shoot off a text, but a handwritten note says you value the other person more than your time.

The note I left Claire this morning was amusing, at least to me. I'm hoping it'll lighten the mood and help her feel less awkward about what happened last night. It's important to me that she understands, despite her hazy recollection of the evening, that I am one hundred and ten percent in on this thing between us.

And yes, I know that's not a real score, but it's a genuine reflection of my feelings. I'm all in . . . and then some.

Surprisingly, I slept like a baby on Claire's floor. Had I gone upstairs, I would have worried about her all night. Even though she sobered up quite a bit by the time we turned in, my medical training has taught me one thing: you can never be too careful. I've seen lots of stuff in the hospital that was initially tagged as nothing, only to end up as something major later on, so I'm overly cautious about this type of thing.

I just wish I wasn't at the hospital for the next five days straight, because it means I won't be able to see her much. Thanksgiving is one of the busiest times when it comes to surgeries and the department needs all hands on deck. I might be a walking, talking zombie by the time this week is over, but that's how it goes when you're at the bottom of the surgical food chain.

Truthfully though, it's probably for the best that I'm working so much, considering I'm starting to doubt my self-control around her. Our hookup two months ago can easily be explained by ignorance—I had no idea she was Parker's sister.

But would that knowledge have held me back?

Doubtful.

She was so damn electric that night, I could barely think straight enough to respond to her coherently, let alone stop myself from taking things too far.

The biggest issue is that Parker trusted me to look after Claire. And I fully intend to continue to do that. But I also plan on fucking her silly . . . which is why I need to have a conversation with him before I take this any further.

I value the friendship Parker and I have built over the past year, and truly owe him everything when it comes to this residency and my career. He's not just my best friend, he's become like an older brother to me, guiding me through my career and taking me under his wing. With my brother in another city with a family of his own, he doesn't have a ton of time for me, so Parker has kind of filled that void for me. And I don't want to do something that will fuck that up.

If I talk to him like a man and let him know my intentions, there's no way he can have an issue with me dating Claire. In his eyes, I wouldn't think there would be anyone better.

After my first case this morning, I shot Cass a text to confirm that Claire wouldn't be alone on Thanksgiving. Not that there's anything I can do about it directly, but it would make me feel better knowing that her first holiday without her mom was filled with family and laughter, especially because Parker is going to be stuck at the hospital with me.

Fortunately, a few minutes after I sent the message, Cass confirmed that since Caroline is busy studying, Claire is tagging along with her to her parents' house for several days. If anyone knows what it's like to experience their first holiday without a loved one, it's Cass, so I'm glad they're going to be together.

Cassidy's older brother died two years ago in an accident, so she's an only child now. She struggled for a long time and even had to change hospitals because she couldn't go back to the place where he died. It's funny how life works sometimes. Had she not experienced that grief and come out the other side, she wouldn't have met the love of her life. Cassidy wouldn't have met Claire or even me. And all of us are better for knowing her. Every decision we make in life, whether it's one we make ourselves, or one that someone else makes for us, leads us to the exact place we are supposed to be.

We see it all of the time in orthopedics. People with broken bones often ask if they had just made one tiny decision differently, like avoiding a pothole or planting their foot at a slightly different angle, if they would they still be in this situation.

The truth is that we have no fucking clue, and I don't say that lightly because as doctors it's our job to act like we have a clue. The patient may have avoided injury just to suffer a worse one down the road. Or they could never be hurt at all. We just don't know.

As humans, it's our nature to question the whys and the what-ifs. But they don't really matter. Because we don't have control over why things happen. Or what happens to us. But we do have control over how we heal from those things. And as a surgeon, it's my job to put people back together. To take something physically broken and return it to normal.

Which is why with Claire, I'm having a hard time because she's not physically broken, she's emotionally broken. And the only way I know how to help fix her is by building her back up again. Building her confidence. Building her self-worth. I want her to know that she can be her truest self and I'm never going to look down on her for it. If anything, I'm going to praise her for it.

On my way to the ortho lounge to grab a snack, I spot Walker lingering in the hallway, a spacy look on his face.

"You good, bro?" I ask, clapping my hand on his shoulder as I come up behind him.

He jumps at my touch and turns around, his expression snapping back to normal as he sees me. "Oh hey, Buffington," he says, trying to shake off whatever had him so lost in thought. "Yeah, I'm fine. Just thinking."

"Well don't hurt yourself, bud. You looked physically ill there for a second."

He gives a half-hearted chuckle, running a hand through his jet-black hair. "Definitely have had better days."

"Anything I can help with? Or if you need more brains, I think Matt's almost out of his case, and the others will be back tomorrow if you need a full house."

Typically we alternate weekend days, so Matt and I take the same days and the other two ortho interns, Sam and Elis, take the others. It's the same way for night call, alternating two at a time and then we all reconvene for the day shift during the week. I've been through the trenches with Matt at two in the morning, which has just made us closer. I like the other two interns fine, but our relationship is more competitive in nature, whereas Matt has become the person I lean on the most.

"Extra brains won't solve this problem," he mutters, more to himself than me.

"Let's grab some food," I offer, flopping my arm around his neck as I steer him through the hospital hall with brute force. "I'm ravenous and if more brains won't solve the problem, you've got one brain that's happy to listen."

"I swear, you eat more often than anyone I know," he says, ducking his head out of my grip.

Sometimes I forget that nobody here knows that I have diabetes. Technically, I was supposed to disclose health information at the beginning of residency, but when I was in medical school I heard a story that scared the shit out of me. Apparently, this one surgical resident with Crohn's disease got all of the worst cases and barely finished his program because the attendings didn't ever bring him in for their surgeries. Granted, this was a different residency program, and I doubt that kind of thing happens at Midtown Memorial, but you can never be too sure.

So I figured what they don't know won't hurt them and I left it off my pre-employment physical. The program is already competitive enough as it is, and I didn't want to give them a reason to look down on me. And while the rational part of me knows I shouldn't have done that, the prideful part of me refused to admit any weakness.

By the time we get to the cafeteria and pick up our lunches, my phone alerts me that my blood sugar is trending low. As I sit down at the table with Walker, I open a packet of Skittles and toss them into my mouth, thankful for the high sugar content that will be hitting my bloodstream shortly. I'm not in the mood to deal with the shakes today.

"You have the weirdest diet of anyone I've ever met," Walker comments as he eyes his grilled chicken wrap.

"What do you mean?"

"Just that you eat super clean, but then you go and ruin it with shit like that," he says, motioning to the empty packet of tropical Skittles on the table.

I open my energy drink and smirk. "Doesn't seem to matter, still got a hot bod."

Walker's head drops into his hands. "I know and it pisses me off."

"Everything pisses you off," I point out.

It's true. He's even more serious than Parker was last year, with zero tolerance when it comes to incompetence. He's already made me a better surgeon than I ever expected, forcing me to think past the obvious injuries. I almost missed a second fracture last week but caught it because of the way he taught me to constantly assess and reassess.

Walker gives a half-smile, acknowledging the jab with a nod. "Maybe. But I'd rather be pissed off and excellent than relaxed and mediocre. This job doesn't leave much room for error."

"It doesn't leave much room for anything other than work, honestly," I reply before taking a bite of my wrap.

I wouldn't trade it for the world, but being a surgeon, especially an intern, requires an incredible level of sacrifice. You give yourself to this beast for five years of your life. A beast that takes you from your family. From your friends. From everything you love. All for the promise of becoming an exceptional surgeon. And you don't get anything in return other than poor sleep habits and a crippling sense of inadequacy.

Which is why it's not surprising that so many of us end up bitter and depressed. I'm depressed just thinking about the fact that I have four and a half more years of it. I can't imagine how Walker feels.

He studies the table, pushing his fork back and forth through his side salad. "Yep, that's starting to become more and more evident."

I don't press him. I figure if he wants to tell me what's going on, he can. But I'm happy to sit here with him and keep him company. If there's one thing I've learned, it's that silence can be a powerful tool. It gives space for those who are usually reserved, like Parker and Walker, to open up when they're ready.

After a while, Walker leans back in his chair, a weight seeming to lift off his shoulders as he begins to speak. "My wife is, uh, not pleased with me at the moment."

See?

I didn't even know he was married.

Silence is powerful.

"I got an offer to do a sports med fellowship here after residency."

"That's badass," I say, raising my drink to him in a toast. "Why would she not be happy with that? Pretty sure there's only like two spots and you get to work with professional athletes."

He sighs, a look of resignation crossing his face. "Yeah, well, it's just another year that my schedule is insane and we're away from her family."

"Bro, it would be stupid not to do a fellowship. You're the chief ortho resident. She has to know that. Plus, your schedule is always going to be insane. That's what we signed up for."

He nods slowly, his gaze distant. "I know, but right now, it feels like anything I do just adds to the strain. We barely see each other as it is and I'm working more than ever. And then when I do see her, it's awkward. How can it be awkward with someone I've known since I was sixteen years old?"

The sadness in Walker's eyes is palpable as he continues. "I don't know, man. It's like we're drifting apart and I can't seem to bridge the gap. She's always been supportive, but this . . . this feels different."

I put down my drink. "Well you know I'm not a relationship expert, so take this with a grain of salt . . . but have you considered that it's not about the fellowship?"

His brow furrows. "What in the hell could it be about? That's all she's going on about."

"Maybe she's just feeling neglected. And listen, I get it. You have a fuck ton of things on your plate. But have you tried talking to her about how she's feeling? Not just about the job or the move, but about you two?"

Walker lets out a pained exhale, rubbing his temples. "I've tried but it always ends in an argument or with her giving me the silent treatment. I'm not even sure what to say anymore. It's like she's done."

"Maybe start with that? Tell her you're not sure what to say, but you want to make things right. Communication is important, even if it starts with admitting you're at a loss for words," I suggest.

Sometimes it's funny how many physicians struggle with their words. For me, it's the only thing I have going for me. I've never been the smartest guy in the room, always having to work harder than everyone else to prove that I belong. But I've also never once felt like I was unsure of what I felt or what I needed to say.

Walker looks at me with a tiny flicker of hope in his dark eyes. "You're probably right."

I smirk at him. "I'm always right."

CHAPTER 21

CLAIRE

"**C**oco," Cassidy yells across the living room. "Kittens are friends, not food."

The golden retriever looks up at Cass with an expression that says *I can do no wrong* before she lays down, keeping her eyes glued on Frosty.

We've been at Cassidy's parents' house for the past two days, lounging around in matching sweatsuits and eating all of the sweets that our hearts could desire. Because Beau's been stuck at the hospital, I didn't want to leave the kitten by himself and Cass insisted that I bring him with me.

Frosty remains cool and collected under Coco's gaze, occasionally swatting a playful paw toward the retriever, just for the fun of it. Cassidy watches them like a hawk, though, ensuring that Coco's fascination doesn't turn into anything more than harmless curiosity. Apparently, her parents got the dog a few months after her brother died, and they've been pretty relaxed about her training, so I think Cass is worried about Frosty being able to defend himself. If only she knew that he went up against a six-foot-four surgeon and won.

Cassidy plops down next to me in the recliner. "So, how are you enjoying the burbs?" she asks, handing me a cookie. "I never thought I'd like living out here, but it's nice not hearing sirens fly by all night."

"I dunno what you're talking about," I answer with a mouth full before swallowing. "Parker's condo is practically silent. The insulation is amazing."

She giggles. "Probably a good thing since you have a new roommate."

I feel myself blush at the thought of Beau. We've barely seen each other since the night I nearly blacked out at the Mexican restaurant. I thought it would be awkward after our conversation and was perfectly prepared to act like nothing happened, but he made sure I was still on board the moment he returned home from work. It's like confrontation and emotional discussions don't make him feel queasy inside like they do for me.

Unfortunately, Beau's been at the hospital late every day since, and by the time he gets home, he's exhausted. I assume this must be a super busy time for them because one night we were chatting, and he got surprisingly quiet. When I looked over, he had fallen asleep on the couch with his mouth hanging open, as if he had started to reply but couldn't fight sleep any longer. I covered him up with a blanket and lay on the opposite side of the sectional, unable to hide the massive smile on my face at how adorable he looked.

"Would you believe it if I said that he's the best roommate I've ever had?" I gush as I think of the little gestures he performs daily. It's astonishing, really, how he manages to find the time and energy to show he cares in such meaningful ways. Sometimes it doesn't feel like he's real.

"I'm sure your mother would be rolling around in her grave if she heard you say that," Cass jokes, breaking a cookie in half and plopping it in her mouth.

Oh shit—sorry, Mom! You were a great roomie too!

"Dinner will be here in five," her dad calls from the kitchen.

According to Cass, her family doesn't cook on Thanksgiving because her mom is usually working all morning. While I miss the extravagant meals that my mom used to make on the holiday, this is way more relaxing. We haven't moved from the couch all day and it's been heavenly.

As the doorbell rings, signaling the arrival of dinner, Cassidy and I exchange looks of guilt for our indulgent morning. She hops up, helping her dad with the food while I stretch and join her mom in the kitchen.

Surprisingly, Cassidy and her mom look nothing alike. Mrs. Callaway has short, dark hair and brown eyes that contrast sharply with Cassidy's light features. Her mom is wearing black wide-leg dress pants and a formal blouse, like she's conducting a business meeting, not eating Thanksgiving dinner with her family.

Once we all gather around the dining table, a mix of aromas fills the air—spicy, savory, sweet. It's almost like they ordered from every restaurant in the area, because there's an assortment of every variety of food imaginable on the table, and my stomach growls with anticipation.

"We like leftovers," her mom says, likely noticing my expression as she takes her seat at the head of the table. "Though it seems this year we overdid it a bit."

She shoots a pointed look at her husband, who just shrugs and says, "I didn't know how hungry our extra guest would be. Come on you two, dig in."

I smile at Cassidy's dad who shoots me a wink and passes me a pair of tongs.

"Cass, you'll never guess who I ran into at Publix this week," her mom says as she starts to fill her plate. Before Cassidy can answer, her mom adds, "Holly Southerland."

I have no idea who this person is, so I sit quietly and munch on a chicken tender.

"Did you now?" Cass replies warily, crossing her arms and leaning back in her chair like she's preparing for battle.

"I did," her mom confirms, looking proud of herself. "I was in the city visiting a client so I ran in to grab a sandwich, and she was right there in the Boar's Head line. Can you believe that?"

Cassidy's hazel eyes narrow. "Well, they do live in Buckhead, Mother."

"Check your tone," she says, and I stifle a grin. She and Mom would have gotten along. "Anyways, she said that you two went to lunch last week."

"We did."

"And she said Weston joined you. I love that you keep in contact with them. How's that young man doing? I hear he's completing a fellowship in Chicago."

Cassidy shifts uncomfortably in her chair, but her eyes stay locked on her mom. "He's fine."

I knew the name sounded familiar. Weston is Cassidy's ex-boyfriend and award-winning jerk of the century. She shared a little bit about what happened last year, and it sounded like a complete shit show. From what I understand, Parker still hates Weston even though he used to be his best friend, but apparently, Cassidy has forgiven him.

This is starting to sound like the plot of a reality TV show. Suddenly feeling more invested, I spin in my chair to face my sister-in-law and lean in, not wanting to miss a word.

"I know Carter would be so proud that you two still have a friendship," her mom continues, smiling as she takes a sip of her wine.

But it sounds like Parker wouldn't.

I look curiously at Cassidy, a devilish smirk on my face with the realization that there's no way in hell my brother knows about this.

"So, I'm going to assume that they're invited to the wedding?" Mrs. Callaway asks casually. "We need to finalize the guest list soon for Save the Dates."

Cassidy glares at me, as if she can hear my thoughts and is silently pleading with me to keep my lips zipped. "Mr. and Mrs. Southerland are welcome, of course. I know you guys are friends."

"We never get to see them anymore, but we set up dinner for the four of us next weekend at the club," Cassidy's mom replies, gesturing to her husband who lets out a slight groan.

"That's great, Mom. I'm sure you'll have fun."

"Yes, but what about Weston?" Mrs. Callaway presses, not missing the fact that Cassidy didn't mention his presence at the wedding. "He's invited too, right? I know the Southerlands will ask at dinner and I want to assure them that he's welcome."

Cassidy cracks her neck and looks away. "Potentially."

"What do you mean potentially? Clearly, you two are fine if you're willing to get lunch together."

"That was a one-time thing and it's a little complicated," Cass replies, hesitating before she adds, "with Parker."

Her mom scoffs, brushing off Cassidy's comment. "Why would Parker care, darling? You're marrying him after all. Not Weston. I'm sure *you* wouldn't care if an old ex of Parker's came to the wedding, now would you?"

I giggle, unable to help myself. "Parker doesn't have any ex-girlfriends. He was married to medicine."

Cassidy's mom raises an eyebrow, a curious look on her face. "Really? No ex-girlfriends at all?"

"Cass brought him out of his shell and thank god, because he was unbearable before."

Her dad chimes in. "Opposites attract, isn't that right, honey?"

She gives her husband a warm smile. "Exactly. Well, Cass, I'm not sure why Parker would have an issue with him coming to the wedding if he knows you two are still friends. I have lots of men that I'm friends with. It doesn't mean that I want to form a harem."

Her father rolls his eyes, adjusting the ball cap atop his head. "I think you mean reverse harem. Plus, you work too much to handle more than one man. You can barely handle me."

I snicker at her dad's comment but Cassidy seems unamused and deflated. "I'll talk to Parker and let you know."

I'm itching in my seat and can't wait to ask her about this later. Obviously, I know that there's no way she would cheat on my brother. She's obsessed with him for some reason completely beyond me. But I also know that Parker will flip his lid if he finds out that she had lunch with Weston without telling him. And there's no way on earth he's going to be on board with inviting Weston to the wedding either.

My brother isn't exactly the forgive-and-forget type of guy. He's more into holding grudges and cutting people out of his life completely.

"Good. So Claire," Cassidy's mom says, shifting her focus to me as she takes another sip of wine, "do you like Atlanta?"

"For the most part," I reply, taking a moment to spoon some grits onto my plate now that the drama is over. "I'm sure you know about everything that happened with my mom in September."

"Yes dear," she says, sorrow washing over her face. "I'm so sorry about your mother. We spoke several times about the wedding before she passed, and it was a pleasure to know her."

Cassidy looks over at me hesitantly, like she's making sure I'm okay, and I give her a soft smile. I thought I would be triggered by this, given the holiday, but I'm surprisingly fine.

Instead of feeling sad, I just picture my mom and her conversation with Mrs. Callaway. I imagine the way that she would have welcomed Cassidy's parents into our family with open arms. How she probably sent a gift basket of Harry and David pears once she found out about the engagement. And how she probably added them to the Christmas card list that grew longer with each year.

Apart from my siblings, nobody has mentioned my mom to me since the funeral, probably for fear that they would upset me. And at first, that was wise because I wasn't coping well. I didn't want to talk about her. I couldn't talk about her.

But now, as I sit and think about my mom, I find peace. Peace in knowing that I'm finally ready to start to move forward in my life. Peace in knowing that she was proud of the person I am. And peace in knowing that she will continue to be proud of me, no matter what I do in life.

All I ever wanted was to make her proud, and I can't think of a better way to do it than this. So the words that come out of my mouth next are something I've considered but not fully committed to until this moment.

"Thank you, Mrs. Callaway," I respond. "I've actually decided to go back to school to become a nurse."

That day at the hospital changed me. I never thought nursing was something I would be interested in, but I haven't been able to stop thinking about that little boy and how good it felt to help him. Or how interesting it was to hear Morgan talk about her day. Or how alive I felt in the chaos of it all.

I've always been unsure of my purpose in life. I went into advertising because it was fun and it was what my friends were doing. I avoided medicine and healthcare because it was what my family loved, and I desperately wanted to stand out. But now, I can't think of a better purpose than to honor my mom's memory and become a nurse.

I glance over at Cass and the expression on her face is one of pure shock. "Really?" she asks, her lips quivering slightly.

"Really." I nod.

"That's wonderful, dear," her dad chimes in. "I know Cass had to get a second bachelor's degree after she left Athens. Is that something you could do too?"

"Yes, sir," I reply, feeling ten thousand pounds lighter despite all of the food in front of us. "There's a program downtown that only takes twelve months, and from what it sounds like, I can start in the spring."

"Cassidy, honey, why are you upset?" Mrs. Callaway asks.

Cassidy quickly wipes her eyes. "I'm not upset, I promise they're happy tears," she says with a forced laugh before she meets my eyes. "I'm just so proud of you," she chokes out, unable to stop the stream of tears from running down her face. "Sorry for crying."

Mr. Callaway smiles warmly, reaching across the table to give his daughter's hand a gentle squeeze. "It's okay to be emotional, honey. It's a big moment. We're all proud of Claire."

He looks at me and winks as Cassidy lets out a loud sob. "It's just," she pauses, trying to collect herself. "I've just always thought you'd be so good as a nurse. But I never wanted to push it on you."

"It's a good thing you didn't because it would have made me run in the opposite direction, just to spite you," I tease, trying to bring some levity to the conversation. "Thank god you're much more mature than I am."

She chokes out a laugh. "I love you."

I lean in, pulling her into my arms. "I love you too."

Eventually, Cass calms herself down and we finish our feast, discussing everything from travel destinations to which Hogwarts house each one of us would be in. Obviously, I said I was a Gryffindor, because who wouldn't want to be the most badass house?

It feels weird to say, considering I didn't get to spend the holiday with my family, with Parker in the hospital and Caroline busy with school, but it's one of the best holidays I've had in a long time.

Beau even sent me a text, since he couldn't write me a note this morning, telling me that he was thankful I don't yell at him when he leaves the toilet seat up. I told him that he shouldn't count his chickens before they hatch because I almost fell in yesterday and came very close to rekeying the condo.

We've been messaging back and forth all day while he works, and while I'd never admit this to him, I'm glad that he leaves the toilet seat up too because it means he's around.

Chapter 22
Chapter 22

Thanksgiving day came and went in a blur. It turns out that people are really prone to broken bones when they're around their families. First, a guy came in with half of his hand on ice because he sliced through it during a morning woodworking project with his dad. We spent ten hours in the operating room working to reattach nerves, ligaments, and bone so we could give him the best shot at a functional hand. While it probably sucked for the patient, it was by far the coolest surgery I've done so far and made for a memorable Thanksgiving.

Then, I was on call overnight and had to set a ridiculous number of bones after shoppers came in from their midnight Black Friday escapades. It was nonstop, and the only thing that kept me awake after almost twenty hours of work was pure willpower. I'm sure the notes that I wrote in patient charts will be flagged for misspellings, but after everything that happened, I was beyond caring.

The Friday after Thanksgiving has always been reserved for the entire surgical residency program to enjoy a Friendsgiving dinner at someone's house. But the guy who hosted it, Weston Southerland, graduated from his residency and nobody volunteered their house this year, which means all of the surgical interns are spending the weekend in north Georgia for a retreat.

If I wasn't so damn exhausted, I'd be thrilled. But I've only slept a total of twelve hours in the past four days, and my enthusiasm for anything is at an all-time low. Which is saying something considering the agenda for the weekend includes some of my favorite things—camping, shooting guns, and drinking beer.

Fortunately, I was able to get a few hours of sleep in the car with Parker, who decided to drive my truck after I told him that his Tesla would get mud streaks all over the side if we drove it. It turns out that the man may be more protective of that car than he is of his own two hands, which is weird considering he complains about his ride breaking all of the time.

While the long drive would have been the ideal place to talk to him about Claire, I genuinely could not keep my eyes open long enough to get a sentence out, let alone explain to my best friend that I want to date his sister. Plus, depending on how he takes the news, it's probably best that I'm not around him with a gun afterward. I'll talk to him tomorrow night once he's got a beer or two in him . . . and all of the bullets are gone.

Walker's land is set in the foothills of the Appalachian Mountains, with miles of private property just past Blue Ridge. Apparently, it was a recent inheritance from grandfather's passing, which it didn't sound like he was expecting or very pleased by. I'm not sure how you could be upset by a gift like that though, because the views as we pull up to the cabin are truly breathtaking.

Looking around, it seems like the rest of the surgical interns have already arrived and are gathered around a campfire. We have three surgical residencies at Midtown Memorial—orthopedics, plastics, and general surgery. While we often work together on cases, I haven't had a ton of time to get to know any interns other than Matt, so this should be a nice change of pace.

After I help Parker unload our stuff and set up my tent, I pull out my phone to let Claire know that we made it.

> At the site—and before you ask, no I haven't talked to your brother.

Ever since I sent her a message on Thanksgiving, we've been texting nonstop, and I know she's eager to know how the conversation goes. Immediately three dots appear and she replies.

> Don't chicken out. Anyone whose favorite candy is Swedish fish is just a big softie.

True—but his favorite tool in the OR is also a scalpel . . .

***

Last night we went to bed early because the majority of us worked the holiday and were too exhausted to stay awake long past the sunset. Fortunately, that allowed for an early morning, complete with a hike and shooting skeet before Walker and Parker forced us to do team-building exercises.

Surgeons are some of the most competitive people you'll ever meet so group activities tend to get incredibly heated. I'm pretty sure one of the plastics guys almost threw a punch when we taunted him, which made me laugh because they are pretty sons of bitches. I can't imagine they would want to ruin their charm by picking a fight with us. The good news is, though, that ortho won and bragging rights are ours for the rest of the year.

Parker may be leading the retreat, but Walker's outdone himself with hosting. I have no idea how in the fuck he had time to get all of this together with everything else going on in his life. I've wanted to ask him how the conversation with his wife went, but we haven't been alone together and he's been in entertaining mode, constantly on the move as he makes sure people have what they need.

I'm hoping now that we're settled by the campfire I'll be able to chat with Parker about Claire. I deliberately plopped my chair next to his and offered him a Budweiser even though he's not a big drinker. He took it, nursing the beer as he directed the general surgery residents on how to make a proper fire. I couldn't help giving him shit about his instructions—he's a city boy through and through and has absolutely no business teaching people how to make a campfire. Probably not the best move if I'm trying to butter him up, but I just couldn't resist.

Currently, we're playing a game called Truth or Drink. The rules are simple: one person picks a question and asks it to the group. Everyone else has to either answer the question or take a sip of whatever libation they're enjoying. Some of the questions have been pretty funny, actually, especially when someone asked who the scariest attending was, and the general surgery interns unanimously pointed at Parker.

"Buffington, your turn," Matt nudges me from my left. His backward baseball cap looks ridiculous with his thinning hairline, but I know he's just trying to look cool in front of the only female ortho intern he's obsessed with. "You're the last one."

"Sorry, what was the question again?"

Someone across the campfire calls, "Would you rather take call for a week straight or spend a month only debriding necrotic wounds."

I make a gesture of throwing up and immediately respond, "Call for a week straight, for sure. Pretty sure I'll be smelling those debriding cases until the day that I die."

Everyone laughs and one of the girls from general, whose name I can't remember, says, "Okay, my turn to pick the question. Who in the group would you not want your sister to date?" The question sends a ripple of laughter and hushed whispers around the campfire.

Walker leans over to me and whispers, "This is a stupid fucking question. I don't even have a sister."

I smirk, waiting for someone to respond. I'd probably pick Walker just to fuck with him. Although if I had a sister, he wouldn't be a half-bad choice. The man is perfect.

Parker, who's been watching the game with a mix of amusement and detachment, leans forward slightly. "I'll answer that," he offers.

Everyone turns to him with surprise, considering he's flat-out refused to answer every question posed so far.

"Don't look at me like that," he says, shaking his head at everyone. "This is the easiest question you guys have posed all night."

Parker turns to look at me, almost in slow motion, and responds, "Dr. Beau Buffington."

CHAPTER 23

CLAIRE

It turns out the stories where a fireman has to rescue a cat from a tree aren't that unrealistic, because I'm currently standing on the back of the sectional trying to pull Frosty from the top of our ten-foot Christmas tree. I turned my back for less than five minutes to put cookies in the oven and found him batting at ornaments halfway up the trunk of my beautifully flocked tree. When I tried to snatch him, he burrowed himself deeper into the branches, daring me to play his little game of hide and seek.

The good news is, he's adorable and I could never be mad at him. The orange devil brings me so much joy that all of his shenanigans make me laugh rather than yell. Beau on the other hand is having a hard time. His supernatural patience is stretched thin by the kitten and it's hilarious teaming up against him whenever we can. If we were ever parents, I would one hundred percent be the fun one, and Beau would be the disciplinarian because that's exactly how it goes with Frosty.

Once I got back from Cassidy's parent's house, I practically had to force myself to not text Beau. I desperately wanted to know how the conversation with Parker went but have been doing everything in my power to stay occupied. This morning that meant putting on my oversized white Christmas sweatshirt that says "Tis the Damn Season" and a pair of black leggings, and getting to work.

Parker had practically nothing festive at his condo, so I took advantage of the weekend sales and turned this place into a winter wonderland. Almost every inch of the condo is covered in something Christmasy at this point, except for my roommate's bedroom, though if Beau wants help decorating up there too I'd be happy to help him. I feel like stockings would look incredible hanging from his bed.

"Just because you live with a doctor who fixes bones, doesn't mean you should try to break them," Beau's voice calls as he closes the door.

"Almost got him," I grit out, ignoring his warning as I push myself up onto my toes and reach for the kitten. "Come here, buddy."

I hold my breath, as if that will make me grow the extra inch that I need to grab him. Without thinking, I jump slightly, catching hold of his scruff and pulling him down from his perch. Normally the movement wouldn't have been a problem, except my ankle twists slightly on landing and causes me to lose my footing on the back of the sofa.

My stomach drops with the sensation of falling, but before I can even process what's happening, my rapid descent halts abruptly. Two strong hands grip my waist and hold me in the air like we're the main characters in *Dirty Dancing*, only definitely less graceful.

Regaining my bearings on the ground, with Frosty nestled in my arms, I'm acutely aware of Beau's fingers still wrapped tightly around my hips. My heart races, not just from the near-fall, but also from his touch which now sends a distinct thrill through me. It's been too long since I felt him on my skin.

Now that we've had our little revelation, my body seems to have given itself permission to react to everything he does. Even a simple flirty text sends me spinning into a haze of longing, desperate to relive our night together.

It would be easy to be pissed at my brother for complicating things, but I understand where Beau's coming from. Parker doesn't have many friends and seems to have a serious aversion to secret keeping after what happened last year, so I can imagine he would freak out if he found out Beau and I were seeing each other behind his back. Not that my brother has any control over my relationships, but I know both Parker and Beau value their friendship, and having this conversation up front is the right thing to do.

The kitten yells and I quickly bend to the ground to let him scamper away, forcing Beau to release me from his grasp.

"Sorry," I say quietly as I stand up. "Thought I could do it on my own."

The darkness in his eyes quickly dissipates now that he knows I'm safe. "I knew you would the second I saw you up on that couch. It's a good thing I'm still fast as fuck."

He's wearing a backward navy baseball cap, dark jeans, and a white long-sleeve T-shirt that is a tad too tight. The stubble on his face has transformed into a short beard, making him appear much older, even though we're only a year apart in age.

I want to tell him that he looks hotter than ever, that I want him to throw his arms around me and have his way with me. But because I suck at communication, all I say is, "You stink big boy."

He tilts his head to his shoulder, inhaling deeply. "Whew, yeah," he admits, shooting me a sheepish grin that makes my heart melt. "That'll happen when you go two days without a shower."

"Do they not teach you basic hygiene in doctor school?"

He doesn't smell that bad. It just adds to the rugged look that he has going on, like he was out doing manly things. The thought makes my blood stir.

"Oh, they do," he says, taking a step backward, "but I was having too much fun to be bothered."

I pucker my lips. "Well, could you bother to take a shower? We already have one animal in this condo, I don't think we need another one."

He shrugs. "You know what they say . . . you can take the boy out of the country, but you can't take the country out of the boy."

"Go." I point toward the stairs, trying my hardest to muster a scowl despite everything inside me wanting to smile.

"Yes ma'am," he drawls, backtracking slowly and never once dropping his gaze from mine, as if he's daring me to follow him. When he reaches the base of the stairs, he pauses with a smug grin on his lips. "Happy to leave the door open again."

Without thinking, I pick up an ornament from the floor and chuck it at him as he races up the stairs, unable to control his laughter.

Fifteen minutes later, Beau comes down wearing a pair of dark gray joggers, running shoes, and a fitted black T-shirt. His thick, wavy hair is combed but still looks disheveled, like he towel-dried it quickly in a rush.

"Something smells amazing," Beau comments, narrowly avoiding Frosty who has claimed a spot on the floor in front of the stairs. The kitten somehow got hold of a stray ornament and is amusing himself by batting it around with his tiny paws.

I made my mom's oatmeal raisin cookies, and they've been cooling on the counter. They're practically the only thing I know how to make, and I figured they would be the perfect reward for my decorating frenzy.

"Going somewhere?" I ask, trying to hide my disappointment at seeing him fully dressed. I was kind of hoping he would stick around but it looks like he's going to the gym.

It's totally fine, Claire. He has no obligation to hangout with you.

"What?" His brow furrows as he plops into the couch. "No? Why?"

I adjust my body, pulling my legs up to my chest as I turn to face him. "Tennis shoes inside kind of signify that you plan on leaving."

"I've barely seen you in over a week. You think I plan on leaving already?"

"I wouldn't blame you," I admit, working to control the emotions in my chest. It's embarrassing how attached I am to him . . .

"I wore tennis shoes because I figured you needed help with decorating, seeing as the top half of the tree is completely bare."

My heart swells, but I paste a glare on my face. "Why would you need shoes for that? I did it in bare feet."

"And you almost fell," he reminds me, unbothered by my sass. "We're going to use a ladder and on ladders you wear shoes."

"Okay, bossy Beau."

"I like big boy Beau better."

"I'm sure you do."

His tone turns serious. "Let's get a few things straight, Claire," he sighs. "I'm not going anywhere. When I'm not at the hospital, the only place I want to be is here, with you."

"But—" I try to make a joke because his words are making my pulse race, but he interrupts me.

"Let me finish," he chuckles, shaking his head. "Fuck, you really are the worst at emotions."

"Am not!" I protest.

He gives me a look that makes my stomach drop to my feet and my mouth zip completely shut.

"Ever since that first night we met, you've been the *only* thing on my mind."

"Your poor patients," I tease because I can't help myself.

His gaze sharpens playfully. "Am I going to have to gag you to have this conversation? Because I swear to God, woman, I will."

I pretend to lock my lips and zip it, focusing on his handsome face.

"That's better," he huffs, taking my feet in his hands and extending them over his lap. "As I was trying to say, I'm still set on making you mine. When I'm free, I want to focus on you and only you."

"So, Parker—"

Beau's thumbs dig into the sensitive part of my feet, making me yelp from surprise, only instead of pain, all I feel is a thrum of energy between my legs.

"Parker and I didn't have a chance to talk this weekend, unfortunately," he explains, studying me closely with those warm eyes. "But that doesn't mean anything has changed. It just means that we've gotta wait a little bit longer."

I sigh because I don't want to wait longer. I want this man's expert hands to drift along my body right now.

"When?" I ask, attempting to hide my disappointment.

"Soon." He slowly rubs his thumb along the inside of my foot. "Desperate for my touch or something?"

"You're touching me right now, dummy." I pointedly look down at his hands gripping my feet, like he's using them as a barrier between us.

"Trust me," he says, digging his thumbs into that spot once more. "*This* is nowhere close to how I'm planning to touch you."

CHAPTER 24

BEAU

My schedule since the retreat has been surprisingly tolerable, and I'm starting to feel like a human being again rather than a strung-out zombie. I worked four days in a row, with only one overnight call shift, and after I finish up today I'm off for two days straight.

Claire made me promise her that I would watch a reality TV show with her tonight, and while I can't wait to relax together, I also can't fucking figure out what to do about Parker.

I was genuinely shocked when Parker said I was the last person in the group that he'd want his sister to date. Clearly, out of any of those bozos, I would be the best choice. When I pressed him for a reason, he pointed out my med school days—back when I used to have various women on call for my dick almost every night. What he doesn't know is that everything changed the moment I met Claire.

Today in our surgical case I thought about coming clean to him. I figured he couldn't kill me in front of a room of people if things went south. But then I started feeling guilty about how good of a friend he's been to me this past year, so I held my tongue like a fucking coward.

On my way home, I considered lying to Claire and telling her that her brother gave his full blessing. It would allow me to fuck her brains out tonight, which is all I've wanted for months. But unfortunately, I don't believe in starting a relationship built on a lie. Though . . . I'm already lying to her each time I tell her that I haven't had a chance to talk to her brother. I've had ample opportunity, I just know what his opinion will be and don't want to hear it.

I may not know what to do, but what I do know is that I've got to do something soon because the way Claire has been toying with me is going to send me into an early grave. The past few nights I've come home to her wearing even fewer clothes than she normally does, taunting me with a knowing smirk on her face. It's like she's showing me what I could have if I would just man the fuck up and have an adult conversation with Parker.

By the time I make my way downstairs after my post-shift shower, Claire's got her show ready in the living room with Frosty purring in her lap. Her wild hair is pulled back in a single thick braid, and she's wearing some sort of matching two-piece set that stops just beneath her breasts, exposing far too much of her stomach to make me feel confident in my ability to control myself.

The purposeful distance I put between us on the couch did nothing to dampen my awareness of her. Every breath she takes makes my skin prickle and my cock swell. She could have the bubonic plague and I think my dick would still be rock hard if it was close to her.

"Are you getting everything?" Claire asks, eyeing me suspiciously.

"Uh, yeah," I reply, leaning forward to grab my beer. "That chick in the black was pissed because that chick in the yellow hooked up with her boyfriend."

"Beau!" she exclaims, tossing a pillow at me.

"What?" I can't help but chuckle as I dodge her throw. "Isn't that what happened?"

Claire places Frosty on the ground and moves to stand directly in front of me, blocking my view of the television. Her perky tits are right at my eye level and I can immediately tell she's not wearing a bra.

"Are you sure you're a doctor?" she asks, popping her hand on her hip.

"Yes?" I reply, not sure where she's going with her question.

"Because this really isn't that hard to follow. Here, scoot over so I can explain everything during the next episode." Claire leans forward, her breasts nearly popping out of her top as she pushes me to the side, wedging her perfect body between me and the arm of the sectional.

"You gotta focus," she scolds with a frustrated sigh, drawing her knees into her chest as she leans against my shoulder.

Yeah, because it's going to be so easy to focus now.

The next episode plays while Claire explains the background of every single character, even diving deep into their motivations and fears. The only thing she's missing is their social security numbers, and I marvel at how she could know so much about complete strangers.

I try my best to listen, but the only thing going through my brain is how soft her arm feels against mine as she wiggles to get comfortable. Every bit of my brain capacity is focused on maintaining the boundaries I've set for us.

Claire must notice something's up because she picks up the remote and pauses the show, looking over at me with concern. "Did you have a bad day or something?"

"No? Why?"

"You seem distracted, like there's a lot on your mind. I hope I'm not bothering you," she says, her face falling with her words.

I shift my body, meeting her gaze so she knows I mean what I'm about to say. "First of all, you're never a bother. Honestly, I'm happiest when I'm with you, even if you're making me watch this mind-numbing garbage."

She rolls her baby blue eyes but there's still a hint of uncertainty in them. I grab her legs, spinning her body to place them in my lap.

"Secondly," I add, squeezing her bare feet and making her giggle, "I'm sorry for making you feel that way. Forgive me?"

"If I must." Claire tilts her perfect lips into a half smile. "Wanna talk about it?"

"Not really," I admit.

"Seriously?" she presses, her thin brows knitted together as she studies me closely. "You're the one who tells me that I suck at emotions and here you are, practically about to explode."

"Am not," I counter.

"Are too," she cracks a smile. "You're clenching your jaw so hard, you might break a tooth."

I release her feet, letting her stretch her legs out across my lap. Putting my hands behind my head, I lean back against the couch with a massive sigh.

She's right—I've got to practice what I preach.

I just wish it was easier.

"I've had lots of opportunities to talk to Parker about us," I start, shutting my eyes for a second to help me get the words out. "I just haven't."

Claire shifts her legs. "Do you not want this?"

My eyes fly open again and I instinctively reach for her, drawing her body onto my lap. My arms tighten around her, and I inhale deeply, the comforting blend of cinnamon and vanilla calming me down.

"You're the only thing I want," I murmur, resting my chin against the top of her head, "which is why this is so hard."

Claire nuzzles into my chest with a comfortability that I've only ever dreamed of. "You're not saying something."

For someone who sucks at expressing her own emotions, she sure is good at reading the emotions of others. Guess I'm going to have to go ahead and say it . . .

"I don't think your brother is okay with us seeing each other."

Her nose wrinkles as she takes my admission. "But you just said—"

I cut her off. "At the retreat, Parker said that I was the last person that he would ever want his sister to date."

She angles her head, staring up at me with a playful smirk. "Did he say which sister? Because you know he has two right?"

"I think the implication was pretty damn clear, Claire."

She chews on her cheek for a minute, assessing my words. "Well, I frankly could care less what he thinks."

"But—"

"I know, I know, for some reason you're his bestie. And I have no intention of coming between you two. God knows my brother needs all the friends he can get." Claire's sky-blue eyes bore into mine as she tosses one leg over me to straddle my lap.

I have no idea where this confidence came from, but I'm immediately hard as a rock.

"But it doesn't make sense to have him come between us either," she adds. "He still doesn't know about the bar, right? How is this any different?"

"The difference is that I know you're his sister now."

"Semantics," she shrugs, draping her arms over my shoulders casually.

"We don't even know if this is going to work out, so why should we have to tell him?"

She grinds her hips against mine, and I groan as I try my hardest to keep my thoughts straight.

"Come on," she murmurs, her voice dropping to a sexy purr. "Let's keep it between us for a while, and then if things get serious, I promise we'll talk to him together."

The problem is that to me, this thing between us already is serious.

CHAPTER 25

CLAIRE

I may not be the most experienced girl in the world, but I'm not oblivious either. Every time I wear something remotely revealing around the condo, Beau's eyes get this droopy haze to them, like he can't focus on anything but my body. It's adorable and has quickly turned into a new game for me—picking out my outfits to test his limits of self-control.

To his credit, he's held surprisingly firm this past week, steering clear of any physical contact, as if he doesn't trust himself fully. But that's just made me more determined, itching to make him crack.

Now that I'm perched in his lap, though, I think he's finally teetering on the edge of his resolve. I'm hoping that our agreement to keep things between us will loosen his inhibitions enough to finally give in to me; at least now he can blame me for the secrecy and not himself. And while I'm not going to be the one who makes the first move, because this is something he has to work out for himself, that doesn't mean I won't do everything in my power to nudge him along.

"Wanna watch the next episode?" I ask, sinking my full weight onto his crotch. "Or do you wanna do something else?"

I feel his whole arousal beneath me and something ignites within me. Something confident and sexy that's inherently natural in a way that it never has been before.

"Anything is better than this garbage." He shakes his head, letting out a sharp breath as I roll my hips.

"Anything?" I ask innocently, batting my eyelashes.

Beau's brown eyes darken as his hands move from the couch to my hips. "You fight dirty, pretty girl."

His fingers dig into my skin, shooting a sharp pang of lust through my core. All I want is for him to show me that he's longing for me in the same way that I am for him.

"Do I?" I breathe, every inch of my body aware of his.

"You do," he confirms, gently gliding his thumbs along my hip bone in the direction of where I need them the most.

My eyes close momentarily, savoring the feeling of his hands on me. They're strong and practiced, like they could bring me to the brink of ecstasy without hesitation.

As he continues to rub my sensitive skin, slowly inching closer to my arousal, he pauses and releases another pained breath.

I mimic his sound because the loss of his movement is painful, and I'm desperate for more.

I slowly open my eyes and meet his gaze.

"Funny," I mutter, unable to hold my tongue.

"What's funny?" he asks cautiously, as if he knows where I'm headed with my comment.

Beau may be ridiculously intimidating on the outside—the kind of guy you'd never talk to at a bar because you wouldn't think he would be into you—but I've learned that he's more like a gentle giant than a macho monster. Beau might toss you around and exude pure confidence in the bedroom, but afterward, he's still going to make your coffee with a friendly note in the morning. Which is why I have no hesitations about what I'm about to say next.

I shrug my shoulders and stifle the smirk that wants to form on my lips. "I just never took you for the guy who doesn't fight back."

And with those words, I know I've won.

His brown eyes flash darker as his large hands dig into my hips, pulling me so close that I'm pressed firmly against his impressive bulge. The grind of the fabric against my clit makes me gasp, a quick bolt of desire pulsing through me.

Tangling his fingers through my braid, Beau tugs so hard on my hair so that my head is forced to fall against his shoulder.

"I'm going to give you one chance to take back what you just said," he breathes in my ear, his tone warning. "When it comes to you, I've got rounds of fight in me. And if we do this, I'm not stopping, even if you tap out."

My core clenches as he pulls harder at the nape of my neck.

"Let's see what you've got, big boy."

His eyes flicker with the last of his resolve as he takes a single deep inhale and mutters, "Fuck it."

In an instant, his lips are clashing with mine with a ferocity that surprises me. It's feral, like a starving wolf that has finally found its prey. It's a kiss that's completely at odds with his normally carefree nature, and I can't get enough.

I moan into him as he sets the pace, taking whatever it is that he needs as his last band of restraint finally snaps.

It turns out that I need the same thing because I've never been more aroused in my life. The thrum of tension building between my thighs is beginning to get uncomfortable. I attempt to grind myself on him, but he's got me locked in place, forcing me to remain exactly where he wants me.

His tongue sweeps into my mouth, almost taking my breath away with its harshness as I taste him. And it's a taste that I want to remember forever because kissing him tastes like letting go. It tastes like completely forgetting about what I should be doing, or how I should be acting, and just simply giving in to what I'm feeling.

After it feels like my lips have been rubbed completely raw, Beau tugs me back by my hair, forcing me to look at him. His eyes are smoldering with raw desire and I can tell it's taking everything he has to hold himself back.

But I have no idea why.

"What happened?" I ask, trying to catch my breath. "I thought you said when you finally got your hands on me, 'I would feel it in my entire body'?"

He chuckles, his eyes momentarily falling to the area where our bodies meet. "And you will. But a ten-course meal isn't served all at once, is it?"

"Uh, not unless you want to eat cold food."

"Exactly, and I intend on enjoying each course." Beau slowly rubs his free hand up and down my thigh before settling it right at the apex of my sex. "But I want to make sure you enjoy it too."

"Pretty sure I'd be happy with anything you had in mind," I pant as his thumb gently plays with the fabric above my clit.

"Maybe," he muses, adjusting himself beneath me. "But I want to know what you like."

"What do you mean?" I mumble breathily, leaning into his touch.

"How do you normally come? I know you like to watch," he smirks, clearly thinking back to the shower. "But do you like to be watched? Do you use toys or your fingers? Do you come from just penetration or do you need your clit rubbed too? Nobody knows your body better than you do, Claire."

I look away, feeling my cheeks heat from embarrassment because, for the first time in his life, he's wrong. I have no idea what my body likes or doesn't like. Though whatever he's doing right now with his thumb feels better than anything I've ever experienced before, and I wish he wouldn't stop.

"Hey," he says gently, his free hand tenderly coaxing my chin as he directs my attention back to him. "Did I say something wrong?"

My eyes close, desperately trying to escape this conversation. I can talk all day about pretty much anything, but when the topic drifts towards anything intimate or emotional, my brain freezes.

"It's not you," I finally admit, forcing my eyes to meet his once more. "I just, um, don't really know what I like."

He pauses his movement between my legs as he waits for me to continue.

I prod my cheek with my tongue. "I mean obviously I like sex, and kissing, and everything that comes between. It usually feels good," I add, as I consider how to explain myself. "But I don't know how to answer your questions, because truthfully, I've never taken the time to explore myself like that."

Beau's thick brows knit together as he drops his hand from my face, wrapping his big arms around me. I snuggle into him, appreciating the warmth and comfort of his embrace, like he's letting me know that he's a safe space.

"I'm sorry I assumed. That was wrong of me," he says, squeezing me closer. "So you've never made yourself come?"

"No," I admit warily, thankful that my face is smashed against his hard chest because I can feel my blush deepen.

It's not like how to orgasm is taught in schools. We learn how to avoid pregnancy and how to manage your period. Female masturbation is seen as this taboo thing that nobody ever talks about. I honestly don't think my friends and I have once discussed sex, let alone orgasms.

I may outwardly seem outgoing and curious, but I guess I never considered that curiosity in terms of sex. The only reason I remotely know what to do around men is because of previous boyfriends or movies. And that's always been fine . . . until now.

"What about the other guys?" Beau asks, his face incredulous as he tilts my head up. "They never made you come either?"

Now I feel guilty. If I don't know my own body, how can I expect another man to know my body? It's not their fault that I don't know what I like.

"It's not like the sex was bad!" I explain, knowing my words aren't coming off the way I want them to. "Like I said, it usually felt good."

He swallows harshly, like he's considering his words carefully. "Claire, if you take anything from this conversation let it be this. Sex should *always* feel good. If it doesn't, your partner is the problem. Not you."

"I guess I never told them." My eyes close as guilt washes over me.

Beau sighs, slowly running his fingers up my back. "Great sex requires constant communication and checking in. Pleasure goes both ways and I'm never going to take my own unless I know you've had yours. Do you understand that?"

"Okay . . ."

"I'm serious. If I do something you don't like, or I need to move slightly to hit the right spot, you need to tell me. It won't hurt my feelings."

I bite my lower lip, feeling horrible that I derailed our fun. "Sorry, I'm defective."

Beau leans down to kiss my forehead. "You're not defective, pretty girl. You just haven't had a chance to be broken in yet."

"Well, let's crack that whip," I smirk, brushing one hand down his ridiculously sculpted chest.

He winces and stops my fingers before they can get to his waistband. He's still rock hard, and I can't imagine that it's very comfortable. "We're not cracking anything until you take the time to learn about your body. I need to know you're confident telling me what you like."

I groan dramatically as Beau pulls my hands away, placing them around his neck. "First things first. Have you ever watched porn?"

Unable to help myself, I roll my eyes. "Why would I have watched porn if I've never even masturbated?"

The word feels crass coming out of my mouth. For some reason, I can say everything else known to man, but the word masturbate makes me feel like a whore in church.

He chuckles warmly, pushing a stray hair out of my face. "Fair point. What about those books of yours that you leave lying around the condo? I imagine with a naked man on the cover there's bound to be some sex."

"They're half naked, thank you very much," I snap.

He shoots me a look that says he's not playing games and I relent. "I mean, yeah of course there's sex and it's hot. Sometimes super hot. But I don't read any of the wild romance stuff like Cass and Morgan, so usually it's just a little dirty talk and your basic sex."

"How does reading make you feel?"

I consider his question for a moment before responding.

"Good, I guess," I confess, thinking back to the last book I read about a billionaire who fell in love with a farm girl. "I don't know, probably a little turned on."

Beau's lips twitch with amusement. "Have you ever wanted to do something about how turned on you are when you read?"

"Sure, yeah, but—"

He interrupts me. "But what?"

This is so fucking embarrassing.

"I wouldn't know what to do."

His expression softens before he pulls me in for a quick kiss. It's gentler and less hurried than before, like he knows that he has me and can finally take his time.

"Alright, here's the plan," he says, picking me up off him and plopping me down on my feet. "Tonight you're going to go to your room and explore your body. Take the time to touch yourself. Figure out what you like and don't like."

"What about Frosty?" I pout, looking over at the cat lying beneath the shimmering Christmas tree. He's slept with me every night since Beau brought him home.

"He'll be fine out here," Beau assures me. "He's a cat, Claire. Animals don't belong in the bedroom."

"You don't want to watch?" I ask, tentatively shuffling my feet across the cold wood floor as Beau follows behind me.

"More than anything," he answers, spinning me to press his lips to my forehead once more. "But this is about you, not me."

Twenty minutes later I'm lying on top of my comforter in just my panties. My head is on my pillow and I'm contemplating what I should do next. At first, I fingered myself because I know I like that—it's something I've enjoyed since fooling around with guys in high school. While it felt good, it didn't really do anything special for me, so I stopped after a while.

Then I swept my fingers up higher, rubbing my clit in various motions as I tried to relax. That felt even better but still didn't quite get me there . . . wherever there is.

The sensation was warm and enjoyable, helping me to ease the tension still lingering from Beau's expert hands. But I stopped because it still didn't snap away like I was hoping.

I have no idea what else to do, so I lie there frustrated for a moment longer before I finally decide to text Beau and inform him that the deed is done.

I did what you asked. It felt good.

He immediately responds.

Just good? Tell me what you did.

Ugh—what does he want, a full breakdown of the explicit movements of my fingers? I'm not a freaking erotica writer.

I fingered myself and then rubbed my clit.

That's all the detail he's getting tonight.

A text bounces back immediately.

Did you come?

I know he's going to be disappointed with my answer, but I also don't want to lie to him because he asked me to be honest about this stuff.

No

Three dots and a response bounce back.

Why not?

I roll my eyes at his text—as if he thinks this is the easiest thing in the world.

Well, I guess it is for men . . . but women's bodies aren't like a car manual where you see an icon and know immediately what the problem is. They're complex and confusing, and something that works for one person doesn't always work for someone else.

I don't know. I guess I'm not in the mood anymore.

As soon as I send the text, my phone rings. Not a video call, thank god, or I would probably decline and never look him in the eyes again.

Just a regular old phone call.

I can do this.

"You know you don't have to call me right?" I say, putting the phone on speaker as I roll onto my side. "You're literally right above me."

"Claire, I need you to listen to me." The tone of his voice is low and raspy, instantly making the pesky tension in my body pull tighter.

I roll my eyes, though he can't see it. "Isn't that the point of a phone call?"

He doesn't respond with a laugh like I'm expecting. "Take the phone and put it next to your head. Lie down on your back."

His demand sends a spasm of pleasure through my core. Maybe it's the arousal pulsing through me, or maybe it's the commanding drawl of his voice, but I listen to him.

"Alright," I reply quietly once I'm in place.

"Were you in the mood when you were with me earlier?"

"Of course."

I have no problem admitting that now that he's not in front of me, staring into my soul.

"Were your panties wet from rubbing against my rock-hard cock?" he asks, his voice breathy and sexy. "Did you feel how big I was for you? How I could barely control myself? How I had to dig my fingers into your hips to stop myself from going too far?"

My breath catches with his words, like they're caressing the most intimate parts of me. Igniting something within me that I've never known was there.

"Yes."

I can hear Beau's ragged breathing on the other end of the phone and wonder briefly what he's doing upstairs. Is he stroking himself as we talk? Is he just as hard as he was less than an hour ago?

I hope so.

"I want you to listen to my words, Claire. You don't have to respond, but I want you to do what I say."

"Okay," I promise, noticing an uncomfortable ache in my breasts as the chill in the air becomes more prominent.

"Take your right hand and gently circle your right nipple. Don't stop until I tell you to. Keep going."

I've never really explored my nipples on my own. They're cold and hard from being exposed, but as I circle them with my finger, the ache between my legs gets even stronger, like I need more.

"Now I want you to tug on it. Don't squeeze lightly, I want you to really pinch."

I do what he says and let out a tiny gasp at the sensation. It hurts but also feels good at the same time. A bolt of pleasure draws a fiery line directly from my breasts to my clit.

"Keep pinching. Don't let up until I tell you to."

Something about hearing his voice talk me through this is wildly erotic. More than the books. More than any hookup I've had in the past. More than anything, really. It's like he knows what I need but is giving me the power to decide how far I take it.

"Relax," he says, giving me time to follow his instruction before adding, "Take your other hand to do the same thing to your left nipple. Fuck, I bet it's nice and hard like the other one, begging for the same touch. You like a little bit of pain with your pleasure?"

The thought of what he's doing on the other side of the phone spurs me on, and I can't help it when I let out a moan as I squeeze my other nipple harder than the first.

Beau groans. "Damn right, you do. God, your breathy little sounds are so perfect. I can't wait to hear how much louder they get when you come for me."

I let out another cry, more for myself than for him as I continue tweaking my nipples as instructed.

"Keep playing with your nipple, not so hard now," he commands, as if he can see into my room. "I want you to move your other hand very slowly down your stomach until you reach the top of your panties."

I have no idea how he knows I'm still wearing panties, but I don't say anything. I just listen to his heavy breathing and comply with his directions.

"Are you there? Are your fingers sitting right above your clit waiting for me to tell you to continue?"

I murmur a confirmation, though I'm beginning to feel so aroused that my brain feels like mush.

"You listen like such a good girl," he praises, sending a jolt of pleasure through me. "Now I want you to drag those fingers lower. Slide them through your wet cunt and don't stop until you've got one finger resting inside that tight pussy of yours."

All I can think about is how I want to follow his every command as my finger slides through my sex and slips inside. I'm soaking wet, and the little bit of friction from my palm against my sensitive bundle of nerves is surprisingly uncomfortable.

"Drag that finger through your pussy and start rubbing around your clit. But Claire?"

My name sounds like a hesitant kiss, prolonged and desperate for more.

"Yes?" I whisper.

"Don't touch your clit directly. I want you to circle it nice and slowly."

Everything feels more heightened than earlier, like all of the blood in my body has focused itself on this one spot. This one spot that has my body reaching for more.

"Nice and slow," Beau repeats, his voice low, "as I tell you what's going to happen next."

I comply, my breaths coming faster as I rub two fingers around my clit. Each stroke, each circle, only heightens my arousal, like I'm going to combust if I don't have some sort of relief.

"I bet your sweet pussy's drenched right now," he mutters as I let out a whimper of frustration. "I bet it's swollen and begging for release."

"Beau," I groan without even meaning to.

"Fuck—I'm gonna fucking spill my load just from hearing my name on your lips. Does it make you hot knowing that I'm right there with you? Gripping my cock in my hand as you bring yourself to the edge?"

"Yes." I can barely say the words because the pleasure is so intense.

"This is exactly how I was touching myself that night in the shower when you watched me. I was thinking about you then, and I sure as fuck am thinking about you now."

I pause a moment. "You were?"

Even though he's made his intentions very clear to me, his admission still comes as a surprise.

"Hell yeah I was," he confirms. "Your perfect body hasn't left my mind since the moment we met."

The way he's so confident in his feelings for me sends a beat of desire through my sex.

"You didn't stop, did you?" Beau asks, his tone dangerous.

"No." I lie, remembering that I'm supposed to be following his instructions.

"Good girl," he rasps. "Now take those fingers and rub your aching clit. Don't stop until I say so."

I finally rub over my clit, trying different patterns as I feel the tension inside start to escalate to an unbearable level. I cry out, continuing the movement just like he told me to.

"That's right. Don't stop rubbing. I want you to feel the way your body lets go, feel those fingers take you over that edge. Keep going. Keep going. Fuck yeah, keep going."

On instinct, my back arches and I feel a muscle that I didn't even know I had contract in my core. All of a sudden the tension between my legs shatters as white-hot pleasure shoots through my body. I'm not even sure I can hear Beau's voice anymore because blood is pounding in my ears, waves of relaxation pulsing through me.

My hands fall to my side as I try to catch my breath and steady my heart rate. My skin feels tight, every inch sensitive to the air above me and the sheets below me. How have I gone my whole life without experiencing this kind of release? It's so much better than I could have ever imagined.

Slowly, I roll my head to the side and face the phone, still on speaker. All I hear is Beau's heavy breathing, and I wonder if he just experienced the same ecstasy that I did. I hope so.

"You there?" I whisper, imagining him naked as he lays on his crisp bed with his dick in his hand.

"Barely." He chuckles like he's trying to catch his breath. "I think I just burst a blood vessel. That was fucking hot."

"It was?"

"Hell yeah."

I smile as I think of what to say. "Thank you. For doing that with me . . . for walking me through it."

"Don't thank me," he replies and I swear I can hear a similar smile on his face. "You're dynamite, pretty girl. I just lit the fuse."

"Goodnight, Beau," I whisper.

He pauses for a moment before answering me, as if he's holding back from saying something. "Goodnight, Claire."

CHAPTER 26

BEAU

I was up at the crack of dawn this morning despite the opportunity for a solid twelve hours of sleep. I guess my body has finally adjusted to chronic sleep deprivation, though my early wake-up call probably has less to do with the fact that I'm adjusting to residency, and more to do with the fact that I woke up with a painful boner.

On my way to the gym, I left Claire coffee and a note like I always do, though this time I pushed things a little further to see how she would react.

> *When I get back, we're going to continue what we started last night.*
>
> *P.S. I fed Frosty. Turns out that if I give him food he acts sweet. Kind of like someone else I know.*

I want her to know that whatever she says or does, it's not going to make me see her any differently so she doesn't have to hide or feel embarrassed. Last night it was like her last wall of defense began to crumble, and I love that I got to share that with her—got to help her let go of everything she was expected to be.

The breathy little sounds that she made as she touched herself were enough to immediately send me over the edge, but I fisted myself to hold off until she was right there with me, falling over the cliff of ecstasy. And I'm so proud of her for jumping with me.

By the time I finish up at the gym and grab a shower, Claire's reading on the balcony with a cup of coffee in her hand. I'm not entirely sure what she has on beneath the white comforter she's wrapped herself in, but her hair is pulled back into a low bun and I'm desperate to go out there and plant kisses along her exposed neck. I just can't get enough.

Choosing to give her some time alone and let her come to me when she's ready, I prop myself up at the kitchen counter and sip my protein shake. In the past, Claire would've avoided me completely if she was embarrassed, so the fact that she's out of her room at all is a good sign.

As I'm scrolling through my email with our December on-call schedule, my phone rings.

"Hey, Momma," I answer, putting the phone on speaker. "How's Houston treating you?"

I haven't had a chance to hear how their move from Atlanta went. The only reason I know everything went smoothly is because my brother texted pictures of my three nieces climbing all over my dad. It looks like they're in for an exhausting few months.

"Oh, it's fine," she replies, sounding disinterested. "Though I'll never understand why your brother decided to move here. It's got more concrete than New York City. And don't even get me started on the zoning laws. Why in God's name would you put a brewery next to a residential neighborhood?"

I smirk as I think about how my brother has probably heard this rant several times already. "Missing Atlanta already?"

"Oh no," she says quickly, her voice rising an octave. "It's lovely to spend time with the grandkids. Did you know that it's almost December? I'd have no idea because we're out by the pool right now in flip-flops."

I chuckle, imagining the chaos around her. "Sounds like a tough life."

"Have you ever heard of a Kolache?"

"Uhhh," I reply, trying to think about the word. It sounds Polish or something. "I don't think so. Why? Is that something I should know?"

"It's a yeast roll with egg and meat inside. They're everywhere here. Though, it's probably a good thing you don't know what they are because you'd love them too much."

I roll my eyes, waiting for her to comment on the inevitable. Surprisingly, she doesn't mention my health and the sound of a splash in the background interrupts our silence, followed by the hearty laughter of my dad's voice and screams of laughter from my nieces.

"How's Dad handling the move?"

I've been so busy lately and hearing their voices makes my heart sink. My youngest niece was born right as I started residency and I haven't had a chance to meet her yet. She's cute as fuck though, and I can't wait to teach her everything I know about being a fun uncle.

"Oh, you know your dad. He's found a golf course nearby, so he's as happy as can be."

"Tell him that I'm gonna kick his ass one day soon."

"I hope you have a cleaner mouth with your patients," Mom says, probably rolling her eyes.

"I guess it's a good thing my patients are asleep," I joke, knowing that it'll piss her off.

"Honestly, after all of our traveling, it's been nice to be in one place, especially now that the girls are growing so fast. I'm pretty sure that Ansley is going to be a prima ballerina one day. She's so graceful," she pauses, whispering something on the side. "Hang on, Beau, someone wants to speak to you."

"Uncle Beau," my oldest niece shrieks into the phone. "I miss you."

She has a slight lisp and it's so damn cute.

"I miss you too, baby girl."

There's a rustling on the line before she replies.

"Are you at work with Daddy today? He said your job is bones."

I laugh, imagining Brad explaining my job to his daughters. "My job is bones, that's right. But your daddy's job is cancer. Not bones. Only Uncle Beau gets to fix bones."

"What's cancer?" she asks and my eyes go wide as I immediately realize that I fucked up.

I hear my mom jostle the phone. "Alright, Uncle Beau has to go, tell him goodbye, Ansley."

"Bye, Uncle Beau," my niece sings, her voice trailing off into the distance.

"Good lord, Beauregard," Mom hisses into the phone. "You better hope that she forgets what you just said, or your brother is going to be livid."

"Sorry, sorry, sorry. I don't deal with a lot of kids!"

Atlanta has several pediatric-specific hospitals, so I rarely have to interact with children. It didn't even register in my brain that I should've held back that word. *Whoops*.

"You're ridiculous."

"But you love me," I reply in my sweetest tone.

"Sometimes I wish I didn't," she replies before adding. "We miss you. Do you think you'll be able to come out any time soon?"

I glance down at my email. "So, I actually just got my schedule for December. I think I can make it out there for a few days between Christmas and the New Year."

There's a noticeable shift in my mom's tone. "Really? That's wonderful."

I can't help but feel a wave of warmth at the thought of seeing my family, especially my nieces. "Yeah, I'll make it happen. It's been too long. And I might bring a friend along if that's okay."

"Oh? A friend? What kind of friend?" There's a hint of curiosity and teasing in her voice.

The thought hadn't crossed my mind until just now, but suddenly, it's the only thing I can think about. I've never introduced a woman to my family before, but something tells me that once they meet Claire, they'll be just as smitten as I am.

"She's my roommate actually," I state, trying to sound nonchalant. "Don't want her to be alone for the holidays."

If I add any more detail, my mom won't ever let me off the phone. Give her an inch and she'll take a mile.

"We'd be happy to have her," she says excitedly. "Just send me the dates and I'll make sure everything is ready for you two. Bradley's house has plenty of room. Everything really is bigger in Texas."

By the time I hang up the phone, my stomach rumbles again. I swear on my off days, my body tries its hardest to catch up with the lack of proper nutrition during my shifts. I feel like I'm constantly shoving food in my mouth to keep the hunger at bay. Seeing as I've barely been here since before Thanksgiving, there's probably nothing in the fridge, so I decide to head down to the grocery store beneath our building to grab a sandwich.

When I turn to find my keys, I notice Claire leaning against the back of the sofa, staring at me with a curious expression. "Got something you wanna ask me?"

Her lips twitch into a knowing smirk as I draw my eyes over her body. She's still wrapped in that massive comforter, her cheeks flushed from the cold air of the balcony. She looks fucking perfect.

"Come to Texas with me."

She arches an eyebrow at me. "Is that a question? Or a demand?"

"It's an offer," I state simply, though I hope like hell she'll take it.

"Hmmm," she muses, amusement in her tone. "I'll think about it."

I shift slightly, disappointed by the fact that she doesn't flat-out accept. "Well, take your time. I know you're *super* busy reading and doing whatever else you do when I'm not here."

Claire's hand dramatically flies to her heart. "You wound me," she teases, flashing me a wide grin. "What if I had dates planned with other people? I can't cancel them three weeks in advance. That would just be rude."

My lips press into a hard line as I feel my pulse start to quicken. We haven't had a conversation about us being exclusive, so she has every right to make a comment like that, but it fucking rips my heart out to think of another man taking her on a date.

"Claire," I snap, unable to help the coldness in my tone.

She flutters her long lashes, testing me. "Yes?"

"You know that if you wanted to have an adult discussion with me about whether or not we're seeing other people you could just bring it up, right? You don't have to play your little games and dance around the topic."

I know this is how she handles uncomfortable conversations, but it doesn't make me any less irritated. Why can't people just say how they feel?

You like someone. You tell them.

You love someone? You tell them.

We only have so much time and we never know when it's going to be taken away. Of all people, I would think she would understand that.

Claire's grin grows, her light blue eyes twinkling like a pool on a sunny day. "But it's so funny to watch your jaw tick."

I drop my keys on the counter as the emptiness in my stomach is replaced with a completely different form of hunger. "It's not going to be funny when I punish you for it one of these days."

At some point I crossed the room because I now find myself standing flush against her, caging her into the back of the couch with my hands. Even though I can barely see her body, the sharp inhale she takes tells me that she likes what I just said.

Interesting.

"Do you want that?" I growl, my voice lowering as my eyes drop to her heaving chest. "To be punished for playing games with me?"

Her breath catches in her throat as she tries to respond but no words come out. Maybe it's the fact that she taunted me with dating other men, or maybe it's how she gulps as I lean into her neck, but I continue.

"Fuck, I should tie you up right now," I groan, lightly dusting my lips against her ear. "Tie you up, and make you come over and over again until you never so much as think about another man."

Leaning forward, I pin her hips against the couch as one hand reaches up to stroke her flushed cheek.

"You're mine, pretty girl," I murmur into her skin as my lips caress her neck. "Only mine."

"I've been yours."

CHAPTER 27

BEAU

I left Claire in a needy state when I went to grab some lunch. But I know if I hadn't forced myself to walk away, I wouldn't have been able to stop what came next, and I'm desperately trying to exercise a semblance of restraint with her. Just because I've given in and touched her doesn't mean it's balls to the wall. I need her to trust me. And to trust herself too.

When I made it back to the condo with food, Claire was lying on her back, furry socks covering her feet as they rested in the air atop the back of the sofa. Frosty sat purring in her lap as she read her Kindle, and for some reason, I was jealous of a damn cat. Especially considering she replaced the comforter with an oversized cream sweater that hung off one shoulder and shorts that barely covered her ass.

As we ate, I tried to keep the conversation neutral, not daring to remotely enter into flirtatious territory. But everything about this damn woman is sexual. The way her dark hair cascades across her exposed collarbone. The way she sighs before she takes a bite of her food. The way her eyes widen with excitement at the littlest things I say.

I can't focus and I desperately need to be able to think to have this conversation, so I position myself as far away from her as possible. Last night was a completely uninhibited moment and I wasn't thinking clearly, driven by pure lust. Before we take things any further, I want to make sure we talk through what's happening between us.

Claire has turned on Miracle, the hockey movie, claiming that it's a Christmas movie. I've got no fucking clue what she's talking about, but if it makes her happy I'm not going to stop her. She's got Frosty in her lap again, happily stroking his back as she watches the film, and I want nothing more than to climb behind her and do the same thing.

"So," I start, picking up the remote from the coffee table and muting the movie.

She shifts her body to face mine and shoots me a death glare, unamused by my interruption. "So?"

"I know we said last night that if it got serious between us we would talk to Parker," I say, trying to choose my words carefully. "And I completely understand not wanting to have that conversation with him immediately."

She huffs dramatically. "Or ever."

I narrow my gaze on her, ignoring her comment. "But I want you to know that this thing is already serious to me. I'm not planning on seeing anyone else."

Claire rolls her eyes as she rests her head against her hand. "Is this about what I said earlier? It was just a joke, Beau."

"I know," I reply. "But I should have made my intentions clear to you last night."

"Got it. You want to be my *boyfriend*." She sings the last word like a taunt and it takes everything in me not to grin. The word sounds perfect on her lips.

"I'll be whatever you want me to be, Claire," I offer. "But I want you to know that I'm all in."

She nods, her expression thoughtful. "You know you didn't have to say this just to get me to come to Texas, right? I was going to come anyways, I just had to make you work for it a bit."

"I know," I admit. "But I needed you to hear it."

She chews on her thumbnail for a moment before responding. "It's serious to me too. But Beau?"

"Yeah?"

Her chest heaves as she inhales deeply. "Do you mind if we still keep this between us for a little while longer? I don't think I'm ready to tell him yet. Not that his opinion matters, but me and Parker are finally getting along, and I don't want to ruin that. Plus, it feels like we're in our own world here and I don't want to let anyone in yet."

I smile at her because I couldn't agree more. Crossing the room, I finally crawl onto the couch and take her into my arms, giving in to her like I always do. There's no telling what Parker will say once we explain the situation to him, but I'm going to let her take the lead on this. I may feel conflicted because of our friendship, but Claire's needs have always felt more important than mine, and I'm going to respect her wishes.

"Of course," I murmur against her hair as she settles into me. "Whenever you're ready."

We spend the rest of the afternoon watching movies as we lounge on the couch and eat popcorn. While this is probably not the best use of my time off, I can't bring myself to care. Everything feels so natural with her, like I can just let go and forget about the million things I should be doing.

As the hours pass, I find myself completely relaxed. The stress of work and the complexities of our situation fade swiftly into the background. The warmth of her body and the gentle rhythm of her breath against my chest is soothing, and I feel a sense of contentment that's hard to describe.

By the time dinner rolls around, neither one of us is hungry from snacking all day, but I make us a charcuterie board knowing that we both need something more substantial. When I bring it over, Claire complains that it's not a Lunchable and I roll my eyes. The woman would be happy with dinosaur nuggets and waffle fries for every meal if she had it her way.

Despite her complaint, she digs into the food with enthusiasm. As we eat, our conversation swerves all over the place, with her ridiculous stories driving our banter. One minute we're discussing the evolution of Hooters, and the next we're debating the best dipping sauce for chicken tenders. The way her brain works is astounding but it has me laughing more than I have in a long time.

Her childlike joy for simple pleasures is infectious, and I find myself picturing what it would be like to have her in my life forever. There would be no boring days, that's for sure.

Once we settle on a movie for the evening, Claire takes my hand in hers and squeezes it. "Thanks for today."

I lean down and kiss the top of her head. "I should be thanking you. It's the best day I've had in a while."

"Me too," she admits, her eyes fluttering closed as she nestles into my arms. "Though one thing might have made it better . . ."

"Oh? What's that?"

"Well, I got your note this morning," she says, bending her neck to look up at me. Her eyes have a glimmer of wildness in them as she blinks up at me.

"Did you now?"

I completely forgot about the plan I had for us today, though I have no regrets about the turn of events because now there's nothing left unsaid between us.

Claire nods her head, holding her tongue.

"And?" I ask, feeling my cock start to stir beneath her.

"Let's do it," she replies casually, her cheeks flushing pink.

"Do what?"

"You know," she whispers, averting her gaze. "What the note said."

"You're going to have to be a little more specific, pretty girl."

She lets out a frustrated exhale, as the blush on her face deepens. "Continue where we left off last night."

I sit up, pulling her with me so that her back is to my front. Leaning in, I whisper in her ear. "Have you been waiting for that all day? Waiting for me to show you what I had planned?"

"Maybe," she drawls, leaning her head against my collarbone.

Gently, I brush her hair aside, exposing the delicate curve of her neck. My lips hover inches from her skin, the heat of my breath teasing her.

"Maybe?" I repeat softly, my voice low. "That sounds like a yes to me."

Claire shivers, a quiet sigh escaping her lips as I trail a few short kisses along her throat. "Yes."

I pull back and whisper in her ear, "Go get your tablet."

She turns to look at me, brow furrowing with confusion. "Why? My phone is right here."

"Because I said so."

Claire stills for a beat, silently watching me like a hawk. I stare right back, narrowing my eyes on her.

Finally, she relents and gets up with a playful roll of her eyes. "Back to bossy Beau are we?" she teases, turning towards her bedroom.

I swat her bottom as she prances away, giggling as she flicks me the bird on her way out of the room.

While she's gone, I lay several blankets down on the ground before tossing the pillows from the couch on top of them. It's a cozy setup, perfect for what I'm planning.

When Claire returns, tablet in hand, her expression shifts from confusion to curiosity. "You want to make a fort or something?"

"That actually isn't a bad idea," I chuckle as I take the tablet from her, setting it up on the coffee table, "but not tonight."

I pull her down to the ground, feeling my heart soar as she nuzzles against my shoulder, like she's more comfortable touching me than being apart. Leaning in, I wrap my arm around her and ask, "Did you like what happened last night?"

We haven't spoken about the phone call, and while I thought it was hot as fuck, I want to check in with her to make sure we're still on the same page.

"Of course," she replies confidently. I stay quiet, waiting for her to add more. "It was nice having you talk me through it."

"It was," I echo, unable to hide the pride on my face. "Do you remember how I asked if you had ever watched porn?"

"Yep," she answers. As if realizing what I'm getting at, she jerks out of my arms. Her eyes widen as they ping-pong between me and the tablet. "Together?"

I smile at her reaction. "You seemed to enjoy last night better when we did it together."

She chews on her bottom lip. "Yeah, but—"

"Claire, I'm not ever going to make you do something that you don't want to do. But, I want you to be comfortable verbalizing what you like and don't like. And I figured it might be easier to talk about it while we watch other people. Though if you prefer, we can watch from separate rooms like last night."

She snuggles her body further into mine and sighs. "But I'm so cozy."

"It's up to you."

Silence settles between us as Claire considers her options.

"Alright," she concedes, pulling a furry blanket over her body. "But if you blind me with your freaky porn, I'm sending you the bill."

Chapter 28

Claire

While Beau pulls up a few videos on the tablet, I pretend to busy myself on my phone, though all I'm doing is doom-scrolling through social media. I don't know what I thought his note from this morning meant, but watching porn together wasn't anywhere on the list. It's not that I'm opposed, I just genuinely don't know what to expect.

"Is there anything you did or didn't like with your past partners?" He asks the question so matter of factly, like this is the easiest thing in the world to discuss.

"I dunno," I reply honestly, feeling my cheeks heat again. "Nothing really comes to mind."

I know he wants me to be more vocal, but I've never prioritized sex, so I'm not lying when I say that nothing comes to mind. Sex was always something I did because I wanted attention or affection from a man, not because I truly craved it.

"Sorry," I add quickly, now second-guessing myself. "I'm not trying to be difficult. I just can't really think of anything specific."

"Don't apologize. That's why we're doing this." He leans over and softly kisses my lips. Somehow his kiss feels like the most natural thing in the world, immediately dampening any hesitation I was having about this exercise.

Beau pulls away after a moment. He places the tablet on the table, queuing up a full-screen video before he returns to my side.

He lounges next to me with one leg bent, his arm casually draped across his knee, and I can't help but marvel at how handsome he is. He's been growing facial hair for the past month which has only added to the rugged look he's got going for him. Gray sweats sit low on his hips, giving a peak of his muscular stomach when his long-sleeve T-shirt rises.

It's distracting and I want nothing more than to run my fingers along those washboard abs. Hell—I wanted that long before I knew he wanted me back, I just never let myself fully admit it.

Beau catches me staring and gives me a small, knowing smirk. "Focus, Claire."

I draw my eyes back to the screen. A blonde woman wearing black, lacy lingerie is lying on her back as a ridiculously attractive man with dark skin kisses down her body. He takes his time, planting his lips in methodical caresses. Beau turned the sound off, so all I hear are his steady breaths, a stark contrast to my shallow ones.

"What are you thinking?" Beau murmurs from beside me after a few minutes.

I glance over at him but his attention is glued to the screen, somehow making this conversation easier. My eyes follow his and widen as the man has finally captured her lips with his. It's sensual and tender, like they've known each other forever. I had no idea porn could be this beautiful.

"It took him a while to finally kiss her lips," I answer without thinking. "She probably wanted it for a while before he actually did."

Out of the corner of my eye, I notice Beau's lips tug upwards, like he's proud of my observation. "How do you think she felt waiting for him?"

I bite my lip, imagining waiting for a kiss that's everywhere but the one place I want it. It's exactly how I've felt around Beau for the past month.

"Frustrated."

"I bet." He lets out a raspy laugh. "What else?"

"Desperate," I add, because I know that particular feeling all too well. I experienced it last night when Beau stopped kissing me, despite my body craving more.

"What about aroused?" he asks, his voice lowering an octave. "Do you think she was getting wet while he kissed every inch of her skin except the spot she wanted the most?"

"Definitely," I say. "Though I think right about now she wants his mouth somewhere else entirely."

The words surprise me as they come out, but instead of apologizing or getting embarrassed, I relax against Beau's shoulder.

The couple on the screen make out for what feels like forever. Their bodies rub against each other with increasing ferocity but they don't do anything else that I expect. There aren't any dicks. No juices. Nothing other than passion and the clash of tongues.

The woman's nipples are erect, pressed against the thin fabric of her lingerie as she climbs on top of the man and grinds her body against his. The man's large hands hold her face, not allowing her to stray from his lips despite her best efforts. I'm sure if we had the sound on, we would hear her moans of desire for something more than he's giving her.

"I bet she does too," Beau murmurs after a moment. "Sometimes the anticipation of what's going to come next is more important than the actual thing. He's working her up before he feasts on her pussy."

My core clenches at the thought of Beau doing that to me.

Oral sex has never been something I've wanted because the guys I've been with haven't ever spent more than a few minutes down there. I always felt like it was a chore for them, so I never got off on it and I most definitely never craved it. But now I'm curious if the man beside me could completely change my mind.

By the time the video ends and the next one begins, all I can think about is how aroused I am. I can't tell if it's because of the proximity to Beau, or the video, but my skin feels like it's tingling. I almost think I need a bucket of water thrown on me to cool off.

I close my eyes, clenching my thighs together to try to alleviate the ache growing there. When I open them, a naked woman is lying naked on her back in a darkened room. Her eyes are covered with a black blindfold and the camera pans to another naked woman climbing up her body.

Tensing my body, I whip my head to Beau. "You've got to be kidding me. I'm not a lesbian!"

He smiles, still refusing to look at me. "Just watch, Claire."

I cross my arms dramatically but listen, forcing my eyes back to the screen. It's not that I have anything against girl-on-girl action if that's what gets you going . . . but it's just not for me.

The blindfolded woman has way more curves than I could ever dream of. She looks like she's panting as the other woman kisses her collarbone, the same way the man did in the first video.

Surprisingly, my eyes linger on the woman on top rather than the one on the bottom. Her body is more similar to mine—long and lanky with not much to hold onto. But from this angle, her ass looks huge and plump, like all we needed was a change in perspective to appreciate her body.

I watch mesmerized as she takes her time with the woman beneath her, teasing her in a lazy, yet precise way that no man has done for me before. Each time she moves to a different part of her lover's body, the woman on the bottom shudders, not expecting it because of the blindfold.

"What are you thinking now?" Beau asks, slipping his hand beneath my blanket and resting it on my mid-thigh. I'm sure the simple gesture is supposed to be comforting, but it just makes me feel like my skin is on fire.

"Uh," I stammer, trying to collect my thoughts. "That it's like I'm imagining myself from both angles at once. I like it."

"And what about the blindfold?" His thumb begins rubbing my sensitive skin, clouding everything in my head. "Is that interesting to you, or not?"

Somehow a conversation that I expected to be incredibly awkward is instead incredibly arousing. For some reason with both of our eyes on the screen, I feel much more comfortable voicing what I like and don't like.

"I've never done it," I reply, forcing my focus to the screen and away from the expert fingers drawing patterns on my thigh.

The woman on top moves her mouth lower, placing deliberate kisses along the blindfolded woman's navel. My breathing seems to match hers, escalating with each southbound caress.

"I didn't ask if you've done it," Beau corrects, his voice silky, like the blindfold on the screen. "I asked if you were interested."

"Yes," I admit, shifting slightly at the thought.

Beau leans forward and pauses the video, looking at me for the first time since we started watching the porn. "Good girl. Ready for the next?"

My heart flutters at his words, like all I want is to please him even though I know we're doing all of this for me.

I smile at him. "Let's do it."

We spend what feels like the next hour watching videos, sometimes in complete silence, sometimes with Beau's questions peppered through. Who would have thought there were so many porn categories? I'm sure we didn't even get to half of them and I already feel like I've learned so much. By the time we get to rough sex, I start asking Beau questions too.

We go back and forth critiquing and commenting on the different aspects of the scenes that interest us. For example, I know without a doubt that I have no interest in impact play. The spanking scenes do nothing for me other than make me nervous. But surprisingly, I do have a serious gravitation towards sex toys. Each video we watch that uses a vibrator, plug, or clamp makes my stomach drop, and I can't look away. It's like a whole new world has opened up to me.

Beau can definitely sense that I'm incredibly turned on because I'm rubbing against him like a bitch in heat. Unfortunately for me, he's refusing to make a single move. The man has kept his hand firmly planted on my thigh, not daring to inch it even slightly higher.

When the last tab he opened finishes playing, I lean forward and scroll through the website. I don't know that I'd do this on my own, so now feels like as good a time as any to explore something I might be missing. Plus, I'm starting to feel more curious now that I've been enlightened to things that I didn't even know existed.

Clicking the categories button, a whole list of words covers the screen—some that I've heard of, some that I haven't.

"What's DP?" I ask, turning my head to Beau.

His caramel eyes flash with amusement. "Double penetration."

My lips purse as I consider what that means. "Like what we watched with the butt plug and the girl?"

"That's one form of DP, for sure," he replies, watching me intently. "But this is probably going to be two guys, one girl. Maybe three."

My eyes widen. "At the same time?"

That sounds painful.

He nods, unable to hide the smirk playing on his lips. "At the same time."

"How does that even work?" I ask, turning my focus back to the screen before adding, "Logistically speaking, I mean."

I hear him chuckle as I scroll through videos in the category. "You're welcome to watch. But that's one thing that we are absolutely not trying."

I pause, surprised by his comment. He's been so intent on me exploring, it's interesting that this would set him off.

"But what if I want to?" I ask sweetly, turning to bat my eyelashes at him.

"I don't share," he growls, the expression on his face suddenly harsh.

I don't want to share either, but all of my pent-up sexual tension is making me want to push his buttons.

"You might not," I shrug casually, trying to hide my grin. "But I'm sure there are lots of guys out there who would be interested. So sad that our relationship is over before it even really got started."

Beau's eyes flash with a predatory hunger as he reaches for me, pulling me onto his lap so that I'm straddling his crotch, just like last night. "Didn't I say earlier that you'd be punished for playing games with me, Claire?"

I grind my hips against his erection, knowing that I'm taunting him and quite frankly, not giving a damn. "Yes."

"And yet here you are, practically begging for a punishment?" He narrows his golden-brown eyes at me. "For someone who just found out that my kink involves bondage, you're feeling awfully brave."

"Bondage Beau," I muse, turning the words over in my head. "I kinda like the sound of that one."

"I still prefer big boy Beau."

"Do you?" My voice transforms into a seductive purr as I rock my hips against him. "Doesn't feel that big to me."

I'm joking, obviously. The man has a porn star dick.

And I would know—I'm officially a porn enthusiast.

"Now I know you're really playing games," he hisses, pinching my cheeks between two of his fingers. His hips grind against mine and I swear I'm getting dangerously close to orgasm from simply dry humping. "You feel how big I am now?"

I groan as the ache of arousal pulses through me with his dominant tone.

"You think these lips could take my cock?" His fingers tighten on my cheeks, pushing my lips out like a fish as he forces me to look at him. "I bet I wouldn't get halfway down your throat before you gagged."

I swallow, as I imagine taking him in my mouth.

"Trust me when I say that my cock is more than enough for you. You won't ever think about another man once you have it. My cock is going to ruin you for the rest of your life, pretty girl."

He releases his grip on my face and collides his lips against mine, kissing me with a wild hunger. Beau is normally so controlled, hyper-aware of everything I do, and intent on making sure I have what I need before he does. But this version of him is unhinged, as if my taunting has caused him to glitch. He's claiming my mouth like I'm giving him my last breath, his tongue clashing against mine in a dance that only he can lead.

I open for him, letting him explore every inch of me as my body grinds against his truly impressive erection.

He's right, I don't need anything else, nor do I want it.

CHAPTER 29

BEAU

I haven't woken up next to a woman since undergrad. We would both reek of beer and bad decisions, and I would race out of the room, not wanting to make things awkward with post-coital chatter. This morning, however, the last thing I want to do is race anywhere other than between the legs of the woman next to me.

After my little experiment last night, I had every intention of making Claire go to bed needy because of the jokes she made. Unfortunately, my bleeding heart couldn't follow through. When I pulled away from her kiss, once again stopping things between us before they went too far, she looked at me with those crystal blue eyes, and all I could think was how I needed more.

So I carried her up to my loft and did what any reasonable man with a smoking hot woman in their bed for the first time would do—wrapped my arms around her and went to sleep.

Was it painful? My blue balls were painful.

Was it the right thing to do? Regrettably.

I'm being overly cautious not to push things too far or too fast with her, which is ridiculous considering I was crowned the king of one-night stands in college. But with Claire, I want her to know that my first priority is her—her pleasure and her progress. And last night I was so keyed up from thinking about her with another man that I wouldn't have prioritized either one of those things.

Our exercise was a major turning point in terms of her ability to verbalize what she's interested in sexually. The videos allowed us to casually talk through what she might like, plus it gave me the chance to watch how she reacted to each scenario. The way her body language shifted during certain scenes was fascinating, especially considering she'd never watched porn before.

But that's the thing about Claire—she's the most naturally curious person I've ever met. Once you introduce her to something, she wants to know every little detail. I love that she's finally letting down that barrier of who she thinks she should be and embracing who she is at her core—a wild, vivacious woman with a joy for life.

When I slipped out of bed this morning, I left a soft kiss on her forehead before getting dressed for work. I'm on call for the next day and a half, but that doesn't mean I don't plan to toy with her—literally.

On my way out the door, I wrote her a note next to a "Busy watching reality TV" mug that said:

You'll be busy doing something else once you open the package being delivered today.

I just wish that I could be there to witness her expression when she opens the box. She voiced last night that she was interested in toys, so I figured that a vibrator was a great place to start, especially since this one had free same-day delivery.

By the time I have a chance to sit down and pull out my phone, it's practically eight in the evening. On days like this, when my mind is elsewhere, my workload always ends up being the busiest.

All I've been able to think about today has been Claire, but the cases just keep rolling in, pulling my attention away from the only thing I want to fantasize about—her.

I can't help the ridiculous grin that washes over my face when I open the messages she sent me. The first one is a picture of Frosty curled up inside my tennis shoe by the front door. He's got his chin resting on the back and looks incredibly serene even though I know they smell like rotted flesh.

The next text came a few hours later. It's a picture of an opened box on the kitchen counter.

Nothing could keep me from the *Vanderpump Rules* reunion tonight, but I admire your effort.

I quickly type a response.

Nothing? Not even a bribe?

She replies immediately and for some reason that makes my grin grow even bigger.

What kind of bribe are we talking about here?

Hmmm . . . I have to think for a second about how to respond. I want something that'll incentivize her to use the vibrator, but I don't want to take things too far.

If you use your new toy tonight to make yourself come, I'll show you how much better it feels to come on my face.

Three little dots appear immediately, then disappear without a response. Like she isn't exactly sure what to say.

Surprisingly, a second later a text bounces back.

How do you know you'll be better? That thing is powerful.

She's such a tease and she doesn't even know it.

Because, unlike that vibrator, I'm going to lick you, suck you, and fuck you with my tongue until you're begging for release. When I finally get a taste of your perfect pussy, I plan on taking my sweet time.

This time she responds instantly.

That's an awful lot of confidence for someone who has barely touched me since we moved in together.

I know she's desperate for more, and truthfully so am I. My resolve to go slow is cracking at the seams, but I don't want her to know that.

> You know what they say—competence breeds confidence.

She responds with an eye roll emoji and I can just picture her face right now—flustered from our texts, but interested in more. Which is why I can't help myself.

> Send me a picture.

My phone pings.

> Of what?

Just as I'm typing my response, my pager goes off and informs me that I have a consult in the ER. I'm the only ortho intern on call tonight, so the chances that I get more than an hour or two of sleep are slim. All I want is something to take the edge off. Something to get me through this day from hell. Plus, I'm curious how flustered she really is and how far she'll go.

> Anything. I need to see my girl.

I don't expect an immediate response so I call the ER to let them know that I'm coming. As I'm about to head out of the door, my phone pings with a picture from Claire. Her pink lips are wrapped around the vibrator's head with the caption:

Fuck me.

I'm going to be late for that consult.

CHAPTER 30

CLAIRE

For the past week, Beau has refused to do anything other than kiss me. Maybe an ass grab here and there, but nothing remotely like he promised in his texts, which is disappointing because I actually listened to him and used the vibrator. I'm trying not to get too irritated, though, because he's been so busy with work and I know he can barely think straight. Last night he came home from the hospital and practically collapsed into a deep sleep, not even making it up to his loft.

I feel guilty for even being disappointed, but god, am I frustrated. All I can think about is getting my hands on him again, which is a completely foreign feeling to me. It's like I never got to experience the sex-crazed teenager phase, and now it's hit me with full force, even though we haven't had sex yet.

The vibrator that he got me can only do so much, though I now understand why people love them. I want to scream the miracles of the Magic Wand to anyone who will listen. It may be the miniature version, but that thing is powerful and way more efficient than my fingers. It makes me wonder why women don't get each other vibrators as gifts. We could all benefit from that kind of generosity in our lives.

While we might not be fucking, Beau and I have been sleeping in the same bed every night. On the nights that he's not here,

I find myself grabbing his pillow from upstairs to snuggle with it. Somehow over several months, he's become one of my best friends. Beau's someone who I feel completely at home with, which is surprising because sometimes I don't even feel that way with my own family.

Fortunately, I've had my nursing school application to keep me busy while he's gone. If my parents taught me anything, it's that networking can get you pretty far in life. Since Thanksgiving, I've spent hours on the phone with the admissions counselor at Elmridge trying to work out how I can start in the spring. Apparently, since I took a bunch of the prerequisites in undergrad, I'm only one credit short of the admissions requirements. She told me that if I could finish the self-paced microbiology class online before the start of the semester in January, they would likely have no problem admitting me.

But that doesn't mean I haven't been anxiously awaiting the email. This is the only nursing school I applied to, and the admissions decisions are due back next week so I've been on pins and needles. The only person I've told is Cassidy because I didn't want to jinx anything if I didn't get in. I've always been a *put all your eggs in one basket* type of person, so if this doesn't work out, I'm not entirely sure what I'm going to do.

As I'm working on the lab portion of my class, my phone rings, and my brother's baby picture pops onto the screen. He hates that I have it as his contact photo, which only makes me love it more.

"Hello, dearest brother. Long time no talk."

I know Parker has been busy with work and the new house, but I miss him. I thought living in the same city would mean getting to see each other more, but he's barely been around. I've actually spent more time with Cassidy recently than with my brother.

While that's not something I'm complaining about because I love Cass, I just feel a little disappointed.

"Yeah, sorry about that," Parker says, voice slightly muffled. It sounds like he's in the car because the audio isn't great and there's feedback on the line.

"I can barely hear you, just FYI."

"Piece of shit," he grumbles, taking a moment before he adds, "Okay is that better?"

"Much." I smile at his irritation. My brother might be many things, but jolly certainly isn't one of them.

"Had to put the phone on speaker. You made me pay a hundred grand for this car and it has the worst audio."

"You know you love it," I tease, completely immune to his grumpy act. "Did you just call me to complain?"

"No, sorry," he sighs into the speaker. "I heard about your nursing school thing by the way."

Of course he did. I should have known that Cass would spill the beans. Ever since the incident with Mom's diagnosis, she's been hyper-aware of keeping secrets from my brother. Which is why it's strange that she hasn't told him about Weston . . . I need to remember to ask her about that.

Before I can respond, Parker adds, "I think it's great, Claire. Mom would be really proud of you."

My heart sinks with his words. This is the first time we've talked about her since the funeral and in true Winters family fashion, we're discussing emotions over the phone rather than in person. It's more comfortable that way, I guess, and avoiding our feelings runs in our blood.

"I hope so," I confess, closing my eyes to picture her face. It's only been three months but the image I have of her in my mind is already fading.

"I know so," he confirms, pausing before adding, "I'm proud of you, too."

I blink in astonishment, struggling to find the right words. Parker has never said he was proud of anyone, let alone his annoying little sister.

"Did your robot brain melt and turn human?" I ask, trying to add levity to our conversation. "Pretty sure that's the nicest thing you've ever said to me."

Parker's laughter rings through the phone. "I guess my fiancée has finally warmed my cold heart. Speaking of Cass, she's actually why I called you."

"Oh?"

My curiosity piques, though I'm hopeful that I'm not going to be put in the middle of their issues again. Actually, I take that back. I love drama and I'm more than happy to play therapist. As long as it's not a sex therapist because . . . ew.

"I want to do something nice for her and was thinking about having an engagement party at the condo. We would do it here, but the furniture situation is still a nightmare. I've been eating on the couch for months while we wait for the dining table to come in."

"How savage of you," I say, picturing my brother's distaste. He's absurd.

Parker ignores my comment. "Could you maybe help with the planning? Caroline is off school for a week between semesters, so I figured that New Year's Eve would be the best time."

Unable to help myself, I squeal into the phone. "Oh my gosh, stop. A New Year's party is so romantic. It's going to be perfect and yes, I'll do everything. Just make sure that the two of you are there and dressed for the occasion. Oh, and let's make it a surprise. How do you feel about sequins? Black tie? Every man looks good in a tux and I feel like we have to have sparkles on New Year's."

My mind immediately pictures Beau in a tux.

Yes, please.

There's a pause on the other end of the phone and I can practically see Parker's mind spinning as he tries to keep up with my rambling. "I'm fine with anything. But do you think Cass would like it? She's not exactly the sparkle and sequin type."

"Trust me, I know," I huff, rolling my eyes. "When Mom and I went wedding dress shopping with her, I tried so hard to get her to buy something fun, but she wouldn't budge."

The memory washes over me, bringing a smile to my face. It was such a great day until it wasn't. But over time, I've chosen to focus on the happy moments rather than the dark ones.

"Cass will be fine," I add quickly to alleviate his concern. "She might act like she hates dressing up but I know for a fact that she's a big fat liar."

"Whatever you say," Parker grunts. "Do you want to ask Beau about the party? Or should I? Not sure how close the two of you are. I'm sure you hardly even see him."

My brother's mention of Beau sends a ripple of nervousness through me. There's no way he knows what's going on between us, but that doesn't make it any less comfortable. Parker isn't exactly the best at handling things outside of his control . . . but maybe if I plant the seed that Beau and I are friends, it'll make things less explosive when my brother eventually does find out.

"I'll ask him," I reply, trying to sound casual. "We've gotten to know each other pretty well, you know, when he's not at the hospital or sleeping."

Surprisingly, Parker chuckles. "Sounds like the life of a surgical intern. He briefly mentioned that he got you a foster kitten, so I figured you couldn't hate him that much."

Quite the opposite actually—I think I like him too much.

Chapter 31

Beau

Whenever I return to the condo from the hospital, the first thing I do is rinse my body off in an ice-cold shower. It's a way to reset myself both physically and mentally after whatever the day brings.

Being a physician, especially one at the bottom of the totem pole, is overwhelming. You never feel like you can leave work at work. There's always this incessant push for more—more patients, more knowledge, more growth—until you truly are as close to robotic as possible.

I've always felt like my strength as a doctor would lie in the fact that I'm not a robot. I prided myself in the fact that I enjoyed taking the time to get to know my patients and colleagues. It was what made me different, I told myself. It's why I would be a great surgeon one day.

The problem is, in real life, that's just not possible. Because in real life being a surgical intern feels like you're sinking in quicksand, despite doing everything to maintain your footing. There's no time to think clearly, let alone hold meaningful conversations with patients or coworkers. I'm constantly pulled in opposing directions while still being expected to perform perfectly in every situation. But perfect performance requires a level of disassociation from myself that is, quite honestly, exhausting.

Surgery used to provide a thrill that nothing else in the world could. But now, it's become a grueling endurance race that I'm forced to run just so that I can get back to the one place where I truly feel like myself—with Claire.

Claire reorients me to who I am. She has an infectious interest in people, the way that I once did. She takes the time to get to know everyone she meets . . . has taken the time to get to know me. That's what probably drew me to her in the beginning—the way she reminded me what it was like to be human, to be curious about people.

So, every time I return home and step into the shower, it's like I'm cleansing myself of the expectations and pressures of the healthcare system. Even with the constant exhaustion and lack of sleep, this ritual leaves me feeling refreshed and renewed. It lets me reset so that I can be the best version of myself for her.

But tonight, as I step out of the shower, terror replaces that sense of renewal. A blood-curdling scream erupts from the kitchen, sending my pulse through the roof.

I quickly wrap a towel around my waist, taking the stairs two at a time and almost tripping over my own feet on the way down. Everything from an intruder to an injury crosses my mind as I sprint to the kitchen. I have no idea what I'm going to do if someone actually broke into the condo, though. Swing my dick at them?

"What happened?" I demand as I reach the island, trying to catch my breath as my eyes fall on Claire. She looks completely composed, wearing black leggings and a gray quarter-zip sweatshirt like she just came from a casual walk outside, not a traumatic event that warranted a shriek. Her blue eyes cut to my body from the laptop screen in front of her as they assess my soaking wet, half-naked state.

"Oh my god, Beau, I'm so sorry," she responds, trying to stifle her grin. "I didn't mean to scare you. I just got an email and couldn't believe it."

Relief washes over me, though it's quickly replaced by mild annoyance. "You screamed like that over an email? You're fucking kidding me right?" I say, my adrenaline slowly subsiding. "I thought you were in trouble!"

"Nope, not kidding," she squeals, her eyes twinkling with excitement. "Come look."

As I approach the other side of the island, Claire eagerly turns her laptop towards me. On the screen, there's an email with bold letters that immediately catch my attention. It's an acceptance letter to the nursing school at Elmridge University, which just so happens to be the best in the southeast.

"I genuinely can't believe it," Claire whispers, her voice trembling slightly as she re-reads the email with me. "I wasn't supposed to find out until next week."

After a moment, she looks up from the computer, her eyes widening slightly. "Oh god, I'm so sorry I didn't tell you! I just didn't even know for sure if I would get in and I only decided that I was going to apply over Thanksgiving . . ."

Instead of letting Claire continue the ridiculous apology, I pull her into a hug and squeeze her body close to mine. "Don't be sorry, pretty girl," I murmur against the top of her head. "That's the best news I've heard all day."

I don't know why I didn't think of this sooner. Claire Winters was made to be a nurse. Not only is she passionate and outgoing, but she's stubborn as hell and knows exactly how to stand up to know-it-all doctors like me.

Claire's body relaxes in my arms. "I did it for her," she sniffles, her voice muffled against my chest.

Wrapping my arms around her more tightly, I let her feel whatever she's feeling. I don't have to ask to know that she's thinking about her mom. Claire is one of the most resilient people I've ever met, and the fact that she's been able to move forward from the most traumatic event of her life and shape it into something meaningful is beautiful. She's beautiful.

"I think you did it for you too," I reply, placing my chin on top of her dark curls.

We stand like that for several minutes before she pulls away, wiping her damp eyes with her hands. I've never seen her look so vulnerable, not even when she was speaking at her own mother's funeral.

I love that she finally let me in and allowed me to see this side of her. I want her to know that anytime she needs to let go, I'll be there. She has me.

"Thanks," Claire swallows, peering up at me through wet lashes.

I smile, feeling a surge of emotion run through me that I'm not entirely sure how to place. "Give me a second to change and dry off. I'm taking you out to celebrate."

CHAPTER 32

CLAIRE

After my mom died, I felt completely lost. I used to go to her for every important decision I made in life, not because I didn't trust myself, but because I simply trusted her more. She was my best friend. When she wasn't there anymore, I felt like I was in a state of limbo, incapable of making a choice without her.

I sat around the condo for weeks, paralyzed with indecision as I considered how I wanted to spend the rest of my life. Should I go back to Virginia? Should I return to advertising? Or should I take a chance and change everything? How could I decide without her there to guide me?

But as time has gone on, I've realized that my mom never once told me what to do. She listened to my opinions and encouraged me along the way, but every decision I made was inherently my own. Even when she probably should have guided me in one direction, she never did. She let me make mistakes and come to my own conclusions, never once forcing me to take a path that wasn't my own.

I didn't appreciate it until this moment, because I know that I was meant to be a nurse, just like her.

And the reason I know that, without a doubt, is because of the conviction in my decision-making that she silently instilled in me over the years.

To celebrate my acceptance, Beau took me to his favorite diner in Buckhead for dinner, a little place by the highway that I'm sure I've driven past lots of times but never noticed. I ordered us milkshakes and the most unhealthy meal imaginable, which I loved and I'm sure he hated. Even though he told me that I was going to send him into a diabetic coma, he sat beside me and happily chowed down on the best country-fried steak I've ever had.

All I want to do when we make it home from dinner is curl up in his arms and go to sleep, but Beau said he has a surprise for me once I feed the cat. Eager to see what he's got planned, I quickly get Frosty sorted with kibble and fresh water before returning to the kitchen.

"Okay, Frosty's all set," I say as I hop onto the bar stool. "What's this surprise you have for me, big boy?"

His brown eyes flick up from his phone screen, sparkling as they meet mine. "Just give me a sec to set it up," he grins before quickly jogging up the stairs to his loft.

"Why didn't you grab it while I was feeding the cat?" I call after him.

Beau's loft is open to the condo below so I hear him yell down, "Nobody ever said I was Brainy Beau."

A few minutes later he returns with a brown canvas bag, instructing me to cover my eyes. I'm a horrible cheater when it comes to peeking, so he forces me to also face the opposite direction as I hear something that sounds like glass hit the counter.

"Alright, turn around."

I open my eyes to find Beau perched on top of the kitchen island. Though his dark jeans and boots are still on, his broad chest is now completely bare, covered only slightly by his crossed arms.

"Dinner and a show?" I joke, taking a few steps toward him.

He laughs and shakes his head. "Damn, I should have thought of that. No, I just figured that since I desperately need insulin after that meal, I would teach you how to give it. What better time to start learning how to be a nurse than right now?"

Where in the world did this man come from? His thoughtfulness is one of the things I adore most about him.

Well, that, and his banging body.

"Okay, but do I get a show after?" I tease, placing my hands on his muscular thighs. "You know, assuming my first patient makes it?"

Beau rolls his eyes, though he's unable to hide the grin on his face. "You can have whatever you want, pretty girl."

I push myself up on tiptoes and kiss him before pulling back to see what was in the bag. On the counter next to him there's a vial of clear liquid, a capped needle, and an alcohol swab.

"What's the three hundred and eighty for?" I ask, frowning at his phone screen which displays the number and a red arrow.

"It's my blood sugar," he explains, opening the app to show me the graph of his readings. "Even with everything we just ate, the number should be under two hundred. You can see how it's still trending upwards. Not good."

I look down at the graph which shows a steady blood sugar all day, the only exception being our dinner time. "You just have to be a high achiever."

"Always," he replies, grinning at me. "Though not too high, because if I'm over 600 I would need to go to the hospital."

My eyes snap to his with alarm. "Has that ever happened?"

Beau is so invincible to me, so self-assured and confident. I can't imagine anything being able to hurt him. Sometimes I forget that he has an autoimmune disease that forces him to modify his life every single day. Yet, he doesn't let diabetes control his life. He views it as part of his routine rather than a burden.

It's the same with his career as a surgical intern. I know he's exhausted and probably wants nothing more than to sleep when he's away from the hospital. Instead, he uses the time we have together so intentionally that I'm not bothered by the fact that we have less of it than the average couple.

"It's cute how you're worried about me," Beau says with a cheeky wink. "But no. I'm always careful not to let it get too high."

"What about too low?"

"That's definitely scarier," he admits. "But I manage the best I can. You get used to it after almost twenty years."

Beau grabs the needle in his hands and places it between us so that I can see the lines on the thin syringe. "Alright, so insulin needles are marked based on units and not ounces. With everything else, you'll use ounces, also known as CCs, but with insulin, you dose based on units. Does that make sense?"

"A unit does not equal a CC," I repeat. "Got it."

"That's my girl," he says, handing me the syringe as he picks up the vial and an alcohol swab.

My core clenches involuntarily at his words. Damn him and his praise. Now is not the time to feel all hot and bothered.

"So you're going to clean the top of the vial with a swab. Then you'll stick the needle in the part you just cleaned, turn it upside down, and pull back the number of units that I need."

He demonstrates the technique and I watch him intently. His explanation is so thorough and easy to follow that it makes me wonder why he's a surgeon and not a bedside doctor. Surely he would do better with patients who are awake instead of asleep.

"You do all this at the hospital?" I ask, watching him curiously. "It seems like a lot of work, given how busy you are."

"Nope. I use something called an insulin pen at the hospital. Don't have to keep it refrigerated and can store it in my locker or my pocket. Remind me to bring one home so you can see how it works."

I fight a smile at his use of the word home and return my focus to the syringe in front of me.

"Got it. So how do I know how many units to put in here?" It looks like this thing can hold a total of a hundred, which seems like a lot.

"Great question," he says, placing the vial and swab back on the counter before reaching for his phone. "I have a chart that tells me exactly how many units I need to take based on my blood sugar."

He hands me the phone and asks, "How much insulin would you give me?"

"Ummm," I bite my lip, feeling slightly put on the spot. But as I glance at the chart I realize there aren't any calculations required. It simply provides a range of blood sugar readings with corresponding unit values.

"Looks like if you're between three hundred and fifty and four hundred, you'll get twelve units."

I look up at him, and he's beaming with pride like I cured diabetes rather than grasped a simple nursing practice. "Draw it up."

Beau observes me closely, but he doesn't intervene or suggest any changes as I follow his instructions. My hand trembles slightly as I hold the insulin-filled needle.

"Now what?" I ask, my voice steady despite my nerves.

He grabs the remaining alcohol swab from the counter and swipes it over his low belly for a few seconds before meeting my gaze. "Now you give me the insulin."

My eyes go wide. "I just shove it in? No lube?"

"No lube." He confirms, chuckling to himself. "You'll go perpendicular to my skin at a ninety-degree angle. Once the needle is in, you'll use your thumb to push the insulin into the tissue."

He seems to pick up on my thoughts because he quickly adds, "You won't hurt me, I promise. It's a tiny prick, and I'm going to pinch the skin that I just cleaned so the needle only touches fat."

I can't help my snort. "Like you have any fat on your body."

Beau looks like a character straight out of a superhero movie, with his sculpted torso and chiseled muscles. Finding a spot with enough fat to cushion the needle's sting seems like a stretch.

"You'd be surprised."

I take a deep breath, working to steady my hand. Beau's trust in me is both comforting and slightly nerve-wracking, but his confidence boosts my own enough to force me to continue.

As Beau pinches the skin on his belly, I carefully position the needle above the blob of fat. "Okay, here goes," I say, putting on a brave face.

Gently, I push the needle into his skin just like he taught me. To my surprise, he doesn't even flinch. He just watches me with an encouraging smile as I press the plunger, slowly administering the insulin.

"There." I finish and carefully pull the needle out. "Did I do it right?"

"Perfect," Beau assures me, his smile widening. "You're a natural. See? Nothing to it."

"Thanks," I reply, unable to hide my blush as I hand him back the syringe. "So surgery next? Can't be that hard if I have the right teacher."

He shakes his head in resignation. "Oh god, I've created a monster."

CHAPTER 33

BEAU

I hop down from the kitchen counter and start to clean up my medical supplies. The insulin needs to be refrigerated, so I trod past Claire and return it to its proper place. The chill from the fridge reminds me that I'm still shirtless, and I close the door with a shudder.

"Cold?" she asks, watching me intently from across the kitchen.

A loose, white v-neck sweater hangs over leggings that look like black leather. She insisted that we dress up for dinner even though we were just going to a casual diner. I haven't been able to keep my eyes off her all night, and it makes me want to dress her up more often even though we have nowhere to go since we're still keeping our relationship a secret.

"Kind of," I admit, searching for my shirt. I swear I tossed it on the counter before our little lesson.

"Looking for something?" Claire asks, a wicked glimmer in her eyes.

I turn to her, noticing that she's holding my red flannel shirt in her hand, a playful smile dancing on her lush lips.

"That would be mine," I remark, walking in her direction.

She dangles the shirt just out of my reach, her smile widening. "I hardly think it's necessary."

I step forward to close the gap between us. "Why's that?"

She gives a nonchalant shrug, her sweater slipping down her shoulder to reveal more of her neckline. "I like you better without it."

"You've seen me shirtless plenty of times in the past few weeks. Are you turning into a greedy girl?"

We've barely been around each other recently because of my schedule, and I know she's been desperate for more from me. It probably doesn't help that I can't stop myself from relentlessly flirting with her. I am a man, after all.

Claire huffs a laugh. "I'm turning into a *desperate* girl."

I continue crowding forward, forcing her to retreat until her back hits the edge of the countertop. Her breath catches as my arms lock on either side of her body, caging her in like a trapped animal.

The sound of her rasped breathing makes my cock come to life with anticipation.

But I won't continue until I hear her say it.

I need her to verbalize what she wants.

"Desperate, huh?" I whisper, my voice gruff. The air between us is charged, every breath and movement amplified. "And what *exactly* are you desperate for?"

"You," she confesses, her eyes glued to my bare chest instead of my face. I flex my pecs in response.

"You've got me right here," I offer, reaching down and cupping her chin between my fingers. "Is there something else you're *desperate* for?"

Her tongue runs over her bottom lip as her eyes meet mine. "Yes."

"And what might that be?"

She swallows hard, her expression flickering between nervousness and boldness. "You know what I want, Beau."

"Do I?"

Her eyes roll and I can't stop my grip on her chin from tightening. She can be such a brat sometimes, and it's hot as fuck.

I lean in close, my lips just inches from hers. "Tell me what you're desperate for. I won't ask again."

The air seems to crackle between us as Claire takes a deep breath. "Everything. I want everything with you, Beau."

"Everything, huh?" I tease, sliding the hair off the nape of her neck. "Not sure you can handle everything yet, pretty girl."

Her eyes flutter closed in frustration as I place my lips on the thin skin along her shoulder. "At least give me *something*" she pleads, drawing out the last word as my kisses turn to bites.

I chuckle against her, dropping my hand from her chin to the area I just nipped. Brushing my fingers across the reddened skin, I consider how the rest of her body would change color beneath my lips.

"How about I give you what you need, and then we can talk about everything."

She responds by leaning into me as I trail deliberate kisses along her collarbone, slowly inching myself closer to her mouth. I have no doubt that she can handle whatever I throw at her, but being able to handle something and enjoying it are two different things. And you can bet your ass that I'm going to make sure she enjoys this.

By the time my lips find hers, my cock is straining painfully against my jeans. I try to ignore it, instead focusing on how soft her mouth feels as it presses against me. Claire practically purrs when I kiss her, my tongue digging into her mouth and drawing out a sound of pure longing. I could kiss her for hours if it meant hearing that beautiful song of desperation the entire time.

Her hands run down my chest, tentatively tracing my muscles like she wants to etch every detail into her memory. Just the sensation of her skin against mine drives me wild, and I can't resist any longer. My hands find her hips, and I hoist her up in one fluid motion, setting her gently on the counter before us. If she'd made it any lower and started unbuckling my belt, there would be no going back. I would have lost complete control.

"What's wrong?" she asks, blinking at me with confusion as she tries to catch her breath.

Even though we're at eye level, it still feels like she's got the upper hand. It's fitting—she always has the upper hand when it comes to me.

"Nothing," I reply softly as I run my hands along her thighs. "Just checking in before—"

She interrupts me. "Before what?"

"Before we go any further."

I've never been this hesitant with a woman. Normally I'm dominant as hell in bed, controlling everything from the pace of penetration to the number of orgasms my partner has. But I don't want to fuck things up with Claire, and I'm terrified that if I let loose completely, she won't like it. Or that she'll like it too much. Or that the second I'm inside her, I'm not ever going to want to be anywhere else.

Her bony hands land on top of mine, instantly calming my concern. "You want me to be more vocal with my feelings?"

"Of course," I reply, not sure where she's going with that question.

"Well then I give you full consent to do whatever you want to my body. If I want you to stop, I promise I'll tell you. I belong to you, Beau, and that means that I fully trust you to give me what I need. And right now, you're not doing that. So snap out of it."

Holy fuck that was hot.

I lean in, tugging her hips to the edge of the counter. "And what *exactly* do you need?"

"I need you to show me why you're better than that vibrator you bought me . . . unless that was all talk," she smirks, knowing she's poking the bear.

My cock pulses at her taunt, desperate to prove her wrong.

"Lean back." My voice drops to a sultry whisper as I tap the metal beneath her.

Claire complies, lowering herself to the counter as I hook my fingers into the waistband of her leggings and yank them down in one swift motion. Tossing the fabric on the floor at my feet, I wrap my arms around the small of her back and return her to a sitting position.

"You forgot something," she comments, fighting a grin as she looks down at the black lace panties still on her body. I've been wondering for months if her lacy bra had a companion, and now that I know the truth, I don't think I'll ever be able to focus again.

I watch my fingers trace along the smooth inner skin of her thigh, admiring how goosebumps follow in their wake. She's just as affected by my touch as I had hoped.

Desperate for more, my hands quickly drift to the bottom of her sweater, tugging it over her head so she's sitting in front of me in just her bra and panties.

"So damn perfect," I murmur, drawing my eyes over her exposed body and committing it to memory. "Everything about you is so damn perfect."

Her perky tits rise and fall as she works to steady her breathing. I can tell she's getting impatient and that just makes me want to draw this out even longer.

Leaning in so that our chests touch, I reach around and unhook her bra, pulling the delicate lingerie down her arms before I let it fall to the floor with the rest of her clothes. Her nipples form stiff peaks, pointing straight at me like they're pleading for me to show them some attention.

My tongue darts out over my bottom lip, desperate for a taste.

"Let's see how wet we can get you before I mop you up with my tongue."

Slowly, my hands trail up her sides and stop at her breasts, giving each bud a tight pinch.

She lets out a moan, tipping her chin up as her head falls back.

I bend down, capturing her right nipple in my mouth as I continue to knead the other between my fingers. My tongue circles her stiff peak over and over, alternating between flicking and sucking.

If she thinks the pace is torturous, I'm right there with her—my dick is so hard it's painful. But the pain only spurs me on, knowing my teasing will be worth it once I finally get inside her.

My teeth rim her stiff nipple, simultaneously biting down as my fingers expertly pinch the other bud.

She cries out, screaming something unintelligible as her grip tightens on the edge of the countertop.

All I can think about is how I want more from her. How I want it to be my name on her lips the next time she makes a noise like that.

Her hips arch against me, seeking more friction as I continue to play with her tits. Gradually, my free hand drifts to her panty line, tugging the seam upwards through her pussy. The lace stimulates her clit, providing just enough sensation to keep her teetering towards the edge while offering slight relief from the mounting tension within her.

My lips find hers and instead of slow, steady kisses, I finally allow myself to take what I need. My tongue darts inside her mouth, exploring her taste like a starving man stranded on a desert island.

She meets my pace, running her hands through my hair and tugging slightly as if to say that she needs more too.

Taking her lead, my hand slowly drifts beneath the lace of her panties to her warm heat.

Claire gasps into my mouth, sending a thrum of desire through me as I slide two fingers through her pussy. She's soaked, and my cock aches with the thought of how good it will feel to finally slip inside of her.

"Fuck, have you been this wet all night?" I ask, slowly pumping my fingers into her.

She lets out a hum of confirmation as her walls grip me like a vice.

"Oh fuck," I groan against her lips. "My cock is gonna destroy this tight pussy, pretty girl. You want that? To be ruined by me?"

Claire's forehead drops to mine, panting slow shallow breaths as I tease her. "Oh god, please," she begs, hands moving toward my erection.

I stop them before they reach my belt. "Not yet. Lay back again for me."

Claire studies me for a moment before lowering herself down to the counter. Propping herself up on her elbows, she watches me with hooded eyes.

Pulling my fingers out of her, I pop them into my mouth and lick them clean of her arousal, keeping my gaze locked on her.

"So fucking sweet. You taste like everything I've ever wanted."

Claire's eyes go wide, as if she can't imagine a man savoring her taste. Good thing she's about to learn that the only man worth having is one that would prefer to drown in pussy rather than come up for air.

I slide her panties down her long legs and discretely tuck them into my pocket for safekeeping. Planting a kiss on the instep of both of her feet, I place her heels on the edge of the counter.

"Don't move these," I murmur, tapping her feet as I step between her thighs.

"Or what?" Her dilated eyes narrow on mine in a challenge.

This woman kills me. Even in a situation where I'm in control, she doesn't let up.

"We'll go again."

Claire bites her bottom lip and nods as I begin to trail kisses along her legs.

My hands roam higher, gently kneading her tits as I tease the sensitive skin of her inner thigh. I alternate between sucking and biting as I move closer to her glistening pussy. Her pale skin is flushed, like all of the blood in her body is pooling at the surface beneath my lips. With each nibble, she gasps and tenses like she's in pain, but she doesn't ask me to stop. Instead, her body arches further into my mouth and desperately begs for more.

By the time my lips reach her bare sex, I'm practically drooling. Her arousal drips from her clit to her ass, teasing me as it glistens around the tight hole.

Flicking my eyes up to hers, I hold her gaze as my tongue finds her entrance. I briefly slip inside her before I lick the full length of her pussy.

Her icy blue eyes have turned almost gray, her pupils blown wide with arousal. I've never had a girl watch me as I go down on them and it's fucking hot. Plus, her confidence in this situation is turning me on even more. I don't know what I expected, but it wasn't this.

Repeating the movement, I begin to leisurely lick from her entrance to her clit, keeping my tongue flat as I savor the taste of her. This won't be enough to get her off, but we're just beginning. We've got all night ahead of us. Plenty of time to keep her teetering on the edge of pleasure.

My fingers continue to tease her nipples as my mouth circles her tiny bundle of nerves. I suck hard before I return to the long strokes of my tongue.

Her thighs begin to quiver after several repetitions of this, and I can tell she's struggling to keep them open. Her feet remain rooted where I left them though, because my girl is nothing if not stubborn.

Sliding my hands down her side, I grip her legs to hold her steady against my mouth. She lets out a breathy gasp as I focus my attention on her clit, alternating between sucking and flicking my tongue over the swollen bud.

Her back arches, thrusting her chest through the air as her fingers wander to her breasts and tease her nipples with a much firmer touch than I expected.

I love that she's exploring her body and becoming confident in what she likes. I need to remember to explore nipple play later on since she clearly likes having them stimulated.

"Ahhh, right there," she pants, legs shaking against my hands as I bring her to the brink.

Adjusting myself for a better angle, I continue to tease her clit with my tongue. Gradually, I return two fingers to her entrance, tracing the rim before thrusting them completely inside. Her pussy flutters around me, giving me a delicious preview of how velvety and tight she'll feel wrapped around my cock.

Claire lets out a soft hum of approval as I massage her inner walls with my fingers. I adjust my pace, slowing down when I sense she's getting close to the edge and speeding up when she's more at ease.

"More," she whines when I reduce my speed once again. "Please, Beau, please I'm so close. I need to come."

I can't help the grin that forms on my lips as I reply, "Yes ma'am."

My mouth starts working overtime, sucking and teasing her clit in the best way I know how. I close my eyes, losing myself in her pleasure as her fingers land in my hair.

Tugging hard, she pulls me against her pussy and starts grinding against my face. Her thighs clamp down around my head, blocking out all sound as she takes what she needs from me.

I don't complain—hearing isn't necessary when I'm buried in the sweetest cunt imaginable.

Her pussy tightens around my fingers, like she's right on the brink of coming undone, so I curl the two digits upwards, massaging the top of her entrance while my teeth graze her clit. She explodes into pleasure, squeezing her thighs against my head as her first orgasm crashes through her.

I maintain my steady rhythm, softly sucking and nibbling her swollen clit, prolonging her orgasm for as long as possible. Her legs fall from the counter inadvertently, unable to maintain their previous tension as she rides out her pleasure.

"What did I say would happen if you moved those feet?" I chuckle softly against her pussy as I begin to pepper kisses along her thigh.

Claire throws her arm over her eyes and whines. "I can't, Beau. It's too much."

I'm sure she's hypersensitive right now, but hey, rules are rules.

"Regretting having me go head to head with a sex toy?" I tease, tossing her legs over my shoulders for round two. "I did warn you."

A small grin forms on her lips. "You did."

"And?"

I can't see her eyes, but I'm sure they roll as she mutters, "You were right."

CHAPTER 34

CLAIRE

I don't like to admit when I'm wrong, but I will confess this to anyone who asks—Beau Buffington is better than a vibrator.

Seriously. The man is the pie-eating champion of the south.

The way he slowly built me up, teasing my body and stroking the fires of anticipation, was unlike anything I'd ever experienced before. By the time he got to the good stuff, I was on the verge of shattering into a million pieces. We might have to sanitize the kitchen after tonight, but it was one thousand percent worth it to experience him like that.

And the second orgasm?

Better than the first.

By a mile.

I can barely feel my body as Beau scoops me into his arms and carries me across the kitchen, heading toward the stairs of his loft.

"Finally gonna make good on your promise?" I ask, nuzzling into his bare chest. It should feel weird that I'm completely naked in his arms, but it's surprisingly natural. His warm body cradles me as he takes the stairs two at a time, as if he's in a hurry for some reason.

"What's that?"

I can't help the blush that forms on my cheeks as I recount his promise. "Of feeling you every time that I walk."

He shakes his head as we reach the top of the stairs. "Do you remember every word I say?"

"Pretty much," I admit, grinning up at him. "We didn't have to go up here, you know. I would have been happy if you had graced me with your girth on the kitchen floor."

He laughs and tosses me on the edge of the bed. "Rain check on that one."

What is it with this man and tossing me around?

And why is it so hot?

I scoot toward the center of the mattress, getting comfortable as I watch him begin to undress. "You really are such a brute, you know."

Beau's eyes narrow on mine, but he doesn't say anything. He reaches down to remove his belt, the muscles in his arms flexing like they're showing off for a party of one. All I can say is, thank god I've got a front-row seat.

"What?" I ask, starting to feel a little less confident as silence settles between us.

His belt cracks through the air as he pulls it loose with one hand and lets it drop to the floor. "You sure you want to say that to the man about to be inside you?"

"Brutish Beau." I tease, watching his fingers begin to work his pants off. "That one might be my best yet."

Beau ignores my comment and bends down. He steps out of the jeans to reveal black boxer briefs that cling to his thick, muscular thighs—thighs that look like they could quite literally break me in half.

"Here's how this is gonna go, pretty girl," he drawls, moving toward the bed with a lustful hunger in his eyes. "You're going to come one more time on my fingers. Then, I'm going to make good on my promise. Once I'm inside you, I'm not holding back, so I'm trusting you to tell me if I need to stop."

"Got it," I swallow, my core clenching at his tone. It's so at odds with how he speaks to me normally, and I love it. "But you won't need to stop. You're not *that* big."

His jaw clenches as he crawls on top of me and whispers, "Famous last words."

Before I can respond, he's capturing my mouth in his and forcing his tongue down my throat. He tastes different than normal, kind of sweet but a little tangy. Suddenly, I realize that it's because he was buried between my legs for the past half-hour, and I'm the one on his lips. Surprisingly, that turns me on even more.

I moan into his throat, letting him in further as I run my fingers through his hair and arch my hips. I'm desperate to feel him. To give him the same pleasure that he's already given me.

"Cut it out," he groans against my lips.

I don't listen, choosing to rub myself against his hard cock so he can feel my arousal. "Cut what out?"

Beau abruptly pulls back, seizing my wrists and pinning them above my head while his legs secure mine.

I attempt to squirm free, but he's significantly larger and stronger. He easily restrains me with just one of his hands.

"I'm trying my fucking hardest to do this the right way with you," he says, voice dangerous. "But if you don't hold still and let me give you another orgasm, I swear to God I'll tie you up and force you to come."

The idea of being entirely under his control, immobile and helpless, sends a shiver of anticipation through me. I know that's one of his kinks from the porn we watched together, but experiencing it firsthand is way more arousing than I had imagined.

Beau never struck me as the controlling type. He's typically so easygoing and fun to be around. But this side of him, this dirty-talking, dominant man, feels like an unleashed alter ego.

And now all I want is to experience Bondage Beau.

"So do it," I taunt, my eyes locking onto his in a challenge. "Or are you all talk?"

He sucks in a forced breath, like he's trying to decide if he's going to take the bait or not. The energy between us grows palpable as I hold his gaze, not intending to back down. He's mine, and that means embracing all of him—his desires, cravings, and fantasies. They're all mine now too.

After a moment, he releases my arms and sits back on his heels, peering down at me with irritation in his eyes. "You just love to poke the bear, don't you?"

I bite my bottom lip to stifle a grin. "You're so easy to rile up."

His jaw ticks as he sucks in a labored breath, climbing off the bed and freeing my legs from his weight.

I move to my side so that I can watch him, but he flashes me a stern glare that makes my stomach flip. "When I turn back around I better see you on your back with your hands above your head. You want to be tied up? You're about to get your wish."

Heat pools between my thighs as quickly I follow his instructions. I've learned when to push him and when not to, and something tells me that I've gone as far as I can with him this evening.

A moment later, I feel the bed dip above me, and something soft wraps around both of my wrists. Whatever it is, it binds them together, positioning my hands on top of each other. I try to tilt my chin to get a glimpse of what he used, but my arms are stretched so tautly above my head that I can't see anything beyond the concrete ceiling of the loft.

Beau steps off the bed, and I hear the sound of his nightstand opening and closing before he appears beside me again. My skin prickles with anticipation as he leisurely draws his eyes over my body, like he doesn't know where to start.

His tongue clicks as the bed dips, and he straddles me at my hips. "I was going to have you come on my fingers, but since you decided to push me, you'll come on my cock."

My eyes widen as they drop lower. He removed his boxer briefs and is slowly stroking himself with one hand from base to tip. A bead of precum glistens on the head and my tongue runs over my bottom lip, suddenly overcome with the desire to taste him.

Beau notices and smirks. "I guess the question now is . . . should I fuck your face or pussy?"

"Both," I whimper, beginning to grow needy.

His pupils blow wide, clearly not expecting my answer. "Open those pretty lips. I'll start there."

Crawling up my body, he positions himself above my face. His cock hangs heavily between his legs, the tip resting on my bottom lip as he peers down at me with fire in his eyes.

My tongue flicks out, swirling over his massive dick as I get the first taste of his arousal. It's salty and warm, but not overwhelming like I was expecting—I like it.

I breathe through my nose like I learned from the videos, and lift my head to take more of him into my mouth. My lips curl around his cock, barely able to take his girth despite my mouth being fully open.

"Oh fuck," he rasps breathily as I slide more of him down my throat, desperately trying not to gag. "That's it. You're doing so well, Claire. I wish you could see how gorgeous you look taking my cock."

My core clenches at his praise and I feel a slick arousal between my thighs. I've never been turned on by giving a blow job before, but holy shit this is hot.

I flatten my tongue, opening my throat as I guide him deeper into my mouth. Beau's large hands thread through my hair as I arch my neck further, taking him as far as the angle will allow before I suck hard on his length.

He's barely halfway inside and I swear his massive cock just tickled the back of my throat. His size is overwhelming and I close my eyes, focusing on his taste to distract me from my imminent gag reflex.

"Claire." My name escapes his lips in a whisper as his hips inch forward. "I knew you could do it. Such a good girl."

My eyes fly open, wanting to experience his expression more than I want to avoid choking. Beau's light brown waves dust over his forehead, his wide jaw clenched tight as our eyes meet. His brow furrows like he's in pain, and his chest heaves with every pass of my tongue along his length.

He groans, leaning back to pull completely out of my mouth. His hand flies to his cock, clenching it with almost white knuckles.

I catch my breath as he fists himself, working to steady his breathing.

"Was it not good?" I ask quietly, suddenly feeling self-conscious. He seemed like he was enjoying himself, but maybe I accidentally bit him. My mouth was literally open as wide as it could go just to get him fully inside, so I wouldn't be surprised . . .

Beau's eyes find mine and soften. "Best head of my life."

I bite the side of my cheek, not understanding. "So then why—"

He interrupts me with a chuckle. "Because I was about to blow my load down your damn throat. I made you a promise, and I intend to keep it."

My lips tilt upwards as I bat my eyelashes at him. "What promise was that?"

"That I'm going to bury myself so deep in that tight pussy that you'll need fucking surgery to ever walk normally again."

Heat blooms through me, not doubting his promise for one second.

"Good thing I know someone." I wink at him playfully.

"Damn straight you do." Beau grins, leaning over to grab something off the bed next to him. "I'll break your body and then put it back together."

My eyes fall to the foil packet in his hand and for some reason, my heart sinks.

I shouldn't care that he wants to use protection. That's the responsible thing to do. It's just that something about a condom feels so sterile, like you're not really feeling the other person. It's a barrier in all senses of the word, and Beau has knocked down every single one of mine that it feels wrong to have something between us. I want to feel all of him, raw and wholly, even if I'll regret it in the morning.

"I'm on birth control, just so you know," I mutter, hoping that he'll take the hint.

He pauses with the foil and angles his head slightly.

"Oh, good," he replies quietly as he drops the partially opened packet on the bed next to him. "And just because I can tell where your mind's going, I haven't touched anyone since we hooked up months ago. My last test was clear, and I've never not used a condom."

I look over at the discarded rubber and then back at Beau. "You don't want to now?"

He shakes his head, reaching down to brush a stray hair off my lip. "I remember everything you say too. And you told me that you belong to me, which means I'm going bare in this pussy. That okay?"

I nod, unable to stop a smile from forming on my lips. His hands caress the side of my face. It's intimate and so at odds with the filthy words that came out of his mouth just moments ago.

The air changes, a noticeable tension rippling between us. He's looking at me like he wants to say something more, but nothing comes. Instead, he leans in and softly kisses me, gripping my head between his hands as his lips caress mine with a tenderness that tells me we're not about to fuck, we're about to make love.

His tongue pushes into me and slowly tangles with mine as his hands run from my face to my breasts, setting my skin ablaze all over again.

All I want is to reach up and touch him in the same tender way that he's touching me, but whatever he has around my wrists isn't budging.

A quiet gasp escapes my lips as he squeezes my nipples between his thumbs and forefingers, a familiar tightness creeping throughout my body.

He continues to kiss me, playing with my aching breasts as I writhe beneath him. His hips pin mine in place, and I'm completely at his mercy. All I can do is moan into his mouth as each expert touch brings me closer to my breaking point.

Planting a tender kiss on my forehead, Beau sits back on his heels and meets my gaze with soft eyes. "You ready?"

"I've been ready, big boy," I practically pant as my eyes drop down his sculpted chest, fixated on the V between his thighs that points to his hard cock.

His hand grips his shaft as he adjusts himself between my thighs. I try my hardest not to think about how he's going to fit, instead focusing on the carnal need to have him inside me.

Slowly rubbing his hard length against my center, Beau lets me feel him as he drags his cock through my wetness. His biceps flex with each stroke and he pivots his hips slightly to tease me, not fully allowing himself to push inside. His jaw hangs slack as he watches the torture, chest heaving as he repeats the movement over and over again.

I can feel my arousal heighten, centered right on the spot where his cock finally lines up at my entrance.

His warm brown eyes find mine once more as he leans down, propping himself above me with one arm, his chest only inches from mine. Shifting his weight, he slowly feeds the head of his penis inside me, a soft groan coming from his lips at the initial push.

Just the tip alone is enough to make me screw up my face. I don't want to, but I can't help it because the searing sting of his cock inside me is unexpected. I'm more aroused than ever, but the way he's stretching me definitely makes me rethink taunting him about his size.

His cock isn't big—it's a behemoth.

Sensing my trepidation, Beau pauses, allowing me to acclimate to his size as the tip rests inside me.

"Need me to stop?" he asks, concern knitted on his brow.

"You're really big," I whimper, closing my eyes as I feel a tear fall from my cheek. I'm not sad, just overstimulated and terrified that I won't be able to keep going.

He strokes my face, wiping away the wetness with a gentleness that makes me actually want to cry. "We'll make it fit. You were made to take my cock, pretty girl."

I lean into his touch, opening my eyes. "Just go slow."

He kisses my lips, momentarily distracting me from the slight pump of his hips.

I groan, trying to focus on my pleasure. The initial sting has already subsided, and I can feel myself fluttering around him.

"Open up for me," he whispers against my lips as he stills inside me for a beat. "Come on, Claire, open up for me."

I attempt to relax my body and give in to him. All of my nerve endings are screaming for more, desperate for their own release despite the initial pain of his intrusion.

"That's my girl," he praises, pushing forward once more. "Let me in."

I moan, already feeling so full and overstimulated that I'm not sure how much more I can take. There's absolutely no doubt in my mind that Beau is going to get his wish and have me come on his cock. I feel like I'm already so close that even the slightest sensation might tip me over the edge.

Beau kisses my jaw as he gently pumps forward again. "Halfway there," he murmurs against my pounding pulse. "You're taking me so well."

My eyes fly open. "Halfway? Are you sure?"

There's no fucking way the man has anywhere to go. I'm pretty sure I already felt him tickle my tonsils.

With a sly grin, Beau lifts one of my legs over his shoulder and shifts his body weight to his elbow, lowering himself onto the bed beside me. His arm snakes beneath my back, giving his hand room to tug on my nipple.

He hasn't moved any further inside me, but he already feels deeper in this position. Reaching around my leg, his fingers dust down my inner thigh before they fall on my clit. I try to wiggle, knowing exactly where he's heading but not entirely sure I'm ready for it. Everything down there is still so sensitive.

His mouth nips my earlobe right as his fingers smack my pussy. "Don't make me tie your legs down too."

My body stills as a small whimper escapes my lips. I attempt to focus on anything other than the way his fingers begin to lightly dance around my clit. I think about the way his facial hair grazes my skin as he's peppering kisses on my neck. The way he always smells fresh, like the ocean's breeze, despite the sweat beginning to bead on his brow. The way he's gentle with me, despite the fact that I know he needs more.

I bite my lip to keep from crying out again as his expert fingers begin to increase their speed. My body feels so tightly strung it's almost painful, yet I need more too. I need to feel him fully inside of me, not just halfway.

"Give me everything," I say, turning my head to face him. "I need all of you, Beau."

"You want all of me?" His eyes heat as my words break some invisible barrier of control within him.

"Yes, yes, yes," I scream right as his hips finally pivot forward, seating his cock deep inside me.

Unable to stop it, a wave of pleasure crashes through my body, shooting ripples of warmth to every part of my being. A dull roaring fills my ears as I feel myself spasm around him while his fingers continue to rub me through my orgasm.

"You already had all of me, Claire," he whispers, placing a soft kiss on my lips as he begins moving inside me again to find his own release.

CHAPTER 35

BEAU

"**W**hat am I even looking at here?" Walker's voice interrupts my thoughts, snapping my attention back to the case in front of us. It's only our third of the day, and based on how things are going, I won't be getting any sleep tonight.

"Looks like that's the talus," I state.

His question was likely not aimed at me, but he's been one moody son of a bitch lately so I don't chance it.

Blazing green eyes snap up to mine. "No shit, Buffington."

I glance at the scrub tech, who just shrugs his shoulders.

Walker continues, his tone harsh, "Why does it look like there's a second fracture on the tibia? Someone pull up the imaging."

The OR nurse's eyes widen as she pulls the blanket off her lap, quickly rolling the computer over to us. I can't see shit from my vantage point, and I'm busy holding a retractor so I'll just have to take Walker's word for whatever he sees on the scan.

If it really is a missed fracture, we're going to be here even longer and I'm already starting to feel a little shaky. In my unwillingness to leave the condo this morning, I didn't grab anything to eat and have been surviving on only a protein shake and gum.

For the past two weeks, every night I haven't had to spend at the hospital has been spent inside Claire. I can't get enough of her and it's been fucking miserable to pull myself away from her in the mornings to come to this hell hole.

I've been trying to look on the bright side—at least I get to spend the day with Walker. He may be a grumpy son of a bitch, especially lately, but we balance each other out well. Plus, I learn a ton from him and have started to genuinely enjoy his company.

Walker steps back from the table, holding his hands up to remain sterile as he pivots to look at the computer.

"Zoom in there," he tells the nurse as he lets out a dramatic scoff. "This image is shit. ER should've done a CT."

While that's probably true, we also should have checked before we started the case. This patient was handed over to us by the resident on call overnight but that doesn't mean we aren't also at fault here. Medicine is just a constant game of checking and rechecking until you have enough information to move forward.

The thing that people fail to understand about surgery is that no decision is ever perfect or without risk. There might be a perfectly healthy person who goes down for a routine procedure and doesn't wake up. But there also might be someone with every comorbidity out there who does great.

We can predict and counsel, but the truth is—we have no fucking clue what's going to happen with each case.

I like to equate it to driving a car down the road—you could get in an accident on a drive you take every single day, or you could arrive at your destination safely on the most dangerous road possible. All you can do is react and rely on your instincts to get you there because things happen in real life that are nobody's fault other than fate.

Unfortunately, in medicine, someone is always at fault for an outcome, whether it's expected or unexpected. And doctors love to blame other doctors, especially when it's a different special-ty. Which is exactly why Walker has been on the phone for the past minute cursing out the ER resident.

While he may be the most serious guy I know, Walker is also a strong leader. He's always going to protect his own, regardless of if we're in the wrong. He treats us like a team, and while he'll berate us for the losses in private, he's also going to make damn sure those losses never go on our record.

"Sorry." I peer over the blue drape at the head of the pa-tient. "Looks like the case is gonna last at least another hour longer than we thought."

The anesthesiology resident looks up from her phone. She can't be much older than me and looks bored as hell.

"No worries," she says, removing the blankets she's hidden be-neath to stand from her chair and stretch. "The next case was with Dr. Baker and I'm not exactly rushing over there. Plus I'm off for Christmas after today. Four whole days of bliss."

I peer down at the crossword game on her phone. "I don't know, you already look pretty damn blissful over there playing Wordle."

We don't know each other, so I try to crinkle my eyes to let her know that I'm smiling behind my mask and not being a complete asshole. If anything, I'm jealous. Everyone knows anesthesia has the cushiest job in the hospital.

"Hard to appreciate my bliss when I'm bound to you jerk-offs for hours on end," she retorts, winking at me.

"Hey now," I reply, shaking my head. "I'm bound to them too."

"Pure incompetence," Walker mutters, stepping back to the table. "Get the X-ray up. We'll reshoot."

Each OR has a machine attached to the wall for instances like this where we need to get additional scans during surgery. Time is precious, so it keeps things flowing rather than having to wait for the portable machines.

"Uh," the OR nurse stutters from the corner of the room.

"What?" Walker snaps, his head swiveling like a possessed demon to face her.

The nurse looks terrified to continue, as if she knows what she's going to say will only make the situation worse. "The, uh, C-arm is broken in this room. We can't rescan."

"You've got to be fucking kidding me."

Walker isn't mad at her, he's mad at the situation. While it's unfortunate that we have to wait, I can't help but see the silver lining in the delay. The extra time will give me the opportunity to break scrub and grab some sugar. My hands are on the verge of trembling, and I'm beginning to feel a touch lightheaded.

"I'll call for the portable team STAT," she offers, fumbling at the desk for the phone.

A few moments later, she hangs up and I ask, "How long did they say it would be?"

"They'll be here soon."

"Sure they will," Walker scoffs dramatically. "They love to take their sweet-ass time."

The anesthesiologist looks uncomfortable, like she's going to get yelled at for this change. I think Walker realizes and says, "Get Dr. Baker on the phone. I'll explain to him why his precious case is being pushed."

"You sure you don't just want to close up and go back in another day?" I offer.

"Fuck no," he replies, looking at me like I have two heads. "You do realize this shit costs money, don't you? Even if we fixed the first fracture, they would need another surgery."

That's another thing I appreciate about Walker—his perspective. Most surgeons would say fuck it, resolve the original issue, and then go back in another day. But Walker understands that each time a patient goes under, there's a ridiculous number of medical bills that will follow, so he does his best to finish each job efficiently and effectively. He doesn't come from money, and though he never really shares about his childhood, I suspect his worldviews have a lot to do with what he experienced growing up.

"Got it," I state, handing the retractor to the tech beside me. "Mind if I break scrub for a few while we wait for the scan?"

"Fuck yeah, I mind. Get over here and look at this original image with me. I want you to tell me what you would do if there's a tibial fracture, too. CT won't take long."

I sigh, trying to clear the brain fog that's creeping in. Handing the retractor to the surgical tech, I step away from the sterile field and take Walker through my plan.

By the time the radiology team comes through and finishes the imaging, it feels like it's been ages, and I'm doing my best to hold my shit together. Based on the results of the scan, we've got at least a solid hour of work before we're done. Walker likes to have his residents do his dirty work and close. Normally that would be appreciated but I need to get the fuck out of here.

"You okay, Buffington?" Walker asks a while later, looking up as he hands the drill to the scrub tech. We just finished plating the tibia, and I'm praying my body holds out just a little longer because we've still got to close. "You're looking a little pale."

Before I can reply, my vision blurs. Walker fades out of view completely and I feel my body falling forward.

Fuck diabetes.

CHAPTER 36

CLAIRE

Ever since I was young, Christmas has always been my favorite day of the year. Not only because of the presents, which I will wholeheartedly admit that I love, but because of the traditions that my dad started for us before he passed away. Traditions like building snowmen, making eggnog, and going to the afternoon showing of a movie in the theater. Some of my very best memories with my family fall on the twenty-fifth day of December.

But this year, I can't even get out of bed.

Grief is a tricky thing because it sneaks up on you. One day you're decorating a Christmas tree, not the least bit sad, and the next day you're practically catatonic. There's no way to anticipate what will trigger you, and there's no way to stop that trigger from snowballing into a complete day ruiner.

Beau and Parker are working today so I was supposed to go over to my brother's house this morning to open stockings with Caroline and Cassidy. Instead, I woke up at six in the morning, texted them that I wasn't feeling well, and went back to sleep. The last thing I want to do is stifle their joy with my misery.

I like to think that I've handled my mom's death well. I went through the stages of grief like a normal person. I was mad. I was desperate. And I was depressed. But truthfully, for the past few months, I haven't felt any of those things because all I've felt is happy. I hate to admit it, but all of the books and videos were right—my life has moved on. And I genuinely haven't felt guilty about my progress until today. Because why should I be happy when my mom isn't here to experience that happiness with me?

As the third episode of *Great British Bake Off Holiday Special* comes on, Frosty stirs in my arms and arches his back. He's gotten huge and it's been nice to have him as a companion while I work through this online class for nursing school. I know Beau initially brought the kitten home as a temporary bridge between us, but now I can't imagine my life without the big furball.

Frosty jumps down from the bed and paws at the closed door. With a groan, I slide out of my blanket enclosure to pad across the floor and let him out of my room. My eyes catch on my reflection in the glass window, making me cringe. The bags under my eyes are trench-like, and my hair resembles a rat's nest on top of my head.

I sigh, reminding myself that it doesn't matter because I'm just going back to bed.

"Merry Christmas!" a voice immediately calls as my door opens. "Sorry if we woke you. We really tried to be quiet."

My eyes land on Caroline and Cassidy in the kitchen, flour coating their guilty faces. Red Santa hats are propped on their heads and they've got matching red flannel pajamas on.

"Didn't I tell you guys I was sick?" I fake a cough to corroborate my story as I lean against my door frame.

Caroline's deep blue eyes narrow on mine. "Those are *not* the pajamas I wear when I'm sick."

I blush, remembering what I've got on. The silky red pajamas were an early Christmas gift from Beau, and I tried them on last night before he left for the hospital. He's on-call until tomorrow morning and wearing them makes me feel like he's here with me. They're more revealing than my usual sets, with my ass hanging out of the bottom, hence the curious look from my sister.

"Look good, feel good," I shrug, a sly smirk forming on my face as I walk toward the kitchen. The smell of cinnamon and oats fills my nostrils and my stomach growls inadvertently. "But seriously, what are you guys doing? It smells delicious."

Caroline wipes her brow with her elbow. "We're making mom's cookies."

Cassidy drops something on the ground and yells an obscenity, causing my sister to roll her eyes and add, "Well, *I'm* making Mom's cookies. Cass keeps messing up the melted butter. It's really not that hard."

"I have no idea why Parker calls you his angel sister," Cassidy glowers, picking up whatever she dropped and tossing it in the trash can. "All you've done this morning is boss me around."

Leaning across the counter, I swipe my finger through the mixing bowl. "It's because they're the same person, Cass. And all demons think they're actually angels."

Caroline shoots me a cranky glare as I pop a glob of cookie dough in my mouth. "Sorry this demon is just trying to make Christmas nice for everyone!"

I can't help the grin that forms on my face. I love that they're spending time together, especially since none of us have seen my sister since the funeral. She's been ridiculously busy with medical school, and she handles grief and emotions much like the rest of my family—by avoiding it.

The problem is, when you avoid emotions for long enough, they decide to come to visit on your favorite day of the year.

Rude.

"Cass, do you not want to spend the day with your parents?" I ask, seating myself on a stool as I watch them work.

"No, they went on a cruise," she replies casually. "Something about their new traditions being spent in the Caribbean."

"Oh my god," Caroline squeals as she runs out of the kitchen. "Who is this?"

She pulls Frosty into her arms, squeezing him tight as she spins around in circles. I've never seen her this excited about anything, and honestly, I'm not sure how to respond.

"Uh," I pause, flipping my head upside down to tame my wild hair into a bun. "My roommate got him for me as a foster but that plan failed, so we kept him."

She takes his paw in her hand and waves it. "I'm Auntie Carol. You're a precious angel baby, aren't you?"

Cass and I both give each other perplexed looks as my sister proceeds with baby-talking to my cat for the next minute. I guess I know what to get her next Christmas . . .

"So how's everything going with Beau?" Cass asks casually as she sips from her coffee mug. "Parker told me y'all are going to Houston in a few days, and we're both kind of pissed we didn't get an invite."

My cheeks heat at the mention of Beau.

I casually mentioned the trip to my brother last week after we had gone over the plans for his engagement party. Each time we talk I try to drop hints about my relationship with Beau, attempting to test the waters before actually having the conversation. Parker didn't really say much at the time, but I also think he was distracted because he had just pulled up to the hospital. If he's telling Cass, though, he clearly can't be that upset.

"You're both working, moron," I reply with all the love in the world.

"Why didn't I get an invite?" Caroline chimes in from the floor. She's got the laser pointer out now and is making Frosty chase the tiny red dot in circles around her.

I sigh, crossing my arms over my chest. "Because *you* don't even know him."

"I met him once! But he was so attractive I could barely look him in the eyes."

Oh god, just what Beau needs—another Winters sibling obsessed with him.

"He's not that hot," I say flippantly, hoping she'll change the subject.

Caroline stands, crossing the room to pull a Diet Coke from the fridge. "Ugh," she whines, the can cracking open with a slow hiss. "Why are there no good-looking guys at my school?"

"Because you go to the best medical school in the southeast, my dear sister," I state, planting a kiss on the side of her head. "Looks aren't an admission requirement, except where you're concerned."

"Parker went to the best medical school in the country and he's attractive," Cassidy points out with a glow of amusement in her hazel eyes.

I fake a gag as I snatch her coffee from her hand and sniff.

"What're you doing?" she asks, looking at me like I'm insane.

"Just checking for drugs," I state, handing her back the mug. "Because there's no way any person in their right mind would say that."

Cass grabs the Santa hat off her head and tosses it at me. "You should be happy I'm in love with your brother."

"Oh trust me, I am," I reply, easily dodging the flying object. "I just don't want to hear how *much* you love him, or what *exactly* that love entails." I shudder dramatically to get my point across as a timer on the oven dings.

Cassidy turns to take the cookies out and nearly trips face-first into the oven, sending me into a fit of giggles. I'm glad she's an ER nurse—with her lack of coordination, she probably gets paid in free visits rather than real money.

"So what's the game plan for these bad boys?" I ask, eyeing the warm tray in her hands. Suddenly, my stomach feels like a bottomless pit that could easily devour the whole batch.

"That's the reason we came over," Cass explains, placing the cookies on the counter. "We're gonna take them to the hospital."

"And here I was thinking you visited to make sure I didn't spend Christmas alone," I say, pretending to be hurt. "Turns out, you just needed my oven."

Cassidy's eyes widen, clearly feeling guilty.

"Oh no, Claire, that's not it at all," she rushes to clarify, her voice laced with genuine concern. "We were going to force you to hang out regardless. The working oven is just an added bonus."

I give her a playful wink to show I'm only teasing, and she releases a relieved sigh.

I love the two of them with my whole heart; their unexpected arrival and kitchen takeover this morning was the best kind of surprise, pulling me out of my head when I needed it the most.

As I reach for a cookie, Caroline springs up from the floor and swats my hand away with ninja-like reflexes.

My bottom lip pushes forward, giving her my best pout. "No cookies for me?"

"Not if you keep eating the dough before we can bake them."

I turn to Cass, lowering my voice conspiratorially. "See? Demon."

She stifles a grin and then adds, "I'm just looking forward to seeing Morgan and the boys. Nothing says Merry Christmas quite like cookies."

"You do realize Parker doesn't eat stuff like this, right?" I ask, raising an eyebrow. "He's a robot when it comes to food."

"Pretty sure mom's cookies are the only sweet treat Parker eats," Caroline counters, bumping her hip against mine playfully. "And this is the perfect chance for you to reintroduce me to *Beau*."

I blink, trying to figure out what happened to my sweet, baby sister. Is her coffee also drugged?

"Absolutely not," I snap, feeling my pulse begin to race. "One, he's too old for you. And two, he's *mi*—" The words almost tumble out before I can stop them, and I feel my eyes widen as I stammer. "My, I mean, my . . . he's my roommate."

The room falls into a brief, awkward silence as my sister and Cassidy exchange knowing looks.

"So because he's your roommate, I can't date him?" Caroline's smirk transforms into a devious grin.

My sister, though often seeming innocent and poised, knows exactly how to stir the pot—something she definitely learned from me. Unfortunately, now she's using my best moves against me.

"No, you can't date him because he's our brother's best friend!"

Oof—really put my foot in my mouth there.

Caroline merely shakes her head, her straight shoulder-length brown hair swishing back and forth with the motion. "I doubt Parker would mind," she counters casually.

Cassidy gives me a look that silently conveys the opposite—he absolutely would mind, which only reinforces my decision to keep things with Beau under wraps for now. After all, if my brother's own fiancée can keep secrets from him, I see no reason why I can't do the same.

CHAPTER 37

CLAIRE

As I shift the car into park, my sister wraps up her lengthy monologue about how she never wants to see another cadaver again, and I make a pointed effort to bite my tongue. She chose the wrong career path if she's already feeling that way one semester into med school, though I have no doubt that she'll make a great physician—her brilliance is matched only by her empathy.

Shooting off a quick text to Beau, I hop out of the car.

> About to pull up to the hospital with the gang. We come bearing cookies and joy.

Beau immediately responds, and this time I really am biting my tongue, though for a completely different reason.

> It would bring me great joy to eat your cookie.

The pure confidence of this man is truly astounding.

> What does that even mean...sicko

As we walk up to the staff entrance, my phone buzzes.

It's provocative—gets the people going.

Suppressing a grin at his reference to *Blades of Glory*, one of my personal favorites, I keep the door open for my sister and Cassidy. They're doing the heavy lifting, carrying the twelve dozen cookies we spent the morning baking.

The only thing you're provoking is my gag reflex.

Merry Christmas, ballsy Beau.

I tuck my phone away and trail behind them, navigating the maze-like hallways deep within the hospital. Compared to the pristine corridors that are patient-facing, this area looks like it's seen better days. Beige walls, marked and scuffed, line our path as we make our way deeper into the hospital.

As we round a corner, my phone pings again. I pause for a moment, a hint of a smile tugging at my lips in anticipation of his next witty text.

My cock is about to provoke your gag reflex.

(Merry Christmas to me)

My stomach drops and I look up to make sure that Cass and Caroline aren't able to see my screen. He's insane if he thinks I'm going to be able to sneak away for a quickie with the two of them practically babysitting me . . . but it sure will be fun watching him try.

I quickly scan for the closest marked door, shooting our location to Beau just as Morgan appears, bounding energetically around the corner.

"Oh shit, I almost didn't recognize you," the petite brunette exclaims, pulling me into her tiny arms and squeezing tight. "Merry Christmas to my future little nurse!" she sings out, drawing out the last words as she steps back. Morgan clasps my hands in hers and makes me hop up and down.

Her outfit is a mixture of professional and festive—light blue scrub bottoms paired with a white sweatshirt that says "gRiNch", highlighting her nursing role. Reindeer antlers, blinking excessively with colored lights, bob on top of her head, smacking against me as we jump.

"Doesn't she look good in scrubs?" Cass chimes in, beaming at me.

"Hell yes, she does," Morgan agrees, releasing my hands to pry open a container of cookies Cass is holding.

"I had to look the part," I explain, popping my hip and striking an impromptu pose.

To avoid any issues, Cassidy had me change into something inconspicuous—her spare scrubs. The only problem is, my sister-in-law is a solid four inches shorter than me, making the top fit fine but the bottoms a tad snug. I can practically feel them riding up my ass, and while they're definitely not what I would wear normally, now that I know I'm seeing Beau, I'm not complaining.

"Seen Parker anywhere?" Cassidy asks Morgan.

"Nope," she replies with a mumble as she swallows a cookie. "And as much as I love you two together, there are some days I want to avoid that fucker."

"Tell me about it," I chime in, giving her a conspiratorial wink.

Cass chews on her bottom lip, torn between staying to chat and leaving us to search for my brother.

"Go on," I urge her, waving my hand in the direction of the hallway. "Take Carol and find brother dearest. Morg and I will handle the cookie distribution."

Obviously, I have an alternative reason to stay, but I'm not telling them that.

Left with the majority of the cookie containers, Morgan and I make our way to the ER break room, handing out the pre-packaged sweets and making conversation along our way. Somehow Morgan convinces her charge nurse to consider me for an externship in their department, which basically is like an internship for nurses. I didn't even know that was a possibility, but the idea of getting more experience while I'm in school sounds incredible.

As I offer a cookie to a handsome police officer at the coffee machine, he squints at Morgan. "Why is it that you never seem to be working?"

"Work smarter, not harder," she quips, abruptly grabbing my hand to whisk me away. "First rule of being a nurse: Never, ever, date anyone whose job title starts with the letter 'P'."

I wrack my brain for other professions that fall under that rule and come up short. "And who else does that include?"

"Policemen, for one," she answers with a dramatic shudder. "They might be charming and kinky in bed, but then you discover that they're secretly married with kids. Pass."

I give a forced smile, acutely aware of the second policeman by the door who seems to have caught every word of Morgan's candid summary.

"Then you have the Paramedics," she continues, handing a cookie to one with a sly smile. His eyes linger on her tiny body as we walk away, practically salivating over the self-assured nurse. "Sure, they can place a damn good IV, but that's pretty much where their expertise ends. Otherwise, they're all bravado, yet bafflingly clueless when it comes to what a G-spot is."

To be fair, I had no idea what that was until recently either.

"Got it," I respond, appreciating her candor. "That's all the P's, right?"

"Nope. Still got two more. Firefighters are up next."

I give her a skeptical look.

"It sounds like a P, grammar police," she retorts playfully, making me laugh. "The firefighters are *always* going to be the hottest. But that's because they spend all day sending naked pics to their endless queue of side pieces. Definitely a high-risk, high-reward scenario—I'd recommend a thorough health check if you take a ride on that truck."

Morgan guides us toward the expansive central desk in the bustling ER, tossing her feet up as she gestures for me to take a seat next to her. I follow her lead and settle in comfortably, my gaze drifting to the elevator doors which promptly chime open.

Beau steps out, dressed in navy scrubs that cling to his stocky frame. He's deep in conversation with a dark-haired man who somehow manages to outstretch even Beau's considerable height.

Glancing to the side, Beau catches my eye and winks discretely before returning to his conversation. My heart races at the sight of him in his element, exuding control and confidence. Obviously, I'm already attracted to him when he's relaxed and at ease at home, but in this professional setting, he gives off a different kind of energy that makes a warm heat settle between my legs.

I watch unashamedly as Beau nods and claps the other man on the back, his golden brown waves peeking out of the edges of his scrub cap. It's official—my panties are soaked. He can have a blowjob. He can have sex. He can have whatever he wants . . . as long as he has me.

"And then we have the physicians," Morgan remarks, pulling me back to reality. Her face twists into a scowl as she watches Beau approach us. "The worst of all. If you're going to hook up with any of the P's, do *not* let it be a physician."

"They're not all that bad," I retort, attempting to steady my erratic pulse.

"What's not that bad?" Beau asks, his accent somehow more pronounced in this environment.

Morgan shoots him a glare. "Nice scrub cap."

"Thanks," he responds, completely unphased by her attitude. "Someone special got it for me for Christmas."

His honey eyes lock onto mine, and I can feel my cheeks burning. He's wearing the scrub cap I gave him last night, covered in little orange cats that look just like Frosty.

"Didn't take you ortho bros for cat dads," Morgan muses, crossing her arms as she looks up at him. "I would've assumed you preferred something more along the lines of a rottweiler."

Beau leans on the desk's edge, grinning down like he's used to bantering with her. "And I assumed you were a pint-sized bundle of sunshine. Looks like we were both wrong."

She cracks a smile, unable to help herself. "Where are my orders?"

"Already in. Feel free to discharge away."

He snags a cookie from the counter, narrowly avoiding Morgan's wrath as he pops it into his mouth.

As Morgan opens her computer screen, Beau turns to me. "You staying for a bit longer?" he asks. His tone is casual but his eyes convey a deeper question.

I glance at Morgan, who's now fully engrossed in her patient's chart, and then back at Beau.

"Um, yeah I think I've overstayed my welcome in the ER," I respond casually. "I should probably head to find Cass and Caroline."

"I'll, uh, walk you out," Beau offers.

"Thanks for hanging with me Morg. I'll see you on New Years?"

Her green eyes peer up from her screen, first at me and then at Beau.

"You two," she hisses, her eyes quickly flickering between us in warning, "need to get your *shit* together before anyone else catches onto what I just saw."

Chapter 38

Beau

The past few days have been hell. On top of a hectic schedule, I've been grappling with the embarrassing fallout from my incident in the operating room. According to Walker, I fell face-first into the patient, ricocheted off the arm board, and landed on the floor with a thud like a tree hit by lightning. Thankfully, the patient wasn't harmed, and the only thing broken was my ego.

Waking up to a nurse rapidly pushing dextrose into my veins was a sobering experience. My blood sugar had fallen to a whopping forty-one. If it had dropped any lower without intervention, I'd probably still be comatose and in the ICU.

Walker refrained from bombarding me with questions at the time, though I could sense his concern. He insisted I take time off until I felt better, but I stubbornly returned to work the next day, unwilling to admit that the episode was more than just a one-off accident. But after a few suspicious looks and pointed comments, I finally came clean to him about the situation today.

He admitted his surprise, though, in hindsight, my frequent Skittles consumption suddenly made a lot more sense to him. He even offered to adjust my schedule, but I was quick to dismiss the idea. I'm perfectly capable of doing the job like anyone else, and I refuse to let this incident define me or my abilities as a surgeon. That's the kind of special treatment I was trying to avoid, which is why I chose not to disclose diabetes in my residency physical in the first place. I didn't want to be seen as the weakest link.

What most people don't realize about surgeons, particularly surgeons in orthopedics, is that we are some of the most prideful assholes to ever exist. We study for years, working our asses off to finish school and graduate at the top of our class. Then, we fight tooth and nail to get into one of the most competitive specialties in the country, and once we're in we have to keep battling ourselves for the next half-decade, just to prove that we're worthy.

Weakness isn't an option, which is really fucking challenging when your body betrays you.

What's difficult about diabetes, and any other chronic illness that isn't outwardly visible, is that they're riddled with silent struggles. To the outside world, we don't appear any different. There's no indication of the constant effort we put into managing these uninvited, life-altering conditions. These conditions that take from us, statistically shorten our lifespans and offer nothing in return. It's a war that we didn't volunteer for, yet we're forced to fight for the rest of our lives.

Most of the time I just pretend that it's not there. I learned how to adapt diabetes into my routine, to the point where I almost forget about it. But sometimes it's just so damn frustrating because all I want is to be impenetrable. To be the guy that everyone thinks I am—the guy I've worked so hard to portray. And it kills me that I can't.

Walker, understanding the gravity of the situation, agreed to keep this between us. At this point, coming clean about my omission on the health exam would only do more harm than good. While I know now that nobody sees the information other than human resources, and that disclosing my diagnosis doesn't impact my ability to practice, it still could be a massive black mark on my record if I retroactively change the details. Hospitals are driven by policy, and regardless of your intention, they tend to look unfavorably upon someone who blatantly ignores the rules.

After Walker and I had a lengthy chat this afternoon about lessons, we both feel like I've learned mine. He's protective of his team and I'm incredibly grateful for that. But that doesn't mean that it's been easy coming to work each day, wondering if I'm the subject of rumors and hushed whispers—the idiot ortho bro who passed out during surgery. Like I said, pride is a tough thing to overcome.

The only thing getting me out of my head since the incident has been Claire. Her enthusiasm took root in my heart the moment I met her, reminding me of everything beautiful in life. She tended to my withering soul, bringing me back from the brink of complete automation. Every time I look at her, I'm instantly reoriented to what truly matters.

"Do you think she'll say anything?" Claire asks, drawing me out of my thoughts as I close the door to the call room behind us. Her eyes are wide with panic as I press her against the wooden door, clicking the lock on the handle. I'm glad I found her in the ER with Morgan instead of anyone else. It's getting almost painful to stifle myself around her, and while she's adamant that she'll tell her brother soon, my control is waning.

"I don't give a fuck if she does at this point," I reply, dipping my head to graze my teeth along her neck. She smells like cinnamon and oats, exactly like the cookie that I put in my mouth moments ago. All I want to do is taste her.

"Beau," she sighs as I kiss the spot I just marked. "I'm serious."

Her tone makes me pause. I draw back to meet her gaze, gently brushing a stray hair from her face. "She won't say anything, Claire."

"How do you know?" she presses.

"Trust me, I just know." I place a soft kiss along her furrowed brow. She relaxes under my lips as I add, "Morgan is a lot of things, a pain in my ass being high up on the list, but she's not a snitch."

Claire's icy eyes find mine, melting into a cool blue. "Nice scrub cap," she teases, running her fingers along the edge of the fabric. "From someone *special*, huh?"

I smile down at her, glad her mood is improving. "Someone *super* special and *super* hot," I grunt, leaning in to kiss her neck again. "Those fucking scrubs have me in a vice."

Claire scrunches her nose and giggles beneath my embrace. "Hotter than the lingerie you bought me? That's hard to believe."

"Everything you wear is hot," I murmur breathily against her pounding pulse. "You could be wearing a straightjacket and I would think it was the sexiest thing in the world."

She tilts her neck to give me better access, letting in a sharp gasp when I nip at her chin. "I hear that's kinky to people like you."

I pull back again, arching my eyebrow at her. "People like me?"

"You know," she says quietly as her cheeks flush. "People into bondage." Claire practically whispers the last word like it's sinful, and I bite the inside of my cheek to stifle a grin.

I grip her chin between my fingers, forcing her eyes to mine. "And how would you know that, pretty girl."

"I've done some research," she admits, biting her bottom lip before she adds, "Is that something you might like?"

Unable to help myself, I let loose a laugh. This woman constantly surprises me.

"Not particularly. Especially when I have far more creative ways to keep you restrained that actually let me see you naked."

My mind flicks back to last week when I introduced her to the fundamentals of rope ties. In an effort to make sure I didn't go too fast, I showed her how the system worked and reviewed the safety of it all, allowing her to ask questions and try various materials. Once she seemed comfortable, I stripped her down and played with her body until she had come so many times she practically passed out.

"Interesting." Given Claire's whispered response and quickening breath, I would guess that she's recalling the very same memory.

"What's interesting?" I ask, releasing her chin.

She purses her lips momentarily before responding. "I'm just trying to imagine your creativity. Everything we've done so far has been kind of . . . vanilla."

My teeth grind, knowing that she's trying to get a rise out of me. But my cock isn't having it. It flexes in my scrubs, desperate to show her how very un-vanilla I can be.

Leaning in, I grab the sides of her face with both hands and plant a rough kiss on her lush lips.

She moans into my mouth, desperate for more. I sweep my tongue against hers, satiating my need to taste her sweetness before I pull back, snagging her lower lip between my teeth.

"Be careful what you wish for," I say with a wicked grin as an idea comes to me.

Turning my back to her, I stride towards the twin bed nestled in the corner of the call room. I slept here last night and didn't have a chance to make the sheets back up, so they're strewn about on the mattress.

Grabbing the flat sheet, I grip each end and circle my arms. The motion twists the linen, transforming it into a makeshift rope—the closest thing I can find to bondage in the sterile on-call room. I spread my arms, snapping the fabric tight, testing its strength as I pivot back to face Claire.

She's leaning against the door with a smug look on her face. A look that I intend to wipe right off her.

"Turn around," I instruct, my voice lowering.

Claire's smug expression shifts to one of curiosity before she complies, slowly spinning her body to face the door like I asked. Her desire to obey when she chooses never ceases to fascinate me. It's like there's a complete shift in her persona as she hands me complete control. It's fucking sexy.

I approach her, gently lifting her long braid to drape it over her shoulder.

"Hands behind your back," I say, my tone steady yet charged with an unspoken promise.

She laces her fingers together as her breathing escalates.

Leaning down, I wrap the makeshift rope around her wrists and forearms, improvising my knot to accommodate the width of the sheets. It should be firm enough to hold her in position, but not tight enough to cut off her circulation. I push my fingers beneath the restraint, taking a second to check in with her.

"That okay?" I ask, my breath warm against her ear.

Claire's arms shift slightly, trying to get out of the hold. She sighs when she's unsuccessful. "Yep."

"Good girl," I reply, grabbing hold of her shoulders and spinning her to face me. "I know normally we do take care of you first, but right now you're going to open that delicate little throat of yours and let me fuck your face. Swallow me down and if you're good, I'll make it up to you afterward. Now get on your fucking knees."

Her gorgeous eyes widen like she wasn't expecting this, but she doesn't say anything as she slowly sinks to her knees. The tension between us crackles, and I feel my cock flex at the sight of her in front of me.

"Listen to me," I say softly, my voice firm yet filled with affection for the woman in front of me. "If it gets to be too much, I need you to snap your fingers, and I'll stop."

She snaps her fingers loudly and my brow furrows.

Before I can say anything she rolls her eyes. "Just showing you I can do it . . . isn't that what you were going to ask for?"

We've gone over several safe-word communication techniques and each time we try something new, I always have her verbalize the term before we begin. The fact that she's enthusiastically offering before I have to ask makes me proud as hell. It shows just how far we've come in terms of her confidence with sex.

I reach down, gently cupping her face in my hands.

"God, you're perfect," I praise, stroking my thumb over her bottom lip. "Now open these pretty lips of yours and show me just how perfect you sound when you're choking on my cock."

Claire beams, her gaze eagerly dropping to the noticeable erection directly in front of her face.

I step back, slowly undoing the drawstring of my scrubs. At this point, she's seen me naked enough times to know exactly what she's getting into, but the way her crystal blue eyes still widen when they land on my hard cock never gets old. It's like she's trying to remember how she took it in the past while mustering up the courage to do it again.

Pulling my briefs and pants down my thighs, I step forward and position myself directly in front of her waiting lips. They're open and expectant, like she's ready for whatever I'm going to throw at her. The way her hands are tied behind her back pushes her chest out, and I wish like hell that she was naked in this position—completely submissive and at my mercy.

Unfortunately, that fantasy will have to happen another day because I'm running out of time.

Reaching down, I slide my fingers through her hair and tighten my grip, knowing that if she's going to stay balanced in this position, I'll have to hold her steady. Giving myself a few slow strokes from base to tip, I ease myself into her hot mouth.

She lets out a hum as her lips widen, allowing me to slide my length along her tongue. I pause a few inches in, momentarily letting her adjust to my size before pushing forward again. Her hips shuffle beneath her, like she's trying to alleviate tension between her legs.

"Does sucking my cock make you wet?" I ask, knowing she can't answer me with her mouth full. "You like being used? Letting me fuck your face? Does that greedy little pussy want to come?"

A garbled moan surrounds my dick as she tries to respond. The vibrations of her acknowledgment ignite something within me. I tighten my grip on her hair, briefly pulling myself out of her mouth before I thrust forward again.

This time, her reddened lips close around my cock and she hollows out her cheeks, sucking as much as she can. Her eyes remain glued on mine, and there's a flicker of a dare there, challenging me to take things further.

There's no way in hell I'm going to last long, so I might as well just go for it. I try to steady my breathing in case I need to hear her snap as I begin to fuck her face, taking what I need from her. Each time I advance, she opens her throat a little more and breathes steadily through her nose, swallowing me down like a fucking pro.

Claire whimpers as the tip of my cock bottoms out in her throat, but my perfect girl doesn't gag. Instead, a single tear runs down her flushed cheek as she closes her eyes in pure submission.

Pride swells through me, but for some reason, I feel the urge to taunt her. "Not going to choke on my cock?"

Her lips curl upwards as best as they can and I respond by rocking my hips forward, shoving myself as deep as I can down her throat. She lets out the hottest little moan I've heard in my life and I lose all control, increasing the pace of my thrusts.

"That's my girl," I grit, feeling my balls start to draw up close to me. "God, you're sexy. Keep fucking making noises like that, and I'll have to come on that delicious tongue of yours instead of down your throat."

She purposely repeats the sound and I'm done. I pull all of the way out of her mouth, relishing in her surprised expression as I grip her cheeks hard.

"Open up," I grunt, clenching my shaft to hold off my release. "You're going to taste every fucking drop."

Her swollen lips part as she complies with my instructions, her chest heaving with anticipation.

I'm barely able to make it back to her mouth as my orgasm rips through my body, painting her tongue with my release. And I know one thing without a doubt—having Claire on her knees in my on-call room is the best Christmas gift I could ever receive.

CHAPTER 39

CLAIRE

By the time I make it home on the evening of Christmas, I'm exhausted. A day that started out so poorly was quickly turned around thanks to the family and friends in my life who knew exactly what I needed. Even though the holiday looked different this year, we started new traditions and made lots of memories. I feel more at home here than ever before, surrounded by people who lift me up despite the grief that constantly threatens to bring me down.

After we left the hospital, Cassidy, Caroline, and I visited Cassidy's brother's grave. Surprisingly, it was her first time visiting since his death two years ago, and it made me happy to know that we could be there for her in the same way she has been for us. Cass doesn't talk about him much, but I know that he was her very best friend, and I can imagine that she misses him every day, in the same way that I miss my mom.

The thing is, you would never know that she carries that baggage around with her if you saw her on the outside. It's the same way that you wouldn't know that Beau struggles with his chronic illness. Invisible demons are still just as terrorizing as the visible ones, and we all handle the battle differently and at our own pace.

After almost four months, I'm finally starting to feel like myself, and that's okay. But, even if I was still hurting and grieving, that would be okay too. There's no timeline for grief—no right answer or formula to normalcy. And just because you take several steps forward, doesn't mean you won't also take a few back.

Today may have started as a step back, but it definitely ended as a leap forward.

Since Parker was going to be home later tonight, Caroline offered to stay with me at the condo for the night so I wouldn't be alone. While I would have normally taken her up on the offer, I promised Beau that I would video call him before I went to bed so that I could open his real Christmas present.

I had no idea he left me anything until he casually mentioned it to me on the way out of the on-call room this afternoon. It's been tormenting me all evening as I've debated what it could be. Given his previous gifts of pajamas and lingerie, the gift is probably something equally as intimate and playful. Though, I'm not complaining because everything the man has purchased for me has gotten lots of use.

Slipping into my Christmas lingerie, adorned with red velvet and bells, I settle myself in front of the festively lit tree and press the call button on my phone. Catching a glimpse of myself on the screen, I can't help but giggle at the sight—I look absurd with my tits pushed up and dark curls falling over my shoulders. But, I also look hot.

"Hey, pretty girl," Beau answers, not looking at his phone as he walks through what looks like a hospital hallway. His brown eyes quickly glance down and widen before he abruptly hangs up.

A minute later he calls back.

"Give a man some warning before you call me half-naked. Anyone could've seen you." He runs his fingers through his facial hair before a devious grin forms on his lips. "You look fucking sexy though. Damn, I'm lucky as fuck."

I feel my cheeks blush at his praise. "Oh, this old number?" I tease, drawing the phone down my body slowly before I snap it back up to my face. "Someone *special* gave it to me."

Beau hisses and bites his hand like he's in pain. "Claire."

"Yes?" I giggle, batting my eyelashes at him.

"You may think it's fun to tease me now, but I've got all day tomorrow, and nothing better to do than punish you for it."

My core clenches at the thought, and I kind of hope it's something similar to what he did today. I loved how he had me in his complete control, using me for his own release before he gave me what I needed. He's always prioritized my pleasure, and having him take his first while I was at his mercy was super hot. His skilled fingers didn't have to touch me for long before I combusted on his hand.

I tilt the screen to my tits again, knowing it'll only provoke him further. "Oh? And how exactly will you do that?"

"A few things come to mind," he contemplates, hesitantly flicking his eyes away from the screen to somewhere in the room. A moment later he says, "Sorry, just got paged."

My heart sinks. I know he's busy, but I was really hoping to chat. We've barely talked in the past week and I miss him.

"Go ahead," I murmur, trying to hide my disappointment.

"No, I've got like five minutes," Beau reassures me with a soft smile. "It's not urgent, and I want to see you open your Christmas present."

"You sure?" I ask, wanting to be considerate of his responsibilities.

"Of course I'm sure," he replies, his voice warm.

I set the phone on the television stand to give him a clear view and scurry to the back of the tree where the gift is hidden. It's unexpectedly heavy, wrapped in rich red paper, and topped with a pristine white bow.

"Careful," Beau warns as I give the box a gentle shake. "It's kind of breakable."

"Oops, force of habit," I admit with a sheepish grin, ripping into the wrapping without a thought to preserve the high-quality paper.

"Well, well, well," I muse, lifting the lid to reveal a coffee mug nestled in crinkle paper. "What do we have here?"

"Wait!" Beau calls, causing me to stop mid-action. I quickly glance back at the screen. "There's a note inside. Make sure you read it before you open the gift."

I smile and shake my head. "Of course there is."

Carefully lifting the paper out of the mug, I find a small, folded note nestled inside.

> *The most important nickname you've given me*
> *is Boyfriend Beau.*
> *I bought this mug weeks ago, and it never felt*
> *like the right time to give it to you.*
> *But because it's Christmas, and at Christmas*
> *you tell the truth, you deserve to know how I*
> *feel.*

My throat catches as I finish reading his note. Not only did he quote *Love Actually*, my favorite Christmas movie of all time, but his words are beautiful.

"Boyfriend Beau," I whisper, drawing my eyes back to look at the phone. "You can't be serious. There's no way that's your favorite nickname."

"Without a doubt it is," he responds, clearly not in the mood to joke around. "Take out the mug."

I set the note aside and gently lift the mug out of its crinkled paper nest. It's simple and white, but the words written in Beau's handwriting on each side take my breath away:

I love you.

The stark honesty of the gift sends a surge of emotions through me. Just three simple words, but they carry so much weight and meaning.

I never considered that what I've been feeling for him was love, mostly because when I've told people I loved them in the past, it never once felt like this. Love never felt comfortable and uncomfortable all at the same time.

Love, or what I perceived to be love, was always comfortable because it was housed by a wall of deceit. A wall of pretending to be someone I wasn't, and funneling myself into the person that I thought I had to be. But that isn't love—it's a cage.

Love is supposed to challenge you. To make you uncomfortable. It's supposed to force you to bear your ugliest parts to someone. The parts that you've been told to hide your whole life. The parts that you've been told are too loud, or too embarrassing. The parts that make you different.

And the thing is, once you let go and remove all of your masks, a new form of comfort arises. A comfort that only comes from knowing that you've been as vulnerable as possible with another person, and they still chose to stay.

So I guess that's what love is in its most pure form—a swirling mix of comfort and discomfort.

And it's exactly how I feel about Beau.

"You've had this for weeks," I ask, arching my brows at him.

"Yep," he confirms, his lips curving into a knowing smirk.

I stifle my grin, trying desperately to avoid the emotion swelling in my chest. "And you didn't have the balls to say it to my face?"

He barks a laugh. "Well, you never called me big balls Beau, now did you?"

"No I guess I didn't," I concede, appreciating the way he effortlessly diffuses tension between us. "But now I'm totally going to start. Those things are huge."

"I know talking about feelings makes you uncomfortable, so I figured that this was a good middle ground." His eyes hold mine through the screen, filled with acceptance and affection.

A smile blooms across my lips. Beau's actions are always so deliberate and mindful. His intentionality was one of the things that drew me to him initially, and moments like this only reaffirm his thoughtful nature.

He's right . . . I am uncomfortable. But, it's the best kind of discomfort there is, which is why I tell him, "I love you, too."

Chapter 40

Beau

"Do you think I should wear the dress with the blue sparkles or the black sparkles?" Claire calls out from her bedroom.

I groan, taking a final swig of my beer. People are supposed to show up in thirty minutes for Parker and Cassidy's engagement party, and she's still not dressed which is ridiculous because we've barely done anything all day. I warned her about our timeline ten times, and yet here I am, gently reminding her again.

Fortunately, everything is already set up on the expansive balcony, so even if she isn't dressed yet, we're essentially ready for guests.

As I reach the door, my eyes widen. "It looks like a bomb went off in here, Claire. What were you doing when you said you were cleaning up?"

We got back from visiting my family in Houston last night, and while it was a great trip, I'm now regretting leaving her without supervision this afternoon. Clothes and suitcases are strewn haphazardly across the floor and bed, making it impossible to see anything other than complete chaos. At this point, we're going to have to lock the door and hope nobody needs to use the spare bathroom.

"I was cleaning myself up," she yells from the closet, her tone laced with mischief. "You didn't specify *what* needed to be clean."

I run my fingers through my short beard—this woman is going to be the death of me.

"Don't I look good?" she asks, exiting the closet in nothing but white lace panties and stiletto heels as she holds up each potential dress. Her chocolate curls are halfway pinned back, allowing the rest of her hair to fall over her shoulders. A rich red lipstick outlines her mouth, making my cock swell with desire.

It's going to be a long night.

We agreed to break the news to Parker in the new year, which means maintaining boundaries around each other tonight. Something that is going to be really fucking challenging with Claire looking like that.

Her perky tits bounce as she hops over a pile of clothes. She almost loses her balance, and lands on Frosty who meows at her in annoyance.

Same dude.

"But seriously, which dress? Because I think—" She pauses mid-sentence, drawing her eyes along my body as a sly smile forms on her lips. "You look good."

I fold my arms across my chest, trying to maintain a stern demeanor. "And you look naked."

If I wasn't so exasperated, I would smile back. I'm wearing a full tuxedo that happens to fit me like a glove, even though I haven't worn it in two years. Put any man in a monkey suit and women get their panties wet. Coincidentally, that's exactly how Claire's looking at me as her tongue traces over her bottom lip.

"So observant," she teases, walking towards me with a glimmer of heat in her eyes. "Is that the first thing they teach you in doctor school?"

I feel my jaw clench. Claire has a knack for playful teasing and likes to poke at my habit of stating the obvious. It's something I typically find charming, but in this moment, it's grating on my nerves.

"In doctor school they teach us about the importance of punctuality, which is something you clearly seem to struggle with," I retort, stepping towards her and selecting the blue dress. "Seriously, get dressed. People are on their way."

She's practically invited the entire hospital, not to mention several of her sister's med school friends who barely know Parker and Cassidy. As of this morning, the guest list had ballooned to around fifty confirmations, and she's been talking about it nonstop. I'm glad she's excited, and I would echo that same sentiment if she would just get ready.

Claire lets the black dress fall from her fingers and giggles, a dangerous expression on her face. "You're kind of hot when you're mad."

Something in me snaps. I don't know how to explain it, but my patience with her games evaporates and I lunge forward, taking her body over my shoulder in one motion.

She protests and I swat her bare bottom hard with my free hand, closing her bedroom door and stomping up the stairs to my loft. Tossing her on my bed with a thud, I take the dress from her arms and walk into the closet, placing it on a hanger for safekeeping.

When I return, Claire has made herself comfortable, lounging back on my pillows with a hopeful expression on her perfectly made-up face. An expression that I want to fuck right off of her.

I crouch down and pull out a box from beneath my bed, placing it on the nightstand.

"Whatcha got there?" she asks, batting her eyelashes at me.

"Wouldn't you like to know," I snarl, reaching out my hand.

Claire hesitantly purses her lips before she places her palm in mine, allowing me to slap a padded leather cuff around her wrist. I repeat the process on the other arm, pushing two fingers between the leather and her skin to ensure she has room for circulation.

She'll be here a while.

I lean onto the bed, sliding a pillow beneath her low back before I take her wrists and fasten them to the ties on either side of the bed posts.

Her brow furrows as she pulls on the restraints. They allow for slight movements, but no more than an inch or so.

Moving down the mattress, I take her feet in my hands and secure matching leather restraints to each ankle, making sure to leave the stilettos on. That's more for me than for her, because seeing her tied up wearing only a thong and four-inch heels is officially a new fantasy of mine.

Stretching her leg straight, I clip in the ankle cuff to the bottom bedpost and adjust the strap to provide the slightest amount of give. Again, only an inch because I don't want her moving for this punishment.

When I make it to the other side of the bed, Claire's eyes widen with sudden understanding.

"Uh, Beau?" she whispers, her tone suddenly less confident. "We don't really have time for this."

I pull her final limb taut, securing the cuff to the other post so that she's in a starfish position, her back slightly arched due to the pillow I placed beneath her. Her hips twist, trying to hide that pretty pussy from me as I stand from the bed.

"We don't have time for what?" I ask, walking towards the nightstand once more.

Claire's blue eyes track me as I move. "Whatever games you have planned."

Ignoring her, I take out what I need from the box and place it on the bed.

I climb on top of her and lean down, kissing her neck. "Oh, but I thought you were the one who wanted to play games? It certainly seemed that way to me when you acted like a brat."

I slide a silky white blindfold over her eyes—a perfect match to her panties. It'll completely deprive her of the ability to see, which is ideal for what I'm planning. I want her guessing.

Claire's breath catches when my fingers find her hard nipples, like she wasn't expecting my touch. I give them a quick tug before I pinch the silver clamps onto both buds at the same time. This is the first time we've used this toy so I reduced the tension, not wanting to overdo it.

She cries out when I tug on the chain connecting the clamps, her chest heaving beneath me. I silence her cries with my mouth, kissing her hard before I pull back.

"Alright." She huffs a hesitant laugh, rolling her hips to try and wiggle out of the restraints. "Point made, Beau."

I look down at her, my blood still boiling. "And what point is that?"

She sighs in resignation. "You turned me on. You win. Now let me go."

"While I'm glad that you're on, that's not the point."

Shuffling down her legs, I pick up the black rabbit vibrator and turn it to the lowest setting.

Claire's neck cranes as if she's trying to figure out what I'm doing, despite her sense of sight being taken away.

"Beau!" She flinches, her breasts heaving as I touch the tip of the vibrator to the center of her thighs.

"Yes?"

"I need to get ready," she whines, attempting to shimmy away from the toy.

Unable to help myself, I remove the vibrator and slide a finger through her pussy. She's dripping, exactly like I thought she would be.

"Feels like you're already ready."

"Okay, okay, okay, fine. Just fuck me, and then let me get dressed. People are gonna be here any seco—"

She yelps, not able to finish her thought as I return the vibrator to her pussy, this time sliding it beneath her lace thong.

"Oh, so now you're worried about time?" I ask, dipping the base of the toy inside her.

She whimpers but doesn't protest as I slowly fuck her with the vibrator, eventually pushing it inside her soaked pussy. The part that goes inside of her curls up to massage her G-spot, while the exterior sits directly on top of her clit, teasing her with little sucking sensations. It's not as good as having me personally edge her for the next hour, but it should do the job while I'm occupied with our guests.

"Here's a game for you, pretty girl," I say, snapping her panties back in place. "Let's see how much you appreciate time when it seems to drag on and on."

Claire moans, attempting to arch her hips as I run my hands up her chest, playing with my food. "I've got this vibrator on the lowest setting. So low that it'll massage your pussy just enough to keep you on edge while never quite taking you over."

My fingers tug on the chain between her tits again, her beautiful cries echoing through the condo.

"That won't do," I tut, smearing her arousal across her lips. "We have guests coming over. Can you stay quiet?"

She shakes her head and groans, loose curls falling over the pillowcase beneath her. A tear streams down her soft face, and I run fingers from her lips to her cheek, gently wiping it away. I may want to teach her a lesson, but I'm not a monster.

My phone buzzes in my pocket, alerting me to the fact that people are at the door. We told the concierge to let everyone up, but now I'm glad I never unlocked it.

I lean in and kiss Claire's reddened cheek. "Well you're gonna have to keep that loud mouth shut, because our guests are here. Wouldn't want them to hear you. That would be embarrassing."

As I'm getting up, I place a small circular button in her right hand. "If it gets to be too much, press this and I'll immediately come get you."

My phone instantly pings with a loud horn and I look down. The app paired with the button I just put in her hand is alerting me, a red stop sign covering my phone screen. My wide eyes flash to Claire, who has a small smirk on her face. "Just checking that it works."

Stifling a grin, I stand from the bed and adjust myself to hide the massive erection pitched in my tux pants. This is starting to feel like as much of a punishment for me as it is for her, and I'm seriously doubting my ability to hold out as long as I planned.

Fortunately, I have the guests to distract me. My goal is simple: get everyone in, spring the surprise, and then discreetly go fetch her.

By the time Parker and Cassidy arrive, our condo is buzzing with energy, the whole damn hospital in our living room, cocktails in hand. Claire's strategic timing—having guests arrive thirty minutes earlier than she told Parker—worked perfectly. They were completely clueless and nearly had a heart attack when we all shouted "surprise."

I haven't heard so much as a peep from upstairs, though I know Claire can hear everything below. Luckily, there's no risk of anyone stumbling upon her on their way to the bathroom—I made sure to triple-check the lock on the loft stairs before anyone arrived.

This probably wasn't the best time for such an adventurous experiment. You should never leave someone restrained without supervision, and even though this was relatively tame in terms of bondage, I'm still distracted. I've been obsessively checking my phone to ensure she's alright, completely neglecting my hosting duties.

In addition to giving Claire a safety button, I also set up a small camera trained on the bed. At the moment, she looks more frustrated than anything; her mouth is pressed into a hard line and her heels are discarded on the floor, like she kicked them off in retaliation. I stifle a grin, enjoying her torment.

Once the guests begin to gradually migrate outside after the big reveal, I catch up with Parker and Cass.

"Happy engagement, man," I offer, bringing Parker into a hug as the commotion settles. "You look dapper as fuck."

He's wearing a tux similar to mine, only it's definitely way more expensive than my department store getup. His dark hair is slicked back and he smells like pure affluence. I guess that's what a trust fund and an attending surgeon's salary will get you.

Parker's face lights up, pulling me in close. "And you look like shit."

"Still better looking than you, though," I shoot back, giving him a friendly pat on the back.

"Not with that beard you don't. It looks like a damn yeti took over your face."

I brush off his insult, knowing deep down that he's just jealous. My beard is dope, and his sister loves it. Especially when she's riding my face . . . .

"Hey—play nice," Cassidy chides, pulling us both into a hug, her face nestled between us. "That's supposed to be his New Year's resolution."

I arch an eyebrow at Parker as we step back. "I'll believe that when I see it."

He shakes his head, turning his attention to his fiancée. "And what about your resolution, sweetheart?"

Her cheeks flush the same color as her lipstick. I can't resist the urge to tease her, knowing that it's got to be good if this is her reaction. "Yeah, Cass, what's *yours*?"

Cassidy glares at me with those striking hazel eyes of hers. Her blonde hair is swept back from her face, highlighting her embarrassment. "It doesn't matter," she mutters, darting her eyes back to Parker. "Because it *isn't* happening."

I look at Parker who's got a shit-eating grin on his freshly shaven face. "Her resolution is to let me fuck her ass."

Unable to help myself, I burst out laughing. That's the last thing I thought would come out of his mouth.

"Hey, Cass," I offer, trying to catch my breath. "There's plenty of interns who already get fucked in the ass by him on a daily basis. I'm sure they could coach you. Just gotta relax into it."

"I hate you both." She snatches a full flute of champagne from the counter and strides toward the balcony.

"Love you too," I call after her, still laughing as she flips us off on her way out.

Parker watches her go, the playful smirk still lingering on his lips, but there's only fondness in his eyes. "She loves you too," he says confidently.

"You two really are perfect for each other," I admit, hoping one day he'll feel the same about me and his sister. "Never a dull moment."

Parker nods. "Speaking of never having dull moments. Have you seen my sister? I want to thank her for putting this all together."

"Uh, yeah," I respond, trying to sound nonchalant. "Actually, Claire's a little tied up at the moment."

Literally.

"Oh?" He arches a brow, reaching for a glass of champagne.

"Yeah you know, just been in hostess mode," I say smoothly, glancing at my phone. I should probably go grab her now that the guests of honor are here. "Last I saw, she was outside and deep in conversation with Dr. Wilson. I think they were talking about his houseboat."

"Oof, I don't envy her," Parker grimaces, taking a sip of the bubbly as Cassidy waves him over from outside. Her short, white dress is definitely not made for winter, so I'm glad we got heaters.

"I'm being summoned. Come save me in a bit. I want to talk to you about something."

"Sure thing," I agree, only half listening as my mind drifts to Claire. "Just gonna grab something from upstairs, and I'll be back down."

CHAPTER 41

CLAIRE

I've had what feels like forever to plan what I was going to say to Beau when he came back for me, but all of it flies out of my head when he pulls the blindfold from my eyes and peers down at me, looking like a freaking James Bond villain.

I'm dead serious.

Beau's face is cast in shadows, backlit by the light spilling in from downstairs, and he lets out a laugh that's unmistakably sinister. Plus, he's in a tux, and I'm pretty sure every villain wears black tie at some point.

"Something funny?" I ask, trying my hardest to sound bored as I train my eyes on the concrete ceiling.

I can sense him still towering next to me, but refuse to turn my head out of spite. Well spite, and the fact that every time I attempt to move my body, the vibrator shifts inside of me. I've finally managed to tolerate the overstimulation, and I'm not eager to test my limits further.

"Just that your cheeks look a little flushed," Beau teases, his fingers reaching down to caress my cheek. "Something got you worked up, pretty girl?"

"No," I snap, closing my eyes to avoid the temptation of his touch.

"You sure about that?" he probes, his tone filled with sinful challenge.

Before I can answer, I feel pressure between my legs as Beau pushes on the toy's exterior, kicking the vibration up another level.

I want to cry out, to do anything to alleviate the uncomfortable tension my body has been enduring for too long, but I know better. Even if everyone is outside, it's possible they could hear something.

My eyes fly open, landing on Beau. He's standing beside the bed with a grin plastered on his face, watching me like his own personal captive.

My nipples harden, tightening the grip that the clamps have on me as a burst of pleasure shoots to my sex. I inhale sharply, and all I can think about is how I need release more than I've ever needed anything in my entire life. My body feels like it's so tightly wound that I can barely breathe.

Beau's fingers lightly trail across the bare skin of my thighs. "Did you come while I was down there?" he asks, his voice low and sexy.

"No," I admit, arching my hips into his hand. Despite the additional stimulation, I still need more. I need him.

"Good. Are you done playing games?"

"Are you?" I grit out, knowing it's not the answer he wants, but I can't help myself.

He kicks the vibrator up another level and I whimper, trying to handle the additional stimulation.

"Please, fuck, please."

His eyes meet mine and flicker with arousal as he holds the toy in place. "Do you know why you're being punished, Claire?"

God, the sound of my name on his lips will never get old.

"Yes," I gasp, feeling my legs begin to shake as my orgasm approaches.

"Why's that?" he drawls, moving his other hand up my chest to give the clamps a quick tug.

I wince, my body tightening further. "Because I made a funny joke."

Beau's eyes flash darker as he clicks his tongue. "Wrong answer."

I feel the speed of the rabbit escalate once more, my chest heaving as I try to handle the sensation. Everything in my body feels heavy, and I can feel myself rapidly running towards the cliff I've been teased with for too long. My whole body clenches, all of my blood rushing to that one spot between my legs as I feel my orgasm finally crest.

Just as I'm about to let go, Beau abruptly pulls the vibrator out of me, turning it off and tossing it on the floor.

I bite my lip to stifle a cry, frustration running through my veins. The loss of the orgasm is practically painful, and I've reached a new level of desperation.

Begging it is.

"I'm being punished for playing games," I pant. "It wasn't funny."

His brow arches at me, waiting for more.

"I'm sorry?" I try.

Nothing.

"I was wrong?"

Nothing.

"I love you," I whisper, hoping those three words do the trick.

Beau's lips finally curl into a proud grin as he walks to the head of the bed and plants his lips against mine. "Fuck yeah, you do. You wanna come?"

"Yes, please," I reply, practically salivating. Now that the vibrator isn't inside of me, I can feel my arousal dripping onto his sheets.

"Listen to those manners. Such a good girl," he praises, pressing another quick kiss on my lips before he reaches into the night-stand.

Jeez—How many things does he keep in there?

I try to angle my head, but his body is blocking my view. He reaches over me with whatever he grabbed, and all of a sudden I feel air where I didn't before.

My thong.

He must have cut it off.

"Open," Beau orders, returning to my side. His thumb runs over my lower lip, and I sigh. Just his simple touch feels incredible after too long without it.

I part my lips as my ruined lace panties are shoved into my mouth, muffling my cries. My body is so overstimulated that the idea of him destroying my expensive lingerie doesn't even upset me. If anything, I'm thankful to have something filling my mouth as he crawls between my legs.

"You're drenched," he hums against my sex. "Don't hold back for me, pretty girl. Soak my face with your cum."

Stifled screams come from my lips as his skilled tongue joins his lips, flicking my clit with insane precision as he sucks hard. I feel myself building again, legs straining at the ties that bind them apart.

The fact that I'm going to come on his face, with no control whatsoever, makes this even hotter. I'm forced to take what he gives me as his hands roam up my legs, one grasping the bottom of the nipple chain, and the other resting gently on my low stomach. The friction of his facial hair against my bare center only adds to the sensation, drawing me closer to ecstasy until I'm teetering on the edge again.

"Give into me," he groans against my core, the vibrations of his words shooting shockwaves of heat through my body.

If I could reply, I would tell him that I have no choice but to do just that. I'm not holding anything back. I'm terrified of my release because I've never been so tense in my life. A gust of wind could break the dam of my orgasm.

I suck hard on the panties to keep me from making noise as his hand pulls on the clamps. The other presses firmly on my abdomen while his teeth graze my clit, and a roaring release explodes through me, deafening all of my senses as pleasure flies through me. My body soars through the abyss, leaving me completely unaware of anything around me, especially the party happening downstairs.

Faintly, I notice the tension in my breasts ease as Beau quickly removes the clamps and circles the bed, untying each of my limbs with practiced ease. If only it had been that easy for me to get out of them . . .

I lie there feeling exquisitely boneless as Beau places a tender kiss on my forehead. "Ready for the party?"

I offer him a hesitant smile. "If we must."

Turns out that an earth-shattering orgasm will temporarily alter your ability to perform basic tasks, like standing. Beau helps me dress, holding me upright as my legs regain their strength.

Glancing at myself in the mirror, I'm pleasantly surprised that my hair and makeup is still intact. Thank god for waterproof mascara or else I would be moonlighting as a clown for tonight's party entertainment.

As I'm stepping out of the bathroom, Beau's blazing eyes linger on my body, as if he didn't just see me naked. We didn't have time to take care of him, and I'm counting down the minutes until our guests leave so that we can go for round two.

"Did you bring me fresh panties?" I ask, suddenly aware of the slick wetness between my thighs.

A devious smirk plays on his lips. "Nope, and you aren't going to wear any. I want that soaked cunt dripping down your legs all night, reminding you of your lesson."

Ugh—if I wasn't already drenched, I am now.

"Fine," I concede, stepping into my heels as I hold his steady arm. "As long as you promise to teach me another one when everyone leaves tonight."

He chuckles, taking my hand in his as we head for the stairs. "Deal."

With just an hour left until midnight, we merge back into the party and no one is the wiser to our nefarious activities in the loft. Beau veers off to find his co-worker, Walker, while I busy myself in the kitchen and replenish the appetizer trays.

The chill of the evening is kept at bay by the rented gas heaters, creating a cozy atmosphere for everyone to savor the night air. The guests, dressed to the nines in their formal outfits, all look like they're enjoying themselves as they mingle and drink. I give myself a pat on the back—I totally killed this party.

Once the food is ready, I make my way through the crowd to find my sister and her friends from school. Despite Caroline favoring Parker, she'll always be my baby sister, and I love her immensely. It makes my heart soar to hear her laugh again. We've had a tough year, and I know Mom would be proud of how we've banded together as siblings. And I can't explain it, but something tells me that this next year will be our best one yet.

As I'm chatting with Caroline, Morgan comes bounding up to me, definitely tipsy as she complains that the outdoor bar is out of champagne. According to her, it's too much effort for her to go inside and get more bubbles.

"You good, Morg?" I ask, narrowing my eyes on her as I take in her disheveled state. The dark wisps that frame her face are clinging to her forehead, and the thin strap of her silver dress hangs off her shoulder, the sequins in a complete state of disarray.

"Just hot," she replies, fanning herself with her hand dramatically. "Alcohol blanket, you know?"

"Are *you* good?" she asks with a sly smirk as her eyes flick to Beau and back.

"Yep," I answer, avoiding her insinuation. "Gonna go get the bottles. Be back in a sec."

Rushing away from her, I make my way to the kitchen to restock and regroup. I haven't had a proper conversation with Morgan since she pieced together the situation with Beau and me. While I would love to have a more in-depth chat, something tells me that drunk Morg is not the most subtle individual.

As I'm pulling bottles of bubbly from the fridge, Cassidy exits the guest bathroom. Her eyes narrow on me in an expression I can't quite decipher.

"You look stunning," I squeal, choosing to ignore her look as I place the champagne on the counter and pull her into a hug. "God, do I have the best taste, or what?"

Her dress, a shimmering white mini, hugs her curves like it was tailor-made for her body, and the flowing, feather-trimmed sheer sleeves add an almost ethereal touch. I had it sent to her house yesterday, instructing my brother to keep it hidden until the party. Thank god I did, because I'm officially obsessed with the dress, and might steal it from her.

A slight blush creeps onto Cassidy's cheeks, though her lips remain pressed into a hard line. "Thanks for everything tonight. You didn't have to do all of this."

I frown as I begin to open a bottle of champagne for us. "Of course I did. As your maid of honor and bestie, it's part of the contractual duties."

Her hazel eyes roll as she fights a smile. "The maid of honor is also in charge of the bachelorette party, you know."

A shrill shriek escapes my throat as her words sink in, drawing concerned glances from a few people on the balcony. I wave my hand apologetically before turning back to Cassidy.

"Wait, are you serious right now? Does this mean I'm the one? You're honoring me as your maid?"

"If you still want to do it," she replies.

My hands fly to my mouth as I bend forward in my formal gown like a pageant queen. "Oh my god, yes. Cass! Wait—I have so many ideas. Let's get a glass of champagne and start planning. How do you feel about Cabo? Or we could do Las Vegas? They have those male strippers, and I've always wanted to go because they look so fun—"

"Claire," she cuts in, halting my audible train of consciousness. "We can definitely go through everything soon. But right now we need to chat."

Her expression shifts back to the serious, unreadable look from earlier, and a sense of unease settles in my stomach.

"Hang on," I say, managing to keep a smile on my face. "This feels like a conversation that requires champagne."

Cassidy gives a small, almost agonized nod as I pour two glasses of bubbly.

"Okay," I say, sucking in a deep breath to brace myself for whatever she's about to reveal. "What's up?"

She looks around the kitchen, ensuring we're alone. "How was Houston?"

I blink rapidly, trying to determine if I heard her correctly. "Uh, it was fine? Really hot for December, but it was a nice change of scenery."

The truth is, the trip was amazing. Staying at Beau's brother's house, lounging by the pool with his family, not having to keep our relationship a secret—all of it was perfect and made me fall even deeper for him.

But obviously, I can't share any of that, so I simply smile and add, "We had fun."

Cassidy's eyes are like lasers boring into me as she loudly whispers, "Are you out of your mind?"

My face falls, not understanding her. "Um . . ."

"You guys are hooking up," she states bluntly.

My legs wobble, threatening to give out. I definitely wouldn't have worn four-inch heels tonight if I had known this was how the evening would turn out.

"Who told you that?" I stammer, struggling to maintain my composure.

"Morgan," she admits, studying my reaction.

Not a snitch, my ass!

As I'm about to blurt out a nasty comment about Morgan, Cassidy interrupts me. "Don't be pissed at her. I forced her hand earlier tonight. She practically turned green when I casually mentioned something about you and Beau."

I roll my eyes, trying to redirect the conversation. "She would make a horrible spy. You're not even intimidating, and she cracked. Remind me to never give her any government secrets."

Cassidy ignores my joke. "Is it true?"

I sigh, knowing there's no way out of this.

"Okay, yes," I quietly hiss, pulling her close to me. "But it's not what you think. We're actually dating."

Her eyes widen as they shift to the floor. "Shit, that's worse. Since when?"

I step back, taking a long swig from the champagne glass before I respond. Now that the cat's out of the bag, I might as well be completely honest.

"A month or so . . . But please, don't tell P. We're planning on talking to him soon. You know how he can be."

She draws in a deep breath and releases it slowly, rubbing her temples as if a headache is brewing. "Why is it that I'm always in the middle of your family secrets?"

"Are you kidding me, Cass?" I quietly sneer, my eyes darting around us to make sure we're still alone. "You want to play that card? Want to tell me what the fuck is going on with the Weston thing?"

Her own secret keeping has been on my mind since Thanksgiving, and now seems like the perfect opportunity to address it. If she wants to toss blame around, I'll toss it right back.

Cassidy hesitates. "Not really."

I roll my eyes, offering her a small smile as a truce. "Too bad. I told you mine, you tell me yours."

She turns away briefly, reaching for her glass of champagne and downing it in a single gulp.

Oh, so it's that kind of secret.

"Okay, so you know everything that happened last year, right?" she starts. I nod, remembering the tangled web of drama between her, Weston, and my brother.

Cass crosses her arms and leans back against the counter. "And you know how Parker is very . . ." she pauses, trying to get the words right before continuing. "Parker sees things in black and white."

I laugh because of course I know that—it's what makes him a great doctor but an incredibly irritating older brother. "Yes, dummy. I know that all too well."

She lets out a long, deep exhale. "Well obviously, things with Wes are shades of gray."

I can't suppress a small grin at her choice of words, and she shakes her head. "Stop it, Claire! Not like that, good god!"

"Sorry, sorry. You've corrupted me!"

I refill Cassidy's champagne, tilting the flute to ensure the drink doesn't sizzle over the rim. "So what's the status?" I ask, handing her the cold bubbles.

She takes a tentative sip, shutting her eyes briefly before she speaks. "Something happened that made Wes leave his fellowship. He didn't elaborate on what it was, but he's been home in Atlanta trying to figure out what he's going to do next. Wes and my brother were best friends growing up, so naturally, his mom and I developed a bond. When Mrs. Southerland reached out, I felt obligated to meet up with them, despite everything that happened last year. It was like something was urging me to go. So I listened, and I don't know how to explain it . . . but he seems genuinely different. He showed glimpses of the person I remember from our childhood, not the arrogant jerk he had become."

Cass stops, a wave of emotion fogging her eyes as she looks away.

I watch her, wishing I could take her pain away. I know she's thinking of her brother.

She gulps, choking down a sob. "Carter and Wes were like brothers, Claire. I have to forgive Wes for his sake . . . it's the right thing to do. And it's not like there's anything between me and Wes other than friendship. You know I love Parker more than anything. You *know* that. But, I'm also desperately trying to cling to anything that keeps my brother's memory alive. Despite everything, Wes does that for me."

I pull her into my arms, my hand soothingly stroking her back. "I know. I completely get it."

"But Parker," she chokes, burying her face into the crook of my neck. "He—"

"Cass, it's okay," I reassure her firmly, my arms tightening around her. "Trust me, Parker will understand."

We stand there for a moment as silence settles between us. This is probably the worst place to be discussing this, but I'm glad we were both able to get things off our chests. I already feel a million times lighter, and I'm sure she does too.

Eventually, Cassidy steps back, her face flushed with the rawness of her emotions. "Sorry."

I brush away her apology with a light-hearted wave. "Hey, that's what maid of honors are for," I say, trying to inject a bit of cheer into the somber moment. "Well, that, and holding your wedding dress up when you have to pee."

Her chin wobbles as she stares at the floor.

Desperate to add some levity to the conversation, I add, "How about we team up and spill our secrets to Parker together? Hit him with a double whammy."

Cass lets out a forced laugh, her fingers dabbing beneath her long lashes to keep the tears at bay.

"No, no, you go ahead," she insists, reaching for her glass to finish the rest of the champagne. "I've got plenty of time to talk to Parker. And it sounds like you guys aren't as secretive as you thought, so it's probably best that you break the news before he finds out through the grapevine."

I playfully swat at her arm. "We're the *most* secretive."

"Uh-huh. Where were you earlier?"

My cheeks heat. "Don't worry about it."

She gives me a knowing glance and teases, "Oh yes, *so* secretive."

I ignore her comment as Cassidy straightens her posture and takes a deep breath. "How do I look? Ready to brave the crowd again?"

"You're perfect," I assure her, my words carrying more meaning than she knows. "Let's get drunk."

Cassidy is everything I could have ever asked for in a sister-in-law. Not only is she an amazing friend and confidant, but she loves my brother fiercely. She's changed him for the better over the past year and a half, and I know he realizes it too, which is how I know everything will be fine between them.

Cassidy reaches out, her fingers gently squeezing mine. "If it matters, I'm genuinely happy for you. But, I'm still pissed that Morg knew before me."

I can't help but grin as we join the party a few minutes before midnight. She'll forgive me—after all, I am her favorite sister.

CHAPTER 42

BEAU

Once I rejoined the party, Parker pulled Walker and me aside to ask about the incident in the operating room. Walker remained stoically silent, leaving the decision to divulge the details to me. Considering Parker isn't just a colleague, but one of my best friends, I saw no harm in giving him a rundown of the event. I even told him about my diabetes and how I taught his sister to inject me with insulin, hoping it might win me some favor when the time comes to tell him about our relationship.

As I expected, Parker's response was nothing but supportive. He even shared a story about a similar experience one of his residents had to make me feel better. The great thing about our career path is that we all understand the expectations and struggles of surgery. It may be a ruthless journey, but there's comfort in knowing we're all on the same team, fighting the same enemy.

By the time our conversation ended, we realized we were far too sober compared to the rest of the guests. Walker insisted we each down a shot of whisky for each year we've been practicing surgery. With only one year under my belt, the alcohol barely fazed me, thanks to my size and naturally high tolerance. Parker, however, was sloshed after his six shots, and Walker wasn't too far behind him.

Drunk Parker is genuinely one of my favorite things in the world. His personality does a complete transformation, evolving into a man overflowing with compliments and affirmations for everyone around him. I couldn't help but laugh as I watched him approach a physician hates and begin showering them with praise. It's like stepping into a bizarre, alternate universe, but I'm not complaining one bit because it's entertaining as hell.

At the moment, Parker and Walker are locked in an enthusiastic argument about the worst insurance company for prior approvals. I'm only half-listening as I nurse my beer. Truthfully, I don't really give a shit. They all suck.

"Buffington," Parker drawls with a heavy slur, looping his arm around my shoulder. "Back me up, bro."

"You're both right," I respond. Choosing between two of the most stubborn people I know isn't going to win me any favors.

Walker animatedly throws his hands in the air. "Fucking cop-out. You suck, Buff."

He's never shortened my last name like that, nor has he shown this much emotion in conversation, which is how I know that my chief resident is also very, very drunk.

I was surprised to not see Walker's wife tonight since significant others were on the guest list. He hasn't said anything about her recently, but he's not a sharer so I haven't wanted to push it. I'll just assume things are getting better unless he tells me otherwise.

Parker gives my shoulder a friendly squeeze. "Yeah, you suck, Buff."

My hand scrubs over my face. I'm definitely not drunk enough for this.

Parker suddenly grins, as if struck by a moment of intoxicated inspiration. "Hey Walker," he says, his smile broadening, "what's the definition of a double-blind study?"

Walker blinks at him, his dark eyes flashing with annoyance, as if he's just been asked the most absurd question. "What is this, a pop quiz?"

But Parker, undeterred, delivers the punchline with glee. "It's two ortho interns looking at an EKG together."

There's a brief pause as Walker processes the joke, and then he erupts into a robust, genuine laugh. Parker joins him, slapping him on the back as they struggle to catch their breath.

I let out a resigned sigh, letting my eyes wander along the balcony in search of Claire. I haven't seen her since we rejoined the party, and even though our relationship requires discretion, I'm hoping to at least catch a glimpse of my girl before the ball drops.

"Did someone say Jimmy's after we ring in the new year?" Morgan calls to the crowd, drawing my attention as Cassidy sneaks up next to me.

Jimmy's, a notorious bar in Buckhead, is a melting pot of diverse clientele, with a notable inclination towards the sugar daddy scene. While it's a great time for people-watching, there's usually a massive line and a cover, making it miserable on a busy night. There's no way in hell you could convince me to go on New Year's Eve.

"I'm game," Walker shouts, his voice carrying through the crowd as he takes a hearty sip of his neat whisky.

"Nah," Parker adds, pulling Cass into his arms as he nuzzles his bride-to-be. "I've got the only woman I need right here."

Cassidy's cheeks bloom bright red as Parker murmurs something in her ear that makes Walker wince and swiftly down the rest of his scotch.

"Hey, roomie," Claire says casually, bumping her champagne glass against mine. She looks fucking phenomenal tonight in the shiny, form-fitting dress, and it's taking all of my willpower to not react to her.

"Isn't that sweet," Parker gushes, his glassy eyes settling between us. "My sister and my best friend, getting along. Who would have thought?"

I manage a nod, carefully avoiding his probing eyes. "Yep, definitely a surprise."

Leaning in, Cassidy whispers to Claire and me, "Speaking of surprises, would you mind if we crash at the condo tonight? I don't see Parker making it anywhere other than to bed after this."

"It's no prob—" I start saying as Cassidy blurts, "Unless you two are using the master bedroom . . ."

Her expression conveys a deeper meaning, and my eyes flash to Claire for clarification.

She simply shrugs before scrunching up her nose in a look of disgust. "Oh god, stop. You know I don't dare set foot in that sex room. The ghosts of orgasms past probably haunt the walls."

Parker's ears perk up, a mischievous twinkle in his eyes as he draws Cassidy closer again. "Someone say orgasms?"

Claire nearly sputters her champagne, and I quickly pat her back, my hand lingering just a moment too long at the base of her spine.

Morgan's voice pierces through the air. "One minute to midnight!"

She's standing on top of a makeshift beer pong table, commanding the crowd's attention. Walker, breaking away from our group, has made his way to the party queen, taking alternate pulls from the Makers Mark bottle with her. I have no idea how they're getting along—Walker barely likes me, let alone anyone else. But for some reason, he's been staring at her all night like a damn psycho.

With Parker distracted and nuzzling sweet nothings into Cassidy's neck, I take the moment to lean into Claire.

"You're the only person I want at midnight," I whisper, my voice barely audible. "This midnight. And all of our midnights."

Claire's cheeks flush a delicate shade of pink as she meets my gaze, her eyes shimmering with desire. The countdown continues around us, voices growing louder as the seconds tick away.

Raising her glass in the air, she clinks it against mine as she murmurs, "To all of our midnights."

Chapter 43

Beau

"I swear to God, Buffington, if you sew any slower that wound is going to heal on its own," Parker sneers from the other side of the table.

I pause and mutter an obscenity under my breath before returning to my work. This is one of the most complicated stitches in surgical practice, so fucking forgive me for taking my time with it.

Casting a glance at the large, clinical clock mounted on the sterile white wall, I note the time. We still have thirty minutes until our monthly surgical meeting where we discuss department updates and difficult cases. That's plenty of time to finish up here and make it without rushing.

Parker's been on my ass all morning for some reason completely beyond me. It makes absolutely no sense, especially considering he was the one who requested my assistance. Typically when I'm on his service, we have a blast. He's relaxed, and we joke around throughout the cases. But today, he's been inexplicably harsh, treating me worse than his interns.

"What was that?" Parker probes sharply, clearly hearing what I mumbled.

As I secure the final stitch, deftly tying it off, I set down the needle holder with a controlled clink on the tray next to me.

"Wasn't your New Year's resolution to be nicer?" I ask, nodding toward my sutures so that he can check my work. "Because we're already a week in, and I see no evidence of change."

The scrub tech standing next to me tries to stifle a laugh, and I'm thankful for the mask covering my own smirk. I'm funny as fuck.

This is my first day seeing Parker since the engagement party. I've been ridiculously busy with trauma service, and the plan was to stay there for the month, which is why I was surprised that he requested me this morning. Typically, when we don't see each other at work, we still talk shit on our favorite chess app, but he's been unusually silent there too. I've just assumed that it was because he was working a shit ton, but now I'm starting to wonder if something else is going on.

Parker leans in to inspect my work, his eyes narrowing as he examines the sutures. For a moment, I'm convinced he's going to find some fault, but then he grunts in approval, his eye twitching as he looks up from the incision.

"We're done here. See you at the meeting," he announces briskly, turning on his heel and exiting the OR with an air of urgency.

I exchange a quick glance with the circulating nurse, who's been quietly observing from her station.

"Alright, guess we're done. Happy New Year, everyone," I say before I book it out of the surgical suite.

By the time I catch up with him, Parker is waiting for the elevator, his foot tapping impatiently as he stares straight ahead.

I clap my hand on his back. "Everything good? You seem a little off, buddy."

Parker shrugs away from my touch, keeping his gaze fixed on the closed metal doors in front of us. I know we joke that we always look like shit, but he really does look terrible today. Deep bags shadow his blue eyes, and a week's worth of stubble covers his jaw, as if he hasn't bothered with a razor since the party.

My stomach drops. Did he find out about Cassidy's meetup with Weston? Claire filled me in on the situation the morning after the party, taking over an hour to intricately describe the dynamics of their history. While I can't say that I care for the drama as much as she does, it definitely sounds like a nightmare. Not that Cass would ever do anything to hurt Parker—she's madly in love with him.

The elevator dings open, breaking the heavy silence between us as Parker steps on, still not acknowledging me.

I follow him in, reaching over to press the button for the top floor where our department meeting awaits.

"Seriously, man, what's up?" I press, turning to face him.

Parker's eyes remain rooted in place as if in a trance, though his hand digs into his pocket. As the elevator announces our arrival with another chime, he hesitates for a moment before finally turning to face me, his nostrils flaring with a deep breath. Instead of offering any words, he takes a crumpled piece of paper from his scrub pocket and hands it to me before stepping out of the elevator.

My heart pounds as I stand motionless, holding the note. Somehow I know what it contains before I even look. In theory, it could be one of the early, harmless notes that I wrote to Claire, but the look in Parker's eyes tells a different story. With a forced breath to steady myself, I carefully unfold the paper, bracing myself for what's written inside.

> ***Got you a new coffee creamer called Italian***
> ***Sweet Cream.***
> ***Doubt it's as sweet as the cream that's gonna***
> ***come out of your pussy when I lick that perfect***
> ***cunt.***
> ***See you soon,***
> ***Bad boy Beau***

Fuck me.

Claire started calling me Bad Boy Beau as my alter ego, a subtle nod to one of our first conversations when I first moved into the condo. She only uses it in a sexual context and I fucking love it—I love showing her how bad I can be.

But, of course, out of all of the notes I've written her with sweet nothings on them, Parker had to find the most sexually explicit one. It makes me look like fucking pervert, not a man so deep in love with his sister that I'd literally give up everything to make her happy.

When Parker and Cassidy stayed at the condo after the engagement party, it didn't even occur to me to hide the notes. I actually had forgotten Claire even kept them in the drawer beneath the coffee maker. What are the chances that out of all of the cabinets in the massive kitchen, he would open the one with damning evidence?

Apparently, very high . . . because it fucking happened.

Claire was planning on talking to him only two days from now at their family dinner. Their youngest sister's New Year's resolution was to have a monthly meetup, and I know Claire was probably hoping her sister would mediate and soften the blow.

Unfortunately, it looks like that won't be necessary because Parker definitely knows.

I jog after him, trying to figure out how to clarify things.

"Wait up," I call, brushing past a few colleagues on their way to the large conference room.

Parker's pace slows when he rounds the corner to an empty hallway, fury practically radiating through the air. He turns to face me, knuckles cracking as his hands grip into tight fists at his side.

There's no fucking way he would hit me. Right?

Not here, at least . . .

"I can explain," I start, my voice controlled like I'm diffusing a ticking time bomb. "Claire planned on telling you this weekend."

His fingers flex, eyes burning into mine. But my best friend still doesn't speak, he just watches me like a general sizing up their opponent before battle.

"I swear it's not just just sex," I continue, considering how much to say. "I promise, man. I fucking love her."

Parker's jaw clenches before he asks, "How long?"

I pause, not expecting the question.

"Uh, well, we hooked up once months ago, but then your mom died, and I thought Claire hated me. I wanted to talk to you about it before we got together again in November, but after your joke at the intern retreat . . . I wasn't sure how you'd react. Plus, she asked if we could keep it between us."

The words come out like a waterfall of relief. I've been wanting to have this conversation for so long, but I had to respect Claire's wishes. Even if he's pissed, it feels good to finally have everything out in the open.

"Un-fucking-believeable," Parker mutters, more to himself than to me. His death glare stings after everything we've been through, and I can't tell if he's angry with me, his sister, or both of us.

I shift my feet, suddenly feeling less confident as I let him work through his emotions.

Finally, Parker lets out an exaggerated breath that rattles on his thinly pressed lips. "End it."

The muscles in my chest tighten. Surely he can't want that—not after everything she's been through this year. Out of anyone to be with his sister, there's nobody better than me—nobody who will cherish her like I do.

"Sorry?" I ask, certain I misheard him.

"End it," he repeats in a carefully controlled tone. "That's a fucking order."

Without hesitation, I reply, "Fuck no."

The air between us feels cold, filled with an icy tension that's on the verge of cracking into a thousand pieces. Parker's not used to being told no, especially not in his hospital, on his domain. But right now, it doesn't matter that he's more tenured or more experienced than I am—there's no fucking way I'm following his bullshit orders.

This has nothing to do with work.

This is personal.

A thick vein on Parker's forehead pulses as his eyes narrow in challenge. "Then you leave me no choice," he sneers, storming away in the direction of his meeting.

I have no idea what he's getting at, but I take a few moments to collect myself in the quiet hallway before going to join my coworkers in the auditorium.

Despite the massive confrontation we just had, a wave of serenity washes over me as I slump into a chair at the back of the room. It feels like a glorious weight off my chest now that I no longer have to sneak around with my girl. I've been wanting to take her out, to show her off. Sometimes when I'm in a long case, I'll picture my future with Claire. Undoubtedly, some of those images are kinky as hell—I am a man after all—but there are so many things I want to experience with her.

And I'm just so thankful that we finally can.

Parker will get over it eventually, I'm sure. He's just in shock right now, reacting with the emotional capacity of a two-year-old. Once Claire explains, he'll have to come to terms with our relationship.

"You good, Buff?" Walker asks, settling into the seat next to me.

"That's the stupidest fucking nickname," I grumble, crossing my ankle over my leg to get comfortable. "How do you even remember it? You were hammered."

"I'm a drunk ninja" he replies as he leans forward to pull out his notebook. "You think I'm on one level, but really I'm somewhere else."

"Yeah, you were really somewhere else when I found you in the kitchen funneling beers with Morgan."

He grimaces, drawing his eyes to the department chair who has walked up to the podium. "Yeah, that one hurt the next morning."

I let out a soft laugh before focusing on the presentation. Typically we go over the department initiatives first, reviewing new policies and procedures before diving into the cases. There's some bullshit about billing and insurance that I only half listen to, because I don't really have to worry about it until next year when I start taking cases on my own.

"I'd like to welcome our newest attending, Dr. Parker Winters, to the podium. He's going to review our safety case of the month," the department chair says after a while. "We haven't had one recently, but he graciously agreed to step in at the last minute with a great example for discussion. Dr. Winters, the floor is yours."

My eyes snap up to the stage, landing on Parker's smug face as the room claps for him. "You all know how this goes, but for the new kids on the block, this is similar to the difficult case list discussion-wise. Feel free to chime in as we review."

Parker changes the slide, projecting redacted patient information onto the large screen. I scan the details, nausea beginning to twist through my stomach as I realize which case we're reviewing.

"Dr. Chastain, I believe this was your patient," he says, flicking his eyes in our direction. "Would you like to present? Or should I?"

Walker's body visibly tightens next to me as he stands, clearly not expecting this.

"Thank you, Dr. Winters. I didn't prepare anything, but would be happy to give a brief overview to the class." Hush laughter fills the room at his sarcasm, though his tone is anything close to humorous.

"This was a thirty-year-old male with a double fracture to the tibia and talus. We went in to do an ORIF, but found a second fracture and had to get repeat imaging once the patient was on the table. As of today, the patient is almost one-month post-op and recovering without issue."

Parker's eyes narrow in a silent invitation to continue, but Walker defiantly sits down, cueing that he's done discussing the case.

"Dr. Chastain, did anything unusual happen during surgery?"

Walker dryly states, "Not that I'm aware of. As I stated, the patient is recovering without complications."

Parker doubles down, leaning into the podium. "Is that so? Because from what I understand, one of your interns collapsed at the table, placing the patient at risk for infection."

Hushed murmurs fill the room. I guess if everyone didn't already know, now they do.

"I don't see what that has to do with the case," Walker challenges, his tone controlled despite the slight tick in his jaw. "The patient was unharmed and given standard antibiotic prophylaxis during the post-op period."

"It was a safety incident. We're here to discuss the safety of our patients and our physicians. Let's discuss how this could have been prevented."

My mind goes hazy as several physicians pipe up, asking questions and providing suggestions. Walker fields all of them with his usual composure and expertise, not giving off that he's bothered in any way.

Once Parker decides that he's had enough, he thanks the audience for their input. As he turns to leave the stage, he pauses to add, "Before we conclude, I'd like to remind everyone that it is against hospital policy to refuse to disclose a medical condition on your employment health exam. Blatantly refusing to follow the policy may result in probation, or in severe cases, dismissal."

My heart practically stops.

The fucker is blackmailing me.

Chapter 44

Beau

In the elevator on our way to the ortho locker room, Walker breaks the silence. "You good to take the consult in the ER? I've got a mountain of paperwork in my inbox thanks to Parker's little tantrum."

I sigh, exhaustion washing over me as I lean against the elevator's back wall. "Sorry about all of that."

He doesn't look up from his phone. "Not your fault."

It's actually entirely my fault, but I don't say that. If I hadn't gotten involved with Parker's sister, Walker wouldn't have been put on blast in front of the entire department, and my best friend and I would be on speaking terms. I have absolutely no idea how I'm going to get out of this one. Either I break up with Claire and keep my job, or I stay with her and lose the one thing I've worked for my whole life.

"Thanks for sticking up for me back there," I say as the doors open to the floor of the emergency room. "It means a lot."

Walker's chocolate eyes meet mine briefly before returning to his email. "You're my guy."

The ER is a beehive of activity, with doctors and nurses moving around with urgency. As I approach the nurses' station to check in, I notice Morgan sitting casually at the desk, typing away on her computer as if the chaos around her is nothing more than white noise.

"Happy New Year," I greet her, leaning my elbows on the counter across from her. "How was your hangover?"

Her green eyes glance up at me, clearly unamused by my interruption. Normally she'd be eating up the distraction, bantering back and forth with me for a while, but today her gaze quickly returns to the screen.

"Hangovers are for the weak," she states simply.

I chuckle, pulling out my pager to check my patient's location. "I think being young helps too."

"You're only a year older than me, dumbass," Morgan retorts, tucking her hair behind her ear before adding, "Sorry, busy day."

"Someone finally making you work around here?" I tease.

She lowers her mask and sticks out her tongue at me. "I just feel bad for Claire. Shitty day to start her externship. I've got her running around looking for a bladder scanner right now because I think the fucking ICU nurses stole ours."

The morning's been such a whirlwind that I totally forgot Claire was around today. The nurse manager called her a few days ago and asked when she could start. Since school doesn't begin for another week, she suggested today to get her feet wet before her schedule gets hectic.

"I'll make it up to her tonight in bed," I joke, trying to put us both in a better mood.

Morgan rolls her eyes and waves me off. "God, you're so fucking gross. Get out of here."

I chuckle, already feeling slightly better as I navigate through the chaos to find my patient. I'm looking forward to getting home so that I can hear about how Claire's first day was. She was so excited when she got the job offer, immediately rushing out to the store to buy an arsenal of scrubs and supplies. Her enthusiasm is infectious and one of the things I love the most about her. There's no fucking way I'm letting her go.

Fortunately, the consult isn't an ortho case so I passed off the patient to general and snake back through the ER. On my way out, an idea pops into my head.

I called Parker's bluff and lost the hand. Now I've got to play my ace.

"Is Cass working today?" I ask Morgan while she's frantically trying to untangle the EKG machine leads.

Letting out a pained sigh she says, "Yeah, the lucky bitch is on triage probably reading her damn Kindle."

Thanking her, I maneuver around a group of med students with overwhelmed expressions on their faces.

Been there guys—it'll get better.

True to Morgan's prediction, Cassidy is stationed at the triage desk, but she's far from lost in her Kindle. Instead, I find her attentively engaging with a middle-aged woman who's raising her voice at her. I momentarily think about stepping in, but Cassidy seems to have everything under control, exuding a sense of calm and empathy as she handles the heated exchange with remarkable poise. The woman eventually exhausts herself and offers an apology before retreating to the waiting area.

"Hey, Cass," I say, leaning against the open door of the circular triage desk.

She spins in my direction, looking just as drained as I feel. Glad to know everyone's having a shitty day, and it's not just me.

"Hey, Buff," she teases, knowing how much I hate the nickname. "Come to take some of this shit off my hands?"

I grimace, imagining the day she's had. "Well, you're definitely not reading your Kindle with your feet propped up like Morgan suggested."

Cassidy rolls her brown-gold eyes, her hands running through her hair to tighten her high ponytail. "She's so clueless. I don't know why she thinks triage is the easiest assignment."

"Wanna take a break?" I suggest, hoping she can find some time or get someone to cover for her. I'm not one to let emotions fester, so I need to nip this shit with Parker in the bud before it goes any further.

Her eyes light up with the idea. "It's like you read my mind. Give me ten to grab our charge, and I'll meet you by the elevators."

I take the time to write a short note about my consult and catch up on my emails. Fortunately, I haven't been bombarded with shit like Walker has. Technically, I still practice under his license until next year, so he's responsible for everything I do within the walls of the hospital. It sucks that Parker's outburst added another thing to his plate, and I'll definitely have to take him out for drinks once this storm passes.

When Cass meets up with me, I quickly explain the situation to her now that I know she's aware of my relationship with Claire. She listens attentively, allowing me to get it all out before she simply scoffs and takes my hand, leading me through the hospital in the direction of Parker's office.

His door is closed, but Cassidy barges right through, not bothering to knock or check for visitors. Her boldness doesn't surprise me one bit—she's not one to shy away from confrontation. It's something I've always admired about her.

As we enter the office Parker looks up from his desk, his expression unreadable. When Claire described him as robotic, she was spot on. The man maintains an iron grip on his emotions, like a damn monk.

"This had better be a fucking joke," Cassidy snaps, her grip tightening on my arm like a protective mother.

Parker squints at her, assessing the situation. "I'm a little busy here."

"The fuck you are," she snarls, kicking the office door partially closed like she knows this is about to get heated. "Are you out of your damn mind? Because you'd have to be clinically insane to threaten your best friend's career just because he's dating your sister."

"It wasn't a threat, per se," Parker clarifies, casually leaning back in his chair as if he's amused by her rage.

Cassidy releases my arm and moves closer to him, her eyes blazing with fire. I want to chime in, but right now the two of them are locked into their own version of a dogfight, and I know better than to intervene.

"Oh really?" Cass challenges, refusing to back down. "Not a threat? Want to tell me what it was then?"

The corners of his lips twitch as he holds her gaze. "A suggestion."

Cassidy takes a deep breath, like she's summoning all of the patience in the world. "You're so fucking delusional sometimes, Parker. Haven't you seen how happy Claire's been in the past few months?"

Parker shrugs, not responding to her question.

"Do you want to know why?" Cass continues, her voice shaking with frustration. "Because of him! Your best friend!"

She points at me, her chest heaving with frustration as she snaps her head back to her fiancé.

"You can't control every aspect of your life, and you certainly can't control your sister. God knows you've tried." Cassidy lets out an exasperated laugh before continuing. "She's as wild as they come, and perfectly capable of making her own decisions."

Parker's eyes flick to mine, and he remarks, "He's just a playboy who's just going to hurt her again."

The words drive a knife into my heart. He can't really think that, can he?

Cassidy's voice escalates as she argues, "And it would hurt her more to force him to break up with her? Did you even fucking think that one through?"

I can't hold back any longer. I lock eyes with Parker and speak earnestly, "I haven't touched another woman since I met your sister, months ago. I haven't even thought about another woman. Claire has me in a goddamn vice, man. She's all I think about. All I dream about. She's become the most important thing in my life. She's always going to be the most important thing in my life. You don't understand. I don't just love her—I adore her."

Parker's eyes flash with emotion but quickly darken again. "Doesn't matter. You'll never change."

I don't know why Parker has this playboy image of me. Sure, I hooked up with women, but I didn't do anything more outrageous than he did. It's irritating that he's just as guilty of sleeping around, yet somehow, I'm the one saddled with the reputation.

"You changed when you met me," Cassidy offers, her tone more controlled.

"That was different."

"Oh, was it?" she snaps, leaning against his desk. "Because I actually think they're in much better shape than we were at this point."

Cassidy's voice lowers as she adds, "Do I need to remind you of that morning in the penthouse hallway?"

I have no idea what they're talking about, but Parker's expression shifts as he redirects his anger to her.

"Do I need to remind *you* of that morning?" he retorts, throwing her words back at her. "Because right now I can think of several ways to do that. You just might not like them."

A tense silence hangs in the air, neither of them willing to back down as they hold each other's gaze. I have to hand it to Cass, she handles his rage with grace, clearly experienced in de-escalating his moods. Most people would retreat under his icy glare, but she actually moves closer to him.

"The point, my love, is that they're clearly serious," Cass says, gently rubbing her hand over his shoulder. "They respect each other, and are acting a hell of a lot more mature in their relationship than we did."

Parker visibly relaxes under her touch but grumbles, "Oh, so keeping secrets is mature?"

I had a suspicion that my best friend's frustration was more related to the fact that we didn't clue him in on our relationship and less about my character. If Claire's bad about verbalizing her emotions, Parker is even worse. It makes sense that he would deflect the hurt and instead hurl insults. So while his words sting, I completely understand.

"Can you blame them?"

Parker's shoulders slump as Cassidy's words sink in. He seems torn between his frustration and his love for her.

Eventually, his navy eyes flick up to mine, softer than they were moments ago. "I really will ruin your career if you fuck this up."

I grin, a wave of relief washing over me. "And I'd happily let you, because she's worth ruining everything for."

Chapter 45

Claire

I've been running around like a chicken with its head cut off all morning, learning the ropes in a whirlwind of activity. The ER is overwhelming yet exhilarating, and for the first time ever, I feel like I truly belong somewhere.

All of the staff members, especially the nurses, have been incredibly welcoming. It's a wildly diverse group of people from all walks of life, and I can't wait to get to know them better. Most of them have no filter, just like me. They throw out curse words as often as they use normal words, and while my vocabulary isn't quite as colorful, I feel right at home, knowing I've finally found my people.

Even though I start school next week, I'm planning to pick up a shift once a week, assuming it works with my schedule. The manager has been incredibly accommodating, offering flexibility without a strict commitment. She told me to take my time and do what was best for me, but I'm already obsessed. I want to be here all of the time.

I've been shadowing Morgan all day because Cassidy is working at the triage desk. We've seen a ridiculous number of patients, and it baffles me how much knowledge Morgan has about various diseases. She'll see a patient and instantly diagnose them, almost like she has some sort of telepathy with their organs. It's intimidating, but I try to remind myself that it's only my first day and she's been doing this for years.

I just spent the last thirty minutes searching for something called a bladder scanner. Morgan accused another department of stealing it, but it was really just hidden behind a bunch of other machines in the corner of an equipment room.

"Found it," I announce, wheeling the scanner over to her.

Morgan's emerald eyes light up, like I've just delivered a block of gold, not a machine to check urinary retention. "You're my angel. Thank you so much."

I can't help but smile, feeling useful despite my inexperience.

"I'll show you how to use this later. Could you go check on Cass? She went AWOL with Beau a while ago, and she promised to help me put in this damn foley. I don't understand how I can put a twenty-tw0 in a severely dehydrated patient, but I can't find the fucking urethra."

My lips purse, wondering what they're up to. I assumed I would see Beau at some point today, but he's apparently been in surgery all morning. I must have just missed him when he came to talk to Cass.

"Sure," I nod, dropping to the floor to re-tie my new tennis shoes. They're cute, but not very comfortable, and definitely not practical if the laces won't stay tied. "Know where they went?"

"Parker's office," she responds, her gaze flicking to mine in warning. "She looked pretty upset."

A wave of anxiety washes over me and I try to steel myself for whatever I'll find. If my brother upset her, I'll kick his ass.

The hospital corridors feel like a labyrinth as I navigate my way toward the physician's offices and on-call rooms, relying on the faint memory of our Christmas Day visit to guide me. As I turn a corner, I hear raised voices filtering through a partially open door nearby. The unmistakable southern drawl of Beau's voice drifts into the hallway, but his words are muffled and indistinct.

Pushing open the door, I see Cassidy sitting on my brother's lap, her arms wrapped around his shoulder. Beau leans against the wall opposite them, his hands in his pockets as he says, "She's worth ruining everything for."

Three pairs of eyes land on me and I feel all of the blood drain from my face. The tension in the room is palpable, and I find myself whispering, "He found out."

The words come out of my lips as a statement, rather than a question. I don't know how I know, but I do.

Beau nods, his eyes meeting mine with a warmth that puts me at ease. Everything must be okay if he's looking at me like that.

I step further into the room, my heart racing with a mixture of fear and relief. Slowly, I turn my gaze to my brother who begrudgingly mutters, "We worked it out. Though you should probably start calling him bitch boy Beau based on how whipped he is."

Parker gives Beau a salacious wink, only to receive a head shake and a chuckle in response.

My eyes snap back to Parker, a hesitant grin forming on my lips. "You're okay with this, then?"

"I wouldn't use the word *okay*, exactly. But Cass so aptly reminded me that I've never been able to control you, dear sister. Nor should I try."

Parker pauses for a beat, looking over at Beau in warning.

"Plus, he knows that I hold the keys to his kingdom in my hands, should he decide to fuck anything up."

I ignore my brother's protective threat and rush over to pull him into my arms. "I love you, P."

We stand there for a moment before Beau chimes in. "Yeah, love you *brother*." He drags out the last word teasingly.

Parker steps back from our hug, shooting Beau a glare. "Easy there."

Beau's face erupts in a cocky smile. "What? You don't wanna be my *brother*?"

"Shove it," Parker snaps, tossing a crude gesture in Beau's direction.

Laughter fills the room, dissolving any lingering tension. I'll have to grill Beau later about how my brother found out, but for now, it's a relief to return to our normal interactions. While I haven't felt guilty for living in our bubble of love, it'll definitely be nice to not have to keep secrets anymore.

"How'd you find us?" Cass asks, looking at me curiously.

"Morg mentioned you guys were in Parker's office," I respond with a casual shrug. "Figured it was near Beau's."

Parker narrows his eyes on mine. "Isn't today, like, your first day? How could you even know where . . . you're fucking kidding me." He pauses as the realization dawns on him, a mortified expression washing over his pale face.

My eyes find Beau's as I giggle. "Don't ask questions you don't want to know."

A proud grin forms on Beau's lips, clearly enjoying the shock wave we've sent through my brother. "You're the one who put two and two together, man."

Parker finally snaps out of his daze, his hands raking through his hair in exasperation. "What is this, a double team? Come on, Cass, take my side here."

He turns to her, seeking an ally, but she just shrugs, uncommitted. "After today? I'm not sure you've earned my support."

I glance at her, curious for more details, but she's locked in a silent exchange with her fiancé. Whatever they're communicating, I just hope it's not anything sexual.

Parker's attention shifts back to Beau, as he lets out a heavy sigh. "I'm sorry for what happened this morning. I overreacted—"

He hesitates, loathing emotional conversations just like me.

I have no idea what happened between Beau and Parker today, but I can count on one hand the number of times I've heard my brother apologize to someone else, so it must have been serious. I'm sure Beau will fill me in on the details later, but the fact that he's standing here with an amused expression on his face rather than one of rage, speaks volumes about his character. Beau's not one to let conflict wedge itself between the people he loves. And for some reason, one that I'm forever grateful for, Beau loves us.

"I hope you know what I said at the intern retreat was a joke," Parker continues. "There are a shit ton of people who I wouldn't want Claire to date. You're not even on the list."

I scoff. "Like you have a say."

Cassidy rolls her lips over her teeth to stifle a grin as my brother looks over at me. His face is pained, and he looks like he needs a long nap. "I'm sorry if I made you feel like you couldn't talk to me, Claire. You need to know that you can come to me with anything. You can tell me anything."

"What if I told you that you can be a real asshole sometimes?"

Parker lets out a deep exhale. "You'd be right."

My lips turn upwards, not used to hearing those words from my brother. "What if I told you that you don't always know everything?"

His blue eyes narrow in warning, but he admits, "You'd be right."

A full smile forms on my face. "And what if —"

"Claire. My patience has already cracked once today, do you want to keep testing it?"

"What patience?" I ask, taunting my brother, like any little sister would.

"I feel like now's a good time to take your side, man," Beau chuckles, shaking his head at me. "She tests my patience every damn day too."

I giggle, noticing the admiration in Beau's eyes. "It's too easy sometimes."

Beau grins as he shifts his attention to Parker, stretching his massive arms out. "Come over here and give brother Beau an apology hug."

Parker rolls his eyes but there's a reluctant smile tugging at the corners of his lips. He steps into Beau's embrace, and they share what might be the most awkward yet heartfelt hug I've ever witnessed. I'm pretty sure I even hear my brother apologize again, and I just wish I could get this on camera to replay when he no doubt reverts to his domineering ways.

As they break apart, Beau claps Parker on the shoulder. "We're all good, I promise. It's water under the bridge."

Parker gives a nod, his expression betraying a fleeting surge of emotion before settling back into a composed calm. Alright," Parker says firmly, shifting his gaze between the three of us. "We're done with secrets, understood?"

I'm about to respond with a sassy comeback when a man with neatly swept sandy hair appears in the doorway. He's dressed in navy scrubs, standing taller than Parker but not quite as tall as Beau. His eyes are identical to Cassidy's in color—a deep, rich hazel.

"What did I miss?" he asks, a sly smile on his thin lips as he stares directly at my sister-in-law.

Cassidy's face drains of color the moment their eyes meet, like she's staring at a ghost. Sure, the guy's a bit pale, but so is everyone in January.

All of the oxygen seems to have evaporated from the room as her lips part and close wordlessly. After a few attempts, only a whisper escapes her lips, barely audible but filled with a multitude of unspoken emotions.

"Wes."

ACKNOWLEDGEMENTS

First and foremost, I'd like to thank my readers. This book would not exist without your enthusiasm and continued support. Seriously. I was never expecting the intense vulnerability that comes from publishing a book. In truth, I almost stopped writing after Dr. Resident. As an oldest daughter who is used to succeeding, Dr. Resident felt like a failure in so many ways. Criticism and feedback have never been things I handled well, so at first I was overwhelmed and depressed. But because of your encouragement, I kept going. Dr. Resident may have been for me, but Dr. Intern is for you guys (though we may still have to fight over Beau).

To Alli and the Morgans, my Texas besties, thank you for living up to the main theme of this book—acceptance. You love the true me, and not the version of me that sometimes I fear I have to put on in order to be loved. I've never once felt like I had to be anyone other than myself around you guys. Please know that I cherish our friendship every single day. So much so that I named my favorite character after two of you (Alli, you will get your turn one day . . . don't sass me).

To Mallory and Katie—I don't know how to describe what you are to me. I've probably never verbalized this, but I look up to the two of you so much. You are both so driven and intelligent that it can oftentimes be intimidating to be your friend. These books were never intended to be a work of literary genius, but you have treated them like they are. As someone who has always felt like a joke, your support means the world to me. Thank you.

To Sasha, Tabitha, and Andrea, my beta readers and biggest cheerleaders, I would not have made it through the release of my first book without you. The fact that you took the time out of your busy lives to provide encouragement, feedback, and praise is astounding to me. Thank you for all of it. And thank you for getting it.

To Sadie, my new friend and editor. I can't believe we found each other, but I'm so glad we did. Your support and understanding has made this second book as joyful as it can be. Thank you for your patience as you explain independent and dependent clauses to me for the hundredth time, and thank you for your enthusiasm. When I parsed through your manifesto on this book, I sat there "chuckling" for far too long at your comments. Finally, thank you for going along with my crazy idea to release Dr. Intern early despite the chaos in both of our lives. I can't tell you how much I appreciate it. Cheers to the next. I'm writing it for you.

To my mor, the only member of the family who knows about this little hobby of mine. Thank you for giving me insight to what it's like to have T1D. (This isn't against HIPAA because you don't know her real name. She's Mrs. Woods to you guys). It was so fun to shed light on your struggles while talking through how it could impact my character. I love you and please know that one day I will convince you to go to Bravocon. I wrote Claire and her mom's relationship based on us. Thanks for being my best friend.

To my husband, who has now been in my life for ten years. One of our first dates involved me running around your fraternity house in a bumblebee costume yelling "put it in my ass". For anyone still reading, he did not do that at the time, don't worry. You've seen me for who I am since the beginning, and never once asked me to change. Thank you for allowing me to be myself. I love you.

To Andy, the OG ortho bro. Thank you for your guidance with this book. I know you'll probably never read this, nor should you, but please know that there are so many character traits of Beau that are based on you. You're the kind of person that everyone should aspire to be. I hope you know how proud we are to have you as our friend.

Finally, to Claire and Beau, my main characters. You two were so concrete in my mind the entire time I wrote your story. I love you for so many reasons, but the biggest is for your unwavering acceptance of one another. Claire, you allowed me to work through my deepest insecurities while portraying a very personal life decision that we shared. Beau, you reminded me of home and showed me what it means to be proud of who I am. Thank you for being my friends for the past several months. I think about you all of the time and love the two of you endlessly.

About the Author

Lexie Woods works as a nurse and writes medical romance novels from the comfort of her air conditioned home in Texas. With approximately twenty failed ADHD hobbies sitting in the graveyard of her attic, her husband is hopeful this might finally stick. When she's not questioning her friends about their most unhinged fantasies, she can be found floating in her backyard pool with a margarita in hand.